Praise for *American Skin* by Don De Grazia

"It is the American story American literature is not complete without. In fact, without Alex Verdi's story, American literature is a lie. A heavy book. An important book. Full of images and humor and action and questions. And truths. America needs to know this story. About the tenaciousness of decency within the character of so many of America's youth. To entertain and to teach. A book can't get any better than that."
—Carolyn Chute, author of *The Beans of Egypt, Maine*

"It's a terrific book and De Grazia is a wonderful writer. . . . *American Skin* is not an exposé, but a story about separation and alienation, and the search for friendly soil where roots can be put down and, hopefully, nurtured. The story of this search is beautifully narrated. The book is structurally sound, perfectly balanced, and the writing is direct, simple, and clear. Mr. De Grazia does not intrude himself between the people he has created and the reader, but allows them to tell their story in their way, and to live the life they must. Mr. De Grazia is not a propagandist; he is an artist. Grazie Don Gennaro!"
—Hubert Selby Jr., author of *Last Exit to Brooklyn*

"This book deals with a particularly American subject in a manner that has not been done before. The writing is fast, tough, and beautiful and goes deeper and deeper beneath its own surface."
—Jim Carroll, author of *The Basketball Diaries*

"A powerful debut from a young Chicago writer. Get your bets down now."
—Andrew Vachss, author of *Flood* and *Safe House*

"*American Skin* is a fiery and bracing thrill ride filled with the unlikeliest of heroes. It is wild yet wise, darkly violent yet shimmering with themes of the power of friendship and the need to belong. A terrific book."
—Scott Heim, author of *Mysterious Skin* and *In Awe*

"Don De Grazia writes like a lyrical bulldozer, relentless and gorgeous at once."
—Maggie Estep, author of *Soft Maniacs* and *Diary of an Emotional Idiot*

"*American Skin* is about skinheads the way *Oliver Twist* is about pickpockets. . . . Alex Verdi is a young man searching for a home and anything resembling a family. With its Holden Caulfield–like narrator, it illustrates the dangers of tribalism while showing its allure."
—*Chicago Reader*

AMERICAN SKIN

Don De Grazia

Scribner Paperback Fiction
Published by Simon & Schuster
New York   London   Toronto   Sydney   Singapore

SCRIBNER PAPERBACK FICTION
Simon & Schuster, Inc.
Rockefeller Center
1230 Avenue of the Americas
New York, NY 10020

First Scribner Paperback Fiction edition 2000
First published in Great Britain in 1998 by Jonathan Cape

SCRIBNER PAPERBACK FICTION and design are trademarks
of Macmillan Library Reference USA, Inc., used under license
by Simon & Schuster, the publisher of this work.

Manufactured in the United States of America

1   3   5   7   9   10   8   6   4   2

Library of Congress Cataloging-in-Publication Data
De Grazia, Don, 1968–
American skin / Don De Grazia.
p.   cm.
I. Title.
PS3554.E11158 A84 2000
813'.54—dc21   99-048500

ISBN 0-684-86222-0

For Lisa, Mom, and above all, Dad. Also for John Schultz.

Very special thanks to Diann Sickles, Virginia M. Johnson, Sophie Martin, and Matt Walker. Also Zak Mucha, Tony Fitzpatrick, Lauri Coup, Frederick Levy, Andrea Newman, Stacy Codikow, Daniel Yost, Louise Quayle, Ellen Levine, Bill Hamilton, Dan Franklin, Charles Johnson, Hubert Selby Jr., the Metro crew, and the Rogue Scholars. Much gratitude to Randy Albers, Gary Johnson, Andy Allegretti, Shawn Shiflett, Betty Shiflett, Wade Roberts and the rest of the Fiction Writing Department at Columbia College Chicago.

PART ONE

The woods are full of wardens.

Jack Kerouac, *Lonesome Traveler*

WHEN THINGS GOT TOO crazy with the cops I suggested to Timmy Penn that we go to college, but he just laughed and said skinheads were working-class for life. Aside from my dad, who was in prison at the time, I looked up to Tim more than anyone. Aside from my dad.

When I was a kid my dad made a stack of cash, sold his all-night diners, and moved our family from Taylor Street in Little Italy out to an old farmhouse surrounded by thick woods, hidden meadows, and an overgrown orchard. In a hilly clearing beside the house sat a red barn, and a long, white-roofed stable where we kept the animals – Shetland ponies, some sheep, a gander, a goat, and an army of dogs. My mom was pregnant with my sister. My parents spent their time raising me and Stacy, and my dad wrote poetry. Haiku poetry. I'm serious. As I grew up he became very well-respected in the Haiku world.

The locals were American Gothic, with strip malls and attitude. They thought we were hippies. My dad grew a beard and my mom let her platinum Jackie O hairdo grow out to natural brown, and wore it in two braided ropes, like an Indian. It might sound funny, but my dad didn't consider himself a hippie at all. The sixties had their own effect on every man, I guess.

Have you ever seen a lilac bush in bloom? My dad liked to call our place 'Lilac Farm'. Back behind our house there were so many lilac bushes that, from inside, they filled up every windowpane in spring. Purple and flowery with that candy scent floating all around. It only lasted a very short time though, before all the little flowers turned brown and stank like shit. Lilac Farm was a good name for that place.

The house sat beneath a grove of giant oaks, and on fall nights we would drift asleep to acorns lightly raining on the roof. Summer mornings I'd cross through the wild flowers and rolling hills of our south meadow to a spring-fed pond, wade through the cattails near the shore to a tiny island, and dive through the sun-warmed surface to the chill underneath, down to the smooth clay bottom, to the silent icy gush of the spring.

We went on long walks exploring our woods – crossing little streams on rocks that stuck out of the water – and picked apples off the trees. We milked the goat, and drank wine at every dinner. My dad would make a fire and play guitar at nights. He'd play 'The Wabash Cannonball'. It was some kind of place to live.

But one day things went badly for us out there in the woods. I was at the high school when it happened. That November it stayed dark as dusk all day. It's a very strange thing to walk out of natural darkness into electric light in the middle of the morning.

I skipped first period study hall as usual to hang out in the library, so when I heard my name over the intercom just before second period, I assumed I'd finally been caught. No big deal. In-school suspension. I'd get to spend a couple days just reading instead of going to class.

I decided to grab some books before going to the office. I turned the corner and saw a gym teacher and a uniformed cop with a dog going through my locker. I stopped and back-tracked in shock, but I can't say it was a total surprise. I'd seen the packages of marijuana in my dad's desk, and Jack Wappler came up from the city with the stuff about this time every month. Those men sifting through my locker gave shape to a vague uneasiness I'd always had within me.

The hundred steps or so down that empty hallway felt like a

walk across a lunar landscape. The bell rang and kids poured out of every room. I reached a door and slipped outside.

I ran home and I remember it being so terribly cold that my face burned and the wind whistled. But aside from that there was no sound or pain or weight or anything for the whole four miles.

I thought only of the bricks of pot I'd seen in my dad's desk, and knew I was just scaring myself – this was something minor or a mistake and my dad would know what to do – but when I was nearly home, about to collapse, I saw a cop car parked at the end of our driveway. The woods were so thick, and our house was set so far back that you couldn't see it from the road. So I ducked under an old barbed-wire fence and into the woods, and trudged through the snow and between the branches of the apple trees that hung heavy with white. After about four hundred yards I could see our house. There were a bunch of cops and men in suits (IRS, I was later told) strolling in and out, some of them carrying my dad's business files and stuff. I wasn't thinking clearly, but I knew not to come out of the woods. I pictured them rummaging through my locker and remembered my dad scoffing as his Beatnik buddy Mickey Silver told stories of police planting drugs on war protesters – sending them off to prison where they were gang-raped for years.

They stayed the whole day, and so did I, staring out from the woods. All I had on was jeans and a sweater and gym shoes and no gloves. To this day my fingers and toes hurt badly when it gets cold out.

By nightfall they were gone. I crept back to the end of the driveway. The squad car had left. Lying in a blue-plastic sleeve, half-buried in snow by tire tracks, was our afternoon paper. I've always wondered if the delivery man felt any kind of irony as he tossed it, or if he even knew at all.

With numb fingers I slid off the plastic and read by the moonlight. It made the bottom of the front page.

For years no one listened, but following a significant drug bust this morning in unincorporated Harding County, a group of concerned community members say persistence finally paid off.

Alex and Teresa Verdi, of 90405 Dairy Lake Rd., were arrested, along with Jack Wappler of Chicago, and charged with intent to distribute nearly 2 Kilos of marijuana, with an estimated street value of $75,000.

Later, even after I met Tim Penn and learned the business end of drugs, I always wondered how they came up with a dollar-amount like that from three pounds of weed. The nearest I can figure now is 'street value' meant what three pounds was worth if you rolled it all into toothpick joints and sold them in prison.

If convicted the three face a possible maximum sentence of 12 years. Wappler's black 1985 New Yorker and the Verdi's 1980 Ford Van were seized. The vehicles, authorities stress, along with the Verdi's property – three buildings set on 40 acres zoned for farming – can and will be sold at public auction upon conviction under current statutes.

'We want to send a clear message that the trafficking of narcotics will not be tolerated in this community,' says Harding County Sheriff's Investigator Lt. Dennis Richter, who headed the investigation in conjunction with the Illinois State Troopers and Cook County Sheriff's Police. Community members – including a mail deliverer and a former employee of the Verdi's – say officials only paid heed to their suspicions after they took matters into their own hands, reportedly keeping the Verdi's residence under surveillance as part of an unofficial neighborhood-watch initiative.

The Verdi's 17 year old son, a Junior at Harding High School, is being sought for questioning regarding the possibility that marijuana was funneled into the school, which has reported a marked increase in drug abuse. If charged, Richter says, the son will be tried as an adult. The Verdi's daughter, 11, was brought to Cook County and placed in State care until relatives are reached.

'*What* relatives?' I mouthed, lips thick with cold. I tore the article out and dropped the rest of the paper in the snow. Them seeking *me* seemed ridiculous. I didn't do anything. But I was seventeen. Was I custody of the State too?

When I got back to the house I saw right off that they shot Lovie, the queen of all our dogs – a massive bitch mastiff, fiercely protective of our family. She wouldn't let them in, so they shot her. They could have used a knockout dart or something, but why bother, right? Half her head was caved in and her brains had spilt out into the snow. I went right down to the stable and came back with a wheelbarrow, a shovel, and a pickax. I turned the barrow on its side and rolled Lovie's big body in. Then I righted it, and shoveled the bloody snow and brains up on top of her. I remember that I started to cry as I was burying her in the woods by a frozen stream, but I only started. The clay I was digging in was rock solid, and I thought my fingers would break off every time I swung that pickax down from over my head with both hands as hard as I could.

After it was done I walked back to the house and broke through the yellow tape the police put across the door. It was dark inside, but I could see by the moon that the furniture had been turned over and there were papers scattered everywhere. The electricity was out – a branch somewhere in the woods had fallen on the lines again – and a faucet had been left running in the kitchen, so there was no hot water left. There was cooking gas though, so I found some matches and lit the old stove's pilot light. I boiled big kettles of water and poured them into the bathtub until it was full. Then I stripped off my wet shoes and socks and wet clothes and climbed on in.

I was scared. In the water I decided it didn't matter that I'd never sold any drugs, or that my father was only part of a little communal buy. My dad laughed at Mickey, but I believed what he'd said about cops. There was a feeling falling and rising inside of me, tightening and relaxing – like everything out there was over, but nothing was settled. I stayed in the tub, seething in the dark, till long after the water'd turned ice-cold. Then I dressed and left.

But before I left I thought of something. For all their searching, they didn't find my dad's small shotgun. He kept it with a box of shells in the tackroom, wrapped up in a horse blanket underneath my sister's little red saddle for the pony that had once been mine.

I loaded the gun and paced around out front of the house for a while, blindheaded, shouting things I can't remember, then headed down to the stable and unlocked all the pens. I let the ponies out and the dogs could pretty much go as they pleased but the Irish wolfhound who was goofy we had to chain up so I unlatched his collar. Still holding the shotgun in one hand, I grabbed the handle of a five-pronged digging-fork and went out to the shed where we kept the feed and ripped big holes in all the bags and left the door wide open. Then I went to the barn and climbed the ladder to the loft and tossed all the bales of hay out onto the snow. I kicked the loose hay strewn on the loft floor into a pile, and felt for the matches in my jeans.

When the fire was burning good up there I went down to let the sheep out, but they wouldn't leave. I don't know where I expected them to go – it was freezing cold out – but the sight of them huddled there in the corner of the pen baaing set me off and I chased them outside with the fork.

With an armful of hay I started another small fire in the stable around an old dried-out wooden beam which caught pretty quick. I went back to the house to the tackroom and lit one there too. As the same blue-black smoke poured from the windows of all three buildings I grabbed the shotgun and started off through our north woods towards the highway. I heard something behind me and saw the wolfhound following and smiling with reflective eyes and without thinking I roared at the dog and fired the shotgun up in the air. It released a bright blue fountain of flame and sparks in the black woods and I saw nothing but spots for a full minute. I heard the wolfhound yelp and bolt back towards the house and when I could see right again, I heaved the gun into the dark and crashed my way through the bushes and branches and, covered with snow and burrs, I ran across the neighboring cornfield to the corner of 73 and 41, where the truckers slept.

An old fellow was pissing up against the side of his eighteen-wheeler. His name was Virgil Sickles, as I recall, and he said he could take me as far as Chicago.

I TOOK A ROOM at the Y and found a job at a West Side electroplating factory. The second shift at Brand H Plating let out at two in the morning, and in my first month there I had already been mugged twice going home. The first time was quick and simple. I walked out the side door of the plant to the street, some guy stuck what was presumably a gun against my kidney and demanded my wallet. I didn't have a wallet, but I told him in a weak whisper that I had a few bucks in my jacket pocket. He took the money, said if I turned around he'd kill me, and ran. I stood there motionless till long after his footsteps died away, then walked on towards the train, grateful that he hadn't searched my jeans pockets and taken my tokens. The second time didn't go so smoothly. I'd just received my first pay envelope – Brand H paid me in cash – and, after stuffing it in my crotch, I trotted warily towards the train. As I reached the street viaduct underneath the Ashland El platform I stopped at the foot of the steps and looked behind me to see if I'd been followed. The streets were empty, to my relief, but when I turned to the steps again I was greeted by a black man swinging what I think was the edge of a brick into my mouth. A few seconds later, when I awoke on my back on the sidewalk, salty blood was pouring from my smashed and swollen lips and I could feel tiny chips of what I thought were pieces of the brick sticking to my gums. A man was crouched over me, rifling through my pockets, and I immediately remembered the envelope. I tried to leap up at the man and felt something hit the back of my head. This blow didn't knock me out though, so I continued trying to get up. I heard several voices swearing at me as they kicked me from all sides.

I swore back at them at the top of my lungs and managed to get up to a sitting position but the kicks and blows seemed to come from everywhere, and again I lost consciousness.

When I awoke again, both front pockets had been torn off my jeans and the envelope was gone. I realized that the tiny chips in my mouth were pieces of my lower front teeth. Calling the cops or an ambulance seemed out of the question – I was afraid the warrant in Harding County would show up. Besides I would still be seventeen years old for a few more weeks, and I felt such action would only jeopardize my work situation. My main immediate concern was the envelope of money, without which I'd lose my room at the Y. I staggered back to the plant and found the general manager – a dour little man with nicotine-stained yellow hair – still up in his office working on payroll. Seeing me all torn and bloody like that was certainly what persuaded him to do the unthinkable – after making me swear I wouldn't tell anybody, he gave me a two-week cash advance.

Ironically, it was probably that pay advance that saved my job at the plant. The fact that I still owed the company money no doubt made them reluctant to fire me. My attempts at running the #2 copper line had been an abysmal failure; there were simply too many steps in the process, and, hence, too many opportunities for my mind to wander. Within a week I was demoted to the racker's tables, at which two rival groups of middle-aged women (one group was Puerto Rican and the other Mexican) jammed unplated engine parts onto rubberized rack-trees all night long. The Puerto Rican ladies, who I'd been teamed up with, wanted me off their crew, saying I was bringing their piece-rate down. The Mexicans, of course, didn't want me either, and I didn't blame them – I was a very slow racker, lost in elaborate fantasies, most of which revolved around me somehow befriending an imaginary gangbanger warlord – pulling him out of the path of an oncoming car or some crazy shit – and, as a result of this great deed, being granted general amnesty in the streets. Then the local hoodlums, who were not really such bad guys once you got to know them, but merely victims of circumstance like me, would come to deeply respect me despite our many differences. In fact, the very same guy who had smashed my mouth with the brick, feeling a special bond between us, would introduce me to his sister, a stunning, dark-skinned beauty . . .

The final demotion they could give me at the plant was to de-greaser. The job description strongly resembled that of a fast-food fry cook, only everything was bigger, and hotter, and more horrible. After donning thick heat-retardant gloves that extended to my triceps, as well as a rubber apron and safety glasses, I would scoop parts, still thick with the greasy, rust-resisting black gunk they'd been shipped in, into wire baskets the size of orange crates. After lifting these baskets I'd struggle to ascend a three-step platform built in front of the de-greaser, which was basically a very tall, iron tub divided into two sections. I'd then lean over the lip of the tub and, by means of two short-handled hooks, lower each basket into the first section, which contained a fierce boiling chemical concoction that emitted white-hot steam. I'd jostle the hooks until I was sure the gunk had all melted off, looking away as often as I could – the heat was unbearable. Still the solution often splashed on my face, leaving red welts which lasted for days. After then dunking the parts into the second section which contained a fresh water rinse, it was on to the next basket, and so on through the night. From a management perspective I was born to de-grease. The sheer hell and ever-present danger of the situation was such that all daydreaming was completely out of the question.

For whatever reason, I was never mugged again, but one night, after a particularly bitter bout with the de-greaser, in which I'd lost a glove and, in the process, been steam burnt on the forearm, I found myself embroiled in a confrontation on the train ride home.

I boarded the car that the conductor – a young black woman – was in, which had become my custom, as it seemed safer. I picked up a discarded Tribune sports section from the car floor and began to read, when, at the next stop, three black guys – two in their late teens and one maybe thirteen at most – got on the train and greeted the conductor with hand signs and hoots. It became apparent that they knew each other pretty well, as they spoke of mutual friends, and, it seemed, flirted back and forth. The two older guys, one tall and one short, and both in LA Raiders caps and jogging suits, stood behind me, where the young woman leaned against her open window and announced the stops into a microphone. The younger kid, who wore his hair combed back in long, greasy waves covered with a translucent blue shower cap, sat directly in front of me, sideways across two seats that faced the aisle, with his knees pulled up to his chest. Shortly after he sat down, he pushed his legs out straight and rested his leather gym shoes on my knees. I heard the two behind me guffaw and turned to look at the conductor.

She just kept talking about whatever it was she was talking about, all the while looking at us vaguely, like a mother absent-mindedly watching her child engage in an inconsequential playground argument. I felt the kid rocking his feet back and forth on my knees, so I turned around and pushed them off. He put them back up on my knees, and I pushed them off again, this time a little more violently. I heard the words 'mothafucka' behind me, and then more snickering. I tried to concentrate on the paper, but just as I realized I was holding it upside down, the kid snatched it out of my hands. His eyes looked painfully bloodshot. I looked back at the conductor again but she avoided my gaze. The two guys were laughing, and I, for some reason, smiled sheepishly. The sight of my grin turned their own expressions grim and stony. I turned back around and heard them burst into laughter again and resume their casual conversation with the conductor. As we neared the next stop I snatched the paper back from the kid.

'Awwwwshit,' I heard one of them say, and I felt the back of my neck prickle, anticipating a blow. I sat glaring at the kid, but he barely existed as far as I was concerned – I was afraid of the two guys behind me, and burning with hatred for that conductor. I don't know if it was reflexive memory of the night I'd been mugged, or just plain nervousness, but I pressed the tip of my tongue down against the lower front tooth that had been shattered by the brick and the instantaneous pain brought tears to my eyes which further embarrassed and infuriated me.

It was at that stop that five teenaged guys with shaved heads boarded the train. Four were white, and one was black, and they all were loud and passing back and forth quarts of beer in brown paper bags. They wore black nylon bomber jackets and blue jeans cropped tight above the ankle, exposing high leather work boots the color of dried blood. The black skinhead and one of the whites – the largest guy in the group, who carried a black guitar bag by the neck – slumped down into seats across the aisle from us, while the others stood by the doors laughing and jostling each other. The train stood still and the doors stayed open for what seemed like a long time.

'C'mon, get this piece o' shit movin'!' shouted the big guy with the guitar. He had a slurred, but definitely British, accent. The rest of them sounded American.

I glanced back at the conductor who, rather than speaking directly to them, leaned up to the microphone and said:

'There is absolutely NO DRINKING OF ALCOHOLIC BEVERAGES ABOARD THIS TRAIN!'

She said it with such indignation, like the fucking bitch I felt she was, that, without thinking really, I cried out incredulously:

'What the fuck do *you* care?'

She eyed me angrily and said, rolling her head forward in a circle with each syllable:

'You can get off the train too if you want.'

I felt the urge to slap her across the face.

'I can't hear you,' I said. 'You aren't speaking into the microphone.'

The skinheads roared at this, and the taller of the two black hoods standing behind her took a step towards me. He didn't say anything, but flared the nostrils of his wide, flat nose, pointed a long black finger at me, and nodded with menace. If his intent was to scare me, it worked. But a heated wave had washed over me, and once again I spoke without thinking.

'Stick that goddamn finger up your ass.'

They roared again, and as the black hood took another step towards me, one of the white skinheads reached between us and said, looking him straight in the eye with feigned awe:

'Excuse me, sir . . . are you in a *gang*?'

The skinhead and the black guy stared directly into each other's eyes as they slowly straightened up to their full height. Both looked around six-three, but the black guy was heavier, and angrier, whereas the skinhead, with a crooked grin spread across his handsome, angular face, looked maniacally amused.

Despite the barrel-chested black hood's slight weight advantage, the skinhead's broad-shouldered proportion seemed to tilt the scales of physical superiority his way. Though he had the long arms and legs of, say, a power forward, and looked as if he might have years ago passed through a brief adolescent stage of lankiness, he was nothing short of strapping now. And there was the calm of an alley cat in his movements that seemed to hold together all that length and strength effortlessly and harmoniously.

'I'm gonna call the po-lice you don't get *off* this mofuckin' train right now!' the conductor shouted. The emphatic head roll she'd used earlier to punctuate her speech was no longer in effect. I glanced over at the kid who'd been fucking with me and saw that his overall look had changed to blank attentive-ness. The shorter black guy, who still stood by the conductor, had the same look, and fondled the silver handle which led to the next car.

The skinhead took a step back from the black guy and unzipped his bomber jacket, letting it fall off his shoulders. Without breaking the stare he tied the sleeves of the jacket around his waist, and jammed his fists into the pockets of his jeans. Each part of the process seemed like a naked dare for the black guy to make a move on him. He wore thin, red suspenders and a sleeveless white T-shirt, displaying muscu-lar, tattoo-covered arms. What stood out most about these arms were the prominent triceps, which seemed packed on, like extra clay – as if some sculptor, having already completed his vision of the male physique, felt compelled to use the leftover slurry in his bucket.

''at's it, Timmy!' the British guy roared, getting up from his seat with his guitar and standing beside him. 'We'll kick all yer black asses.' The two other white skinheads crowded in close behind them and sneered.

For the first time, the black guy broke from Tim's gaze and rested his eyes on the black skinhead who still remained seated.

'You gonna play me like this, brother?'

At this, the black skinhead dropped his chin and stared between his legs at the train floor for several seconds. Then, before looking up, he spoke.

'Now everybody just hold on here, goddammit . . .' His voice was deep and scratchy. He stood up, stepped between the two, and, a full head shorter, faced the skinhead Tim. The black hood stepped back a bit to let him through, and Tim pulled his fists out of his pockets. 'This is all wrong, Tim, all wrong . . . you see?' As the black skinhead spoke he grasped Tim's fists and worked to uncurl them until the white skinhead's fingers were interlaced with his own. The black skinhead stared deeply into his eyes for a few seconds before Tim hung his head in what looked like defeat. From where I was sitting though, I could see the curl of a smile on his lips.

'Now you see, brother . . .' the black skinhead said as he started to turn around, then, in one fluid motion, dipped down quickly as if scooping something from the floor, sprung straight up, and drove his fist into the black hood's chin. The sound of his open jaw snapping shut resounded like a rifle crack, and he literally flew off his feet and landed flat on his back.

The black skinhead uncurled his own fist and stared, open-mouthed and bug-eyed, as if amazed to discover the roll of quarters that rested in his palm.

'Haw!' he cried, pointing at Tim, 'I never seen this before in my life. This ugly-ass white skinhead planted it on me. I swear to mothafuckin' God' He whirled around and faced the other black guy, who still gripped the silver handle leading to the next car. Leaning back against Tim, the black skinhead cried: 'You want some of this, motherfucker? C'mon.' Tim laughed and grabbed him in a playful headlock, pulling him backwards and slapping him on his bare black scalp.

'Naw,' he protested, 'you ain't pinnin' this on me!' And with that he tossed the roll of quarters in my lap.

'*He* did it!' he cried. Surprised, I caught the roll with both hands and slipped it into my jacket pocket. As the conductor frantically radioed for police, the skinheads poured off the train. Tim was the last one off and before he left he turned to me and said:

'You better come on, man.'

And I did.

*

Out in the street one of the white skinheads who'd stood and silently sneered behind Tim now spoke with rapid-fire excitement. He was the shortest of the bunch, with olive skin and a long straight nose. I later learned his name was Jason.

'Ah shit, guy,' he was saying to Tim, 'this is just like in *The Warriors*, dude. We're in enemy territory. The streets are hostile. We gotta get back to home base. Some of us will make it, and some of us won't.'

The rest of them laughed and told him to shut the fuck up.

'Did you see that black bastard fly?' the British guy crowed to the group, and then, holding the guitar bag aloft with both hands, howled up at the El tracks that hung over our heads: 'Skiiiinhead!'

Everyone echoed his cry and laughed. There seemed to be something consciously parodic about everything they did and said.

'We gotta get outta here,' Tim said, throwing an arm around my shoulder. 'Homey here's concealing a deadly weapon.'

'Aw fuck that,' the black one said, holding up his fist. 'This here's the deadly weapon.'

'We gotta go,' Tim said again, and then, after a few seconds, added, 'Where we gonna go though?'

Everyone faced him and talked at once: 'Better not take the bus,' 'Shit, the cops'll be here any second,' 'We can't go back to the party, it'll be crawlin' with Swazis,' 'Thay gonna deport me ass,' and so on until we heard the sirens way off in the distance.

'C'mon,' I said, and started running towards the plant – the train had only gone three stops east. I yelled that we could stay in the break room until this blew over.

There were just two old Mexican guys working the third shift, and when I told one of them we were going to wait in there for a ride home, he shrugged, as if to say he could give a shit.

The skinheads talked and drank there all night long, popping various cassettes into the break room boombox –

quick, amateur rock; snide, boastful rap. They were both impressed and sarcastic about the fact that I worked in such a place, as if the lowliness of my job made me a loser, but a loser was something admirable to be.

'You're just a regular Joe,' Tim kept saying, his arm around my neck constantly. 'A regular Joe.'

I gathered from much of what they talked about that there were two main groups of skinheads in the city of Chicago – a multiracial group that included themselves, and the Nazi-skins ('Swazis') who they fought with constantly. I sat there in the break room and imagined the life of an anti-Nazi skinhead to be several times more romantic than that of a First World War ambulance driver or a freedom fighter in the Spanish Civil War.

In the morning, just before the first shift crew came in, we left out the side door. As we rode the train back to the North Side, and neared parting, I wanted to cry out to Tim and the rest of them: 'Take me with you!' But instead I just stood and held the bar in gloomy silence. As they crowded toward the door to leave though, Tim handed me a flyer for a club that he and the olive-skinned guy worked at as bouncers. It read, in part:

Fuck Art, Let's Dance!
at
The Gorgon
(The Latest in Industrial Sounds)

'Stop by sometime,' Tim said, as he and the rest of them stepped off the train at the Belmont platform. And then, before the closing doors shut out the sound of his voice, he turned to me, brought his fingers to his breast and recited – still in that half-parodic tone – the lyrics of some rap song:

'*Lotta beer, lotta girls, and a lot of cursin'/.22 automatic on my person.*'

That night, I returned to my work at the de-greaser as usual, and, for the first time, despite the steam and heat and boiling hot splashes, found myself daydreaming again. The roll of quarters Tim had forgotten hung heavy in my front pocket, and over and over again I imagined myself swinging at some anonymous jaw – the tautness in my fist exploding on impact in a shower of silver.

I WOULD GET BACK to my room at the Y, generally speaking, at about 3:30 in the morning. I could never go straight to sleep though; the completion of each night's shift left me very tired, of course, but wound up as well, and filled with the desire for some sort of leisurely celebration. I generally celebrated by sitting at the edge of my bed, staring into the bureau mirror, watching myself smoke cigarettes. Or, rather, watching myself *pretend* to smoke cigarettes. I had not yet mastered the art of inhaling all the way into my lungs. Actually, it never occurred to me that I was doing it wrong.

I just liked the way I looked with a cigarette dangling off my lip, as I blew gray clouds around me, and, occasionally, usually by accident, achieved a minor ring or two. On nights that I hadn't caused any major catastrophes at the plant, my young and roundish face seemed to take on temporary definition, and caused the rise in me of certain ambitions. Every night, as crushing images materialized from that Lilac Farm apocalypse, I'd distract myself with heroic fantasies of job promotions, of scrimping and saving, and – slowly, steadily, through undetermined (but uncannily wise) investments – rising in the world. I'd get an apartment and find out where they had my sister, steal her away, and she'd come live with me. I'd somehow contact my parents in prison without betraying the warrant for my own arrest, I'd hire a lawyer, a really good one . . .

I thought also of Tim and the skinheads. I kept the club flier Tim gave me taped up to my bureau mirror at the Y, and the roll of quarters sat beneath it, upright, as a sort of monument to the night we met on the El. There was a strong desire to cash in on Tim's invitation to come see him, but, much as I desired all the camaraderie and contact with girls it seemed to promise, I was, at the very root of it all, as frightened of the whole thing as I was excited. As dismal as my current situation was, it did provide a certain structure to my life, and I was afraid to do anything that might interrupt that rhythm of security.

That rhythm was broken abruptly one night when I got canned.

We were very far behind on an order of bolts, and my job duties suddenly doubled. Located at the end of the copper lines were what looked like a pair of heavy, leaden garbage pails. These machines, which operated much the way an upright clothes dryer would, were built for the purposes of drying newly-plated industrial parts just pulled from their final rinses. That night old Juan had his hands full – operating both of the plant's parallel copper lines simultaneously, pulley-hoisting and lowering both barrels into their respective vats with the masterful dexterity of a champion yachtsman handling his riggings and checking gauges. And, as behind as we were, as soon as he reached the end of the lines, he had to start all over again with another pair.

I was left to dry. I still had to de-grease as well, mind you – quickly enough to keep Juan busy with parts to plate – and, being that de-greasing and drying were the first and the final steps in the plating process, the two stations were located at opposite ends of the building. My night consisted of a seemingly endless sprint between the jobs, at a pace that quickened with every interval. I had just emptied and reloaded the dryers for about the eleventh time that night, and was halfway back to the de-greaser, when I heard a clanking cacophony behind me.

In my haste, I had overloaded one of the dryers and forgotten to latch its heavy lid. As the revolving cylinder started to pick up momentum, the lid flew up and the machine began hurling out parts like a skeet machine gone berserk.

Juan caught a hot bolt square in the forehead, and in my attempts to remedy the situation the lid came down on my index finger and smashed it. After finally shutting the thing off, I got what I needed in the way of bandages from the first-aid kit on the lunchroom wall, but poor Juan had to go get stitches.

Before the shift was even half-over the plant manager called me into his office and told me brusquely that production was down and they were 'cutting back'. I solemnly went and hung up my rubber apron on a hook in the locker room, put my gloves and safety glasses back on the shelf, and left Brand H forever.

Now what? My twin gods of Sensible Thrift and Lofty Ambition, cowed by this unforeseen failure, could only silently watch in horror as I cracked open the roll of quarters on the bureau's edge, bought a pack of cigarettes at the Mexican restaurant around the corner, and headed for The Gorgon to see Tim.

If I ventured much more than a stone's throw from the El back then, it sent the needle on my internal compass spinning wildly, so, even though the club's Sheffield address was not that far from the Y, I ended up taking some long, meandering route to The Gorgon that night. I suspected that I was getting close, however, when I came upon the Dunkin' Donuts at Clark and Belmont.

It was warm and humid for an early spring night, and the parking lot was packed solidly with kids of every imaginable race – all in some sort of distinct costume. As I reached the corner, I leaned back against a newspaper box and took it all in. Punks with colorful, bristling Mohawk hair and metalhead types in black leather biker's jackets. Girls with strangely applied eye make-up that gave them the appearance of exotic birds. Morbid-looking characters dressed all in black with amazingly sallow skin that stood out like moonlight in the night. All laughing and swearing and milling about amidst the

23

sputterings of a few scooters and mopeds that slowly threaded their way through the sea of black vinyl and olive drab, fishnet and bleach-spattered denim.

One girl in particular took my attention. She was small and dark and beautiful – in a monstrous, slutty kind of way. High-laced, black leather army boots and a very plain, short yellow sun dress that left her entire back bare, exposing a grand tattoo of what looked to be some epic Japanese battle. Red and black swordsmen and Geisha-types in robes. Scaly green dragons that slithered through pale pink flowers . . .

I suddenly became conscious of my own, hopelessly styleless appearance. Jeans and a gray, short-sleeved work-shirt that I'd taken from Brand H. Longish, dirty blond hair I wore combed back and kept trimmed myself at one, unimaginative length.

I figured I'd better light a cigarette.

Not long after I did, a huge kid emerged from the crowd, tall and fat and hunched over at the shoulders. He was bald and booted in the mode of the skinheads I'd met, and, as he approached me, I made hopeful eye contact with him, thinking momentarily that perhaps he had been there that night on the El.

'Could I get one of those off ya?' he said, pointing to my cigarette.

I nodded vigorously and extended to him my open pack of Marlboros. He grabbed the pack, dropped it to the sidewalk, and ground it into the cement with the heel of his black leather boot. As I looked up at him in shock he turned and made his way back into the crowd. Sewn across the back of his burgundy bomber jacket were the words (which meant nothing to me at the time):

S.I.U. STRAIGHT EDGE

You cannot imagine how this crushed me.

I sulked away down Belmont and turned right on Sheffield anyway. I'd come this far, I figured, I might as well see this

24

thing through. The closer I got to the address of The Gorgon, though, the more inclined I was to turn around and head back to my room at the Y. Groups of characters similar to the ones I'd seen in front of the Dunkin' Donuts were meandering about everywhere and congregating in small alleyways – arguing and laughing raucously and playing loud music on boombox radios. As I passed the parking lot of a shuttered glass-factory, I saw a black guy – shaved bald except for a short strip of bleach-blond Mohawk – smashing his head repeatedly against a 'No Trespassing' sign bolted to the chain-link gate. Nobody paid him much attention except for a couple of very young punk girls who were laughing in encouragement and taking pictures with a small Instamatic.

The groups of weirdoes thickened and I realized that I was standing in front of The Gorgon. It was a square brick building – maybe five stories tall – with blacked-out windows and one, small entrance in the middle. Several skinheads stood in the doorway checking IDs with hardassed indifference, while a jumble of people – five or six abreast in some spots – stood against the wall in a line that extended fifteen yards or so to the next side street, then wound around the corner out of sight.

I looked quickly at the bouncers, and, seeing that none of them was Tim, followed the line around the corner where it extended east for at least another thirty yards or so. It seemed as if every person I passed was staring me down, and, when I reached the end of the line I couldn't bring myself to stop. I just kept walking slowly, without looking back, until I found myself alone again, standing beneath the north-south El tracks. I leaned up against a steel girder, slid down on my haunches, and watched the line from that safe distance through a web of my own fingers, which seemed to put everything even further away.

With bitter scorn I silently laughed at the vague fantasies of

25

good times and friendship I'd envisioned myself finding amidst this freak show.

'You certainly lack balls,' I concluded, and then, as if to show myself in some small way that that was not entirely true, I pulled the second pack of Marlboros from my breast pocket and lit one up.

Almost as soon as I did though, I heard the sound of a car engine humming close behind me. I twisted my neck around and saw a beat-up old Pinto with its lights off creeping up to where I sat. Even in the dark I could see the damned thing was filled with skinheads.

'Jesus fucking Christ!' I said aloud, stamping out the cigarette, and quickly slid back up the girder to my feet. What the hell was this? Some kind of goddamned anti-smoker skinhead vigilante squad?

As I fumbled to stuff the Marlboros back in my pocket, and considered whether or not to run, the Pinto pulled up alongside me and stopped.

'Hey brother, how's it going there?' the driver said, smiling with familiarity. The skinhead who spoke wasn't any of those I had met, so I was wary, but I took a step towards the car anyway and peered in.

'How's it going there, brother?' the driver said again, shutting the car off and nodding with a wired sort of energy. He was square-headed and stocky, and not quite bald; his hair was about the length of felt and he sported a pair of enormous muttonchop sideburns. There were several guys crammed in the dark back seat, and sitting shotgun was a big sullen-looking skin with a skinny bleach-blonde girl in his lap.

The driver asked me how it was going again and I shrugged and told him 'all right'.

'Excellent,' he said, approvingly, as he opened the door and got out with a quick, wary glance at the Gorgon line. Then, turning his back to that sight, he looked at me, still smiling, and stuck out his hand, which I shook with some hesitation. It was a warm handshake though; not at all the bonecrusher I'd somehow expected.

'What's going on tonight?' he asked, as if we'd all made previous plans to meet here or something. I smiled and shook my head. I could feel myself loosening up a bit.

'I don't know, man,' I said.

'Yeah,' he laughed. 'I'm Frank Pritzger by the way.'

We shook hands again.

'I'm Alex Verdi.'

'Okay, great, Alex. Let's see. *Ver*-di.' He chewed each syllable and rolled it around in his mouth, unable to identify the taste. '*Verdi*. What is that?'

'Italian.'

'No kidding,' he smiled, peering closer in the dark. 'Northern Italian?'

'I'm half Irish.'

'Ho-*ho*,' he laughed. 'Whose got the worse temper – your ma or your dad?'

I laughed and shrugged, thinking of them.

'Well, they were *both* half-Irish, half-Italian . . .'

'What? Ha ha, that's great. What do ya do Alex – you have a job?'

I told him I was an electroplater.

'Union?'

'Nah.'

'Nah,' he said. 'Payin' you shit, huh?'

I nodded.

'Well, but you're lucky though. Mexicans got most of those jobs.'

I nodded, remembering with a strange pang that I'd probably never see Juan again.

'I mean, say *you're* the boss,' Pritzger continued, with an energetic tone of compassion. 'Who are you gonna hire? The American, who you have to pay minimum wage? Or a Mexican who'll work for a dollar an hour? Yeah, a dollar an hour. What's some illegal gonna do? Call the Better Business Bureau? Nah, he'll take his eight dollars home every night, put them in a jar, and dream about going back to sunny Mexico where he can roast goats every night and live like a king. *He*'s happy, the *company*'s happy, and the white American man is out on his ass.'

He stood there before me, stocky and resolute, his feet planted shoulder-width apart, waiting for my response. I nodded.

'Yeah,' I said, 'I never thought about it before but . . . there shouldn't *be* a minimum wage.'

He looked at me curiously for a second, then grinned and chuckled:

'No, Alex . . . listen to me. The white man's problem is not the *minimum wage* for God's sake, okay?'

I nodded, a little confused, but the shape of a vague realization was forming in my mind.

The passenger door of the Pinto swung open and the guy got out, leaving the blonde girl sitting in the car. He was huge. Much bigger and more muscular than even the skinhead who had squashed my cigarettes. And shirtless, displaying a giant, black, iron-cross tattoo that covered his entire chest.

'Frank,' he said, in a rumbling voice. He nodded towards The Gorgon.

Frank and I looked and saw a group of three or four skinheads standing separate from the line of freaks. They stood in the middle of the side street, pointing at us and motioning back to some other skins leaning against the building.

'Ah, forget them,' Frank said good naturedly. 'Alex, man, you want to party tonight, my brother? Have some beers?'

I hesitated and he quickly went on talking.

'Here,' he said, reaching into his pocket and pulling out a folded-up piece of paper. I took it without really breaking my gaze at the growing group of skinheads by The Gorgon. It suddenly became clear what the situation was here. I felt my guts contort and my brow moisten as I began unfolding the paper.

'Are you aware, Alex, that it says right in the Jewish Talmud that God *smiles* upon those that cheat a gentile in a business transaction? That's *you* they're talking about, Alex. That's me. That's you and me and all our white brothers and this is our country.'

'Let's go!' the girl inside the Pinto implored.

'Nah . . . fuck that,' the big guy said, suddenly reaching in the back seat of the car. He produced a polished wooden walking cane.

'Fuckin' Swazis!' I heard someone shout from the Gorgon group. There were about ten of them now, and they were walking steadily in our direction. All the freaks in line had turned to watch.

'Yeah?' the big guy said, and trotted a couple quick steps towards them. The group abruptly stopped and drew back en masse. There was rustling and motion in the back seat and the door began to open when the big skin turned quickly. 'No!' he said, and made a threatening motion towards the car with his cane. Then, turning back towards the group he laughed with derision: 'You gotta be fuckin' kiddin' me!' and added, with an exaggerated lisp, 'Ohhhh, look at the little Bomber *Boys*, don't they look cute in their little skinhead outfits? Don't you just wanna take 'em all home and fuck 'em in the ass?'

Frank looked at me and jutted his jaw with knowing confidence towards the big guy. I should add again that this guy was *big*.

A couple of skinheads in the group began to take tentative steps towards us again, until the distance shrank to less than ten feet. I felt a quiver in my knees and took a step away from Frank without thinking. The faces of those coming towards us were indeed boy's faces – similar to my own – whereas this giant with the cane was clearly in his mid-twenties; clearly a man.

This little drama unfolding before me was compelling of course, but even more compelling, I must say, was how, exactly, *I* fit into the whole equation. Frank, and the giant, and all those in the Pinto (it now was clear) were the Nazi-skins – the bad guys I had heroically battled against night after night during my Brand H reveries. But Frank's interest in me seemed genuine. This had just been, quite frankly, the first even half-friendly conversation I'd had with another human being in what seemed a very long time, and . . . what was I supposed to do? Suddenly run over to the others and announce my immediate allegiance? As I watched them flinch at every stroke the giant Nazi made through the air with his cane, it didn't seem like the wisest of decisions.

A brief flash of Tim came into my mind, a realization that I'd certainly had my ass kicked before, and – with a strange, but very definite sense of guilt – I decided to do it anyway.

I hadn't gone three steps towards the anti-Nazi skins, though, when I saw one of them raise his hand in my direction. Something the consistency of jism arced through the air and I was blind with burning eyes and nostrils. I grabbed my face and fell to my knees, heard pounding footsteps, felt a kick to the temple, and red and deep-green colors filled my head. I fell to my side. There were shouts, car doors slamming, unidentifiable thuds, a kick in my ribs, another. More thuds, more shouts, more car doors slamming, the sound of the engine, tires squealing, and I suddenly felt someone grab a fistful of my long hair and pull my head back. The person wrapped his other arm around my neck and I was pulled blind and staggering to my feet.

'We got us a little Swazi boy-*yee*!' I heard someone shout.

'No!' I shouted back, 'FUCK!' I managed to twist around in the grip, and bear-hugged whoever it was that had me by the hair. He tripped me behind the ankles and I fell backwards on the pavement – with him on top of me – but I didn't let go. De-greasing had given me a pretty good grip, if nothing else.

'Get off me!' the guy shouted. I could smell lunch meat on his breath. 'Get the fuck off me!' His request seemed absurd – he was on top of me, wasn't he? He was indeed, but between the sweat and the mace, I couldn't quite open my eyes to verify.

As we struggled someone else suggested that they 'curb' me. The others seemed to like the idea. I didn't know what 'curbing' was, but it didn't sound like a good thing.

I still had my arms locked around the guy's torso, and they tried to peel my fingers off, but I was stubborn. Finally they broke my grip and, though my vision was only blurrily coming back, I could see that they were dragging me towards the curb. I fought of course, but they got me to the sidewalk anyway, and began pushing my head down towards the white concrete lip that rose above the gutter.

'Make him bite it! Get his mouth open and jump on his fuckin' head!'

And then, though it seemed idiotic at the time, I said it: 'Get Tim!'

Everything stopped.

'What'd you say?' someone asked, as the hands released me. During this momentary reprieve I gasped to get enough breath to say it again.

'I'm here to see Tim!'

'Tim who?' someone wanted to know.

'Tim,' I said again.

'Timmy Penn?'

I nodded, hoping to hell it was the right answer.

'Yeah, right,' someone finally said, but they let go of me.

I stayed there heaving for breath on my hands and knees as they continued to ask me questions. Dull aches all over my body began to sharpen into distinct and separate pains. My temple throbbed, my ribs, my tailbone where I'd fallen. My cheeks and eyelids still burnt with the residue of the mace.

'How do you know Timmy?'

'We're old friends,' I said, looking up at them all for the first time. There was a circle of panting skinheads tight around me, and a large crowd looking on behind them.

'Tim's not on the white power trip no more, fucker,' someone said and pushed me over on my side with his boot.

'I'm not white power!'

'Whaddya doing hanging out with the Swazis then?' an angry young Latino skinhead asked me. He was holding the flyer Frank had given me.

'I wasn't hanging out with them, they just . . .'

'We'll find out,' the Latino kid said, and reached down to grab me by the shirt sleeve. I yanked back and got up to my feet.

He slapped his chest violently with both hands.

'You wanna go again right now?' he asked, 'I'll kick your dirty ass all the way back to the *South* Side motha . . .'

'Fuckin' back off, Dario,' I heard a sarcastic voice say behind me. 'All of a sudden you're a *tough guy* now? Where the fuck were you ten minutes ago?'

A splash of sheepish hurt doused his face, and for a moment, he looked about five years old.

'Oh fuck you, Jamesey . . .' he said.

'Fuck me? Bitch, I'll . . .' And as they began to argue, a couple of skinheads about my size, one white and one Asian, told me to come on, and led me back around the corner, past the line and the bouncers at the door, and into The Gorgon. It felt like we were all a bunch of kids playing army.

The doorway led directly to a very wide and steep dark stairway. The heavy bass beat of dance music seemed to vibrate the walls, and lightning flashes of white and red strobe sporadically exploded from above. As I made my way up, still flanked by the two skinheads, I tried to adopt something of a cool demeanor, seeing that I would soon face Tim. But the thought occurred to me: what if he didn't even remember me? Or, what if he got pissed that I'd been telling people we were friends after I'd just been seen hanging out with Nazis? There wasn't much time to contemplate though, for as soon as we got to the top of the stairs, there he was.

He had some pale kid backed up against a podium. The kid had swoopy black bangs with shaved sides, and behind the podium sat an old lady in a cardigan sweater who seemed oblivious to her surroundings. The kid was shaking as he looked up at Tim, who stood there with his arms crossed, looking more bored than anything. Me and my two escorts stood back a bit to watch.

'Were you making fun of her?' Tim asked the kid, and pointed to a chubby girl in some sort of black smock who stood a couple yards away looking deeply hurt.

'I . . . I don't want any trouble with you, Tim.'

'Well . . .' Tim said, and seemed disgusted that he had to waste his time with this.

'It's cool,' the kid assured him.

'Well . . . just stay away from her.'

The kid nodded hopefully.

'Alright?'

'Yeah.'

'Okay . . .' and as the kid scurried away past the girl towards an inner dance floor, Tim called her over.

'What'd he do?'

She began with rapid-fire indignation: 'He was laughing at me and I went over to him and got in his face and he told me to . . . he said to stick it up my ass!'

Tim dropped his head and laughed with exasperation.

'Ah c'mon, Marcy,' he grinned, 'you act like you never stuck nothin' up your ass before.'

'Fuck you, Timmy,' she said, swatting him lightly across the shoulder with an open palm. She started to leave, then stopped and looked demurely down at the toes of her patent leather oxfords. 'Hey, y'know Kim? From Schaumburg?'

He grinned and nodded, as if he knew what was coming. 'You think she's cute?'

He shrugged.

'Oh fff . . . you *know* she's cute,' Marcy continued. 'She's *beautiful*. She's modeling for *Elite*. She came over last night and we were watching TV and this old John Wayne movie came on. Like, when he was super-super young. And we were like: "Who does that look like?" And she figured it out. Do you know?'

Tim shrugged with a half-grin and scratched the stiff stubble on his head.

'I don't know . . . *me?*'

She growled sourly at his cockiness, and adopted a snotty tone: 'Maybe you *would* . . . if it weren't for the broken nose. You really oughta get that fixed. Me and Kim both agreed — it's *ugly*.'

'Get outta here,' he laughed, pushing her away. 'It's not becoming for a skinhead to be seen consortin' with you filthy punk rockers.' She cackled and disappeared back into the flashing dance room.

'Tim,' I heard myself saying, and he turned around. He stared at me blankly for a second, and then screwed his face up with what seemed to me at the time to be confused annoyance. The strobe flashes from the dance floor half-illuminated his face. I hadn't really noticed the slight meandering of his nose-bone before, but now it added to my fear.

'Hey,' I said, and nodded upwards as if to try and jostle his memory. I was steadily filling with a numb sort of dread.

'You know this kid, Timmy?' the white skinhead behind me said, stepping forward into the strobe light. His right eye and cheek were swollen and bleeding. Tim came closer and peered at me with that same aggravated look.

'We saw him with Frank Pritzger and those guys from

34

CLASH, and he just told us that you and him were . . .' the guy began, and a small tick of realization seemed to put a dent in Tim's mean mask. Suddenly he was smiling with amusement.

'Degreaser!' he shouted, and laughingly embraced me. He smelled like a brand new shirt.

I heard the Asian kid behind me asking Tim again if he knew me.

'Yeah, yeah we're old buddies,' Tim said, pulling back and looking at me, nodding. He kept both hands on my shoulders. 'How ya doin', Degreasey?'

I shrugged and opened my mouth to say something cool and ironic, something tough, but with all the events of the night still swelling up unresolved inside me, it occurred to me suddenly that I was safe, and that I'd found my friend, and that he was indeed my friend − after all he'd just said it hadn't he?

I couldn't help it. I burst into tears.

As I PAWED THE tears from my eyes, Tim took my shoulder and steered me towards a door in the black hallway wall. Above the door was painted, in chipped gold cursive: 'Cloakroom'. As he pulled the door shut behind us and muffled out the club sounds, streetlight and moonlight shone through a window and illuminated a bedroom.

Oh, it was a cool bedroom.

In one corner, suspended at chin level, was the bed. One end of the bed frame hung from the ceiling by two lengths of heavy silver chain, and the other end was bolted to the wall. Beneath the bed was an enormous fish tank, aglow and pulsing with splashes of vividly colored marine life.

'Want a brew?' Tim asked, sitting down on a small fridge near the window. He produced a sweaty forty-ounce bottle of Midnight Dragon malt liquor and handed it to me.

He had a stereo, a television, a video-recorder, and a small shelf of books. A samurai sword hung on the wall and a poster-sized photograph of himself standing in front of The Gorgon with his powerful arms crossed. Beneath the windowsill, like dark reflective pools, stood a row of highly polished boots. Oxblood, brown and black boots, all arranged by height. The tallest rose to just below the kneecaps.

'Come on, that's mother's milk, Degreaser, drink up.'

I unscrewed the cap and looked at Tim.

'You *live* here?'

He shrugged with mild embarrassment.

'For now,' he said. 'I'm lookin' into some real estate you know, but . . . it's a place to crash. A place to bring the Bettys. Whatever.'

'*No*,' I said, 'this is a *great* place.'

He smiled wryly at my reverent tone. 'Yeah? You like it?'

He gave the room an exaggerated yeah-I-*am*-pretty-fuckin'-cool once over, then shot me a look of mock annoyance.

'So what's up? Eh? I invite you out to come see us like two months ago and what? You got such a busy schedule you can't visit your friends? Boy-oh-boy . . .'

'Nah,' I said. 'You know. Work.'

'Oh, so de-greasing is more important,' he laughed. 'How's *that* goin'?'

'Ahh, you know . . .' I sighed, then sat down in a beanbag chair by the door, and took a sharp bubbly sip of the cold malt liquor. When the liquid hit my broken tooth (which had started to abscess) it sent an instant ache through my lower jaw, but I covered the tooth with my tongue and kept on sipping as I told Tim my sorry tale. After a few sips the ache went away, and things in general didn't seem half as dire.

'So the job's history, eh? *Now* whattya gonna do?'

I shrugged and chuckled. I had no idea.

'Well . . .' he said, glancing at the door, as if remembering he had other places to be, 'we'll take care of ya, Degreaser. We'll take care of ya. Let me see what I can do . . . Hey, you gonna *drink* that? Come on, you look about a quart low.'

As I tipped back another sip, he stood up, clapped my shoulder, and told me to hang out for a while. Then he went back into the club. As I sat there alone, drinking and thinking, my carefree buzz melted into melancholy, and embarrassment at the tears I'd shown. I stood up from the beanbag, and slouched to the window.

I looked down to where I'd nearly had my already fucked-up teeth completely curbed out of me, and all my aches and bruises suddenly complained in unison. Dark streams of kids were leaving the club and branching out, piling into cars, scuffling, making out. Suddenly I yearned for my spartan room at the Y. I was scared. I had wanted change, and it was coming.

We'll take care of ya.

Aside from Tim, I hated this place, these people. My temple throbbed and it seemed that if I took one more sip of beer I'd puke, but Tim expected me to drink, and I wanted to make up for the tears, so I opened his window and began pouring the beer out to the sidewalk three stories down.

I had just about emptied the bottle when I heard the door open behind me.

'De . . . hey! Whateryou? Getting sick?'

'Hunh?' I said, pulling in quickly. 'Nah, I thought I heard something out there.'

'Nah, don't worry,' he laughed, 'nobody's gonna fuck with you again, bro. I talked to those guys. Just a big misunderstanding . . .' He eyed my beer. 'What'd you . . . kill that thing already? Shit, Degreasey . . .' He knelt down, and pulled another forty-ounce bottle from the fridge.

'C'mon,' he said, handing me the bottle, 'I gotta introduce you to somebody.'

*

The club was dark and empty now. As we left Tim's room a girl sat by his doorway with her chin on her knees. She looked about sixteen. Pug-nosed and cute, but sullen, with black lipstick and heavy mascara; a long, concert T-shirt stretched over her knees. Tim held up a one-minute forefinger to her, and led me across the hallway to another door – the Gorgon office.

A long wooden table took up most of the room, and around it sat many of the same skins who'd attacked me in the street. They hunched over cardboard boxes of cold pizza, drank beer from big bottles like mine, and took turns packing weed into a small bowl and sucking on it, squinty-eyed.

There were others in the crowded room, teenage freaks and punks, and one middle-aged man in a suit made out of some reflective, silvery stuff. The man stood bent over a small rolltop desk, punching numbers into an adding machine, and scribbling on a note pad. He was tall and chubby, with frameless bifocals, and sported a slick, blue-black ponytail, though his hairline started halfway back on his head.

'Hey Jason,' Tim called out, slapping my back, 'You remember the Degreaser?'

Jason was too busy to respond with much more than a quick sneer. He was rocking back and forth on a piece of papier-mâché art meant to look like an asteroid, or a sea-mine – it had long spikes jutting out of it. Jason straddled it so that the longest spike, which must have been about five feet, projected out from between his legs like a giant cock. Holding two of the shorter spikes as handles, he cackled evilly, and hopped towards the knot of punk girls.

The girls swore, and laughed, and I recognized the one I'd seen at Dunkin' Donuts. The mocha-skinned one in the yellow sun dress, with the epic Samurai battle tattooed across her back. She grabbed Jason's faux cock and swiveled it around until it almost poked the silver-suited man in the ass.

Everyone in the room – the punk girls, the skinheads at the table, Tim – roared at the sight. Encouraged, Jason began rocking back and forth on his papier-mâché steed, making faces of exaggerated ecstasy.

The silver-suited man glanced back, then arched his buttocks out towards the point and lisped bitchily,

'Ohhh . . . is that all you've *got*?'

Everyone roared again and the tattooed girl squealed with scorn and delight, 'You're so *greedy!*'

'Hey, Punch,' Tim said, addressing the silver-suited man. Jason swiveled back towards the tattooed girl, who kicked at the prong with her army boots and bellowed for him to get away. She pulled the spike up with both hands and dumped Jason on the floor, adding to the general uproar.

'Punch!' Tim said again, 'I got somebody here I wantchya to meet, alright?'

Punch pushed himself up from the desk, folded his arms, and gave us both a supercilious look.

This was Alex, Tim explained. He and I were cousins. I was a good guy. Etcetera.

The skinheads went back to their beer and pizza and weed, and Punch went back to his note pad, nodding occasionally to show he was listening, but barely. Closely monitoring the situation, however, was the tattooed girl, Marie, though she continually looked away with a catlike feign of disinterest.

'I would assume, Timothy,' Punch finally said, without pausing from his work, 'from your *splendid toast* to Mr Alex here, that he wants to become one of our *minions*. Am I right?'

Before Tim could answer, Punch leered at me over his frameless bifocals, and asked, lasciviously,

'Is he willing to go above and beyond the call of duty?'

This got a roar of laughter from everyone in the room. Everyone but Marie. Her big, baby blues, wide and childlike, were glued on me, and her thick black brows were arched in warning.

'He's probably not even *kidding*,' she said. 'What are you? Like sixteen years old?'

'Seventeen,' I quickly corrected her.

She looked at Punch with disgust.

'Ohhh,' she said, 'you're sick . . .' Though there was genuine disdain in her tone, it was clear from Punch's smirk that he considered her pugnaciousness charming. 'How can . . . ohhhh! Do you know what a sick old faggot you are?'

Punch raised his eyebrows and placed his hands akimbo.

'Marie,' he said, with well-I-never indignation, 'this is for *you*. I saw the way you fairly *lit up* when this . . . this . . .' He looked me up and down with mock awe. I suppose, standing

40

there meekly, hunched a bit with my knees still involuntarily trembling, I did not cast the most magnificent figure. ' . . . this *Greek God* entered the room.' Another roar of laughter from everyone, though I didn't see what was so goddamned funny. Marie scoffed and her chocolate-milk cheeks flushed deep and dark as he continued. 'Mr Alex is hired. Happy Birthday, Marie.'

'It's your birthday, Marie?' one of the punk girls asked – eager, it was obvious, to ingratiate herself. Marie's face still flushed in a twisted scowl.

'Yeah, on this day, nineteen years ago, my mother shat me out of her cunt. Big deal.'

The room erupted again. 'Marie . . . fuckin' Marie,' people laughed, shaking their heads. 'C'mere Marie,' Tim said, grabbing the doorframe with both hands and leaning towards her. 'I'll give you your birthday spankings.'

Averting my eyes she ducked under Tim's arm as he aimed a pretend slap at her shapely rump, and exited with a heavy stomping of her army boots.

'Oh, Lordy,' Punch said, fanning himself with the notebook, 'I need air. This room is thick with hormones.'

'She's got the hots for you, Degreasey,' Tim said consolingly, clapping me on the back.

'Who?' I asked, alarmed.

'Marie,' Tim and Punch answered in unison.

'That black girl?' I asked.

Punch nodded. 'Part black . . . Polish? Greek? Italian? Who knows? A veritable Taste of Chicago whatever the case. Heaven help you, my son . . . and Timothy . . . if this boy goes wandering about the club with a flashlight professing to be some sort of authority figure, looking like *that*, word will be that The Gorgon has contracted out its security duties to Charlie's Angels or something.'

Another roar from the room. I was beginning to hate Punch.

'Nah,' Tim laughed, 'Alex is a skin. He's a skin. Who's got the clippers?'

'They're cutting hair up on the roof, Jones and them,' one of the skins at the table said.

'Well, I gotta take care of some shit,' Tim said impatiently, looking out the doorway towards the pug-nosed punk girl waiting in the hallway. 'Somebody show him how to get up there.'

He grabbed hold of my bruised cheek and said, as if psyching me up for the big moment: 'We're gonna make you a skinhead boy-ee!'

I didn't feel I was in any position to object.

*

Jason led me out through the main dance room to a fire escape. We were followed by all the other skins in the office. As I stepped into the cool night air, out onto the clanking, swaying catwalk, and looked four stories down to the alley, I teetered, dizzy with vertigo. When I saw Jason swing his leg over the edge railing and grab the rung of a ladder that led to the roof, I felt paralyzed. But when you're on a catwalk followed closely by a dozen drunken skinheads, all of whom are eager to get to a rooftop, vertigo or no vertigo, your only thought is 'up'.

I reached out and grasped the ladder with a fear-weakened fist, swung my legs out to it, and began to climb. The ladder was anchored to the bricks at such an angle that by the time I neared the top, I was leaning out backwards over five stories of air. I felt triumphant, though, when I clambered to the safety of the tin-covered roof.

There was a party of sorts going on up there. Not very far away stood three young guys dressed in three-button suits, narrow ties, and thin-brimmed little fedoras cocked back on their heads. With them, I noted with some fear, stood Marie. She glanced over at me, scowled her inimitable scowl, turned back to the suits, and laughed uproariously at whatever tale they were telling. She went on, giving two or three extra gestures wherever one was needed, as a girl who knows she's being watched will do. Further on, dangling their legs over the edge of the roof, sat several bald kids looking down at the north-south El tracks. They were joined by the skins that had come up with me. One of them had brought up a pitbull puppy on his shoulder. Sitting near them, atop two plastic milk crates, was Jones – the big British skinhead I'd met on the El with Tim and Jason. Brawny and handsome and rosy-cheeked with booze and rugged health – like some jolly rogue in an old-time pirate flick – he sat there strumming simple, but amazingly quick chord changes on an acoustic guitar, and bellowing a drunken sing-along, with the other skins:

Oi! Oi! Oi! The chosen few!
This is what we think of you!

This was from a song by an apparently anti-semitic English skinhead band, I later learned. But singing it now were many of the same kids that had fought tooth-and-nail with the Nazis in the street. It was absurd, but I realized, with time, that most of them didn't even know (or care) what the hell they were singing. The vigorous pleasure of aggressive rhyme was all that mattered.

I heard a screaming whistle which died off in the distance, followed by a short crackling report, and saw a small, white flash on the El tracks. It was followed by another, and another, as several of the skins shot off bottle rockets, singing all the while:

Oi! Oi! Oi!

The pitbull started yapping, and other music – sweet, almost corny trumpet, with slower lyrics and a strange,

Caribbean, or perhaps New Orleans feel to it – rose up from where Marie and the boys in suits stood:

> *Stop your messin' a–round.*
> *Better think of your future . . .*

> *Ru–*dee . . .
> *a mess–age*
> *to you . . .*

'Turn it off!' Jones yelled. 'Can't ya see we're havin' us a . . .'

'Piss off, Jones!' Marie yelled back, and turned up the volume on a portable yellow boombox she was cradling like an infant.

> *Ru–dee . . .*
> *a message*
> *to you.*

'Alright then,' Jones growled, getting up and leaning the guitar against the crates, ' . . . ya cunt.' He wore thin, red suspenders, like many of the others, but before charging at Marie, he pulled his down, so that they hung at his sides in two loops.

Marie screamed and ran laughing behind a huge air-conditioning unit in the middle of the roof. She turned the music even louder.

> *Stop your foolin' a–round . . .*

Jones chased her around the thing three times before she tripped and sprawled out flat on her stomach. She held on to the radio though, and curled her body up tightly around the blaring music.

'Gimme that,' Jones demanded, briefly attempting to wrest

the box away from her. She swore and laughed from somewhere deep in her gut.

'Alright, smarty,' he said, and bent down to grasp her ankles. He began dragging her towards the ledge. The skins who were sitting there hustled out of the way and shouted in encouragement as Marie screamed at the top of her powerful lungs. When he reached the edge, he suddenly swung her up off the surface of the roof, and began whirling her around in a circle. If she slipped loose, or he let go at the wrong time, she'd go flying out over the alleyway that ran behind the club, five stories down. My legs lost nearly all musculature, my breathing stopped entirely, and then it got worse.

Tired of whirling, he began to swing her back and forth over the ledge like a pendulum. Marie's yellow skirt had fallen up around her torso, exposing her plain white panties. The other skins cheered louder and louder as the arc she made through the air increased with every swing.

Marie was howling, laughing, swearing, and trying to pull herself up enough to nail Jones in the head with her radio, which still played:

Stop your messin' a-round . . .

She nearly took his head off with one swipe, and in avoiding the blow, Jones leaned and slipped and fell backwards.

I closed my eyes tightly and, just like with the bottle rockets, there was a dying away of sound followed by a short report. When I opened them again I saw Jones flat on his back, still holding Marie's boots. She was still in them, thank God, twisting around between his legs to see the corpse of her radio.

'Fuuuuuck!' she cried, pulling herself up on top of Jones and beating him about the face and head with her small fists.

It had all been too much for me. I was definitely going to throw up now. My only hope was that I could avoid being seen. I quickly crossed the roof to the unoccupied side facing Sheffield. I passed Jason, who knelt (oblivious to everything that had just happened) in front of a board that lay across two

45

upturned plastic buckets. On the board were six tiny, potted marijuana plants.

'How are my little babies?' Jason cooed, as if addressing his own sextuplets. 'Yes . . . it's springtime, isn't it?'

As I walked closer to the ledge, my vertigo kicked in again and the sick feeling in my gut was forgotten. I stopped and sat down a full six feet from the edge.

'Jesus fucking Christ,' I muttered to myself, and pulled out a cigarette, taking several of the quick puffs that I took to be actual smoking.

The bottle rocket shrieks and Jones' strumming sing-along and the pitbull yapping all started up again on the other side.

'Hey,' someone behind me demanded, 'let me get one of those from ya.'

It was Marie. After fearing for her life so, I was actually happy to see her, and she seemed that much less frightening now for some reason. But I did feel a little resentment towards her for having been a part of that goddamned spectacle, however unwillingly.

'Could I have a cigarette, please?' she asked again, still panting hard from the ruckus.

'What're you . . . gonna take my pack and squash it?' I asked, sullenly.

'No,' she said, sitting down beside me. 'Who did that? Fat Moe?'

I nodded. The guy who had ground my smokes into the sidewalk with the heel of his jackboot looked very much like a Fat Moe.

'Well . . .' she said, 'once he finds out you're down with Tim, he won't do that anymore. Those suburban straight-edge wannabes only get righteous on little kids like you who don't have anybody to watch their backs.' She shook her head. 'It's all these, like, *hordes* of misfit skinheads nowadays. The Bomber Boys are into jumping little pussy-boy punk rockers now for their leather jackets and their shoes – like a bunch of fuckin' *gangbangers* and shit. And now straightedges are jumpin' on kids like Narcs. Pff . . .'

Remembering the back of Fat Moe's jacket, I asked Marie what 'Straight Edge' meant. She briefly described a clique that listened to hardcore punk rock, but didn't smoke, drink, do drugs, or sleep around, and considered anyone who *did* their sworn enemy.

'So . . . *you're* not straightedge, right?' I asked her.

'Why?' she scoffed, smoking, and checking her legs for scratches and bruises. 'You think I sleep around? Is that what Timmy told you?'

'No,' I said. 'I mean . . . you're smoking.'

'Yep,' she said.

We sat and smoked in silence, looking out over the North Side of the city. After a few minutes, I felt her staring at me.

'Um . . .' she said, in a certain tone of false politeness girls often use when addressing a boy who is in some way being absurd, 'what are you doing?'

'Huh?'

'What's this?' She pulled at her cigarette with loud wet smacks in a flurry of short, mouth puffs.

'Don't you know how to *smoke?*'

This was before I developed an almost reflexive habit of lying to girls about virtually everything, so I just shrugged with embarrassment, smiled weakly, and said that, well, I *thought* I knew how to smoke but . . .

This tickled her, and she resolved, on the spot, to teach me.

'Okay, blow all the air out of your lungs . . . don't breathe. Now pull some of the smoke into your mouth. Not so much.'

I gave a short choking cough, and she said, very quickly: 'Now open your mouth and breathe all the smoke into your lungs right away.'

I took an enormous puff and felt a sudden rush of something rising towards the inside of my skull. As if pulled

47

by that rush, I stood up, and began swooning around in a dizzy dance.

'Blow it out,' she squealed with delight. I nearly fell over, headlong towards the edge, but she braced me by the shoulders with her palms.

'Whoa there, buddy!' she laughed sweetly. I laughed too.

'Whoa . . . *man*,' I said.

We stood there for a couple of seconds like that, smiling while she held my shoulders. Then, as I lost the head rush, I lost my nerve. I looked down at the tin roof beneath our feet as if I'd dropped something, and saw a small smoldering. I realized that I had, in fact, dropped the butt, and as I reached down for it, a commotion arose from the skins at the other end of the roof.

'Look at it! Fuck! Sh*iiit*!' they were yelling with a mixture of fear and delight. Marie and I walked over towards them and saw that they had started a small fire on the El tracks with their bottle rockets. The flames grew slowly and spread out along the garbage that lay between the tracks.

'Oh! They gonna deport me ass!' Jones cried, and all the skinheads clambered towards the ladder, scooping up the guitar and the pitbull as they ran. I started with them, but Marie caught my arm.

'Where you goin'? You didn't do anything.'

'But the cops . . .'

'They won't come,' she said lightly. '*That* little fire?' But it was growing. Small flames were licking at the wooden ties, and I could smell the smoke of wood and garbage.

'Look at it,' she said, 'it's beautiful.'

But I was looking at her.

When she caught my soft-eyed gaze she sat down on the roof to watch the fire, and yawned with exaggerated boredom. More and more she was reminding me of a cat.

'I gotta go to bed,' she growled.

I asked if she'd like me to walk her home.

She rolled her eyes up and gave me a fishy look.

'What do you mean?'

I just meant what I'd asked, but cursed myself for saying it anyway.

'No,' I said, 'I meant . . .'

'I live *here*,' she said, pounding the tin with her fist like a gavel.

A thought occurred to me, and my heart sank.

'With Tim?'

'Pfff,' she laughed. 'Yeah, I sleep on the fish tank while he screws tragic whores three at a time on that trapeze bed of his. *No*, I don't live with *Tim*. I have a real room upstairs.'

'Jeez,' I said, 'you both live here?'

'Yep. And Jason. And Kirk. And fuckin' Jones. Did you just *see* that asshole? This is like Timmy's personal zoo: he sees some nutter he thinks is interesting, and Punch gives them a storage closet to sleep in. Doesn't it seem like the bad cliché B-movie gang? He's got Jermaine the token black . . . Aladdin's like his Asian karate sidekick guy . . . Jones is the organically-grown true-blue old-school East End London skinhead, Jason's Jewish, Kirk's white-trash Americana . . . Just watch – you'll end up living here. This place is a flophouse for freaks.'

She yawned again.

'So, I guess you don't need me to walk you home,' I smiled.

'Yeah,' she said, stretching her hands to my belt to pull herself up, 'I do. I need you to walk me home, and then I want you to sleep over so we can have a slumber party. You wanna?'

I couldn't tell if she was speaking facetiously or . . . metaphorically.

'You want to?' she asked again.

'Uh . . .' I said, my heart pumping uncomfortably now, 'I'm supposed to get my hair cut.'

She gave me a dubious look, then said, still holding on to my belt, that she had some clippers in her room. She could cut my hair.

'Okay?' she smiled, leaning close.

As I felt her soft mouth close on mine, I shut my eyes and I could hear the crackling and could smell the sweetish smell of wood and garbage burning and all I could think was Marie was right, she was right, what a strange and beautiful thing was a set of burning El tracks.

Then her probing tongue found my broken tooth and I pulled back in pain, my eyes still squeezed shut. Way off there were sirens.

'*What?*'

'I gotta sore tooth . . . I . . .'

'Hey . . . *buddy* . . . wake up. You gonna come down to my room, let me cut your hair?'

I opened my eyes and nodded.

*

Marie's room was off the railed balcony that overlooked the main dance floor. Her window faced the El tracks, and as we walked in we could see the growing flames and the red-blue glow of police lights as they reflected off the street. Marie pulled down the shade, and switched on a tiny lamp that sat on the windowsill. Her room was a little bigger than Tim's and filled with all sorts of polished chests and cabinets, a futon-couch, and a white presswood desk stacked high with plastic containers and shelves. The floor was smooth, well-waxed hardwood and the whole place smelled of lemons. The cleanliness and order was startling, especially compared to the rest of the moldering nightclub. She even had her own adjoining little bathroom, set off from the back of the room, and through the open curtain which served as a door, I could see it was cramped with not only a sink and commode, but a hanging nozzle shower with a tiled drainage area. Everything sparkled.

Her walls were precisely arranged with punk-rock posters

and flyers, and, as she rummaged around on the desk to find
her electric hair clippers, I saw that one such flyer featured two
bald-headed guys who looked a lot like Tim and Jason. I stood
up and saw that it was, indeed, a photocopied picture of them,
but there were tiny swastikas scrawled across their foreheads,
meant to look like tattoos. Both of them were baring their
teeth and Jason pointed the barrel of a .45 at the camera.
Below the picture read:

*********WANTED********

For the bombing of several synagogues
and the attempted assassination of
the Honorable Mayor Harold Washington,
not to mention assorted child molestations
of several children of color. These two
vicious SKINHEADS are armed and dangerous and
thought to be mildly retarded.

********SHOOT ON SIGHT!********

'I thought they *weren't* Nazis,' I whispered to Marie,
confused.

'It's a *joke*,' she sniffed, dragging a folding chair into the
bathroom. 'That's just what people think right away when you
say "skinhead". Jesus. I mean, Jason's *Jewish* don't you know
the deal at *all?* Come in here.'

I could hear her running a faucet. As I entered the
bathroom she jammed the chair-back up against the sink bowl.

'It's better to cut clean hair,' she said, pushing me down in
the chair and bending my head back under the weak stream. It
seemed like a strange theory – a waste of time actually – but as
the lukewarm water flowed down the sides of my neck, and I
felt her fingers massage the apple-smelling shampoo into my
hair, I stopped thinking so rationally. As she leaned over me, I

could occasionally feel her breast, beneath the fabric of the sun dress, flatten a bit against my forehead.

'I *do* know the deal,' I told her with eyes closed. 'There's the *regular* skinheads, and then Tim and them are like . . . the *anti*-Nazi . . . the *other* kind of skinheads, right?'

'No,' she snapped. 'Tim and Jason are just *skinheads*. You don't even know *anything*, do you? I shouldn't even cut your hair.'

Despite her irritated tone, her fingertips still danced lightly across my scalp.

'Move your big feet,' she said, shifting in front of me a bit. 'Jesus, what size are your shoes?'

'They're just eight and a half.'

'You're gonna be just like *all* these other weekend-warrior suburban fresh-shaves,' she said. 'You wanna be a skinhead, but you don't know shit about the history. Do you even know who the Mods were?'

I shook my head, and she shook hers.

'They were white English working-class kids in the sixties who listened to black soul music, like Smokey Robinson . . .' she began, as if reciting from a constitution. 'And they rode around on motor scooters. Most of them tried to dress up, you know? Like they were rich? But they weren't rich. So they looked like poseurs. Wannabes. But some of the Mods were like: *Why the fuck pretend we're something we're not? We're working-class, factory lifers, and we're always gonna be working-class, factory lifers, so what the fuck?* So they just wore jeans, and flannel shirts and kept their hair short and wore Doc Marten work boots. The guys, I mean. The girls dressed like girls and kept their bangs, like me. *They* were the first skinheads, and they hung out more with the black Rude Boys who were immigrants from the West Indies than they did with the other Mods. I mean, Alex . . . you should know about this. It was totally fuckin' cool. Black kids and white kids dated, and if anybody didn't like it the skinheads would beat their asses.

Nobody fucked with them. They had their own bands, their own music . . . you know what we were listening to on the roof? That's ska. They *invented* that. Then, when the flower-power shit started at the end of the sixties most of the Mods turned into hippies, but the skinheads were like: fuck that. Skinheads *hate* hippies . . .'

'Why?'

'Cuz hippies are filthy, limp–dick scum.'

'Oh,' I said.

'My parents were hippies,' she added.

I almost replied that mine were too, but stopped myself, as it didn't seem entirely accurate, or fair. To the locals we were hippies, but my dad didn't sound like one when he tutored me in Nietzsche and told me that strength was the most important thing in life – never accepting defeat and all that. I'd always thought of my dad as simply a great man. And, I reminded myself, I would be a great man too.

'I mean . . .' she went on, 'my *mom* was a hippie. I don't know *what* the fuck my dad was.'

A soft, strange chuckle escaped my lips.

'Besides some white son-of-a-bitch I never met,' she continued, irritated by my interruption. 'What's so funny, fagboy?'

'No, nothin'',' I said quickly, 'I . . . it's just, right when you said that, I was just thinking to myself whether or not *my* dad was a hippie.'

'Well it's *not* that complex. What was his deal?'

'Anh . . .' I began reluctantly. '"What was *his* deal?" Well . . . in the sixties he owned some all–night diners on the Northwest side, and made a pile of cash. Then he sold them all and moved our family way up to northern Illinois . . . almost to Wisconsin.'

'What, to evade the draft?'

'Nah . . .' This conversation turn depressed me. 'I was just a kid, and my mom was pregnant with my sister. It was an old farmhouse in the middle of forty acres of woods . . . and meadows. There was a big red barn and a long, white stable. My dad bought a couple of ponies, and some sheep, and a goose, and a goat, and a bunch of dogs for us to play with.'

Marie seemed confused.

'And . . . '

'And, that's it. The idea was that he wouldn't work – him and my mom would just spend their time raising me and the baby. And he'd write.'

'Write *what?*'

'Haiku poetry.'

There was a slight pause.

'Uh,' she said, with that mock-polite tone again, 'I'd say you could pretty much call him a hippie.'

'Yeah, but . . .'

'*Haiku poetry?*'

'Yeah,' I said, trying to hide my rising anger.

'How old's your sister now?'

'Eleven.' I said it through clenched teeth.

Marie seemed to sense something in my voice, and there was only the sound of the trickling water for a few minutes.

'So, *anyway*,' she finally said, resuming her lecture, 'it was black and white skinheads hanging out together, listening to ska music – totally cool scene, proletariat all the way. Until the seventies when the motherfucking British National Front Nazi cocksuckers started recruiting working-class white kids to be their little *stormtroopers*, and pretty soon there were all these *racists* calling themselves "skinheads". And now people call *us* the "other" kind of skins. That's bullshit! *We're* the original skins, man. Fuckin' Frank Pritzger and those jagoffs – *they're* the "other" kind.'

Lost in different thoughts, I mumbled that I had met Frank earlier that night.

'Watch out for *that* guy,' she said, those blue eyes widening again. She shut the faucet off and wrung out my hair. 'That is one sick motherfucker. He says that after his "revolution", all race mixers will be lined up and *shot*. Seriously. He'll talk all nice to you, but those CLASH guys' idea of a good time is to get all liquored up and jump white girls walking down the street with black guys. I heard he broke his own girlfriend's *arm* once when she was working as a waitress, because she got a *ride home* from a Mexican busboy . . . pfff, she's like eighty pounds! Oh, *big man* Frank . . .'

All at once she swung her leg over and sat down on my lap, straddling me. She put her arms around my neck and pulled my head up so that we were nose-to-nose.

'Aren't you *afraid*?' she whispered with mock foreboding.

'Whaddya mean?' I gulped. As a matter of fact, as she hooked her boots around the back chair legs, and slid her smooth buttocks up my thighs until our groins were flush, I could feel the warmth beneath her thin white panties, and I *was* kind of afraid.

'Aren't you afraid to be race-mixing? I mean when Frank takes over . . . we'll both be *shot*.'

'Oh,' I laughed nervously, and she kissed me hard. A sinking feeling, a hollow depression I'd been fighting, suddenly seized me fully. I kissed her back, weakly at first. Then I closed my eyes and kissed her harder, and harder. As if to shake off all the gloom that was dogging me I tried to think only of her lips. I slid my hands up her dress and cupped her breasts. The pads of both my thumbs touched warm, erect flesh for an instant. It was a lasting instant. Think of the burn of a snowflake as it's dying on your cheek.

Then she yelped in surprise and hopped up off my lap.

'Hey there, buddy!' she scolded. 'Whattya thinkin'?'

I was confused.

'I . . .'

'Is that why you came down here?' She looked mildly disappointed. 'To get some?'

'What are you *talking* about?'

'Boy-oh-boy,' she chuckled, as if impressed. 'You act all nice and polite, and then . . .'

I stood up to go. This place was a house of fucking mirrors.

'Where you *goin*'? I thought you wanted your hair cut.'

I looked into her eyes and for the first time her face seemed to flicker with recognition at how distraught and confused and utterly non-threatening I really was. As I walked towards the door she blocked my way.

'Nonono,' she apologized. 'Ohhhh . . . I'm sorry. I just don't *do* that, okay? I'm straightedge. I am. Except for the smoking. I'm sorry.' She paused. 'I mean, my whole goal is I want to be in rhythm with the universe, you know? And . . . and the way people go around just *fucking* each other, with their rubbers and their sponges and their pills, it's . . .' She grimaced. 'I made a promise to my mom before she died . . . I'm sorry, I didn't think that's what you wanted when you came down here.'

'But *you* were . . . !'

'I know,' she said, sighing with mild self-exasperation. She pushed me down gently back into the folding chair. 'I know. I swear to God, what I need is a fuckin' clitoridectomy. Pff . . . what am *I* talkin' about? If I lived in *Africa* I'd probably *have* one. It's almost like, thank *God* for the slave trade, you know? I don't know . . .'

She continued muttering to herself as she prepared the clippers for my head.

'I don't want my hair cut,' I announced.

'What's the matter?'

I just shook my head and felt my nostrils flare as I fought to keep from crying for the second time in one night.

'What's the matter, Alex?' she asked softly. I took in a deep breath through my nose and told her again that I didn't want my head shaved.

'Why not?' she asked, brushing my damp hair back from my face and massaging my temples with her thumbs. There was affection in her voice, but it wasn't amorous anymore. It was sober, and it was comforting, and it was humiliating – as if I'd lost at something.

'What's wrong?'

The first time I saw my sister Stacy was in the van, when me and my dad brought her and my mom home to the farmhouse from the hospital. As we drove, her head fell to one side and she looked up with bright blue eyes that shocked me, like some absolutely real thing that had somehow snuck its way into a dream. They were my dad's eyes, and it just gave me the creeps, I guess, to see a grown man's eyeballs looking out from a bald little baby girl's head.

And my dad grew his beard and my mom wore her hair in two braided ropes like an Indian. I don't know if we were hippies or not. That's not the point. The point is this: I missed my family but I was afraid. I came back to the city alone to find my sister, but I was afraid. Every night, as I lay in bed at the Y, I recited those plans. I would do well at my job, and get promoted. I would scrimp and save and move to an apartment. Somehow I'd find the strangers she was living with – and I'd take her away. They weren't just plans, they were ballast. But I had failed and now I was veering, veering . . .

'Your sister might *like* the people she's living with. You ever thought of that? A kid doesn't care who their family is, so long as they *got* one.'

That's what Marie told me in the morning when I was bald.

MOVING OUT OF THE Y was simple. I stuffed my two pairs of jeans, my sweater, my Brand H shirts, my half dozen or so pairs of socks and underwear, and my alarm clock into a plastic garbage bag and left. I carried my toothbrush and toothache drops in my jacket pocket, along with two paperback books, *Siddhartha* and *Fools Die* by Mario Puzo. Seeing how I could buy books at white-elephant shops for a dime, tear through them in a night or so, and then sell them at used book stores for as much as half a buck, reading was more than a diversion; it was cigarette money.

I arrived at The Gorgon at a little past seven. I wasn't supposed to start work until nine, but I was anxious to check out my new room.

The massive front door to the place was unbolted and when I reached the top of the stairs I found Tim lazily sweeping up the main dance floor with a push broom. He wore only a pair of light blue Hawaiian shorts and gave the bleary-eyed impression of one who'd just rolled out of bed. But even in pajamas he looked like a fucking gladiator. Marie said that a camera crew had come to The Gorgon once to film a beer commercial and ended up centering the whole thing on shots of him slam-dancing naked from the waist up.

I stood in the arched entrance and marveled at all his tattoos. On the side of his freshly shaven scalp was a realistic blue-ink rendering of dog's head, beneath which was written in cursive: *American Pitbull*. Tim's hide was just as illustrated as Marie's, but instead of one thematic mural, he was a wall of random graffiti – here a dragon, there a skull. On his calf a man in a black fedora and sunglasses was slamdancing against a checkerboard backdrop, on his shoulder a skinhead was hanging crucified on a cross. There on his back was a grinning skull in a cowboy hat and Texas string-tie – 'Hank Williams R.I.P.' Looking at Tim, I resolved on the spot to do two things – get a tattoo, and pump a lot of iron. Actually, I'd been lifting weights at the Y, but my broken tooth had grown so sensitive that every time I ate something, I had to soak my mouth first with the toothache drops. My clothes had begun to hang on me a bit. I knew I needed to see a dentist, but rather than figure out how to get enough money, I decided to wait things out, as if the tooth were angry about something, and would forgive and forget with time.

Thinking of the tooth, I dropped my bag down in disgust. Tim looked up, as if angry at the noise.

'Oh,' he said, then went back to his sweeping. 'Hey, Degreasey.'

'Hey,' I said.

He coughed, and said, without looking up from the broom: 'You're a bald-headed motherfucker now, aren't ya?'

'Yep.'

'You got the closet off the hallway to the fourth floor video room.'

He turned his back to me and worked the pile of dirt toward the stage at the rear of the room.

When I reached the fourth floor I saw Marie behind a corner juice bar unpacking squat, rounded bottles of Orangina from a cardboard box. Next to her a kid with a brick-red flat-top was doing the same. He was a sinewy, pale and veiny sort and it bothered me that he was standing so close to her just in his dago tee.

'Hey,' she said, without looking up. It was an inscrutably casual 'hey', as if she just vaguely remembered meeting me, and it hurt like a sock in the gut. In those last few nights at the Y, she'd been the major player in every dream.

'Hey,' I croaked back.

I walked down the hallway and found a sliding wooden door. My new room was half the size of the one at the Y, barely big enough for the sheetless twin mattress on the floor. I pulled a rope that lit the room's one bulb, dropped my bag, and sat down on the bed. As I slid the Puzo book out of my jacket I saw, sitting in the corner, a pair of worn, but well oiled, ten-hole Dr Marten work boots. I reached over, picked them up, and smiled. They were eight and a halfs.

After lacing up my Docs and admiring them for a while, walking around and convincing myself that they were not at all too tight, I lay back on my mattress with my hands behind my neck and stared happily at the high ceiling of the closet, forgetting altogether that I started work as a Gorgon bouncer that night. Lost in reveries of how I'd polish these boots and bleach the heavy sole stitching, and fix the loose brass eyelets, I soon fell into strange, non-narrative dreams replete with skinhead Siddharthas.

At a few minutes before nine the door slid open, waking me up. Tim stuck his head in.

'Ah ha! Caught ya jackin' off!'

'What?' I said, still drowsy.

'C'mon, Degreasey,' he said, eying my boots. He seemed about to ask something, but shifted gears. '*C'mon*! Here . . .' He bent down and handed me a long black flashlight as thick as a club and left.

'C'mon, Degreaser!' I heard him yell again.

I forgot the flashlight on the bed and hustled after him down the stairs, casting a furtive glance at Marie who was standing behind the bar with hands on hips, conspicuously not looking at me.

When we reached the podium at the top of the front stairs, I saw the same old lady sitting there in her cardigan. On the podium before her was a cash box and a thick roll of theater tickets.

'You're gonna stamp hands,' Tim said, handing me an ink

pad and a rubber stamp. He vanished into his room, reappearing with an olive-drab, nylon bomber jacket and a pair of handcuffs.

'It's gonna be too cold up here for just that,' he said, eying my Brand H work shirt. 'That's fresh though . . . you got any more of those?'

I nodded nervously, looking at the cuffs.

'Don't be flashing these too much,' he said, stuffing them in the pocket of the bomber after I'd put it on. 'These are, like, sex-cuffs I found in Punch's desk. See the safety?' He grinned. 'I mean, they'll do the job, you know, it's just . . . we'll get ya a pair of Smith and Wesson's when you get paid, okay?'

The front door at the bottom of the steep steps pushed open and Jason called up:

'We ready?'

'One minute,' Tim said, reaching behind the podium and dimming the lights real low. Then he turned towards the main dance room and called for music.

'Tim . . .' I said.

He stopped and looked back at me.

'I . . . I mean, what do I do? Whattya want me to do?'

'Whattya mean?' He asked, impatiently, and stepped right up to me. 'What's *to* do? You take this stamp, you make sure everybody buys a ticket from Violet here. Violet this is Alex, Alex . . .' Violet and I exchanged polite nods. 'You take the ticket from each person and stamp their hand, then you give the ticket back to Violet. Nobody gets a stamp without a ticket, nobody gets into the club without a stamp. After this first bumrush it's gonna be real slow tonight, don't worry.'

Tim left, and it still seemed hopelessly complex. He just wasn't aware of my ineptitude with details, and, as the flashing lights and heavy bass dance music had already started, this didn't seem like a good time to tell him.

Before I could sweat it too much though, they were filing up the stairs – all the same freaks I'd seen at Dunkin' Donuts, in full punk regalia. Most of them were so accustomed to the process that they all but led me through each step – handing me their tickets, extending their wrists – and pretty soon I had it down. Take a ticket, stamp a hand, let one in. Take a ticket, etc.

After the initial rush at the door, the pace did slow down to a trickle, and I'd just gotten comfortable enough with the situation to light up a cigarette when I heard Tim shout my name from behind. I turned to see him with Kirk and Aladdin – the two skinheads who had escorted me in that first night. They were pushing five Asian kids in blue headkerchiefs and long black jackets towards the podium.

Tim seemed pretty pissed.

'Alex, man, you lettin' people in without a stamp?'

I shook my head guiltily, but I was telling the truth – I hadn't seen these guys before. I would have remembered them.

'He says he's never seen you,' Tim said.

'We paid,' one of the Asian kids said angrily, his blue bandanna pulled down so low you couldn't see his eyes.

'Well, I gotta believe my guy here.'

'We paid the kid out front with the Vespa,' he continued, 'and he took us up the fire escape.'

A barely distinguishable tic of realization appeared on Tim's face, then he sighed.

'You snuck in then,' he said.

'Yeah.'

'So that's your excuse? You tried gettin' over on the club and got caught?' Tim made a disgusted hissing noise. 'Fuckin' *good*night guys. Walk these gentlemen out wouldjya, Alex?' Then he and the other two skinheads walked back into the dance room.

I looked at Violet pleadingly, as if, perhaps, she might explain to me exactly how I was going to go about kicking out these five Vietnamese gangbangers by my lonesome. She was a lot of help. After raising her eyebrows and shrugging, she looked down at the pile of tickets I'd handed her and began to count them in her lap.

I turned towards the five of them and, without once meeting my eyes, they trudged down the stairs all cursing in a tongue that sounded like banjo to me. I followed them at a four-stair distance, fearing at any minute they'd whirl around and cut me down in a cyclone blur of expert chops and kicks.

One of them did, in fact, open the door with an angry front kick, and they poured out into the streets still cursing.

'Give us the money,' their spokesman said to Jason.

'Nah man, no fuckin' refunds, man,' Jason said, as big burly Jones loomed up behind them. 'Look guy, we both took a risk. You got caught . . . and I didn't. Tough luck.'

'So solly,' Jones grinned behind them, squinting, in a Cockney imitation of an Oriental accent. 'No tickee, no dancee.'

Despite the fact that the odds had been raised to 3-to-5, I was still trembling a bit, and dismayed at Jason's and Jones' fearlessness.

They left though. They walked backwards down the side-walk yelling: ''s fuckin' bullshit, man!' then turned round the corner towards the El tracks.

No sooner were they out of sight, it seemed, but they were out of Jones' and Jason's minds. And they turned their attentions to me.

'Well lookit the little fresh-shave,' Jones said running his hand roughly over my scalp. 'What 'appened to your be-u-tee-ful blond locks there, ay?'

'Yeah guy,' Jason sneered. 'Why'd ya do that? Jones was all set to make you his bitch.'

'Yeah,' Jones said, 'I got tired of puttin' a wig on Jason here every night. He ain't got no ass on him at all.'

'Guy,' Jason said, grimacing, unable to take his end of the

dogging, 'You know what? I'd never be anybody's bitch man. If I found out I was going to prison, I'd go out in the garage, take my belt and — kkkkk.' He twisted his neck unnaturally to the side. 'Just like my old man did.'

'Well, you better get that belt ready, 'cause that's eggzactly where yer headed — the stripy hole Jasey, the stripy hole.'

Jason hardened his sharp black eyes into a look of grim but undeniable satisfaction. Jason Diamond, I'd learn, was a rich kid who grew up in various Northshore suburbs. He was also a liar of such extraordinarily absurd dimensions that he was appreciated by all as a form of convenient entertainment. As eternally sour and insincere as Jason was, I soon grew sick of him and several times we nearly came to blows. That night in front of The Gorgon, though, I found him nothing less than petrifying.

'Hey, where you goin', guy?' he asked, stepping in front of me as I attempted to enter The Gorgon and get back upstairs to my post. 'Jones still wants to make a date with you.'

'Yeah, I'm gonna bring 'im over to your mother's house, Jasey, and watch them fuck while I jack me knob all over your picture.'

'My mom doesn't have any pictures of me,' Jason sneered with satisfaction, and then I heard the squeal of tires and saw the small blue sedan careen around the corner.

It is inaccurate, I believe, when people say that time stands still during dramatic circumstances. I think it would be closer to the truth to say that time becomes distorted. Certain things freeze, certain things proceed at a slow-motion pace, and other things maintain their normal speed.

As the car swung in front of The Gorgon that night and screeched to a halt, before one of the Vietnamese had even begun to hang his body halfway out the backseat window to point his pistol at us, I caught in my periphery the hunched-down blurs of Jason and Jones on either side, diving as if in a dream into the doorway behind me. As he opened fire I heard a distant pop and saw a strobe-quick flash of light in his hands. Then another, and another.

The sound of a rat running through the walls of a room is a curious thing. Often times they only make a noise at the corners. As quick as rats are, before you can really focus on the place the first sound came from, the next sound projects from somewhere else, and so on, disorienting the senses.

That was one thought that ran through my mind after the bullets – all in one abstract millisecond – sliced off of the doorway wall to my right, the steel door behind me, the wall to my left, then ricocheted out towards the street – *there are rats in these walls*.

Then it occurred to me that the kid with the pistol had shouted 'Asian world!' at the top of his lungs before shooting. Then the car squealed off and was gone.

'Ah shit, they shot him in the fuckin' neck man, oh shit!' I heard Jason cry, and I turned around in horror to look at Jones. Jones though, was staring at me with a similar look, and his neck seemed fine. Then I touched the sweat running down the side of my neck, and my hand came back red. I felt myself begin to lose consciousness, but before anything faded out completely, Jones was shouting that I wasn't shot at all.

'It's his ear,' he said, standing up and examining me closely. 'It's just a little . . .' He suddenly filliped my ear pretty hard and I located the sharp sting of a scratch. 'Just some of this brick here musta flied up and nickt yeh,' he said. 'Yer all right . . . look at this . . .' We all examined the three chips in the black paint of the right brick wall, the three dents in the steel door, and the scattered scratches on the left wall.

'That's a pretty tight grouping,' Jason marveled. 'That chink had a steady hand.'

'Yeh, but he was too squinty-eyed to hit this stationary target here,' Jones said, slapping me on the shoulder, making me realize how rubbery my legs were.

'You gotta duck, man!' Jason admonished. 'Jesus Christ, guy!'

'Nah, he ain't gotta duck. He's ee-*lek*-tro-plated in nickel, ain't ya Degreaser?'

'"Asian world,"' Jason scoffed, looking off in the direction the sedan had driven in. 'What the fuck is *that*?'

The Gorgon door kicked open and Tim burst out.

'What the fuck are you doing, Alex?' he said, throwing up his arms in exasperation. 'You can't leave Violet up there all by . . . why the fuck are you bleeding?'

'Degreasey got shot in the ear,' Jason said.

'What?'

'A . . . a brick chip. The bullet made a brick chip,' I stammered, 'and it hit me in the ear.'

'They were really shooting out here?' Tim asked, with a smile that betrayed excitement as well as dismay. 'Ah fuck . . . If the cops come you saw nothin' . . . actually, Jonesy, you go float around inside before you get deported, and I'll send Kirk out here. Degreasey man, come on.'

He threw his arm around me and led me back up the steps, talking incessantly to take my mind off of what had just happened: 'You got somethin' with your tooth right?' I nodded. The only person I'd told was Marie.

'Punch's gonna give you an advance and I'll take you on the bike tomorrow to Northwestern. They got a dental school . . . C'mon, you'll be alright, your ear's not even bleeding anymore,' he said, handing me back my rubber stamp and ink pad as we reached the podium. 'Violet, give this man a cigarette.'

Violet took the Virginia Slims she was smoking out of her mouth and handed it to me. Though it was stained with her rosy lipstick, and though I still had a few of my own left in my pocket, this seemed like the route to nicotine that would require the least amount of motor functions. So I shakily took it.

66

In the following minutes, as I gradually digested all that had just occurred, a strange mixture of dread and euphoria – nervous energy and sinking weakness spread throughout my body. When a couple of patrons finally arrived – a little washed-out punk girl and her boyfriend, a big guy in a thrift store Chicago Police jacket – I took their tickets, barely aware of their existences, until the girl looked up at me, as if mildly aware of being there herself, and said: '*Owww . . .*'

Regrettably, I had just stamped her hand with the burning end of Violet's Virginia Slims. I looked down at her ash-smeared wrist, and then quickly up at her hulking boyfriend.

'Oh . . . man,' I said, begging for mercy basically. 'I'm . . . I'm sorry.'

He shrugged and told me not to worry about it. His girlfriend, as if coming more fully out of whatever stupor she'd been in, said again: 'Owwww!'

I looked at her boyfriend as he ushered her into the club, and something was apparent. He was afraid his girlfriend was about to get him into something he wanted no part of, and . . .

'I hardly know this chick,' he whispered and winked, and it hit me: he was terrified of me. At first it seemed unexplainable, and then I remembered the boots and the bomber and my fresh-shaved skull. That's why those Vietnamese had left so readily too. I was intimidating. Not as Alex Verdi, but as some anonymous Gorgon skin. I immediately inherited the collective scummy ass-kicking reputation the minute I'd donned that costume. Eventually the unearned nature of this rep would come to secretly bother me in an almost pathological way, but at that particular moment, and for some time afterwards, I must admit, I had no complaints.

'A LITTLE TO THE RIGHT, boys,' Punch called down to us, playfully. He was leaning out over the balcony banister to watch as Jones and Jason and I stood in the middle of the main dance floor, pulley-hoisting the giant papier-mâché asteroid up towards the high ceiling while Tim waited in the rafters with hooks and hammer. We were all shirtless and sweaty in our boots and tight jeans, still pumped up from a workout in the Gorgon basement, where Punch had let us set up a bench and a heavy bag. It was at that moment that a certain realization hit me as to this curious partnership of an artsy gay juice-bar owner and a bunch of roughneck skinheads.

Gleaming work boots, close cropped hair, bulging tattooed muscles . . . in a way, the scrupulous skinhead aesthetic was the masculine answer to the Playboy bunny — an exaggerated ode to *la différence*. And though out in the streets skinheads had the fearsome rep of snarling, fag-bashing malcontents, as long as Punch was supplying the pay envelopes (not to mention housing so many of us) we were beasts contained. Now, I don't want to wake up any watchdogs, and I *don't* want to send the subtext sleuths off on any pink herrings, so I'll be careful here and not protest too much.

But the whole thing made me feel kind of funny.

I suppose, though, the increasing discomfort I felt under Punch's lecherous gaze that afternoon had an awful lot to do with the fact that, in that whole seedy universe of orthodox decadence, I had picked the one aspiring nun to fall in love with. An aspiring *Buddhist* nun no less. Marie belonged to a Chicago group of Nichiren Buddhists, but was trying to find a sect with a convent she could join. The stricter and more isolated the better, she said, as to thus ensure her spiritual purity.

Visions of Marie's curvaceous body, her chocolatey, painted skin, and her haunting blue eyes wrapped themselves like transparencies around my every waking thought. And did I dream of her at night? In full color? From all angles? Did I feel what it would be like to cup her smooth round buttocks in my hands? To slide my naked body up against her soft and dewy skin? To taste those nipples? I was ashamed of myself. I knew this inability to get laid must have cast my budding manhood in a very dubious light, especially in the skinhead context, but I had myself convinced that the old in-out-in-out, as it were, was the very *last* thing I wanted from Marie.

Since meeting her on the rooftop that first night, and learning her basic story – the white father who took off before she was born, and the black mother who was dead – I had amplified her orphan status in my mind. I wanted to be with her on all occasions, to provide whatever comfort I could for her, to protect her, and most of all to be her one and only soulmate. And I wanted it in a way that seemed to preclude anything so earthly as sexual intercourse.

Like I said – *I* believed that, but the old courtly love bit couldn't fool a skinchick like Marie.

She tolerated my longings – allowed me to help her stock the juice bar she tended at the club, to run errands for her, and let me tag along some nights to dinner at the local burrito place, where I'd display an intense fascination for even her most trivial comments. Anything to watch those full lips purse and curl into laughter. Anything to watch her bend and shift her ripe body around in those short, tight sun dresses she favored. Anything. But there was always something in her eyes – something openly mocking and ultimately disinterested which invariably tainted these stolen pleasures, and deepened my frustration.

As we were hanging the last of the decorations, with

doortime steadily approaching, Marie came tromping up the front steps with Jermaine, the black skin I'd met on the El, and a couple other skinchicks, who announced in snippets of breathless indignation that a group of *Nazis* were hanging out in the Dunkin' Donuts parking lot, handing out propaganda flyers.

I was so struck with this revelation, this unbelievable opportunity to prove my worth, that I let go the heavy rope Jones and I were holding and almost jostled Timmy from his perch in the rafters.

'What the fuck?' Tim barked, regaining his balance.

'C'mon, fuckin' Degreaser!' Jason snarled, punching me in the arm and taking over my duties.

As I held my arm and glowered at Jason, Marie shouted for us to forget the fucking asteroid and come on.

'Nah, fuck that,' Tim shouted down.

'Fuck you!' Marie shouted up.

'Ah, Marie! For Christ's sakes, come on. Not everybody's got the night off! Get outta here goddammit,' Tim said, starting to laugh. 'Go write a letter about it to Harold Washington or something.'

'What're you – afraid you'll see some of your old buddies?' Marie goaded, but Tim drowned her out with his hammering.

'Well, I'm going,' she said, standing there like some sort of steedless little jockey with her white T-shirt tucked into black stretch-jeans tucked into knee-high black boots. 'And if you all are too much a buncha pussies then fuck ya all!'

I stood there, torn, of course, and, from his all-seeing vantage point, Punch felt moved to intervene.

'Take your swain, Marie, before he splatters Timothy all over my refinished dance floor.'

'Yeah,' Tim called down, 'take The Degreaser.' I looked up at him questioningly. 'Go on Degreasey, go crush the Fourth Reich for Marie whydontchya?'

'Pfff, thanks a *lot*,' Marie said as I walked towards them, and the other two skinchicks rolled their eyes. Jermaine though, bless his heart, greeted me with brutal chest-to-chest bump that made me feel quite welcome, though it almost knocked me on my ass.

When we reached the bottom of the stairs, Jermaine grabbed a heavy wooden walking stick he'd left leaning in the corner and kicked open the front door. Such canes were *de rigueur* for the more combative skins.

Out in the darkening street a small crowd had formed. I recognized Aladdin, the Korean skin with an amazing talent for cartooning and tattoo art, who always carried smooth round stones in his pockets to hurl at his enemies like tiny discuses, along with wiry Kirk, who hailed from the backwoods of Florida and entranced me often with tales of his father, who he claimed had been a knife thrower in the circus. We exchanged rough soul handshakes and clapped each other on the back briefly while the rest of the crowd, all faceless hangers-on in the scene, followed us at close distance as we made our way towards the donut shop.

A group of Black Power skinheads called the SHANC Boys, led by a Marx-spouting former college football player named Sparky Blevins, usually pounced on any Nazi that dared venture into the neighborhood. But when they jumped a young skinhead friend of Timmy's visiting from Boston for wearing an iron-cross pinky ring, and beat him badly, a war of sorts erupted between Sparky's guys and the Gorgon Skins. So the SHANC Boys hadn't been seen for a while, and the Nazis were starting to come around again.

I was so eager to impress Marie, and yet so scared I could barely keep up with them. As we walked though, more skins joined our group and soon my scalp and fingertips were tingling with excitement. Marie had scoffed at my combat abilities; well, I would show her. I'd be the first to leap into the fray. I would grab Frank Pritzger (who no one had seen or heard of since the night he tried to recruit me) and throw him to the ground. I would pummel him with my fists and kick him with my Docs, and the cane blows of that giant guy he traveled with would be useless. I'd wake up handcuffed to a hospital bed and Marie would be there when I opened my eyes, clutching my free hand and weeping. '*There, there,*' I'd chuckle, '*why are you crying? These wounds will heal with time, but long after the sun burns out our love will still remain.*'

*

As the well-lit Dunkin' Donuts parking lot came into sight, I could see the regular hordes of costumed freaks slithering about, but there were no Nazis in sight. We pushed our way through the crowd, desperately looking for our adversaries, and finally saw a ring of spectators pull out around a lone, bleached-blonde skinchick. She was standing next to a rusty blue Vespa scooter clutching a stack of mimeographed propaganda in one hand and the leash of a serene-looking pitbull in the other. Hers was the same bleach-blonde fringe-cut (head shaved except for the bangs, like Marie) I'd seen through the passenger window of Pritzger's Pinto that night, but now, beneath the harsh streetlamp, she looked skinnier, more washed out, with pinkish pancake make-up slathered over a badly broken-out face.

'Where's the rest of the stormtroopers, you nasty cunt?' Jermaine inquired, stepping forward until the pitbull, without changing its good-natured, dullard expression leaped up at him, straining against the leash, and snapped its jaws just short of his privates.

'It's just me!' she screeched defiantly, displaying very bad teeth in braces. 'I got the fuckin' right to free speech, nigger! Back off! Back off!' And she let the dog lunge closer.

Like a railroad worker sinking a spike, Jermaine broke the heavy cane across the dog's blockhead, and, as it crumbled limply to the blacktop, I saw Marie attack. The Nazi girl, with some reflexive burst, grabbed Marie around the waist and tripped her backwards to the ground. I dove at them but was immediately caught by several arms which held me back amidst laughter and reassurances as the girls rolled and scratched and kicked for all they were worth.

'Don't worry about Marie,' I was told, 'she's got it, she's got it,' and sure enough, very quickly, she was on top of the white-power girl, pinioning her arms to her sides, and head-butting her repeatedly, square in the face. I howled for them to let me go, but there was nothing doing. The Nazi girl briefly got one arm free, and suddenly a large crescent of red appeared on the back of Marie's white T-shirt.

'Watch out Marie, she's got nails . . . she's scratchin' you!' they called, and Marie, again in complete control, glanced back to see the damage.

'Oh,' she panted, 'you like to scratch, huh? You like scratchin'? Okay . . .' And with that she grabbed the girl's right wrist and shifted her legs out to the side in a reclining, seated position, leaning her full weight back against the exhausted, bloody-faced Nazi girl's chest, and clamped the girl's right arm between her bicep and breast. Still clutching the girl's limp wrist, Marie held up the pale little hand that had scratched her for all the crowd to see. The captured fingers featured extremely long, white-painted nails that looked capable of all kinds of horrors.

'Ohhh, okay,' Marie said, gulping for air, and reached for the nails with her free hand. Then, starting with the Nazi-girl's thumb, Marie proceeded to bend back and snap the lacquered talons off at their roots.

This drew much applause from the crowd, of course, as well as pitiful screams from the girl, and I stopped struggling altogether, transfixed at the indescribably horrible sight of those long white nails one by one reduced to bloody stumps.

This was certainly the climax and the end of the contest, but Marie began slugging the girl again in the eyes, nose and throat until the sirens and flashing red lights were suddenly splashing everywhere around us. Jermaine and Aladdin and I quickly pulled her off the motionless body and tried to slip her into the crowd but blue uniforms were approaching from every direction telling everyone to freeze.

An older white cop approached the whimpering girl and knelt down close beside her, immediately asking questions, careful not to touch her with any part of his own body. As the pitbull began to stir next to them, his partner dragged it off towards the street. Another cop, who evidently knew Jermaine quite well, saw fit to brace his nightstick across Jermaine's throat and twist him face down to the blacktop. A huge black officer grabbed me by the collar of my bomber and together we looked towards the older cop and the girl.

'Do ya see 'em here?' he asked her. She was now holding her head up a bit and looking in our direction. Marie stood next to me, unrestrained and still panting hard – with smudges of drying blood on her forehead – and stared with those glowing blue eyes directly at the girl.

One of the girl's eyes had begun to swell shut, but with the other she looked over at us, and said to the cop through a red bubble of spit:

'Some nigger. Some nigger gangbanger tried to take my purse. He's gone, he ran, he's gone . . .'

Despite the sickening decisiveness of the fight, there was an uneasy feeling of unfinished business in the air, particularly when Frank's Nazi-mobile – the pale blue Pinto – slowly pulled up behind the ambulance to observe what Marie had done. Though it would be a couple days before we felt them, this cause would have its effects, a whole crazy string of them.

*

Marie and I walked back towards The Gorgon in silence. It wasn't quite nausea I felt, but some kind of emptiness and courselessness and hate. I felt the eyes of all those we passed upon us, and imagined their thoughts: *There they go – the vicious virgin she-beast and her eunuch bootlick.* I could not get the sight of the Nazi-girl from my head and wanted suddenly to be as far from Marie as possible. As far away from The Gorgon and all of this absurd shit as I could walk in one night, and then keep walking when the morning came. I was ready to admit defeat and turn myself into the Harding County cops as a means of having some contact with my family, but still I kept in step with Marie, as if we were magnetized, all the way up the steps of The Gorgon to her bedroom.

She sat down heavily on the end of her futon couch and I stood in her doorway, silently, looking around her unlit room at the shadows of punk-rock posters and thrift store bric-a-brac.

'Well, we're opening up soon,' I finally managed to croak, and took a step out into the hallway.

'You're not even gonna *help* me?' she cried, incredulous.

I looked back at her blankly.

'I'm fuckin' hurt! I'm *bleeding.*'

I drew in a breath, and again fought back the strange desire to simply turn my back and walk.

'Fine,' she said, 'get the fuck outta here. GET OUT!'

I shut the door and went to her and gingerly helped her off with the shirt which was sticking to the deep scratch on her back. As she unclasped her bra and tossed it angrily away, I looked at her firm, bare breasts and seethed, as if this carelessness about being naked in front of me was yet another bit of mockery. She produced from somewhere a bottle of Everclear alcohol which I poured on a clean bar rag. She stretched out on the couch on her stomach, muttering obscenities to herself about the pain, which, from the looks of the jagged scratch, must have been considerable.

As I knelt before her and began to swab the wound, a feeling of suffocating rage seemed to come from within and without. The rage was directed at her and I couldn't quite justify it but didn't care.

'Ahhh OWW! OW!' she screamed and squirmed as I dabbed, 'Ah, you fucker! You fuckin' idiot.'

'WHAT?' I suddenly roared, grabbing her arm so she would look at me. 'Huh? What?'

'Be careful,' she said, twisting her neck around with a taken-aback expression. 'Jesus!'

I grabbed the bottle of Everclear and thrust it at her. 'You want some more of this? Huh?' and splashed some directly on her back. She screamed and shrank and slid away from me up to a sitting position as I raged at her, my voice breaking.

'You don't like this, ya fff . . . ya fuckin' *bitch*? Huh? Huh?' I said, standing up, and hurled the bottle at her window. It crashed through the glass, letting in the sounds of the Englewood-Howard El and distant city traffic. She screamed at me at the top of her lungs to get out, then flew at me with swinging fists. She drove me back against the wall and we grappled for a split-second before she went limp and began to sob with a ferocity that rang in my ears.

I held her stiffly, trying to contain the strange rage that still consumed me, but as she apologized tearfully into my neck, then slid her wet face down to my chest, my hands went to the small of her back, and reached inside the waistband of her stretch jeans.

We kissed hard and sloppily and my fingers and thumbs groped everywhere on her body, squeezing and seeking out entryways to bare skin as if I were on some limited shopping spree. With a mounting feeling of frenzy I pushed her back towards the futon, unbuttoning her jeans on the way. After pressing her down on the couch, I tugged her pants down to her knees before she stopped kissing me and asked, in a tiny voice that seemed alien and detached: 'Do you love me?' I grunted in the affirmative and pushed her pants down to her 20-hole Docs which, I saw, would have to be removed. As I furiously worked to unlace them, she sobbed and said, as if she were slowly coming back from wherever she'd just been:

'Alex, are you gonna be straightedge with me?'

I nodded.

'I mean it. I'll do it. Will you?'

I nodded.

'Totally just you and me – and not drink or smoke or . . .'

'Okay.'

'And tomorrow's Easter,' she continued, sniffling hard as I pulled the first boot off. 'Will you spend it with me? We'll spend Easter together.' I nodded and attacked the second boot. 'Only . . . but let's not eat any turkey. Let's not eat any meat any more. I mean, not even fish.'

Even in my state, that last request struck me as odd, but a dizzy, agreeable feeling was taking hold and I told her that would be fine as I pulled the second boot off, yanked the pants all the way down, flung them to the carpet and went for her.

'Hold on,' she said, as I began fumbling frantically with my own fly. A fuse had been lit, I suddenly realized, and there wasn't much time. 'Hold on,' she said again, and, twisting out from under me, she scrambled across the floor fumbling for something. 'Hold on,' she said and flicked a Bic lighter which illuminated her naked brown body in all its tattooed, scratched-up splendor. Oh, good Lord, crawling like that in the flickering shadows she looked like some strangely-coated, leopard-lady or something – the saddle of tattoos on her back stopping abruptly at her tailbone so that her pale brown rump looked all the rounder and more luminous.

'Hold on, come here,' she said, as she crept towards a tiny old chest of drawers, reaching up to light two small candles that flanked an upright rectangular box. It was constructed of thick cardboard that was designed to look like stained pine. There were two doors on the front which she ripped open from their velcro fastening, and hanging inside the box was some sort of Oriental scroll which she began muttering to.

77

'Come here,' she said shakily, and I knelt behind her in the flickering glow, gritting my teeth as the dike within me groaned with the hopelessness of its task. 'Say it with me,' she said. '"*Nam*" . . .'

'"Nam,"' I spat.

'Myoho . . . Rengay . . . Kyo . . .'

She stared directly at the scroll, her naked ass resting on the balls of her heels, her backbone arching as she prayed. As if punched square in the face by this image, my eyes began to water and a stinging raced up both nostrils.

'Nam Myoho Renge Kyo . . .' she chanted. 'Come *on*.'

I blinked and all but sobbed the whole prayer three times with her, and she leaned forward to blow out the candles. But before she could even exhale, I had pushed my jeans down to my thighs and, as if led by a divining rod, plastered myself up against her back with a slapping sound.

I reached under her armpits and, for the first time, felt the weight of her breasts in my hands. Real tears of gratitude slid down my cheeks, I am telling you. For an instant she reflexively arched herself even more tightly against me and reached back to lightly scrape her nails against the sides of my ass. Oh God, the sands were running down to the final grains! 'Hurry! Hurry!' all my inner voices cried in unison.

I wrapped one arm around her tiny waist and rolled her to the floor, flat on her stomach. I grabbed her hips and nudged, and when I felt the first hint of that moist warmth, I . . . could this be? Was there truly a current of justice in this universe?

Before I could investigate any further, Marie corkscrewed over to her back and pushed out away from me with her legs. There was a desperate, humid moment as the clock ticked towards zero and all seemed lost. But she just lay there, with her wounded back pressed firmly to the smooth, clean floorboards – eyes closed and not fleeing – as if to say: '*This* is the way you'll take me – like *this*.'

I slid headfirst into home, you might say. I released at the buzzer. The shot was good and I scored. She sucked air in sharply through her teeth, as if to scream in pain, but before she could, I let loose with a crazed and victorious throat sound that rolled out of me in delicious wave after wave and finally trailed off into a half-demented sort of chuckle.

She waited until I was through yowling, then burst into tears again. But these tears were different – these sobs were light silvery giggles of relief. At least that's how they sounded to me at the time.

She curled up in my lap as the cool air from the hole in her window washed over us and I held her in my arms for several minutes, repeatedly assuring her that I loved her – yes, yes, I would be straightedge with her. And I meant it, the basic natural pleasures of life were the purest and most intense – why would I need any others? Then the heavy bass beat from the downstairs dance room came pounding on the door, alerting me that it was time to go. I had completed my quest.

I kissed her until her sobs eased off into the occasional hiccup, then pulled up my pants and trotted downstairs to my security post just a few seconds before doortime. It was a phenomenal night at work. I single-handedly broke up a dance floor brawl and threw the biggest of the offenders out without any assistance. For the first time I felt at home in the frenetic atmosphere of the club, amidst wild lights and that throbbing dance music – those driven beats layered with technologically enhanced little girl whispers, sultry moans, and electronic whip-cracks, all speaking of a dark universe where people clawed towards and reached greater and greater heights of orgasmic ecstasy. It didn't seem so ludicrously exaggerated now. I gazed down upon the main dance floor and realized that all the writhing and thrusting of those naughtily half-dressed, sweaty female bodies was not just some sadistic tease – it was an honest promise to he who was brave enough to take what he wanted.

As we cleared patrons out at the end of the night, a short

Puerto Rican girl in a black lycra mini-dress (with thick white racing stripes running down the sides, no less) stuck her hand in my bomber jacket pocket as she passed. I stopped and watched her clip-clop away in high heels. Jason shone his flashlight on the back of her dress where the fabric was stretched to near-transparency by the jut of her globular ass and it glimmered in the smoky beam of light like a disco ball. She was down the front stairs and out the door before I thought to reach into my pocket. Scrawled inside a foil chewing gum wrapper was her phone number.

After work, Timmy had a box of forty-ouncers delivered to the club, and I sat at the main juice bar getting hammered with him and Jones and Jason and Kirk as we rehashed the night's excitements over and over again. When Aladdin arrived I badgered him into breaking out his jerry-rigged, prison-style tattoo kit – a mason jar of bleach, a bottle of India ink and a mechanical pencil wired to a Walkman motor. After tossing some bleach on my right shoulder, then wiping it off with his sleeve, he gave me a simple blue anarchy sign about the size of a silver dollar. The rest of them expressed their disgust as the symbol had long ago become the ultimate punk-poseur cliché. But it had a deeper meaning for me, I explained, and the drunken words flowed out of me . . .

I knew Marie was waiting for me up in her room, and I knew there wasn't any great hurry to get to her. I knew she would wait for me now. I knew this as well as I knew my own name. But when I woke with an unbearable pang late Easter morning, alone and hung-over in the middle of the dance floor, I knew just as well that she was gone.

THERE ARE FEW THINGS more depressing than an empty nightclub in the morning. Like a toy kaleidoscope that's been torn in two, the mute, litter-strewn dance floors and absent flash of colored lights betray a cheesy sham – a contrived device for euphoria and exploration – no more real than a blow-up doll or a tab of acid.

At least that's how I saw it that morning as I grumpily went behind the sticky mainfloor bar, grabbed a squat bottle of Orangina from the cooler, and headed out to the fire-escape for the roof.

I stopped though, suddenly fully aware that it was a holiday. I went into the Gorgon office, sat at Punch's desk, and called my old phone number. I listened to the disconnection recording, then called the Harding County Police and hung up, paranoid that they'd trace the call. There was overpowering guilt, followed by a wave of rage. Momentary hatred – was I wrong to be afraid? Was I the one who let them destroy our family all for some filthy fucking hippie weed? Was I the one? I stood and picked up my folding chair to throw across the room. But I stopped, put it down, and sat again. After a moment or two I pulled out the phone book and thumbed through the white pages for any sort of social service agency that might get me in touch with my sister. But, again, they would want to know my name. And it was a holiday. So I went up to the roof.

It was a gray, cool day, and the sky hung low as I ascended the ladder. Once on the rooftop I paced around for a while, examined Jason's pot plants which were thriving, and found myself sneering like Marie that he wasn't a *real* skinhead. I

81

found a half-empty forty-ouncer of stale malt liquor and poured it all over his hippie shit, then sat and watched a few El trains roll by. After a while I took to seeing how close to the edge I could creep without getting giddy. Before long I was stretched out flat on the roof so that only my eyes extended over the ledge, and looked down to the sparse traffic on Sheffield. I stayed like that, with eleven-twelfths of my body clinging to the roof, until I saw Tim approaching from the east with a gym bag. I remembered him asking me if I wanted to go work out that morning at the Chicago Fitness Center – a local gym where mostly cops and bouncers and skinheads lifted weights, boxed, and practiced martial arts. Tim, a black belt, was showing me the Tae Kwon Do patterns I'd need for my yellow belt test. When I saw him down there I forgot my fear for a bit and stuck my entire head over, yelling to him. From that distance, with his hooded sweatshirt and stubbly head, he looked as much like a big, pretty-boy Wrigleyville jock out for his daily jog as he did the undisputed King of the Skinheads. He looked up and wanted to know what the hell I was doing, and, as I was without an answer, I shouted to him that I was coming down.

'Whaddya doin'?' he asked again, as I entered his room. He was sitting on the beanbag taking off his sneakers. On top of his chest of drawers lay his gi, already neatly folded, with the black belt doubled up beside it.

'Whatta *you* doin'?' I asked him back.

'Nothin' . . .' he said, pulling on his ten-hole oxblood Docs. 'I thought you were going out with Marie somewhere or something.'

I explained to him how she'd ditched me, after insisting that I reserve the holiday for her. Tim noted the dismay in my voice and informed me that she was 'mindfucking' me.

'You're too comfortable with her now. You're getting to know her too well. Chicks don't want that. They're like . . . you ever see those hypnotist guys that come to your school?' I hadn't, but, preferring my wisdom in pearls rather than epics, I nodded so he'd continue. 'Do they ever pick the kids from the audience that know what time it is? Nah, they pick the goofballs and the nice kids – the wide-eyed ones who are in awe of the motherfucker and, like, *believe* he's magic or some shit. A chick is one hundred percent illusion man, that's all she's got. So, either buy into it, or sooner or later she's history.'

In light of Tim's rep as a cocksman – his long list of conquests included aspiring models, actresses, and countless Homecoming Queens gone bad – I knew his advice must be valid, but felt it was directed at the wrong guy. I had no problem buying into the illusion of Marie. I was full-on mesmerized, as it were.

Tim rose on long legs from the beanbag and walked over to the huge fish tank beneath his suspended bed. He'd purchased a new Siamese Fighting Fish – shimmering amethyst in body, with bright red fins – for an upcoming fight-to-the-death against one of Aladdin's Siamese. These fish, Tim told me, would swim peacefully in the same tank with any other breed except their own.

Tim was something of a self-taught naturalist – a voracious reader of sea adventures, wildlife texts, and popular science magazines – not to mention, in Punch's estimation (and he seemed to know such things) an accomplished photographer. Tim confided in me once that his ultimate dream was to sell a picture to *National Geographic*. There was a type of bird in India, he claimed, that had never been photographed. He often told me how the two of us could go to Alaska, work on fishing boats, and make enough money in one summer to pay for equipment and round-trip tickets to Bombay. What *my* exact role in the adventure would be was never quite clear to me, though I pictured myself as a sort of roadie, lugging all the camping gear and water skins through leech-infested rivers. In fairness, though, I think it was clear: he just liked having me around for some reason. Sometimes. Even with me he was guarded about some things. Everybody knew he occasionally did work for some local coke dealers, but nobody knew the details. There were lots of things nobody knew.

He tapped on the glass of the tank and found his fighting fish lurking behind a chunk of reef. 'Ah ha, there ya are, Marie, ya little minx,' he said. It seemed an obvious name choice. After sprinkling in some food, and checking the gurgling aerator, Tim turned to me and grinned. 'She's gonna *destroy* that little *guppy* Aladdin's got, man. I been personally *training* this fish. She's got the Timmy Penn *moves*, friend.'

Unfortunately, the bout was destined to be decided by forfeit, as the aquatic Marie would soon die from some sort of fungus that periodically wiped out Timmy's entire tank. Tim always kept his room as neat and clean as an Army barracks, and he was just as meticulous about that aquarium, but the fish kept dying, and he finally blamed the excessively high mold count in the mildewy club's air which he had no control over.

After putting away the fish food, Tim grabbed a stiff brush and swiped it back and forth across the toes of his Docs, then pulled on his new, nylon bomber jacket – black and shiny with a stiff Chicago flag-patch sewn on the shoulder. He had let me keep the worn olive bomber, saying it was too small for him anyway.

'Where ya goin'?' I asked.

'Me?' he asked, and in one half-second seemed to prepare to brush me off, then seemed to say fuck it, sighed, and told me in an uncharacteristically flat tone that he was going to his mom's, and did I want to come too?

*

As always, we couldn't simply pay for two El fares. According to plan, Tim burst in through the swinging red doors at the Belmont station hollering at the black girl in the ticket booth, while I scampered in behind him on all fours just as they swung closed.

'Yo yo *yo* bay-bee! Whussup? Haw? Whussup?' he brayed in his best street black. As he stopped at the turnstile I bumped my head into his calf. 'Sayyy momma, when's you an' me gonna get to-*getha*? Huh? Whussup? Aw, I get it . . . it's cuz ahm *white* ain't it? Uh huh. Thass it. It's cuz ahm *white*!'

I could hear the ticket girl giggling and sliding him back his change as I snaked my way between his boots – blackening my knees and palms – toward another free ride.

'Oh, so that's howz gonna be,' Tim told the girl in a deeply hurt tone. 'Awright den.'

We got off the train in East Rogers Park at Morse and followed the narrow alley that ran along the El track embankment to Pratt. Timmy's mother lived in Pratt Manor, a rundown monolith of tiny studio apartments.

'Don't mind my ma,' he assured me, as we rode the rickety elevator up to eleven, 'she's a freak.'

When we reached her door Tim grabbed the knob, then thought better of it and knocked.

'God only knows what she's doing in there.'

No sooner had he knocked than a happy shriek went up inside and the door was flung open. A scrawny woman who, with her angular face and blue-gray eyes looked unnervingly like Tim, threw herself upon him and smothered him in kisses. She smelled like a stale gin and tonic.

'Ma, c'mon huh?' he grinned as he ushered me into the apartment. It was one square room – not much larger than my closet at The Gorgon – with a small kitchen off to one side and a bathroom off to the other. There was a broken-down sofa against the wall she shared with the hallway and a round glass table by the window, at which sat an elderly little black man with a sweat-stained straw fedora. He rested his hands on a cane that stood between his legs. His eyes – magnified behind

85

goggle-sized, black-rimmed eyeglasses – floated in our general direction, and narrowed suspiciously as we walked in.

Tim introduced me to his mother while staring at the black man. Ignoring me completely, Tim's mom introduced the man as Mr Allen from the tenth floor, and skipped drunkenly into the kitchen.

'Howyadoin', Mr Allen?' Tim said, pointing at him.

'Mmm hm,' Mr Allen said, nodding, as if to let Tim know he was completely on to him – knew his kind inside and out. 'Thought you'd *finally* come see your mother, huh?'

'Have a seat, Timmy and . . . both of youse,' Tim's mom said, giving me a fishy look as she emerged from the kitchen with an armful of Miller tallboys. 'I was just telling Mr Allen about this guy who ran up to me in the stairwell last night and started . . . JACKIN' OFF at me!'

Tim grimaced.

'Ma . . . Jesus.'

'Mmm hmm,' said Mr Allen accusingly, 'and where were you? Out havin' a *good* time.'

'Ma . . . you fuckin' made that up.'

'I did not.'

'Ma . . .' Tim turned to me for support: 'What are the odds of a woman having, what ma – like a *dozen* different guys jack off in front of her in public?'

'Pretty good if she ain't got nobody 'round to take care of her,' said Mr Allen.

'Maybe they're all the same guy . . . like he's *stalkin'* me or something.'

Tim shook his head and drank his beer. I was startled to see how close he seemed to angry tears.

'Tim and his friend are skinheads,' Tim's mom told Mr Allen.

'Mm hm,' he said, 'I can *see* that.'

'But not the Nazi kind any more, right Timmy?'

'Whattya mean, ma? I told you.'

'They ain't got nothin' against colored people,' she assured Mr Allen. 'Or Jews. Do you Timmy?'

'Do I *what?*' Tim was full-blown sullen now.

'Have anything against blacks or Jews?'

'Do I? No,' Tim said.

'Me neither,' Tim's mom said. 'Except . . .'

She looked at me accusingly. 'You Jewish?'

I shook my head and she continued.

'I hate how those Jewish comedians always go on and on and on about how annoying their Jewish relatives are – like it's *cute* or something. That'd be like Timothy gettin' up there and saying " . . . and then there's my grandpa Pat, he was a big fat Irish cop who drank all the time and everybody told him 'Pat, you better stop drinking' but he kept right on drinking and drinking till one day – *a blood vessel exploded in his head and he died*!" I mean, that wouldn't be very funny, you know?'

Beer suds shot out my nose, and the three of them – Mr Allen, Tim and his mom, turned to me accusingly. I was as horrified as anybody and began to apologize profusely but there was a knock on the door and I was saved.

If it seemed that Tim's mood could not sink to any gloomier depths, the arrival of what turned out to be his mother's new boyfriend – Sammy – proved depression is a bottomless pit.

Sammy was, I would venture to say, no more than (at most) a year or two older than Tim, though he seemed to have entered puberty somewhat later, as his sallow weasel face featured a blooming crop of acne and a peachfuzz mustache – the scraggly ends of which he stroked constantly with his thumb and forefinger. It was an affectation of suavity I found ludicrous, and strangely infuriating. As this was the mid-1980s, I feel compelled to give some detail of Sammy's mode of dress, lest anyone forget what a renaissance of elegance that decade actually was. His shirt was a sleeveless alloy-gray thing, the neck of which unzipped diagonally across his chest so that a giant flap would have fluttered with his every step like an elephant ear, were it not for a tasteful aluminum snap located on the right shoulder. His pants were of the now obsolete, but greatly missed, 'parachute' variety – red vinyl, skintight, and covered with literally scores of silver zippers, not one of which appeared utilitarian.

As his dead-drunk mother and Sammy clumsily embraced, amidst Mr Allen's supportive greeting, I looked at Tim and saw what little adolescence there was left on his already rawboned eighteen-year-old face momentarily melt away, until I wasn't quite sure whether he looked like a weary old man or a sad little boy, or both. Sammy ignored us as he and Tim's mother shared the chair next to Mr Allen and cuddled. For the next half hour or so Tim and I drank our beers in silence while his mother, Sammy, and Mr Allen took turns puffing on a couple of giant joints that Mr Allen, with his crinkly brown fingers, had expertly fashioned out of two cheap cigars and a bag of pungent skunkweed, compliments of Sammy. I'm not sure if it was the contact high I got as the tiny room filled with smoke or just the beer but I had nearly drifted into a serene, all but consciousless, state when I suddenly imagined that I *felt* a strong heat emanating from Timmy's body.

His mother and Sammy were leaning their elbows on the table, staring into each other's eyes, murmuring unintelligibles, and had just begun to nuzzle noses, when I saw Sammy steal a sly glance up at Tim that produced in me the same strange fury as the mustache stroking. I watched him closely now, as they began to tongue kiss, and there it was again – that quick, self-conscious, but triumphant look. I waited for it to come again when suddenly the table-top flew up and Tim dove across the room, pushing Mr Allen, who had nodded off, over backwards on his chair, and grabbed Sammy around the neck with both hands.

As Timmy's mom jumped up shrieking, then tripped over the cursing Mr Allen, I leaped upon Tim and grabbed him round the waist, but only for his own sake as he seemed intent on murdering the chump. His thousand-sit-ups-a-day regimen, coupled with his naturally sinewy musculature, gave me the impression that I was wrestling with a writhing knot of conduits.

I offered about as much help as the mouse that pulled the turnip, but I was just as successful, as Tim suddenly let go of the geek on his own accord, stood up, and allowed him to scamper into the bathroom and lock the door. I let go of Tim and attempted to help his mother and Mr Allen up but they both swatted at my hands and swore at me.

'You . . , you come into my house, you sonofabitch!' Tim's mother sobbed. 'A stranger! And right away you're startin' shit! Timmy I want him *out* of here *now*, do you hear me? Out!'

'We're leavin', ma,' said a sober-sounding Tim. 'Degreasey, c'mon.'

'Come in here and start bustin' up the gott-damn place!' Mr Allen shouted from the floor, thrusting his cane at me with menace.

'Timmy, wait,' his mother cried, as we reached the door, 'hold on a sec.'

'Oh yeah, I forgot,' Tim said quietly, and dug into the pocket of his jeans. He pulled out a plain silver money clip and plucked out three crisp hundreds and a fifty.

'No . . . it's . . . I got your birthday present for you . . . I woulda given it to you on the *right* day but . . .'

'But you couldn't even come see your mom on the day she *birthed* you.'

'Hey Mr Allen,' Tim said, flaring up again, '*shut* the *fuck* up, Ma, forget about it.'

'No, it's right here, Timmy,' she said, reaching under a couch cushion and pulling out an only slightly used-looking paperback.

'Ain't nobody shuttin' the *nothin'* up,' grumbled Mr Allen.

'Ma,' Tim said as he took the book, 'c'mon. This is your book. This is the book you been reading.'

'But I got it for *you*, Timmy,' she said, wiping the tears away and swaying a bit. 'I wrote in it see? It's for you.'

Tim opened the cover of *Ransom*, by Jay McInerney – the story, as I recall, of a young rich kid who renounces American decadence and moves to Japan to become a karate expert. Timmy was more of a Jack London man.

Sure enough, there was an inscription scrawled in red pen.

Timmy,
I thought of you as I read this book because I always knew how you wished you were a Jap. But just think, if you were – you'd have *a little one*!
Love Ma

'Thanks Ma. I'll see ya.'

'Timmy?'

'Yeah?'

She looked wilted and meek now as she reminded Tim about a fifteen–dollar late–charge for the rent. Tim pulled off another twenty which left his clip pretty thin, and we left.

When the elevator came it was filled with piss. An incredible amount of brownish–orange piss that sloshed back and forth on the warped tile floor. Standing in the back were two middle–aged black men who, by the roughness of their clothes and their overall grimy appearance, looked homeless. I had a hole in my right boot, so I rode down with one foot curled up in the air behind me.

'Damn,' one of the men said to the other, 'somebody done pissed on the floor.'

'Who would go and do a thing like that?' said the other.

I looked at Tim, first at his well–oiled Docs where piss beaded up harmlessly on the red leather toes, then to his face as he stared directly at the men with hard–eyed irony.

'Didn't I just say,' said the first man, a little nervously, 'right when we got on: "*Damn*, somebody done *pissed* on the floor . . . who would do a thing like that?"?'

'Mm hmm,' said the second man.

'Musta been a *small boy* go an' do a thing like that.'

When we got out to the street Tim chuckled softly, and bitterly.

'What?' I said. 'Those guys?'

He looked at me with a beat expression.

'Huh? No . . . *you*. Standing there the whole time with one leg up in the air like a fuckin' flamingo. Pfff. That's your new name – "Flamingo".'

With a forced grin I dropped my chin and walked alongside him in silence, as the slushy alley puddles squished in through the hole in my boot. I thought of the advice he'd given me about Marie that morning, and wondered in silent dread if I had gotten to know *him* too well – if I'd failed some secret test today and now he'd stop being such a good friend to me.

We didn't try the two-for-one trick at Morse. Tim just paid for us both and we rode the whole way back to Belmont in gloomy silence. But as we left the train and passed the cute CTA girl we'd tricked that morning, she smiled up coquettishly at Tim. And out in the street the gaggles of punk kids greeted him eagerly, but cautiously, like royalty. We passed the burrito joints and pizza places where, like cops, we ate for free in exchange for our good will. And I felt the leaden gloom of that Easter Sunday lift slightly, and continue to lift as we approached The Gorgon – all lit up and full of people again, its brick walls throbbing with heavy sound.

Out front, a bustling crowd had formed where a line of girls were getting their heads shaved. A caustic industrial punk band was shooting a concert video upstairs and they needed more bald people. So girls with big hair, bobbed hair, Mohawks and ponytails were trading in their locks for a chance at a few seconds of infamy in a video that would never be aired on MTV because Jason Diamond kept leaping up and sieg-heiling the camera out of sheer nihilistic spite.

The music was relentless, like an amplified phone left off the hook. Upstairs looked like a street riot. The strobe-lit mainroom dance floor was a twisting, turning knot of kids that moved around like dark water in a pail. Punk kids splashed up on stage to dance with the crazed band, then dove back in like freeze-framed suicides.

As we approached, the air got hot and thick and Tim tied his bomber around his waist, preparing to jump right in. My heart leapt to see that his cocky visage had returned and I grabbed his arm.

'Tim!' I shouted over the driving guitars.

He stopped and cupped his ear.

'I don't want to be "The Flamingo", man!'

I wanted to stay The Degreaser, strange as that may sound.

He laughed his regular laugh and put an arm around me, as if to say: 'Sure, Degreasey, sure,' then shoved me violently into the crowd. I was slammed from all sides, and I slammed back, shoving and worming my way through the sweat-slick bodies, towards the cleared-out center of the room, where the skinheads dominated, circumventing the slam-pit in a counter-clockwise pack, like the eye of a storm, knocking down anyone in their path.

Everyone was there – Jones, Aladdin, Kirk, Jermaine and Jason. Tim's friend, Jim Shea, from the hardcore band Worth Less, was there too, with his crew of skins. A dozen sweaty scalps, a dozen tattooed bodies. Spit flying, all high knees and elbows flailing, like evil parodies of warpath Indians, they danced the skinhead stomp.

When I reached them I flew shoulder down into Jason's back and sent him sprawling across the floor. I was hit from behind by Jones and Kirk simultaneously and flew face-first down after him. As I tried to get up, some big punker with a Mohawk stepped accidentally on my face, and got knocked on his back for it. Suddenly hands were reaching down, grabbing me from all sides. Jason had one hand and Jones the other. Once I was up and safe again they shoved me into the pit where I collided with Tim. I bounced back against the crowd, panting ecstatically. I tasted blood in my mouth and spat it up towards the band. Across the slam pit Tim and Jones shouted at me. They were crouched with their hands intertwined and cupped. I ran at them, stepping into their hands, and they sprung up, catapulting me up and backwards like a high jumper, high above the sweat-soaked crowd. I closed my eyes before the crowd caught me, then saw in my mind's eye an image of a laughing Marie, and wondered where she was, and when I'd see her again. Then, buoyed up there by a dozen strange hands, I rode around in darkness and thought of nothing and let the whirlpool take me where it may.

THE NIGHT WE CAME back from Tim's mom's apartment, I saw a sweaty skinhead, spent with drunken exhaustion, leaning heavily on the front stairs banister as he left the club after the video shoot. His whole back was covered by one tattoo – a blue-inked depiction of an arm-wrestling match between Satan and what appeared to be a bald-headed Saint Michael the Archangel (as Skinhead). For an instant, I felt a little bravado thrill of appreciation for this kindred spirit. Then I just felt a little embarrassed for the kid, and for me.

Being a skinhead was never really about anyone's conceptions of Good vs. Evil. There were just some skins who thought that if they did their violent things for a 'cause', it would be okay. I was certainly a little that way, and Marie was entirely that way, and Timmy Penn was not that way at all.

Frank Pritzger and his neo-Nazi Chicago Land Area Skinheads (CLASH) were definitely that way, and Sparky Blevins no doubt valued CLASH as the raison d'être for his black-power Skinheads Against Nazis in Chicago (SHANC). But most street skins were free-floating apolitical packs of thugs like the Anti-Societal Skinheads of Lake Zurich (ASSHOLZ).

I am not saying, though, that for all its considerable sound and fury, Skinheadism signified nothing. I mean, I'm no expert here. I don't know much about instinctive patterns in human behavior, but I do know one thing. In addition to the slew of other farm animals we had after my father moved our family out to the old house in the woods, we raised from a pup a small black-and-white border collie named Billy. He was by far my sister Stacy's favorite dog. Long before Billy reached maturity (though we never taught him anything beyond basic paper training), he began herding things. All kinds of things. Anything in fact would do. He herded other dogs, cats, geese, children, even, on occasion, I swear, kitchen chairs. As he grew older, and the other farm animals learned to avoid him, Billy began to stray off in search of greater things. Through our north woods and past the neighboring cornfield, Billy discovered, across the four lanes of rural Route 41, a meadow where thoroughbred horses were let to roam during the day. From dawn till dusk you could find him there, faithfully herding the horses, who tried at first to kick him to death, but, failing at that (he was quite deft), eventually resigned themselves to humoring him in his purposeless passion. We found Billy one day, dead on the gravel shoulder – struck, I'd guess, by a passing semi. My father remarked soberly that he'd died with his boots on.

Would you permit me to say the youthful skinhead was a lower-class inner-city white manifestation of the young-warrior archetype in the human psyche? All throughout history when young men reached a certain age, they were ritualistically made into the warriors they instinctively thirsted to be.

Until this so-called post-modern age.

Then again, everyone has their own reasons for doing things, their own demons, perversions as unique and detailed as thumbprints, so maybe I shouldn't say. Maybe all my life I've been trying to live by what I've read in books, with only half my heart in it. My father 'home-taught' me before high school, with mixed results. At thirteen I knew the Russian Masters and Shakespeare – intimately – and could draw an aesthetic bridge between the Japanese poets Zeami and Basho. But math, beyond basic algebra, was a black abyss. My dad tried to jazz it up with many a martial pep-talk, telling me equations represented the complexities of *life itself* – I must *confront* them and *never* accept defeat. But it was still just fuckin' math to me. When my father got busted with the weed and everything fell apart with my family, I never once doubted that there was an answer – a solution that would put everything back together again. But it was too complex for me, and I was bitter, and I was ashamed, so for a while there I just blocked it all out. Or tried to. I had already run away from home in body; I think for me Skinheadism was just my mind catching up.

After we cleared everybody out of the club that Easter night, me and Timmy went to his room, where I collapsed in his beanbag chair. He sat down sideways on his windowsill, put a Hank Williams Sr. record on the turntable, and proceeded to get drunker than I'd ever seen him. In truth, Timmy was something of a closet straightedge when it came to drugs and alcohol; he just liked to be *surrounded* by rowdy drunks for some reason. But, like I said, tonight was another story.

As we exchanged sneers of appreciation for the melancholy hillbilly lyrics and chuckled incessantly, I asked him why he was a skin. The words just came out of my mouth. I wasn't accusing him of anything, but that's how he decided to take it.

'"*Why* am I?" Dude, c'mon, Marie's brainwashin' you with her Rainbow-Skinhead fantasies. She's a hippie disguised as a Rude Girl and she's *indoctrinatin'* you, friend.' He grinned bitterly and reached down to lower the volume a bit on his stereo, then grabbed a fresh forty-ouncer from his fridge. 'It wasn't some black-white togetherness *statement* they were makin' in England back in the sixties. It was just some young working-class kids hanging out, listening to music, drinking beer, sticking together, watching each other's back . . . And that's bullshit when she says a bunch of English *Nazis* turned the white skins against the blacks. It was the fuckin' blacks themselves, man. They turned Rasta . . .'

'So what?'

'Degreasey, Rastafarians are just dope-smokin' Black Militants with fucked-up funky hair instead of bow-ties and berets.'

'Okay, Archie Bunker,' I said. 'Gimme some of that devil's brew there, friend.'

He shrugged as if I just didn't want to hear the truth and handed me the forty.

'You don't know shit, Degreaser, 'cause all you read is *fiction*, man. You ever hear them Rastas talk about Haile Selassie? *Jah be praised, some day we'll kill dat whitey, mon . . .* It's right in the fuckin' book, friend.' He gestured towards his bookcase, where Nick Knight's photo-history *Skinhead* sat, right next to several well-thumbed old Richard Allen paperbacks. It was primarily from these sources that Chicago kids bastardized countless hybrid skinhead philosophies to match their own ideals.

'I hate that black power shit,' Timmy continued, and got up to start the Hank Williams record over again, then thought better of it, and replaced the album with a 12-inch single of some frantic hardcore song by Last Resort, but turned the volume so low it sounded like a muffled argument down in the street. 'Those SHANC motherfuckers *still* talk shit behind my back because I hung out with Frank Pritzger for like, two weeks, when I was, like, *fourteen*. I was never a fuckin' Nazi . . . I just dug that will to power shit Frank talked about – honor, loyalty, discipline. I still do. I'm not a fuckin' racist, but I'm not gonna slap a FREE NELSON MANDELA bumpersticker on my ass to prove it, 'cause I'm not a Communist either. I'm not a National Socialist. I'm not a fuckin' *Anarchist*, *Degreaser* . . .' He made as if to slug me where my tattoo was. 'I'm an American skin. That's it. Why? I don't know, Degreaser. Maybe if you and me were rich kids, instead of working class, we'd both still be in school and play on the football team and we could hang out together at the mall wearing identical letterman's jackets instead of nylon bombers, and identical hundred-dollar basketball shoes instead of oxblood Docs. And maybe if either of us had any families to speak of, we could get part-time jobs at our rich dads' offices instead of working in this freak-show juice bar where chicks fuckin' *flock* to us in droves, all intrigued and shit by our shaved heads and our bad-ass tattoos. And maybe you could impress your mulatto girlfriend by writing editorials about racism in the school paper, instead of always trying to find some Nazis to fight. And maybe none of this is a good excuse. Maybe you should have stayed at Brand H plating, and hooked *me* up with a *de-greasing* job. And maybe we could have worked real hard and got ourselves little wives and had kids and given them all the advantages we never had. But you wanna know what? Fuck that.'

*

A couple of days after Marie pummeled the Nazi girl (whose name, I learned, was Corny), Kirk and Aladdin and I were standing out front of the Gorgon as dusk neared, when, very much to our surprise, Frank Pritzger's rusty old Pinto pulled up to the curb. Before we could react, the door swung open, and out stepped the mulatto skinhead Jermaine, smiling, and skaking hands with those inside the car. Then he slammed the door shut and the Pinto rattled off towards Clark Street.

'We were cuttin' through the alley,' Jermaine began happily, in response to our discombobulated expressions, 'me and Jason and Marty, and we saw a bunch of these Latin Eagle motherfuckers poundin' on some skins . . .'

The Latin Eagles were the dominant branch of gangbangers in that area and they strongly disliked the skinhead presence. There were several scuffles, with a few on each side ending up in the hospital and/or Cook County Correctional.

'Now, *we* didn't know,' Jermaine continued, 'we just saw

some skins throwin' down with the spics so we went aggro on 'em and they booked off to their section-eights. I fucked one of those muthas up. *Fucked* him up, man. You don't mess . . .'

As Jermaine began demonstrating his feared uppercut combination, we pressed him with the obvious questions.

'Man, when we saw who it was and all that, Frank just stuck out his hand to me and said: "We all skins, brother, we all skins," and said he was buying the beers, so we all went to Aetna Park and got *fucked* up. I am so fucked up man . . . Frank's a pretty cool dude when you sit down and actually *talk* to him, bro. I mean, when you listen to what he's actually *saying* it makes sense.'

'*Naziism*?' I asked incredulously.

'Naw man . . . aw shit man, I can't explain it to you. I'm too fucked up. Shit is deep man,' and with that he bellowed 'Skiiiiinhead' at the darkening sky, and gave me one of his patented chest-to-chest bumps.

About all I managed to mutter was that I could only wonder what Marie would have to say about all this when she came back from wherever she'd taken off to.

'Man, we was just talkin' about her,' Jermaine said. 'You know where she's at right now? You ain't gonna believe this shit. She's down at Thorek Hospital tryin' to sneak into where they got *Corny* an' shit . . .'

*

When I got to Thorek the first person I saw, sitting in the lobby reading *People* magazine, was Frank Pritzger. Before I could disappear he stood up brightly and waved me over. All I could think as I numbly walked over was that, in his red and black Fred Perry polo, and without his trademark muttonchops, he looked almost *preppie*.

'Mr McDago,' he laughed, gripping my hand with that same warmth as the night we met. 'How are you my brother?'

I shrugged.

'Lookin' for Marie?' he smiled.

'Yep.'

'She's up with Corny. It's all right. They're just talkin'. Marie's somethin' else isn't she? A true warrior, brother. She's great.'

'Frank,' I said, eying the many iron-cross and swastika rings on his stocky fingers, 'I don't understand what the fuck is goin' on here. What do you *mean* "she's great"?'

I had him all wrong. The movement he had founded, was not about *hate*. It was just that the white man needed his own thing just like every other group, and the groups shouldn't mix in the Biblical sense. It just wasn't right. Now, yes, he knew that Marie was my girl, but we were still just kids and things would change as we grew up. He was touching on a very delicate area, and he knew it, but he was so earnest and friendly that I found it hard to muster up the proper rage. This was not an argument, he made it clear with every smile, just a man-to-man discussion.

'But Frank,' I said, exasperated, 'what about Marie herself, man? And Jermaine. Both of their dads were white, how can you sit there and tell me Marie's great if . . . ?'

'Alex,' he said, in a confidential tone, 'you know both of them. You know the problems they both have. Jermaine thinks he's *white* for God's sake. He wants to be his father. But he can't. He's not white, is he? No. Will he ever *be* white? I don't think so. And Marie, she's just *all* confused. I feel for them, brother. I really do. This kind of shit shouldn't be happening. Race-mixers never think of the goddamn kids. They never do. It's a sin if there ever was one, my man.'

My debating skills are less than silken now, and back then they were downright clunky, so I just let him ramble on as I waited more than an hour for my Marie.

When she finally emerged with tear-smudged mascara she didn't seem particularly surprised to see me there. Frank asked if Corny knew he was coming to see her next and she shrugged as we walked towards the exit.

'See you later, guys!' Frank called, as the electric glass doors slid closed behind us.

*

'That your new buddy?' Marie asked snidely as we headed back to The Gorgon.

'My buddy? *My* fuckin' buddy? Jermaine tells me you came to see the Swazi chick you almost *killed* two nights ago. I didn't know if you'd gone nuts or if you were gonna rip her IV tubes out, or *what*.'

'I didn't almost *kill* her,' Marie said, flaring up. 'She's getting released tomorrow.'

'What were you doing? Making plans for the rematch?'

'No, asshole. I was *talking* to her. She's beautiful. She's a beautiful person. We talked and I told her what was up with *real* skinheads. I told her the whole history you know – and she listened. She couldn't believe it. She's done with Frank and that CLASH shit now.'

I scoffed.

'Well of course she told *you* that,' I said. 'She doesn't want another ass-beating.'

Marie stopped in her tracks and asked me why I was so ignorant.

'Ignorant?' I said, 'Who's ignorant? You're saying that in one day she's stopped being a Nazi and I'm saying I'll believe it when I see it.'

'Well, you'll see it tomorrow,' Marie said, turning her head forward and walking on. 'When she gets released, she's gonna come live with me at The Gorgon.'

AFTER CORNY MOVED INTO Marie's tiny bedroom, I saw very little of my girlfriend. They disappeared a lot together and whatever private moments I could steal with Marie in her room were marred by the presence of Corny's pet ferret, Fido, who they often allowed to run loose from his cage. The thing was always crawling on me and licking me everywhere at exactly the wrong moments, much to Marie's delight and my disgust.

Marie and Corny's friendship was so tight that the inevitable rumors immediately began to surface, but Timmy was quick to point out a bright side.

'You're gonna have yourself a duo-deal before long, my man,' he congratulated me. The *ménage à trois* was his favorite and regular arrangement with the lovesick Gorgon maidens who would agree to just about anything for a chance with The King. (Hell, I was getting girly action on the sly just for being his best friend.) It was rumored (by him mainly, though I never doubted it for a second to be true) that he'd even, on a couple of occasions, when the pickings were particularly plentiful, experienced the rarely talked about – what shall we call it? – *ménage à quatre*, I guess.

In my view, the *ménage à deux* was complicated enough, with one lifetime seemingly far too short a time to master it. The idea of having to deal with *two* sets of everything made about as much sense to me as, say, 3-dimensional chess.

As it turned out, the only group experiments Corny and Marie ever invited me to take part in were their frequent trips to the local Buddhist Center on Wrightwood.

Marie had initially learned of the place via some smiley

street-corner propagators of the faith, and I was dubious at first, as I sat there between her and Corny in the large auditorium (filled roughly with a third each of whites, blacks and Asians) before a giant, rather ornate version of Marie's bedroom shrine, chanting Nam-myoho-renge-kyo's and stumbling through phonetic pronunciations of Lotus Sutra passages printed in ancient Chinese. But the basic premise of the atheistic religion, as explained to me in extremely broken English by our youth group leader – a tiny, burstingly energetic Japanese lady named Mrs Kabushita – appealed to me greatly; the karmic philosophy being that whatever good or evil you did would come back to you tenfold, thus making benevolent behavior not simply one's moral duty, but the direct route to fortune within this lifetime. *Bonno Sokko Bodai* – or 'Material Desires and Enlightenment Are One' – was a central tenet of the faith that caught my attention in a big way.

I tried explaining it to Tim one night but he quickly closed his eyes and held up a palm that seemed to say, 'been there, done that, but if it floats your boat, by all means continue, friend.' It was a hard statement to counter so I stifled what I was embarrassed to realize had become an almost missionary zeal I felt for a set of beliefs I knew just the barest of bones about.

As she'd become such a fixture in Marie's life, I attempted to get to know Corny, but the snaggle-toothed, pallid little skinchick was quite laconic, if not altogether mute. She hailed from some tiny town near the southern tip of Illinois and had run away to the city with a boyfriend. They hooked up with Frank's ragtag Nazi clan and then, after the boyfriend was sent away to the slammer for assorted crimes, she settled in as Frank's girl.

'So,' I asked her one night as we and several other skins sat in the Gorgon office, waiting for Marie to return from the local burrito joint with dinner, 'how is it that your parents named you "Corny"?'

'That's just a nickname, stupid,' she said, in a squawky drawl.

Well, *I* didn't know. I'd asked Aladdin once why they called him 'Aladdin' and he told me rather indignantly that they called him 'Aladdin' because that's what his parents had named him.

'Mah real name's Cornucopia,' she said. 'Corny's just short for that.'

After a short pause I asked how it was that her parents had named her 'Cornucopia'.

'Well,' she said, in a rare fit of rhetoric, 'I was born in 1969, and my momma wanted to name me Mary Grace after my great aunt, or else Marla, after the neighbor lady, but this was when a lot of folks was namin' their kids things like "Moonflower", and "Rain", you know, and my daddy said he wanted me to have the same advantages as all the other little kids so they decided on "Cornucopia".'

'That's cool as hell,' Jermaine said, suddenly sitting down on the table beside her. 'That shit's cool as hell. Wouldn't that be a cool-ass name for our band, Jonesy? *Cornucopia*?'

Jones was sitting at the head of the table with his glistening scalp down in his arms. He was older than most of us and locally famous for having played in several of the original British punk bands of the late 1970s. He played with Squatter's Rights on their last American tour but got fired by the band after passing out drunk during a performance at The Gorgon, then waking up and mistakenly pissing on the drummer. Timmy gave him a closet to stay in and immediately every surly three-chord wonder in Chicago wanted to start a band up with him.

'How 'bout it Jones? How 'bout we name our band "Cornucopia"?'

Jones grunted, without moving: 'It's gotta have "Oi" in it somewhehz.'

'Well, how 'bout, "Cornuc . . . OI!-pia?"' Jermaine said,

sliding off the table to the empty chair beside Corny. 'CornucOI!pia. That's a fuckin' kickass name, dude. How 'bout it?'

Jones said he didn't give a fuck, and Corny stared demurely at her hands while Jermaine continued to put the moves on.

So it was that a hardcore punk band was named, and a romance of sorts developed between Corny and Jermaine. All involved were greatly pleased, especially Marie who saw this new union as proof of the true spirit of skinheadism – and knew it would deeply infuriate Frank. I was pretty happy too as I figured the development would give me more time with my own Betty.

This was not to be, however, as Marie's self-righteous kick was snowballing. When she wasn't chanting ardently (or bitterly chewing me out for my reluctance to join her two-hour Nam Myoyo Renge Kyo-fests) she was wheatpasting mimeographed condemnations of racism on every lightpole in the city. A blow-up arose one night when the club was closed for remodeling, and she and her cronies were heading out on an overnight trip downstate to counter-demonstrate at some Klan rally.

Marie and I were sitting at the office table again just before she left for the rally, along with several of her friends (but not Corny, who was lying in Marie's room very sick with the flu). Punch was also there, going over his ledgers and periodically peppering our conversation with brief sarcasms.

'Where are *you* going?' she asked me in a withering tone, as I attempted to slip out the door undetected.

'Out with Tim,' I said flatly.

'I thought you were coming to the rally, you cocksucker.'

'I never said that.'

'Yeah, you fuckin' did.'

'Well, I'm not.'

'Goin' out with Tim, heh?'

'Yep, goin' out with Tim.'

'Yeah, what's the big deal right? *You're* not one of those niggers they want to ship back to Africa – you're just *fucking* one.'

It was a low blow, I felt – her playing the race card like that – particularly when I knew what she was really pissed about. I knew for certain that none of the Gorgon girls I had secretly taken out on the fire escape had spilled the beans. In fact, every one of them – terrified of Marie's wrath – had pleaded with *me* not to say anything to anyone. But she knew, man. Somehow she just knew.

'Tim is such a fuckin' asshole and you just *idolize* him, don't you? You're no fuckin' straightedge.'

'Hey, fuckin' yap all you want, have a fun time *wasting* your time. *I'm* going out with Tim tonight. Don't worry, I won't fuck any chicks while you're out shaking your fist at the wind.'

'Hah! Chicks? I'm not worried about chicks. I think you're fuckin *queer* for Tim.'

'I beg your pardon,' Punch said, turning from his books, his bifocals sliding down his nose.

'Well, I just think he oughta come to terms with his latent lust for that jagoff.'

'Look, you fuckin' cunt,' I hissed, 'I'd probably just go to *sleep* tonight, but all the sidestock is stacked in my room, and I can't sleep in *your* bed 'cause that's where your DYKE LOVER's crashin'!'

She was getting mean and irrational, and I was getting meaner and more irrational . . . ah young love.

'I just don't see what everybody thinks is so great about Tim,' she said, toning down and trying another tack. 'He's not that great. He's a selfish asshole is what he is, and all he cares about is himself.'

'I'm sure you remember, Marie,' Punch said, in a voice that was, as always, both serious and campy, 'the way things were on this ship before the handsome sailor Tim Penn came aboard. It's very likely I would have closed this place for fear of someone getting killed. The calming effect he's had on the rabble is as much a benefit to *you* as anyone. Timothy is the cornerstone of this organization, the hub of our wheel, the belly of this beast – you'd all be lost without him.'

'The belly?' Marie sneered. 'He's the *dick*. That's all he is, is one big walking cock. And little boys like Alex think he's King Shit because of all those tragic whores he fucks . . . God, they are such *whores*.'

'We're all whoring ourselves for something,' Punch said, turning back to his books, and the rest of the room gave a collective silent groan as Punch began one of his infamous meanderings. 'Money, self-esteem, security, diversion. No matter what you're after you're a whore. Elegance and refinement and even monogamy only mask the truth. With the lack of mythical details – oh, a push-up bra you know, and the exchange of petty cash, a twirling umbrella . . . whatever – we lose the big picture. But replace the pimp with a marriage/money-minded mother, replace the street prostitute's crude and sinful desire for basic food and shelter with the lofty goals of fame and fortune and esteem – a man with enough money to buy sports cars and cocaine and strings of pearls, a prize woman with teardrop tits and an ass like a firm split honeydew – and you've still got a bunch of whores. We're all whores? So what?'

'Speak for yourself, you old fairy,' Marie said, but when Punch was in the midst of such a soliloquy, there was no stopping him.

'Even if a girl is seeking, say, a man who will be a good father for her babies, what's she doing in essence? Selling her ass for assistance in raising her young. And what's *he* doing? Selling his cock for a steady piece of pussy, for a feeling of worth, for respectability in the eyes of society while, perhaps, he goes out at night and secretly picks up . . .' (He held up rabbit-ear quotation marks here) ' . . . "whores".'

'Punch,' Marie said, with feigned concern, 'you sound

frustrated. What's the matter? Want me to go find some homeless toughboy who'll let you blow him for a quarter-ounce?'

'Baby,' he said, with macho affectation, 'I don't *gotta* pay for it.'

'Then why the hell *do* you?'

'Ah, what a question. I'm mystified myself, dear – unnerved, heartbroken, confused . . .' he said, switching his tone to that of exaggerated tragedy, 'I, too, suffer from the self-delusion that it's love I'm after, when I know in my heart I'm just a whore amongst whores.'

'So you're not coming?' Marie said, softer now, tired of Punch and turning to me.

I sighed.

'That's all right,' she said, like it truly was all right.

'Look . . .' I said.

'No, we'll be okay, um . . . we'll be back around noon. Maybe if Corny's feeling better, you and me and her and Jermaine can go get sushi or something. Bye . . .'

She lightly kissed me on the lips. As she and her little entourage filed solemnly out the door, I sat there alone with Punch, filled with guilt, and silently cursing her for having finally found the right formula to ruin my evening.

*

As usual we spent the night visiting every North Side club and bar that would still let us in. And the numbers were shrinking. We didn't set out specifically to find trouble but we didn't exactly shirk from it either. When we walked into a place, people always stared. And we always stared back. We usually won these blinking contests, but there was always some group of steroid-pumped weightlifters or soreheaded Cubs fans brave enough or drunk enough to say something.

These experiences gave me new respect for all the Tae

Kwon Do patterns Timmy taught me. Initially, I saw them as contrived preparation for a wholly spontaneous phenomenon. But fights, like just about everything else, are all made up of the same stuff, only the combinations are different. There are a finite number of ways a person can hurt you, and after you've been hurt in all those ways enough times over – barring death or paralysis – you learn the forms and start to do your own hurting. In any athletic science, though, there are the certain few who transcend the inherent structures of the game – your Michael Jordan, your Pele, and so on all the way back to Alcibiades. All the Gorgon Boys were good scrappers, but Timmy Penn, without a doubt, was the Michael Jordan of the bar-room brawl.

So, as usual, we held our own.

And, as usual, that night someone knew of an after-hours party which we crashed and stayed at – drinking up all the liquor – till long after everyone else had left and even the hosts had cautiously retired to their bedrooms with their valuables, locking the door behind them, periodically peeking out to see if we had left yet.

When I awoke late the next morning on a foul-smelling, beer-soaked sofa in some art-student's rented coach house on School Street, only Timmy and Jason remained, standing near the front bay window talking in low tones, snickering.

'Once again, Degreaser,' Jason sneered, as he saw me rise from the sopping cushions and grasp my temples, 'you girled-out on us.'

'*Afraid* to party!' Tim chimed in cheerfully. 'What a *coward* you are. Man ... I told you, you can't pass out like that around Jason. I caught him trying to suck your cock again.'

'Shut the fuck up you Irish potato-nigger drunk-ass sonofabitch.'

The late spring sunlight was pouring in behind them horrifically and, if the couch had been any less soggy from the pitchers of warm keg-beer they had poured on my face in futile attempts to wake me, I would have put my throbbing head out of its misery and fallen back asleep.

We silently trudged several bustling city blocks back to The Gorgon, amidst a mocking melody of bird chirps and sirens, car horns and jackhammers, stopping once briefly while I threw up in some hedges that reeked of insecticide.

Once inside the musty, darkened club, we sat for a while in Timmy's bedroom for the obligatory recounting of the night's adventures, drinking from a jug of orange juice I found in his mini-fridge. Jason did most of the talking while Timmy looked through a special fluorescentizing lens at the new additions to his collection of quartz rocks. He knew all the scientific names. Like I said, he was something of an expert on nature. Though Marie asserted snidely that this was all just another tactic of his for getting laid, 'to show his sensitive side', I knew by the way he pored over volumes of rare bird encyclopedias and talked incessantly and in minute detail of his India-by-way-of-Alaskan-fishing-boats plan, that Marie either didn't know Timmy Penn from Adam, or else knew him so well that her energetic attacks masked certain feelings for him I didn't care to dwell on.

When I got up to Marie's room I was not prepared for what I'd find. The room had been demolished, and it reeked of chemical mace. Amidst the broken pottery and torn-up bloodied futon-stuffing I found Corny shivering in a corner weeping softly. When I pulled her hands from her face I saw damage that made the savage beating Marie had given her (what seemed like such a long, long time ago) pale by comparison. Both of her eyes were cut and bloodied and swollen shut, her lips were clownishly red and giant, and her broken, dangling teeth seemed held in place only by the twisted metal braces.

As I screamed at the top of my lungs for Tim and Jason I quickly glanced around the room at the carnage. Marie's Gohonzon scroll lay crumpled in a corner – smudged, like just about everything else, with reddish-brown. Smeared on the wall in its absence, finger-painted in the same dried blood, were the words, written in stupid-looking block letters – DEATH TO RACE MIXERS, along with the white power symbol.

I tried to pick her up in my arms.

'Don't touch her!' I heard Tim yelling from the doorway. 'Don't fuckin' touch her, man! God*dammit*!' he screamed, sidekicking the drywall fiercely as Jason ran downstairs to the payphone and dialed 911.

Timmy produced a switchblade and, for some reason, delicately sliced open her blood-soaked, oversized T-shirt. It was all she was wearing, and, as we waited without touching her, I was struck by a new tattoo she had gotten just to the left of her dishwater blonde pubic area. It was still raised from the skin and bubbling with pus and showed a caricature of Jermaine that Aladdin had designed for CornucOI!pia's new band logo. The wild-eyed likeness of Jermaine's brown face was true to the original, but through some lack of communication or interpretation, what was supposed to be a bullet flying through one of his temples and out the other became a sharpened pencil. It made absolutely no sense that Jermaine should have a pencil sticking through his head, and the absurd immutability of the ink (I thought too of my own anarchy tattoo) strangely overrode all the rest of the present horror. Then I heard Marie and her pals, having just gotten back from their trip, come storming into the room with shrieks and cries.

I could not look Marie in the eye and was grateful when Tim grabbed me by the arm and pulled me with him down the stairs to his room.

He pulled a .45 pistol from behind his bookcase, stuck it in the waistband of his jeans, and handed me the switchblade. Jason came into the room, armed, I knew, with several canisters of mace, not to mention his favorite tool of battle – the thigh bone of a science-class human skeleton that he and

Kirk had carried home one night after breaking into Lane Tech High School. The idiotic caveman connotations of the thing had always appealed to our parodic self-image, but I'd seen him inflict some very real damage with that bone.

Tim seemed to know exactly where we should go. We roused Jones and Aladdin and found Jermaine, then jogged as a group all the way to Lincoln Park. It was a strange and terribly wonderful thing to be so maniacally angry as to forget fear. Circumventing the skinhead hangout – Aetna Park – before the three-way corner of Halsted, Lincoln and Fullerton, we cut through the alley beside the Biograph Theater, and emerged before a tour bus full of yokels who had come to see the spot where John Dillinger was shot. Crossing Lincoln to another alley, we arrived at the back entrance of an old studio-apartment complex (very seedy, especially for that neighborhood).

A Mexican lady was bringing in her groceries through a back door, and Tim slipped past her. As we followed she screamed at us in Spanish. Still behind Tim, we ran up to the fourth and top floor and entered the hallway, when what seemed like a hundred Nazi skinheads (it was actually three or four) came at us, led by the giant with the cane who had taken on a dozen Bomber Boys by himself that night I first came to The Gorgon.

The overwhelming bravery that had filled my veins vanished in less than a blink and I turned and followed at the heels of Jason, Jones, Aladdin, and Jermaine. When we got back out into the alley, though, we stopped. Timmy wasn't with us.

'Oh he's fuckin' dead, guy!' Jason bellowed mournfully, and just enough of that previous fire flared up again to send me back into the hallway on shaky legs, with the switchblade drawn out open in my damp and trembling hand. I heard footsteps coming down the stairs, and halted for a second as the rest of them bumped up against me from behind. Tim jumped down to the landing, holding the giant's cane in one hand, and the .45 in the other, his face bleeding and the left arm of his new bomber jacket missing, cursing at us hatefully to come on.

We charged up behind him and entered the top hallway again. On the floor lay the giant and another skin, both moaning and grasping their heads. Tim stopped before a flimsy apartment door, and began hammering at it with front snapkicks. We all threw a shoulder in, and the lock began to give.

The people inside, however, were trying to push it shut. But Tim got one boot in, and stuck the nose of the .45 through the crack. There were shouts and shrieks from inside and the sounds of scrambling. The resistance from behind the door abruptly vanished, and we all stumbled forward at once.

Inside the pathetic studio apartment stood several of the skins, including the one we were looking for – Frank Pritzger. This was just before the mass pistol fetish began in the late eighties, before the firearms taboo vanished altogether, and even grade school kids started packing – so when they saw Timmy enter the door with his .45, they shrank back against the side wall, unsure of what to do next. The floor was almost completely covered with raggedy old mattresses with disheveled sheets exposing various stains. On one such bed sat several wide-eyed, roly-poly skinchicks, one of whom clutched an infant that wailed at the top of its lungs.

'You need a *gun*, Timmy?' Frank inquired, with that same crazy-eyed friendly smile. 'I thought you were a warrior, but you're no better than a nigger. What am I saying? A nigger's better than you, you coward.'

'You fucked up,' Tim gasped, pausing to wipe the blood from his mouth. 'You think you can come into *my* house like that?'

'Aren't you ashamed to say that?' Frank asked with a concerned laugh. 'Aren't you *ashamed* to call a scummy queer-bar crawling with vermin and race-mixers your *house*? I wouldn't step *foot* in that sty.'

'Oh! You're livin' *real large* here, Frank!' Timmy scoffed, spreading his arms out at the hellhole apartment. He suddenly tossed the cane aside and handed the pistol to Aladdin, who stuck it in his pocket with his smooth round rocks. I closed the switchblade and stuck it in my back jeans pocket. We all gravitated towards Timmy and waited.

'C'mon, Thor,' Timmy taunted, with wide-eyed invitation, 'it's just you and me now. No gun.' Frank's smile broadened and, as he motioned for his sidekicks to step aside, Tim leaped forward and laid him out with a quick jab, then backed up and waited.

Frank sat up and the crazed smile was gone. His nose was bleeding – like Timmy's – and he rose to charge, but his friends, seeing an opportunity, grabbed him and dragged him towards the door.

We started for them, but Tim shouted to hold back. We would take them outside. The Nazi skins dragged Frank kicking and screaming down the hallway.

So we followed them in slow pursuit until they scrambled out the front entrance of the building. They began to cross Fullerton Street towards the DePaul campus, stopping traffic. Tim was a blur as he ran up across the hood of a parked taxi, using it as a sort of ramp, and leaped – tackling the backs of Frank's knees and bringing him down. Tires screeched as the rest of the Nazis turned and fell upon Timmy. Jason got there first, cracking heads indiscriminately with his bone, before he too was brought to the ground. Then Jermaine joined the fray. As I approached with Aladdin and Jones, three of them squared off against us individually.

Aladdin swept the legs out from under his opponent, then stomped again and again on his curled up body. The few seconds I caught of Jones' bout was equally mismatched. He dragged his skinny Nazi in a headlock towards the parked taxi and tried to put his head through the driver's window. The glass wouldn't break, but Jones kept trying.

My guy, not a skinhead, but a tall, long-haired, white trash affiliate of some sort, charged at me, swinging, and backed me all the way up on the sidewalk to the window of a currency exchange. When I felt my heels hit brick and my spine bounce against the plexiglass pane I reflexively brought my elbow up and caught him pretty good under the chin. I put my body into it, and sent him reeling backwards into the street.

As I ran at him he twisted his torso, as if to flee, then blind-sided me with a backspinning hook-kick. It connected so solidly with my head that it sent us both flying in opposite directions.

If he'd been wearing Doc Martens, instead of a pair of battered old Converse high-tops, he would have earned himself some lasting fame. I had been kicked that hard only once before, *barefoot*, by Timmy when we were sparring, and it spun the headgear around on my face. It had infuriated me so much that, though blinded by the headgear, I had charged at him and knocked him off his feet to the mat. It was the one and only time I ever knocked down Timmy Penn.

I was sort of angry this time, too, I must say. As I pushed myself up from the ground, blinking to bring some focus back to my vision, I heard a groan of agony that rose above the ringing in my ears. It came from directly behind me. I got up woozily, and turned to see my assailant using both hands to grasp the ankle that was connected to the foot that was to blame for my current state of consternation.

As his tear-filled eyes rolled up at me, we came to a simultaneous realization, he and I, about the capricious nature of fortune.

He screamed and struggled up, trying to sort of hop-shuffle away on one leg. I followed him of course, rather calmly I might add, and kicked him square in the ass with such force that, had *I* been wearing sneakers, *I* might have injured *my* ankle.

But I was wearing Docs.

He flew forward and skittered on his face. As he tried to get up, I kicked him again, just as hard. I was about to kick him again, but the bastard rolled under a parked car.

I looked up and saw the spectacle we had created.

Traffic was backed up all the way to the Fullerton El stop, and scores of car horns blared as crowds of onlookers – yuppies, DePaul college kids, shop owners – lined the sidewalks.

I turned around to see the Gorgon Skins pretty much mopping up the Nazis, or mopping up Frank actually. The rest of the Nazis had either fled or were lying in the street immobile. But Tim held Frank up by the back of his collar with one hand, wrenching an arm behind his back with the other, while Jermaine, Jason, Aladdin, and Jones stood around them in a circle, and took free shots that Frank feebly tried to fend off with his free hand.

Before I had a chance to join in, the cops showed up with their guns drawn. They dropped us all to the ground and kicked our legs out splay. But they had only come for Frank. They had been looking for a reason to put him away for a long time now, and reasons didn't get much better than what he had done to Corny.

As they handcuffed Frank we slowly stood up and watched the cops hustle him, still struggling, towards a car.

'You fucking cowards!' he slurred, twisting back to look at his remaining friends, who stood there nursing their wounds. I guess they were cowards because they weren't attacking the cops. And then, before getting shoved into the car, he saw Tim and informed him bitterly and predictably, that he was a dead man.

'Get the fuck outta here!' a skinny Asian cop screamed, shoving me so hard that I fell. 'You hear me?' he bellowed at us all, drawing his nightstick. 'Disperse!'

Jason helped me up and we walked back to The Gorgon in silence. I vomited again several times on the walk back, and, upon reaching the club – not wanting to face Marie just yet – sat alone in the alley beneath her window, shivering on the damp blacktop amidst patches of still unmelted snow. It had been a big victory, that fight, but as I leaned my back up against the cold bricks, I still felt desperately unproven. I sat there and endlessly flicked open and closed Timmy's switch-blade, murmuring Nam Myoho Renge Kyo, envisioning what I would do to Frank when he made bail.

But Frank had no one. No one who would bail him out anyway. Frank had no one and he wasn't coming back for a long time. I had to find someone else to be my enemy now.

IT WAS THE NIGHT before Timmy and I were to leave Chicago for a summer of fishing-boat adventures in Alaska. We'd purchased our bus tickets and everything and I started a fight in a nightclub and got us all arrested.

After they finished patting us down, the cops shoved Tim, Jason and me towards the paddy wagon and the paramedics wheeled the Italian character who had sucker-punched me into the back of an ambulance-van that was parked up on the sidewalk. The whole thing had been a silly misunderstanding. When I sidled up next to his doe-eyed date – a comely little mulatto girl who I genuinely thought had smiled at me in a come-hither fashion – how was *I* to know he was standing right behind me? I thought he was in the bathroom or something.

My left eyeball felt crushed and bleeding.

'You're *dead*, you bald-headed fuck!' the Italian character, now fitted with a neck brace, shouted at me just before they closed the ambulance doors.

I managed to shout back, right before I was heaved face-first into the paddy wagon: 'Fuck you, I hope you fuckin' die!' Big mistake. Not the first and certainly not the last of many big mistakes.

They put Timmy, Jason and me all in the same jail cell at the Belmont station, which struck me as odd and depressed me. The last person you wanted to be locked up with for any period of time was Jason. He wasn't happy to be there, and nothing pleased that weasel more than unhappiness.

'Ah, the stripy hole, boys,' he kept sighing mournfully, 'the stripy hole.'

'Would you shut the fuck up?' Tim finally asked. He had a

very fat lip from a policeman's lead-filled leather glove, and he'd never been the sort to be proud of his war wounds. It messed up his leader image.

Jason walked up to the bars of our little holding cell, with one hand bunched around the waist of his baggy chinos (they'd taken our belts and bootlaces, which was fortunate, as we'd probably have ended up hanging Jason with them otherwise).

'Turnkey!' he shouted, clanging his free fist against the bars. 'Turnkey!'

He climbed up on the bars, turned himself upside down, and began kicking the low ceiling with both feet.

'Turnkey!'

'Oh for God's sake, Jason,' I said, holding my eye, which had swollen shut. I was sure they would run a check and my Harding County warrant would show up and this would be the end of the line for me.

'Whutchoo want, boy?' came a voice from down the corridor. A big black jailer came lumbering up to the bars and looked at Jason's upside-down grimacing face.

'When do they feed us around this goddamn joke of a jail?'

'*Feed* you?' the man said. 'This ain't no goddamn . . . boy, you best shut up and I *ain't* gonna tell you again. You want me to come in there and kick yo' monkey ass?'

'I gotta piss,' Jason said.

'Piss in yo' pants, skinhaid,' the jailer said, and shuffled away.

'We fought for you in the streets, man!' Jason cried after him.

Speaking of which – while we sat in jail that night, Frank Pritzger sat in some other branch of the Cook County jails awaiting sentencing for the savage beating of Corny. He claimed he was framed. He made this claim, I suppose, because he was. Sort of. Maybe. The only thing for certain was that he wasn't the one who beat up Corny. It was a couple of other skinheads she didn't recognize. But we were pretty sure they were cronies of Frank's from out of town. The cops, who had been looking for an excuse to get him out of Chicago, told Corny to say it was Frank anyway. We all encouraged her strongly to go along with it, and she testified, with her wired-shut jaw, like a trooper. Then she went back to whatever little town it was she came from, and we never heard from her again.

I fantasized about killing Frank every day. A frost had fallen on Marie – as if she somehow blamed me for Corny's broken, bleeding state that morning. That's why I threatened to go to Alaska with Timmy. But she didn't even have the decency to beg me to stay. So I decided to teach her a good lesson and actually go. Just lucky for her, you know, that I should happen by chance to start a fight and get arrested on the eve of our departure.

The authorities that dealt with Timmy, Jason and I after the bar fight were completely disinterested in the fact that there were different kinds of skinheads. It happened that the man who punched me was rather well-connected in Chicago, and of course, the girl was black, so they were playing it up as a Nazi attack. Of course we had fought Nazis, my girlfriend was black, and Jason was Jewish, but those facts complicated things, so they were ignored.

The morning after our arrest we were brought into a small conference room for questioning to determine what charges would be filed against us. The guy punched me first, remember, but apparently he had taken the doe-eyed girl with him the previous weekend to Vegas, where they got married in a drive-through temple as a kick, so now he was playing up the fact that he was just defending his newlywed wife against my unwanted advances.

'At what time did you first become affiliated with the Nazi skinheads, or any other group associated with Naziism?' the woman from the State's Attorney's office asked us. She was about twenty-eight, and quite pretty, in a mousy, bespectacled way. But she was tightlipped and nervous, as if they'd just locked her in a room with Lex Luther, The Penguin, and The Joker. Well, Jason was the joker all right.

'Let me ask you something first,' he said to her. 'What's the difference between an intelligent midget and a venereal disease?' He didn't wait for a reply. 'Well, one's a cunning runt, and . . .'

Tim was livid. Jason was the only one of us that had not yet reached his eighteenth birthday. He could afford to play like he was Jimmy Cagney.

'Jason,' I said, and then turned to the D.A. 'He got that joke from the Jim Morrison book. Jim Morrison said that once. Everything's from some book or movie with this guy. Ay, Jason? It's a compliment actually. He thinks you're pretty. I mean, you *are* quite attractive, you know.'

'Let me ask *you* then,' she said to Tim, completely ignoring my little attempt, 'What's your connection with the Nazi . . .'

'Fuck that,' Tim said. He had lost his cool. His handsome triangular face was soaked in red. A bad sign. 'Fuck that. Fuck Hitler,' he continued, glaring hard at Jason, 'Hitler gave anti-Semitism a bad name.'

Well, ahem, you see, that's how we pals of different ethnic and cultural backgrounds *often* talked to one another. Jason once called me a spaghetti-nigger. Heh heh. It was a type of *bonding* actually, uh . . .

By the time we got out of that room they had dropped all charges against an unnamed minor, and upped the charges against Alex Verdi and Timothy Penn from Aggravated Assault and Mob Action to Attempted Murder. Nothing was mentioned about my Harding County warrant though, so Punch came and bailed us out, and the headline in the Trib the next morning read:

'Skinheads Attack Interracial Couple on Honeymoon.'

Marie insisted that we run away to Mexico, Jason was kind enough to bring up the fact that prison was guaranteed anal rape and AIDS for guys like us, and Tim just said we'd better start growing our hair out for court.

THE ATTEMPTED MURDER CHARGE was never meant to stick; it was a prosecution bargaining chip from the get-go. But we were still in trouble. A group of drug-dealers that Timmy used to, more or less, break thumbs for I guess, fronted him $5,000 to pay a lawyer who said he could work out a deal with the judge to drop all charges; but only if Tim and I joined some sort of military service. Tim found out that we could cut our losses by joining the Reserves on the "Buddy System" – in which case we'd only have to leave for four months of training, after which we could pay off some sergeant at our local guard unit and be done with the whole business. I didn't relish the idea, but anything seemed better than prison, and besides, we had a much bigger problem to contend with.

Paul Ugo, the man we'd sent to the hospital with a sprained neck, was, apparently, hooked up with organized crime. Not in a big way – it seemed he helped launder cash for several North Side nightclubs which were, in actuality, sinkholes for mob money. But Paul was a notorious hothead, and bent on revenge against 'those baldheaded fucks', as it were.

I believe the only thing that saved us from concrete Docs was our fairy godfather, Punch, who, it turned out, was not without connections of his own.

One afternoon towards the end of summer, on the eve of our alternative sentencing, Punch came into Timmy's room where the two of us sat somberly as we drained his fish tank and packed it away. If the reprieve he had arranged for us was to be sealed in stone, he said, we would have to meet somebody within the hour.

'His name is Nuccio – some sort of mid-level mob manager,

or . . . *I* don't know,' Punch said, looking a little confused. For the first time in my experience, the tone of eternal irony was all but absent from his voice, which only added to my considerable fear.

'He owns the Bobbisox club on Ontario and he's there right now. This whole *meeting* thing came out of nowhere, but I would assume it's some sort of greaseball formality – an opportunity for the two of you to show your *respect*, or *whatever*, I don't know . . . *please* try and make yourselves look somewhat presentable. It could save you a thumb. Or a pinky finger at the very least.'

Unsure if he was joking there at the end or not, we quickly stripped out of our boots and jeans and donned our only formal wear – the ska-skinhead uniform of charcoal-gray, three-button suits, striped Ben Sherman oxfords, and thin black ties. We left our little porkpies in their hatboxes though, as they seemed a bit too jaunty for the occasion. We had, indeed, grown our hair out a bit for court, and, before leaving, each slicked it down to the side the best we could with Wildroot.

We rode to the meeting place on Timmy's sputtering Harley, then brushed each other off briefly before entering the Bobbisox, which did not look like a mob hangout at all. It was a retro, fifties-style dance bar actually. A bunch of these places had popped up in the city briefly in the early eighties, but this was the only one still around at the time.

The interior decorations were standard fare for such joints – bright and plastic. Art deco walls. Red vinyl stools at the bar, and a neon jukebox in the back. The place was not yet open for business that day, but a couple of made-up, middle-aged ladies in evening dresses sat in the dim light at a table near the door drinking highballs. We watched them give us brief, hard looks before we caught sight of the one man sitting at the bar. Nuccio was middle aged, stocky and olive-skinned, dressed in a summer-wool sportcoat and no tie.

Turning towards us just a little bit as we approached, he told us to sit down, then shook our hands with a bored smile. He also drank from a highball, and smoked. A carton of Carltons sat at his elbow on the bar. He offered us a drink or a cigarette, but we declined, saying we were in training.

Though I sat between the two of them, Nuccio leaned over and addressed Timmy exclusively, not once even glancing at me. He said he'd heard we were all right guys and that the thing with Ugo was just a misunderstanding and there wouldn't be a problem now, seeing how we were off to join the service, and, even more than that, how, after we got out, we weren't going to step foot back in the city limits for one year.

Timmy couldn't quite disguise his dismayed surprise at that last stipulation, and, had he looked at me, Nuccio would have seen my own shock. Much as we had talked about leaving the city on our own, for adventure, such a decree was somehow frightening.

'What's wrong with that?' Nuccio wanted to know. 'You don't wanna be in the city anyway. The 'burbs is where it's all happening now. I mean, you wanna live in Cicero, Elmwood Park – go ahead. You wanna take a fuckin' *rowboat* up to the shores of Oak Street Beach with a pair of fuckin' binoculars to look at the ladies – who cares? Just so long as you stay outta Chicago proper.'

There wasn't much we could say, and it was still quite a relief to be leaving with all our appendages, so we thanked him and waited to be dismissed. It was then that Nuccio turned to me.

'Now, your name is Alex Verdi. Correct?'

I nodded and shot an apprehensive look at Timmy who was stone-faced again.

'Hunh,' Nuccio reflected, then stooped to sip from his highball. 'Now, what're you guys supposed to be again? Some kinda skinheads or something?'

I shrugged reluctantly.

'Buncha skinheads came to my niece's graduation party once. Out in Elmwood Park. They jumped one of my nephew's buddies. Ho ... *big* fuckin' mistake. Every one of those bozos went the hospital that night.'

He chuckled into his drink. Then, as he lit up another Carlton, asked:

'Your old man's name Alex Verdi too?'

The question threw me considerably, and, at the time, seemed packed with implications of some mysterious and horrible underworld vendetta. Suddenly, it all made sense. When my father moved our family out of Chicago to that old house deep in the woods, it wasn't *really* so he could write haiku poetry. That was just a ruse. He had, in fact, crossed the mob, and we were part of the witness relocation program. And now, well, I was going to die. But, as a skinhead, at least I'd die knowing that my old man wasn't really a hippie. He was a gangster cleverly *acting* like a hippie.

'Is Alex your old man's name too?'

After a split-second of contemplation I nodded, figuring that, in some worst-case scenario, honesty might earn me a quick end with piano wire, but spare me, say, the blow-torched testicles.

'You grow up on the Nord-west side of the city, Verdi?'

'Not really, you know – no, not really.'

'Your old man go to Steinmetz High School?'

I had to stop and actually re-acquaint myself with the fact that I had a father; it seemed another lifetime ago that I'd run away and come back to the city.

'I think so ... yeah.'

Nuccio smiled inscrutably, like he'd won something, then clapped a beefy arm on my shoulder and laughed heartily.

'I grew up with the sonofabitch. We were pals.'

I about collapsed with relief and could feel Timmy silently sighing behind me.

'How's he doin'?'

I mumbled something vague to indicate that I didn't really know.

'That right?' Nuccio said, as if understanding that I didn't want to talk about it. 'Alex Verdi . . . no shit. Goddamn. We all grew up together – him, me, Steve Pappas, Jack Altieri, Dom Schettino, Art . . . whatsisname? I dunno, all those guys. We were like the local greasers. Hoods they called us back then. We had a . . . you know – social athletic club . . . The Saints. Your father ever tell you about that? We had these fuckin' purple satin jackets with "The Saints" embroidered on the back. It wasn't like . . . nah, I mean, a few fights with those Oak Park cocksuckers maybe now and then, but we weren't bad guys. Not like these fuckin' shmooley streetgangs startin' up with the Uzis and shit. Yeah, no shit, your old man was the Saints' president. Lost all the club's money in a pool game once. Ha ha ha! I ain't kiddin'. I am not kidding you. Mosta the guys just thought it was funny. Smart, though. Smart guy. When Korea came, he got drafted into the Army but he knew he could still sign up for the air force if he passed the test. The Army called me and I woulda had to go straight to Inchon if it wasn't for this fuckin' knee of mine . . . In the air force they put him through so much special schoolin', *he* missed the whole fuckin' war. He came back four years later a *Captain*. You know that?'

I nodded a little. Yes, I knew that. When I was a boy, just after we'd moved out to the country, my father would go into his wardrobe and bring out a small, flat box covered in soft leather. He would flip the lid up on its hinges and let me look at the four little lieutenant's bars pinned inside to the red velvet lining. Each one was less than half the size of a postage stamp. Two were gold and two were silver, and the pairs of bars were lined up next to each other, equally spaced, in a gleaming little row. A half-inch higher on the velvet, with a wingspan that stretched the length of the velvet, was a silver flight eagle, its crevices tarnished like an old quarter. During one of these showings, as I rubbed the pad of my index finger across the velvet and the cold smooth metal bumps, my father made a proposal. If I memorized the Greek Gods and their Roman counterparts, ran twelve lengths of the stable each day for a month, read and studied a chapter each week from the books on foraging and algebra, and, the impossible kicker – made peace with the gander . . . I could have one of the silver bars. When that was done I could work on the second silver, but it'd be twice as hard to get, and then a gold, and so on . . .

'Made Captain and got the hell out of the service when his time was up,' Nuccio continued, more to himself, it seemed, than to me. 'I saw a picture in the neighborhood paper of him in his officer's uniform. That was something else. Something else. I mean, compared to the last time I'd seen him, which was with his greezy hair and Saints jacket . . . shit. Ah shit, Steinmetz High School. You know who else went there? Hugh Hefner. No shit, and the Spilotro brothers.' He paused and seemed to look at me pointedly then. I had read about the Spilotro brothers in the *Tribune*. They were big-time Chicago Mafiosi who pissed off the wrong people. They were beaten to death in some frozen field with pistol butts and the shovels they had just used to dig their own graves.

'I saw your old man once right after Korea, and asked that half-Mick bastard why the hell he was getting out as a Captain, and he said the service didn't seem like a good place to raise a kid. Said he wanted to make some dough too, which made sense. But him talkin' about raising a *kid* . . . it was funny. I mean, you know . . . your old man had turned into a fuckin' *beatnik* for Chrissakes. The hair a little shaggy, and always with some crazy broad – a different one each time I saw him. And not just broads from the neighborhood. Colored broads, hillbilly broads, rich broads from the Northshore. He was a fuckin' ladies man. I mean . . . this was before he met . . . well, your mother I guess. Beautiful woman, your ma. Marilyn Monroe lookalike, I swear to Jesus.' He paused, as if he was going to ask me something, then seemed to reconsider and continued.

'Next time I saw him was a few years later and your old man was already worth a bundle. A bundle. He was living on Taylor Street then, but he still had three all-night diners going in the old neighborhood. He was starting to attract some attention as a guy to watch . . . I'll tell you straight out: there was a lot of opportunity back then – big opportunity and we invited your father to get involved. I went to see him personally, more than once. But he wasn't interested. The last time I talked to him I stopped into one of his restaurants – the one that used to be The Sugar Bowl – which was funny, 'cause that's where The Saints used to all hang out and shoot the shit when we were kids. He was there with your mother. And you. You don't remember, you were just a little shit. He didn't look so beatnik anymore . . . just a little bit intellectual or something. We all sat down in a booth and had some cake and coffee and your old man talked about selling the restaurants and buying a piece of property out in the country. Said he didn't think the city was a good place to raise a kid. And I looked at you . . . I looked at you, and thought . . . well, it was like the song – "Your daddy's rich and your ma's good lookin".'

He paused to take another sip. In the silence I looked down at Nuccio's handmade loafers as they gently tapped against the steel-ring footrest of his stool. There seemed an unbearable weight on my chest whenever I thought directly of my mother, or my father, or my sister – and since I'd come back to the city I'd gradually learned to shake off such thoughts pretty well. It got so even my dreams had pretty much closed their doors to that time and place. And now it was as if those banished thoughts had suddenly revealed that they were only toying with me. Tagging effortlessly behind, nipping at my heels for amusement's sake.

'So you're Alex Verdi's son, eh?' Nuccio finally said, and then, just before he told us we could leave, seemed to sigh a weary sigh for the both of us. 'Ah, well . . . it's funny the way things go.'

*

The only words I spoke to Timmy as we zoomed back north, were to ask him if he'd drop me off at the Buddhist center on Wrightwood. He did and, without even saying I'd see him later, I walked through the swinging glass doors in search of Mrs Kabushita. I found her in the little bookstore, where they sold Buddhist literature and prayer beads and candles and things, and tearfully told her my story. It was impossible to explain all that Nuccio's tale had conjured up inside me, so I stuck to explaining how Paul Ugo had sucker-punched me, and how I'd been forced to join the service and was exiled from Chicago and how much I'd miss Marie and, in short, how *unfair* it all was.

Mrs K. looked up at me with shining black eyes and smiled broadly when I finished.

'Hy!' she said. 'Hohhhh . . . thassa beeg-uh *benefit*! Congra-julashuns Ah-lex!'

I found this response, I must admit, less than comforting. But not a bit surprising. Any challenge in life was seen by these Buddhists as an opportunity – an incentive – to chant more. I didn't much feel like chanting though. I thanked her for listening and left the building.

Tim was still there, leaning back sideways against his bike, arms folded, waiting.

As I crossed the street he swung his leg back over the seat without a word, and started it up. We rode back to The Gorgon, stopping off at 1,000 Liquors to pick up a few bottles of Midnight Dragon. Out in front of the store I borrowed ten dollars from Timmy and said I'd meet him in a few minutes. He said he'd be on the roof.

It was about half past four. I went to the currency exchange

129

and bought a roll of quarters. Then I walked to the payphones underneath the Belmont El. I spent about half my money trying to find the right number, then sank the rest of my change in the slot and called the Department of Children and Family Services.

A young black woman answered and I said, above the din of the overhead trains, that I was trying to locate a girl named Stacy Virginia Verdi.

'I don't have that information, sir,' the woman answered, with a slightly adversarial tone that surprised me for some reason. 'And even if I did, I couldn't release it to you.'

'I just wanna know where she is and if she's all right.'

'I don't know, sir, and I couldn't tell you if I did.'

'Who do I need to talk to then?'

'Who are you, sir? And why do want information concerning this child?'

'I'm her fuckin' brother!'

'Don't you curse at me or I'll hang this phone up right now!'

There was a moment of silence.

'I'm her brother,' I said.

'First of all, I don't know that, and second of all it don't matter *who* you are. If this child is under our supervision we don't release that information to no one. Not a brother, not a mother, not nobody else.'

'You got a boss?' I spat.

'Excuse me?'

'Your manager, your superviser, let me talk to . . .'

'Hold . . .' she said, and left me with Muzak for several minutes.

'Hello?' It was another black woman, sounding older, kinder.

'Yeah, I was just wantin' to know if you had any information about a Stacy Virginia Verdi. She's elev . . . twelve years old. I'm her brother, my name is Alex.'

'Why do you believe this child is in state care, Alex?' There was a maternal patience in her voice – a certain softness – and I relaxed a bit.

'My . . . parents were arrested, and it said in the papers.'

'The officer you spoke with just now explained to you that we can't release any information, right?'

'But I'm her brother, I just – I mean I really am her brother.'

'Well, we don't release information even to family members, Alex, particularly when a crime has been involved. We've had a problem with family kidnapping children. I know that's not your intention – you just wanna see how she's doing, right?'

'Right.'

'Right, I understand, Alex, but see we're not really who you want to talk to. It's a matter for the courts.'

'Can't you tell me anything?'

'No, Alex, I'm sorry. But if you give me your full name again, and a number or address you can be reached at, I can send you . . .'

I pressed the silver tongue down and held it for a few seconds, then I heard the dial tone and hung up. I walked back to The Gorgon, climbed up to the roof, and drank with Timmy in silence.

As the sun dipped down below the hazy gray skyline, the top of one distant mid-rise building seemed to smolder in pale pink, like the glowing cherry of a neon cigarette. Then, after a few minutes, it too went gray.

'What'd those Buddhists tell ya?' Timmy laughed. 'Did they say what a *big benefit* this all was, and congratulate you?'

I laughed in surprise, and then, as he continued, kept laughing till the tears nearly came. I drank more beer and it seemed a particularly good batch of Dragon.

'Those Buddhists,' he said, with a certain affection in his voice, and shook his head. 'You could go in there and tell them you'd just had your *dick* chopped off and they'd go . . .' He squinted hard and suddenly developed a massive overbite. '"Ho! Thassa *beeg* uh ben-uh-feet!"'

I laughed some more and drank some more and Tim suddenly threw a sinewy tattooed arm around my neck and said: 'God, that would suck huh? Getting your dick chopped off. I mean, wait a minute – that's not what happened is it? Is it? Degreaser! Did Marie finally catch you cheating on her and chop it off like she said she would? Ah *shit*, man . . . What about the Army physical? I mean, it's okay that you're an anarchist – you can hide *that* – but they aren't gonna let you in the infantry without a dick, friend! You still got a dick don't you, Degreaser? Huh? Do ya? Well, alright then.'

PART TWO

'In the old days the human race was always making war, its entire existence was taken up with campaigns, advances, retreats, victories. But now all that's out of date, and in its place there's a huge vacuum, clamoring to be filled. Humanity is passionately seeking something to fill it with and, of course, it will find something some day. Oh! If only it would happen soon! If only we could educate the industrious people and make the educated people industrious.'

Anton Chekhov, Three Sisters

ONE TIME LOVIE, THE queen of all our dogs, jumped into a tall, chicken-wire pen we'd built in the barn for sheep. Lovie, the massive bitch mastiff, was so fiercely protective of our family that she'd jump on top of her dog-house and leap up at the dark green helicopters that flew low across our land every other weekend.

Me and my dad were spending a cold and gray winter afternoon by the fireplace playing chess when we heard the dogs. Like I said, we had a lot of dogs — mutts of every shape and size: smooth-skinned, long-haired, pointy-eared, floppy-eared, fluffy black-and-white sheepdogs like Billy, and one huge, idiotic, long-legged Irish wolfhound with scruffy salt-and-pepper hair.

My dad and I threw our coats on and tore outside to the barn. The dogs were up on their hind legs against the sheep pen, barking all at once — yip, yap, rolf, woof, bow-wow-wow; their dog breath puffing through the silver wire.

The sheep were all huddled together in the corner closest to us, except for one, which stood in the far corner, very calmly it seemed, while Lovie chewed and ate the sheep's bloody hind leg like a turkey drumstick.

Lovie saw us, stopped, and got a very (it's the only way to put it) *sheepish* look on her face, like a fat little kid caught with her hand in the cookie jar. My dad unlatched the door to the pen yelling 'Bad dog!' and she crouched down as low as she could get and slinked out, giving us those dog eyes and licking her bloody chops.

The sheep was fucked. There wasn't much left on the leg

but tendons and bones. So my father went into the house and got the shotgun and shot it.

He was pretty mad. He didn't like to see things wasted. We drove way out to a little Kincaid County shop that sold butcher tools – evil-looking blades hanging off of pegboard walls. He selected a few, and even bought a few books on the subject. But they weren't much help.

We got home and dragged the sheep carcass back behind the house and he started butchering it while I read aloud from one of the books. But the whole thing just turned into such a bloody mess that we ended up whistling for the dogs to come and eat the thing which they were happy to do.

But lesser men could butcher, so he practiced until he could butcher too. That was my dad, and I was proud of him, though I did get pretty sick of mutton after a while.

When my sister was born, and we brought her home from the hospital, Lovie wanted to eat her. Stacy stared, her big blue eyes filled with alarm, as Lovie barked and drooled and bared her yellow fangs. But we kept yelling 'Bad dog!' till she stopped, and before Stacy could even walk, we were strolling her around on Lovie's back like a horse, through the yard we never mowed on purpose. That's when things were probably as close as they ever got to being the way my dad had wanted them to be.

Now, anyone with an ounce of suchness in his soul will rail against kitsch, but how does one paint a picture of the moment that matches or surpasses the corny ideal? That old beatnik friend of my father's – the burly bearded Mickey Silver– would drive over with his wife some weekends. He had been a Chicago high school football star turned minor-league bongo-poet, and ended up teaching at a university in Wisconsin. One Christmas Eve, despite an enormous snowfall, Mickey and his wife drove over. While the women prepared the dinner, Mickey and my father and I took a walk through the snow, pulling my sister Stacy on a red sled. Our driveway, which led to a rural dirt road, was a half mile long and lined on both

sides with apple trees. The orchard had so long since been
pruned that the branches leaned over and touched, covering
the drive like a canopy. When we returned from the walk it
was dark and the moon shone through the bare apple-tree
branches all glazed with ice so that it seemed as if we were
entering a crystal land. No one said a word, not even my little
sister, until we stomped the snow off our boots and went
inside and, well, you can expect what it smelled like: roast
turkey and baked breads and spices and incense. We sat down
in front of a roaring fire made of good hard oak that burned
clean and long and sipped some brandy, and Mick looked at
my father and said, quoting a beer commercial, trying to make
a joke but looking and sounding too sincere for it to come out
ironical: 'Guys, it just doesn't get any better than this.'

And my dad chuckled and shook his head and nodded and
said: 'I wouldn't *want* it to.'

*

At dawn my dad would rise. He said the advent of electricity
had thrown man off his natural rhythms. At dawn he would
rise and brew a pot of coffee or chicory tea on our old gas stove
and bring it back with him to the study he built onto the back
of the house. He'd bring oranges, raisins, maybe pumpkin
seeds or an apple, and there he'd remain till lunch, working.
When he emerged, sometimes his face was flushed with
satisfaction, sometimes it was drawn, pale with exhaustion, but
at the end of every month he'd mail out four manila envelopes.
After lunch he'd spend the rest of the day with me and my
sister and mother. Usually the remaining daylight was spent
fixing something – busted pipes, leaky roof – mending a fence,
trimming a branch away from the power lines that plugged us
in to the main road. Firewood was chopped, the animals were fed
and cared for. Dinner. Reading aloud from the classics in front of
the fireplace. Sometimes we'd drag out our little black-and-

white TV from the tack room and watch the latest installment of some thirty-part Channel 11 presentation of *War and Peace*. Sometimes friends like Mickey and others would visit. Their 'weekend commune' they called it. They were very proud of my father. In certain ways they knew more about him than I did. Mickey would tell me that if haiku were Rock and Roll, my dad would be Mick Jagger. 'Paul McCartney!' 'Elvis!' Mickey's wife and my mom would protest.

Then sleep. There were four full seasons out there, of course, but when I think of us sleeping I think of acorns raining all night on the roof. And the smell of burning weeds. For a long time I thought that smell was coming from the Boy Scout camp a mile or so behind us, but one time, when I was about fourteen (I had just started my second semester of high school) I was rooting through my father's desk drawers looking for the key to the tack room, when I saw a plastic-wrapped brick of green stuff and recognized the smell. Well, I knew what pot was. I mean, I didn't, really – but what else could it be? It sat atop five other bricks still covered in manila paper. I'd seen one of my dad's friends from the city bring those packages out every few months and just assumed they were books or something.

So my dad smoked pot. It seemed strange. He was against drugs. All drugs. He said electric light was a drug. And why did he have so much of it divvied up like that? Was he a drug dealer? It didn't seem likely; who could he deal it *to* out there? The next day, after he and I strung barbed wire along the north-east corner of our property, then cut to the road and headed back towards our driveway, I asked him about it.

What was the look on his face? Not sheepish, or ashamed, you know, but, well, as a little kid I never stumbled in on my parents making love – not that I can remember – but it was that kind of look.

'I don't smoke a lot of grass, Alex. If I did, I'd tell you, but

I don't. Think of how often you smell that burning weeds smell . . .'

As he continued talking, I did think. Maybe once a week.

' . . . Norman Mailer says that all of his highs are rewards – rewards for accomplishment. I like that. I couldn't enjoy getting high unless I'd put in a week's worth of good day's work like I did today. Just finished some poems and sent them off. Nietzsche says – how does he put it? – that life should be spent waging wars and that peacetime should be a brief time to celebrate victory in war and as a time to create new wars. I celebrate sometimes by smoking some grass, counting my blessings, and preparing for my next project.'

'Jack brings a lot of it, though,' I said.

'A couple pounds,' my dad said. 'See, he's not going to drive up here just to keep me stocked with celebration grass. So I buy a couple pounds or so from him, take what I need. When Mickey comes out to see us, he takes the rest back with him to Wisconsin, where he has some friends who live even further north, and so on. The way it works out, it doesn't end up costing me anything.' He seemed very pleased by that. I could tell it wasn't the money he saved, so much as the clean economy of the arrangement – like a perpetual motion machine – and the fact that he wasn't *paying* for rewards he had earned.

He really *was* against drugs, he started to say, it was just that . . . but he fell quiet as we turned up the hill of our driveway. It was springtime and overnight the canopy of apple tree branches above our heads had exploded with white blossoms. Petals floated all around us like snow and blanketed the dusty lane white. And we were both silent for a while and then my dad began to speak euphorically of Japanese potentates – emperors who, during special ceremonies, had lackeys trot before them tossing cherry blossoms on their path.

THERE'S AN ANCIENT Turkish proverb that goes: the first time you see a man, look into his eyes and you will look into his very soul. The first time I saw Zack Mustafa he was pissing out a fourth-story window at the Sleepy Bear Motel down on Canal Street and his eyes were closed.

The Sleepy Bear was the no-star flophouse where all Chicago-area military recruits were ordered to spend the night before being shipped across the country to various boot camps. Per the agreement with Judge Dugan, Tim and I were headed for four months at Fort Benning, Georgia. Like a couple of conscripted Catholics on the night before Lent, we brought two cases of beer, two fifths of Jack, and found ourselves two Filipino Navy-nurses-to-be who were staying on the second floor. Now, the mathematics of the situation would seem simple: there were two of us and two of everything else, right? As usual Tim's rawboned magnetism defied all laws of logic, and, as he and the two aspiring Florence Nightingales started getting silly together – wrestling and tickling and unzipping and unclasping – on one of the twin beds, I forlornly slunk out the door with both of the fifths.

As pissed as I was at Tim, it wasn't really his fault. I guess my heart just wasn't in it. The night before, as I packed up my things at The Gorgon, my icy Marie all-of-a-sudden quick-thawed. We fucked all night and when we weren't fucking we were intertwined naked and pledging our eternal love. We tearfully promised each other that we'd be true, though for me it didn't seem like much of a promise, considering where I was headed. But I hadn't even left the city yet and here were these couple of island temptresses putting me to the test. I tried my best to convince myself that Marie was just as full of shit as I was, and would be sending me a 'Dear John' letter within a week, but the thought of *that* gave me a hangdog look guaranteed to scare all females away. Though I had tried hard of late to act the happy-go-lucky nihilistic skinhead, I still wasn't immune to that kind of stuff. Besides, we were being sent into *exile* for chrissakes, who *wouldn't* be too depressed to pursue a meaningless lay?

Timmy fuckin' Penn, that's who.

I made my way out of the Filipinas' room and back towards ours up on the fourth floor; up the dingy back staircase and down the long, smelly, dimly-lit hallway which lay before me like a green shag-carpeted El tunnel. There I saw the profile of a young man pissing out a window into the darkness below. To my drunken, soreheaded sensibilities, this dark and hawk-nosed character was not simply urinating out a window, he was making the ultimate swashbuckler statement.

'Move over,' I said, as I walked up next to him, set one of the fifths of Jack down on the sill before him and unzipped my fly. 'And remember,' I said, glancing down at the blacktop of the empty parking lot, 'do not, under any circumstances, cross the streams.'

That perked his interest. His blackish eyes flew open and flashed with some strange mixture of naïveté and menace.

'Why not?'

There was something very childish in his tone.

'Because . . .' I said, 'because, to cross the streams might very well throw the entire universe off its axis.'

'Whaddya mean "off its axis"?' he asked me dubiously, shifting his cock with his hand so that the streams, until then parallel, now crossed a few feet in front of us before continuing and eventually fraying and splashing into the lot, several yards short of the dark and empty street.

'Now you've done it,' I said, setting down the other fifth

and placing my free palm against the window frame, as if bracing for the downfall of the cosmos.

He sighed as we pissed and shook his head slowly.

'Y'know, one of the reasons I took time off from college and signed up for this shit was to get *away* from campy sons of bitches like you. You shouldn't have passed the physical. You're going to infect the other recruits with irony.'

Oh, a college boy, eh? I turned my head towards him with a twisted grin of whiskey surety, then narrowed my eyes into a look that said: *Prepare to have your mind blown, motherfucker*:

'"Remember, Razumov, that women, children, and revolutionists hate irony, which is the negation of all saving instincts, of all faith, of all devotion, of all action."' I winked, and added, for his edification: 'Conrad, via Milan Kundera.'

He didn't even bat a long black eyelash, just shook his head again and watched his weakening stream of pee.

'Yeah . . . you know what? Kundera's just pissed because he was duped into jumping on the Communist bandwagon, and for thanks the Communists screwed him in the ass, because that's the *nature* of Statism. But could Kundera just admit he'd been a dumbass? A naive, young, intellectual wannabe? No, it couldn't mean that! Kundera's a fuckin' genius! No, it must be that if *Kundera's* ideology was ass-backwards . . . then ALL fuckin' ideologies must be ass-backwards!'

I stood there, mouth already open for retort, drunkenly trying to digest his words, when from seemingly nowhere I heard a deep voice boom:

'Hey, y'all watch where yer pissin'!'

I looked to the other side of the street and saw them emerge from the shadows of a big brick building and into the light of the streetlamp: six big hickish types, all decked out in their best mesh T-shirts and skin-tight acid-washed jeans, and all looking up at us with their chests inflated and thrown out, and, I'd imagine, the hair on the back of their red necks bristling with rural indignation.

'Awwww shucks, whatsammater fellas?' I asked, as they crossed the street towards our window, while Zack and I redeposited our members and zipped up. 'Where y'all from? Iowa? Y'all get lost on the way to Rush Street? Shucks ...'

I nudged Zack, who glanced at me, then shouted to the rabble:

'Yeah, what are you worried about? You're on the other side of the street, losers! Is our piss causing any harm to you or your property, assholes?'

They shouted up at us, shaking their fists. I laughed and, with a four-story height advantage, told them to bring it on, dramatically tilting my head back and drinking down several healthy gulps of the whiskey for good measure.

*

A couple of hours later I was lying on my back in bed, reeling, the empty bottle of Jack somewhere on the floor on its side, talking non-stop to Tim who had finally come back up to our room from his marathon session with the Filipinas. As usual, he went about his business – getting undressed, washing his face – and acted like he wasn't even listening to me.

'This guy's method of argumentation was fucking cracking me up, man. I mean, all these steroid eating hillbillies yelling up how they'll rip our fucking ... and this guy's yelling shit back like: "You're obviously not even *from* this community and now you're citing community standards? Do we come up to Iowa and complain when you guys marry your sisters and fuck goats up the ass?" And they're, like, kicking newspaper boxes and yelling: "We're not from eye-o-wah! Whyo'choo come on down here an' we'll whup yer asses. Sheeeit. Yahoo!"

'And this guy – *Zack* – this guy Zack – he goes to college at Northwestern – he says: "There's five, no six of you, and two of us. How can you fuckers honestly expect us to come down there, you fucking cretins?" And the biggest guy, this – he

143

almost looked like a skin, Tim, boots and bald, but he was just a big jock hick I'm tellin' you – he points up at Zack and says "Just me and you, motherfucker." And Zack goes: "OK, I'll come down just as soon as you tell all your GAY LOVERS to leave!" And they're like: "You're the gay ones playing piss games!" And Zack's like: "Yeah right, why don't you take that ceramic dildo out of your ass and then talk."

'So the big guy's really pissed and he tells his friends to leave and they start walking down the street towards the Post Office and Zack yells down; "Nice try, fuckers, I'm not coming down unless they go over *there* . . . " and he's pointing in the opposite direction, so they start jogging in that direction and he's leaning out over the windowsill going "No, over *there*," so they stop and start running in the opposite direction, and he's like "No, over *there*," and the big guy who just stood there the whole time grabs one of his buddies by the arm, real pissed, and they all stop and start swearing and yelling unintelligible shit.

'So I'm like: "Come up here then tough guys," and out of the corner of my mouth I'm laughing and telling Zack they got the whole place under lock-down, and they're like, "We'll be up there, you fuckers." So they start trying all the doors and they're all locked, and then they disappear around the back and we start laughing and drinking. I ended up drinking that whole fifth, I think. Unless I spilled some. So we're laughing and shit and all of a sudden we hear this commotion stomping up the back stairway and me and Zack look at each other like: SHIT! and we start running down the hall towards the room and I can't find my keys so we just start trying every doorknob and they're all locked except for one and it's this fucking closet with, like, linen hampers and maid shit, so we go in there but it's so small that we can't shut the door all the way – it's still open a couple of inches, so I can see them when they all pour into the hallway looking for us and I start laughing and Zack's like "Shut up" so I do and they all run right past us and up to

144

the window and start saying what pussies we are for leaving and blah, blah, blah, and they leave.

'So as soon as they're gone Zack runs back to the window and waits until he sees them in the street again and yells "Hey you fuckin' faggots – where were you?" And they say, "We just waint up thur!" And Zack's like: "This is the fourth floor. The . . . fourth . . . floor. Can't you count?" And he sticks his hands out the window and starts showing them on his fingers, "one, two, three, four. What're you all from *Iowa* or something?" And they're all like "RRRarrrrr! You fuhkers!" and they start running back around the building again but some security guy comes around the corner and tells them to beat it and we're like "Yeah, losers, beat it! Hahahhahaha!"

'And get this man: this Zack guy's *infantry*. Fort Benning. He'll be with us the whole four months.'

Right then I felt Tim grab me by my sweat-soaked T-shirt and yank me up to a sitting position. When I opened my eyes, the room was teetering and Tim's face and upper body were half-lit by the red glow of the alarm clock next to me.

'Listen,' he said, 'we gotta get through this thing without any fucking problems! Stay away from that guy. You hear me? He's trouble.'

I've just downed roughly a fifth of sour-mash whiskey, and Tim has me by the shirt. He himself is shirtless and all his tattoos are pulsing: the pitbull on his head, the blue spider webbing on his elbow, the green and red dragon all across the left side of his chest, the rest of his skin crawling with various spiders and scorpions and skulls, and actual blood is dripping from various cat scratches that the Filipina girls left on him while he fucked them both. This big, bloody, tattooed, skinheaded, sex-smelling, beer-breathing character is looking me in the eye and saying: 'Stay away from that guy – he's trouble.' I burst out laughing and immediately started to puke, and Tim nimbly jumped back and started laughing too.

The comic relief was good. There was some kind of tension

building between Timmy and I, and, as I looked at him laugh in the dim red glow, I drunkenly wondered what I was doing to make him start resenting me so. In looking back on it, I think it was the other way around. Tim was the King of the Skinheads and it bothered me to gradually realize there were powers greater than that.

Then the alarm went off. It was 3:55 in the morning. Over the course of the next week, while they shipped us and processed us and measured us and fitted us and filled in all the free time with little games aimed at breaking us down and building us up brand new, I would imagine that I got no more than a total of a few hours sleep. The hangover lasted the whole first week, but that pain was nothing compared to the deadening monotony of it all. Throughout, though, there was a certain spark of dissonance that flickered amidst all the olive drab like a knowing sneer, like an unshaped promise of something better somewhere else. That spark was Zack Mustafa.

IT SEEMED LIKE A DAY where we were only pretending to be alive. The tall and crowded pines of the hilly Georgia woods were bare of branches till the very top and seemed to go on and on forever, like posts in endless fences. The sun was going down but the forest floor was one big mat of bleached-out pine needles, so it didn't seem so dark.

'This here is some gen-u-ine Hank Williams Sr. territory, friend,' Timmy drawled lazily, then a voice echoed from the woods.

'Private Penn!'

Tim rose up from where our squad sat waiting for the evening training to begin. He put his hands behind his back in the at-ease position, and stared off into space as Master Sergeant Wills approached, wearing heavy-starched battle greens that snapped like sails in the wind as he walked. Wills was a massively-built good-old-boy. The Army-brat son of a highly decorated World War Two Infantry grunt, Wills himself had served in both Korea and Vietnam. And he loved Timmy Penn.

All the sergeants loved Timmy Penn.

Wills reached forward to push Timmy's plastic-shell helmet-liner back on his head, exposing the blue-ink of the 'American Pitbull' tattoo above his temple.

'Goddammit, boy!' Wills drawled. 'I done *told* you *three times* to *wash* that damn dawg off your head, now didn't I?'

'Yes, Drill Sergeant!' Tim deadpanned. It was a running joke between them. One that Wills evidently found hilarious.

'Front leanin' rest!' Wills bellowed, and Tim dropped to the

147

ground, pumped out fifty picture-perfect pushups, then hopped back up to the at-ease position.

Wills was about to holler some more when a jeep came barreling down the little stretch of dirt road behind him. Lieutenant Rollings, a sandy-haired little wisp of a guy, not much older than Tim and I, stopped the jeep and called for Wills.

'Yes, sir!' Wills called back, with the tone of weary, slightly parodic – yet ultimately real – deference middle-aged men reserve for their wives. Before stepping smartly away, Wills poked a finger at Tim, and said, his weathered face filled with mock rage:

'Boy, ahm gonna *dog* your Nasty-Guard Weekend-Warrior ass till you tell me you're joinin' the *real* man's United States Army.'

'Yes, Drill Sergeant!' Tim shouted, then sat back down beside me.

Regular Army, National Guard and Army Reserve recruits all went through the same boot camp together, but the Drills never got tired of saying how the guys going home to once-a-month weekend duty after graduation were wimps, whereas the *real* men were staying for jump-school, Ranger training and a full-time life-long commitment to the infantry. I hadn't told anyone yet, but that whole first week at Benning I was actually turning over in my head the idea of signing up for active duty.

Where else was life so cut and dried? Here you were given challenges, and, if you just tried your hardest, you got promoted. Guaranteed. A life of pure cause and effect. I thought of Mrs Kabushita back in Chicago. Had my Buddhist practice mystically led me to my true destiny as an infantryman? Sitting there among the pines, I casually leaned over and asked Tim if he'd considered it.

'Nah,' he sighed, watching Lt. Rollings roar off in his jeep with Sgt. Wills. 'No way ...'

'We'd make good soldiers,' I offered.

'Yeah,' Tim said. 'So what? Wills is a fuckin' *great* soldier. Fought in two wars – got all shot up. Thirty-something years after he was first drafted and he's still gotta call punks like Rollings "Sir".'

As I dug an index finger through the sunbleached pine needles, down to the fragrant green ones closer to the earth, I caught a flash-image childhood memory of my father's silver Captain's bars, and said:

'*We* should be officers then . . .'

Tim screwed up his mouth with scorn.

'Pff. Yeah, right. Fuckin' goofy-ass *Zack's* got a better chance of being an officer than us. You gotta have college to get into Officer's Candidate School. Officers are all college kids.' He looked up at me as if he could see the wheels start to turn in my head, laughed, and lightly slapped the side of my helmet shell. 'You're a skinhead, Degreaser. You're working class for life. Get used to it. Can you see *us* in college?'

I didn't answer. I mean, it was true: hard as I tried, I couldn't picture *him* in college, but . . .

'Awright dickweeds, listen up!' shouted the Staff Sergeant assigned to our squad that evening. He was a pale little hillbilly with his garrison cap pulled down so low you couldn't see his eyes, pacing back and forth in front of the long, chest-high bench, waiting to lecture our squad on the chemical-biological antidotes we would carry in a combat situation.

We all trotted over to the bench where there was a bunch of olive-drab plastic packages filled wih heavy-duty-looking metal syringes. The Staff Sergeant launched right into a drone.

'The Soviets' élite infantry, our intelligence tells us, will begin each wave of each assault with an attack of death gas rockets. These rockets or rather this gas will *keeel* you . . .'

After a while he jutted his hatchet chin towards the sets of monster syringes.

'The needles are cocked inside and upon impact spring activate like a switch-blade stiletto. These needles are extra long and thick so as to penetrate yer protective suit, yer Battle Dress Uniform pants cargo pocket and all contents thereof . . .'

Then, following his instruction, I slid the biggest, meanest-looking syringe from its case, held it out at my side aimed at my thigh poised to stab, and froze. Everybody else did too. We looked like a goddamn Busby Berkeley chorus line. I glanced down at the flat, sealed end of my syringe, and imagined a long, rusty spear just aching to shoot out at me.

'These here test syringes're filled with a liquid dose of Vitamin C, but the needles are real, now raise yer hands up like so . . .'

I was about to plunge an iron spike into my leg. For the first time since leaving Chicago I felt fully awake. As I raised my arm up like everybody else, a battle raged beneath my helmet. I was eighteen years old. Was I a man? Or a boy?

A man, I decided, a man!

' . . . and with a vigorous thrust on the count of three bring the nub of your syringe down against yer thigh hard enough to activate the needle, one . . . two . . . three!'

I swung my arm down in a blur and, at the last possible second, figured, ah, fuck it, so I'm a boy then, and halted my swing so that the nub stopped just short of my thigh. Then I closed my eyes and grimaced in what I meant to represent excruciating (but stoically contained) pain.

Tim, who'd been standing next to me the whole time, looked over at me sideways, knowing somehow exactly what I was up to.

'It's a joke, man,' he whispered out of the corner of his mouth. 'Look! No needles.'

I glanced down at his and everybody else's unpunctured legs. Yes, it had been a joke alright. Great joke.

The Staff Sergeant overheard.

'Joke?' he said, looking at me. 'I don't recall any jokes, you dickweed. Get down and give me fifty and yer boyfriend too with the damn puppy-dawg tattooed on his haid! An' elevate yer laigs off'n this here instruction bench while yer at it, ya coupla Nasty-Guard No Go's.'

Tim and I put our hands on the pine-needley ground and swung our feet up on the bench. My chest muscles were shredded from thousands of earlier push-ups so the idea of doing fifty, like this, was a joke. This guy was full of jokes. The best of which were yet to come.

After a few minutes of slight elbow-bending, the Sergeant hollered for us to join the rest of the 130 so other guys in the Delta Company who were lining up at closed ranks on the narrow dirt road. Way off, beyond all the endless trees, I could hear the idling engines of the cattle cars waiting to take us back to our little bivouac campsite a dozen kliks away. We hadn't slept in the barracks since we got there four days ago. It seemed a lifetime ago.

'Awright, dickweeds, line it up! Line it up, dickweeds. Tighten up, Delta Cumpnee.'

We were right on top of each other, the entire company marching in place, seven men across and fifteen deep – clump, clump, clump – and finally he ordered us to advance.

'Whattayou lookin' at, Private?' a Drill howled at me. 'Eyes front, goddammit!'

I fixed my eyes on the back of the helmet of the guy in front of me. He was from the fourth squad – a tall, skinny, zit-necked recruit named Birch.

'Way down in the valley!' I heard the Drill Sergeant croak.

'WAY DOWN IN THE VALLEY!' we all screamed back. Except me, anyway. Fuck it, I thought. My throat was getting stripped raw from yelling silly shit day and night so I decided I'd just mouth the words from now on. Who would know anyway? Perhaps you are wondering: 'What if *everybody* did that?' I was not concerned. If I had learned one thing since joining the Army, it was this: I ain't everybody.

'I heard a mighty roar!'

'I HEARD A MIGHTY ROAR!'

I heard a faint popping noise off to my left, but didn't give it a single thought, just kept staring at Birch's skinny neck.

'It was mighty mighty Delta! Eyes front! Eyes FRONT goddammit!'

'IT WAS MIGHTY MIGHT . . .'

Then Birch suddenly wheeled around and drove the bridge of his nose right into my helmet. His head bounced back like a rubber ball and he stumbled into the soldier in front of him. That popping noise wasn't so faint now and it was everywhere – in front of, behind, and right beneath me. Off about ten yards to the left I saw three guys wearing old-style, olive-drab BDUs creeping out of the woods. They had gas masks on. One was lobbing little shaving-cream-sized canisters at us, one after another, and the other two guys had the same kind of cans fastened to the ends of sticks. Thick yellow smoke was pouring out the ends. The tight wall of soldiers seemed to disintegrate into a swirling, camouflage sea.

In the same split-second, beads of tears just started to squeeze from the corners of my eyes and I felt an acid-hot burning in my nostrils. I looked down and saw a fog of the yellow smoke rising up above my gunbelt.

'Aaaaaaaawwwfuuuuuuuuck!' I yelled.

There wasn't much else to say.

In case of actual wartime gas attack we'd been drilled all day to:
1) Put your rifle between your legs, butt down.
2) Unsnap your chinstrap, remove your helmet, and drape it over your rifle barrel.
3) Unsnap your protective mask carrier with your left hand, remove it with your right hand.

*4) Hold the mask out in front of you, and grasp each side firmly
by the webbing.*
5) Pull it on, chin first.
*6) Cover the air filters with both palms and blow out to clear a
breathing passage.*
*7) Raise both arms straight out to the side and bend upwards at
the elbow repeatedly, each time yelling: 'Gas! Gas! Gas!'*

As soon as I saw the Drill Cadre throw all those CS riot-control gas grenades at us I flung my rifle to the ground so hard that the detachable pieces of it all went flying in every direction, yanked my gas mask out of its case with both hands and tried to put it on over my helmet. It got stuck so I left it up there and ran.

I didn't get far, though. Somebody barreled into me from behind and I tripped over another idiot who was somewhere beneath me on all fours. On the way down I took in a burning yellow lungful. And then ... well, I don't know exactly. Except that for the first time in my life I thought I was going to die. Truly, I could not breathe. I couldn't see. My nose was pouring snot and my squeezed-shut eyes were oozing like two burning cold-sores. All those lessons in Soviet killer-chemicals were jumbling around in my head and ... I've already said it: I thought I was going to die.

Then, through sizzling eye-slits I thought I saw a clearing in the yellow to the right of me. I crawled towards it with lungs about to explode and got all set to take in a breath of real air – sweet, beautiful, real air – when I saw a black jumpboot, with that tell-tale wing-tip strip across the toe, plant itself right in front of my nose. I looked up and saw the legs of a Drill and the barrel of his homemade gas-gun blowing more of the yellow right between my eyes.

This man was obviously trying to kill me. I wasn't thinking much of anything coherently, you know, but I do remember wondering, as I curled up into a suffocating little ball on the path with every sweaty pore and orifice in my body afire: 'Why do you want to kill me, friend? I mean, I can see killing somebody for a reason, but I've never done anything to you. Have I?'

Then it was over. They ran out of gas I guess. When I could open my eyes well enough to see again there were only a few yellow wisps floating off in the trees, and soldiers were getting up off the ground, coughing, dry heaving, stumbling around, looking for their gear. That's what brought me back to reality – my gear! If you lost one tiny strap on your web-belt, or God forbid, a piece of your rifle, God only knows what they'd do to you. I stood up weakly, still burning everywhere, and looked around at the jumbled mess. I heard a violent retch and saw Zack off in the trees vomiting. Everything was scattered everywhere on the dirt – gas-masks, helmets, rifles, camouflage sticks, empty cartridges, pieces of rifles (pieces of *my* rifle!), contraband cigarettes, cans of chewing tobacco, left-over, freeze-dried *MRE* food packets, scraps of love letters . . .

'I'm not gonna make it . . .' I whispered to myself, remembering that this was only day four of a four-month fun-fest. Just that morning some idiot from the Third Platoon had scrawled on the wall of the cattle car: 'Delta Company, 131 Days and a wake-up!'

'I'm *not* gonna make it,' I said again. Then I saw Tim roll up off the ground to his feet. I gave him a wild, distressed look. He came over and snagged two plastic barrel-stocks off the ground (they could have been anyone's) and snapped them on to the naked skeleton of my rifle. As he stooped to pick up more of my equipment, I could see by his shaking back that the whole situation had him in stitches. I had almost died and he was *laughing*.

I was about to drop my end of the deal and lay down right there. Judge Dugan said if we got kicked out he'd go ahead and put us on trial for assault. So what? Prison couldn't be any worse than this. But I figured they'd probably just start gassing me again, so I went on searching for my gear.

*

Before going to sleep that night, Tim and I sat with Zack for a while by a small, three-log fire at the rear of all the neat little rows of two-man tents. This was about as far away as we could get from the Drills' tent, which was the size of a small house and hooked up with electricity to boot. Behind us and our tiny fire was the woodline – miles and miles of forest filled with every poisonous snake in North America and, adding to my morbid, sullen mood, packs of wild dogs that yelped and howled through the night.

Though we'd been there less than a week, Zack was already on every Drill Sergeant's shit list, which made sense, as his sole reason for joining had been to antagonize authority. He dosed up on acid one night in his Evanston dorm room at Northwestern University and watched on TV how Bill Murray's wisecracking supposedly turned the Army on its ear in the movie *Stripes*. The next day, before he even came down fully from the trip, he went to the recruiter and signed up.

Now, after just four days, the novelty had worn off pretty good. That night, after they gassed us, the Drills decided to put Zack on fire-guard duty all night long as an example of what happens to wiseacres in the United States Army. He said he was just waiting for the Drills to doze off, though – then he was going to hide somewhere and go to sleep anyway.

We sat in silence by the fire for a while, reading the letters we'd gotten at evening mail call. Marie wrote me a quick note filled with meaningless street gossip and anecdotes of Jason's latest scrapes with the law and references to new hardcore punk bands I'd never heard of and it nearly made me weep with depression at a Gorgon life so hollow I couldn't even miss it.

The gas attack had been a hard blow for me. I'd lived through worse things, of course, and I was destined for worse things, but I don't think I ever felt as low and weak and without hope as I did right then.

'I'm getting out of here, man,' Zack suddenly said, staring into the little fire that each of us periodically fed with tiny twigs and pine needles. Hot as the days were, it got near to freezing there at night, and my toes were aching beneath the stiff, thin leather of my new combat boots.

'Where you gonna go, Mustafa?' Tim asked, stretching his field jacket over his broad shoulders and pulling up the hood. Unlike most of the recruits, his camouflage BDUs seemed to *fit* him right; he looked like a soldier should. Tim was starting to actually take a semi-liking to Zack, it seemed, but he harassed the hell out of him. 'Where you gonna go, Zack? Out there?' Tim pointed towards the deep black woods where the dogs howled. Even further out you could hear the steady dull pounding of practice mortar rounds. Boom . . . Boom . . . Boom. . . .

'I'm *thinking*, man. I don't know *how* yet, but I'm getting out. Frankly, that gas thing was the final straw.'

For the first time that night I felt the urge to speak.

'They tried to kill us, man,' I said with quivering lips.

'They didn't try and *kill* us,' Tim scoffed. He was sitting furthest from the fire with his hands buried in his coat, and his words came out in white puffs, like tiny smoke signals. 'How else are they supposed to get us ready for war?'

'What war?' Zack asked.

'There could be one, man,' Tim said. 'In South America . . . or, I don't know . . .'

'The Mideast,' Zack offered. 'Eastern Europe. Korea again. So what? Would you go and fight?'

'Right now? Yeah, I'd have to.'

'Why? To die protecting your homeland when it isn't in danger in the first place? That would be a *shameful* way to die.'

'It's a *duty*, dude. Besides, I got no choice. I signed a paper.'

'A *duty*? Listen,' Zack said, 'you gotta read Ayn Rand, friend: "*I swear on my life that I will live for no man, nor will I ask any man to live for me.*" That's her most famous character's credo. I'm telling you this, friend, because right when I met you, you reminded me of an Ayn Rand character. Seriously, like an updated Ayn Rand character. And here you are, a *skinhead*, saying you'd let your government treat you like a bitch.'

Tim grinned, but I saw his lean face get that reddish soak of anger. People didn't generally talk to him like that. He pulled his hood back down and pointed a long, pale finger at Zack.

'Mustafa, first of all, you don't know me.'

'No, you don't know yourself.'

The grin vanished from Tim's face and his gray eyes went hard.

'I know my dad went to Viet Nam and came back with a metal plate in his head. And I don't think it's "shameful". I'm proud of what he did.'

I had never known this before. I looked over at Zack, who nodded vigorously.

'You *should* be, man. He didn't have a choice in the matter and he survived it.'

'He had a choice. He volunteered for the Marines.'

'Well . . . then it's a moot point. He voluntarily put himself at risk for a cause he believed in. If *I* was old enough then, I would have disagreed with the cause, but I *still* probably would have had to either go fight, or go to prison, or become some kind of a fugitive. Listen, the government exists to enslave its people – the draft is just another form of slavery.'

I thought of Nuccio recalling when he and my dad got their draft notices for Korea, and for the first time saw my dad's Captain's bars in a new context. To avoid the fighting Nuccio used his connections. My dad became an officer.

'Slavery?' Tim scoffed. 'Why? Just because *you* didn't

believe in the fuckin' cause? What about World War Two? Hitler's gassing Jews like dogs. Would you have gone?'

Zack shrugged.

'Tim, are you familiar with the term "Red herring"?' A faint smile reappeared on Timmy's lips, and his eyes widened a bit in warning, as if he gave Zack credit for having the balls to talk down to him like that, but might just have to kill him anyway.

'I asked you a fuckin' question, Mustafa . . .'

'You ask me what I would have done in World War Two and the answer is, I would have fought against Hitler *if I fucking felt like it*. But as far as "duty" goes? Again, like John Galt said: "I swear on my life that I will live for no man, nor . . ."'

'Oh, that's cool,' Tim said, suddenly leaning his face in closer to Zack's. 'You're born lucky, so fuck the little Jew girl, *let* 'em stick her in an oven.'

Though I was actually reveling in the energy of their debate, I was starting to get a little nervous, but Zack just gave a blink that seemed to say 'you can hit me, but I won't shut up,' and continued:

'"Born lucky?" Bullshit. People who are born lucky don't *go* to war. They have their well-connected daddies make a few phone calls so they can stay at home. You've got a sucker mentality, Penn. You wanna fight somebody else's battles, go ahead, but don't force me – at the barrel of a gun – to go with you.'

'Pff, Mustafa, you don't even know what the fuck you're talking about. Did you know a bunch of hard-ons from your squad were talkin' about giving you a blanket-party when we get back to the barracks? Talkin' about putting on their gas masks to disguise themselves and holding you down in your bunk and beating your ass 'cause you keep fucking up. Yeah . . . it ain't gonna happen, though, because I *told* them it ain't gonna happen. And I don't even *like* you. You won't *ever* see anybody here even *think* about pullin' shit like that with Alex or me, because we're skins, and we watch each other's backs . . .'

With that Tim leaned back again and shoved his fists back into the pockets of his field jacket. Zack held up a hand in protest.

'Well, I thank you for that . . . even though I never asked for your help. But, frankly, you're confusing the issue! Look what you're defending. The fact is that the government could send you *anywhere* right now and get you killed for any reason. You're their *property*, and you didn't *ask* to be here. You didn't volunteer like your dad. All you were doing was watching Alex's back in a bar. You were *screwed* into joining the Army. You guys told me that yourself!'

His words – and even more so the bitterly sympathetic *tone* of his words – felt like a slap in the face, a wake-up call of some sort. I looked at Tim who stared now at the coals of the campfire, his face pulled tight. He nodded vaguely to acknowledge that Zack was right, then exploded:

'But nobody made *you* sign up, ya fuckin' goofball!'

'It was a mistake,' Zack conceded. 'But I'm getting out.' He reached down, grabbed a big manila envelope that he'd been sitting on, and started pulling out sheets of onion-skin paper and throwing them on the fire. They were pages of a long, rambling letter from his mom, written in Turkish. Just after mailcall he'd translated a couple of passages for us which described, in hilarious detail, what a disappointing loser he'd turned out to be in her eyes. After the letter was burned he pulled out a thin newspaper, but before he could toss that into the flames too, I grabbed it. I'd been dying for something to read. It was a copy of *The Daily Northwestern*.

'Whattya gonna do?' Tim persisted. 'Run away? The FBI will track you down. Punch a Drill? They'll put you in Leavenworth, breaking rocks.'

'I could say I'm a fag.'

'Well, they *knew* you were Turkish when you signed up.'

Their conversation had been filling me with unfocused rage, which, strangely, made me feel better, stronger. But now the talk was taking a futile turn, so I read the college newspaper backwards from the Sports section, describing how NUs teams had all been trounced, walloped, shellacked, etc., through the classified rooms for rent, and the features, to the front page. And there I saw a picture. Not just any picture, mind you. It was a picture that would change my life. Mere ink and paper, yes, but . . . well. But it's true.

It showed two girls standing on a lawn before an old, whitestone building with two pillars and a wide stone staircase. One girl wore a loose and flowery dress. She stood with her legs spread and bent and stared with crossed eyes at a little beanbag ball she had balanced on her forehead. She had kind of a big schnozz, so it was pretty funny looking. At least the other girl thought so. She wore jeans and a T-shirt. Thin. Brown, bobbed hair. Very pretty, yes, but it was something else that sucked the breath out of me. Let's see, she was laughing – but you could tell the sound of her laugh wasn't mean or sarcastic at all. It was a wide-eyed, open-mouthed, surprised laugh. And she was clapping. She had her fingers clasped to her chest, and her wrists were limp, bent to one side. She seemed so genuinely *happy*. I looked to the caption for a name, but all it said was:

At Deering Meadow Friday students took advantage of unseasonably warm weather.

I interrupted their argument to ask Zack if he knew the girl in the picture. He squinted in the firelight and shook his head.

'No . . . wait,' he said, pointing to the girl with the Hackey-Sack on her nose. 'I know that one, a little. I sold her a bag of weed once and she bitched that it was light.'

'What about her?' I asked, pointing to the other girl.

'It *was* light, though. Her? Nah. Wait a minute . . . no. Probably some sorority slut. I gotta get outta here, man.'

Tim stood up to stretch his long legs. His knee had been bothering him ever since the night we got arrested. As he walked a few steps towards the woodline to take a piss, he looked back at Zack and sneered: 'Deal with it.' That was the Delta Company's motto – 'DEAL WITH IT!' It was painted on our barracks wall above a mural showing a huge hand of cards. The hand was a pair of deuces.

'Fuck "Deal With It",' Zack snapped. 'That's such typical American shit – "Deal With It." Do what you're told. Toe the line . . . right face, halt. It's the American Way.'

'Pfff . . . you're high, dude,' Tim said, disgusted, then sat down by the fire again and pulled his hood back up.

'Oh, come on Tim,' Zack said. 'Don't tell me a skinhead's going to defend the *system* here in America . . . Come *on*.'

Though I was still lost in the picture, I felt compelled to join in at this point. Though it may seem strange – highly ironic, even – I, like Tim, felt a strong, unshaped patriotism in my skinhead bones; one that had absolutely nothing to do with government.

'It is *not* the American Way,' I said, folding up the newspaper and sliding it into my cargo pocket. That picture had filled me with a strange, intense vigor. 'It's not the American Way at all.'

'Yeah . . .' Tim said.

'It *is*, though,' Zack sighed.

'Would you rather be in Turkey?' Tim asked. 'There something so great about the Turkish Way? Is that why you live in America?'

'I'm not Turkish,' Zack said. 'I was born here. I'm American. I'm an American citizen. I can criticize my country.'

Tim looked at me knowingly, then narrowed his gray eyes to slits and looked back at Zack, shaking his head with disgust.

'Your people come to this country because it's the *best* fuckin' country in the world, and the free-est, with the most opportunity, and then American colleges teach their kids – like you – that the American Way sucks.'

'I'm not even passing judgment,' Zack said. 'I'm just saying that the American Way is to conform.'

'Ah, bullshit,' I said. I felt challenged, especially with Tim there. I had always been considered the intellectual of the skinheads. Did this guy think that just because he went to some fancy college . . . ?

'You're talking about every *other* way,' I informed him, and Tim leaned over and looked into the fire again, letting me take over. 'How about fuckin' whatshisname from Greek . . . *Greek* mythology. Him and his old man are escaping an island on mechanical wings, and the father says: "Don't fly too close to the sun, son." '

'Icarus,' Zack said.

'Yeah, *I know* it's Icarus,' I said, 'and . . .'

'and Icarus doesn't listen,' Zack said, his voice filled with boredom, 'and the sun burns his wings and he dies and I am so fucking sick of hearing that cliché shit.'

'So am I!' I said, slapping the anarchy tattoo beneath my BDU blouse. 'But don't go sayin' it's the American Way.'

'I don't care what way it is. You know what it fucking reminds me of?' he said. 'That Icarus shit reminds me of those beer commercials that say: "And remember, please don't drink too much."'

'Fuckin' A,' I agreed. I had no idea what he was talking about.

'Because I'll tell you something, friend,' he continued. 'No matter what anybody says otherwise, I'll tell you what the old men have always dreamed of and the old ladies have always prayed for and the best girls in every grass hut and every skyscraper since time began have pined for, and that's an Icarus who *makes it*.'

And every sorority house, I added silently.

'You're goddamn right,' I said. '*That's* the American Way, friend.'

'All right, fine. Then why don't we act like Americans and get the hell out of here?'

'Because this isn't America,' Tim said, spitting on the dying fire. 'It's the Army.'

After a while we left Zack by the fire and went to our tiny tent. A Drill had said that if you tied up the door-flaps real good, and then lit a little candle, it would heat the whole tent. It sounded like bullshit, but we did it anyway. We stuck it in the sand between our sleeping mats, and, at the very least, it gave off a pretty good light.

'Fuck it,' Tim said, and pulled out a glass bottle of Sea Breeze face-astringent from his shaving bag. He unscrewed the cap and took a big gulp.

My momentary shock ended when he handed the bottle over to me. Then I remembered him mentioning some contraband booze Zack had given him for safekeeping because the Drills were about to do a complete search of his personal items.

'Guy's a nutter,' Tim said, as I took a gulp of the vodka. With my tongue and throat still stripped raw from the screaming and the gas, it was like pouring vinegar on a wound. But I took another drink anyway before passing it back to Tim; booze was such a precious commodity there that already some guys were concocting schemes of smuggling it in. Texas Hector, Timmy's big, beefy friend from the Second Platoon – an ex-skinhead from Laredo – started getting the shakes his first day there without beer and had to go through two months of cold-turkey Army-hospital rehab before starting basic training. Then he got a letter from his girlfriend back at home, and in it she mentioned a new kind of 'dry' beer. He had it in his head that the stuff was like powdered milk or something and wrote a long letter back to his girl describing in detail how she should send him fifty letters, each with a tiny amount of 'dry beer' secretly sprinkled in the envelope. When Timmy told him what was up, it about broke his heart.

I felt the vodka warm me up and wondered if the candle was doing any good. I stared at it for a while. It was fat and short and white. The pool of liquid wax on top was overflowing and pouring down into the sand. It reminded me of something and I laughed.

'My old man bought a samovar once,' I said.

'A what?'

'A samovar. It's like a little pot-bellied stove kind of Russian thing for making tea.'

'I know what you're talkin' about,' Tim said. 'I saw it in a movie once. Why'd he buy one of those?'

'I don't know . . . Maybe he saw it in a movie once. I think he read about them in books so much that . . . I don't know, but he got one. An antique dealer brought it over, and right after he left, my dad fired it up and started making some tea. He put some Russian classical music on and had me and my mom and little sister sit around it by the fireplace, and when he figured the tea was ready he said to me: "Let me have your cup, Alex." I gave it to him and he turned the spigot and this tea came out all steaming and my sister and mom were cheering and then I looked and the stream of tea turned silver.'

'Eh?'

'The tea turned bright silver and we were like "What the fuck?" and my dad turned it off right away. The goddamned *lead solder lining* had melted inside. Thing was a fuckin' unusable show-antique, man. Coulda given us brain damage.'

We both laughed and drank some more and Tim asked me when the last time I saw my dad was and I told him as my throat began to swell – over a year now. The realization that it had been that long was followed by a suffocating sense of guilt. I hadn't tried to contact him because I was afraid I'd get caught and sent to prison myself. Even if I could prove that I hadn't dealt any drugs at school, what about burning the buildings? If the property had been seized, wasn't that a crime? But after the fight with Ugo nothing came up about Harding County. Before our swearing-in, the Army had finger-printed us and conducted an extensive FBI background check. When we reached Benning we were all given one last chance to admit to any outstanding warrants. I kept quiet, waiting nervously, and nothing happened. Wouldn't even a local warrant have shown up? This was getting ridiculous, I couldn't just go on not knowing for ever. But it slowly occurred to me that even if I was in the clear, there was something else. I had those vague and childish plans of becoming a great man and somehow saving the day, but time kept passing, and here I was. Even if now *was* the time to act, here I was.

I was always kind of subconsciously getting myself into conversations about my dad, and Tim was a good guy – he always took the bait. But that night in the tent, like usual, I changed the subject once I realized where it was headed.

'When's the last time you saw *your* old man?' I asked him hoarsely, as the swelling in my throat subsided. He had to think.

'The last time I saw my . . . no, the second to the last time I saw my dad was when I was in kindergarten. When my mom was renting a house up in Melrose Park. He just showed up one day and I had no idea who the fuck he was. My ma just laughed and said: "This is your daddy, Timmy . . . you came outta his pee-pee."'

I had to laugh. Tim's mom.

'Her and him didn't act like they'd ever been, you know . . . it was like they were brother and sister or something. She just acted like "Ah boy, here's the big dummy again, what's he got up his sleeve this time?" you know? And he did, he did have something up his sleeve. He quit his job as a pipefitter to become a magician.'

'What?'

'This was when fuckin' guys like David Copperfield and Doug Henning were the shit, you know? Millionaires. And in Chicago there were guys like Ernie Johnson. He was cool. And my old man thought: "Fuck, it's all just a bunch of props, you know? All I need's the props." He had this idea about making a dozen tigers disappear.'

'A dozen tigers? Where the fuck was he gonna get a dozen tigers?'

'Rent 'em. But he had to buy the cages. He had to build some capital. That's where I came in . . . What it was was he wanted to start a magic school for kids. And he was due to go on the Ray Raynor show the next day to promote the goddamn thing, even though he didn't have any students yet.'

'Shit.'

'That's why he came to see me and my ma. He wanted me to go on the air with him – like I was his top student, you know? And before he even got the words out of his mouth my old lady was on the phone telling everybody: "Timmy's gonna be on the Ray Raynor show! I need to borrow some money to buy him a suit . . . " Then my old man took off and I didn't see him till the next morning. I was standing out on the front porch in this real slick brown three-piece deal from Sears, and he finally screeched up in his piece-of-shit El Camino. He was like: "We're late, c'mon." So he drives like a fuckin' madman to the WGN studios, right? and we rush back to Ray Raynor's dressing room – the show's just started, and we're due to go on in fifteen minutes; right after the Clutch Cargo cartoon where only the mouths moved – remember? – and some shit with a duck.'

'Chauncey,' I said.

'Yeah that's right, Chauncey, man. Fuckin' Chauncey. Anyway. When we get back there to the little dressing-room, he's like: "*Yeah*, we made it, dude." He lights up a Kool, and leans back and starts making fun of all Ray Raynor's jumpsuits. The guy had like fifty jumpsuits hanging on the wall, and my old man's pointing at, you know, the pink ones and laughing and all of a sudden he's like "Holy Shit!" He looked like he shit his pants or something, and it scared me you know? And then he was like: "I gotta teach you a fuckin' *trick* to do, man!'

We'd about finished the vodka, and I was rolling.

'So in the next five minutes he tries teaching me this shitty three-card trick with two diamonds and a heart, right? If you turned the heart upside down and put it between the other two, it sort of looked like a diamond too. But I got it down in five minutes and we went out to the set.'

I wanted to know what the set looked like. Even though my father moved us out to the country, intent on raising me on nature and great books, there was that little black-and-white TV in the tack room, and I was a Ray Raynor *junkie*.

Tim shrugged, turning the empty bottle upside down, and closed his eyes to picture the set.

'It looked like nothing,' he said, opening his eyes. 'No audience, everything made out of cardboard. But wait, it gets better. My old man goes on first, and I'm standing off in the wings watching him. He's got this blue tuxedo deal on with a big frilly shirt goin', and he's, like, pulling coins out of Ray Raynor's ear and feather-dusters out of his jumpsuit. And then it's time for me to come out. I walk out there, confident as hell. I know the trick and I know that my whole kindergarten class is watching back at school. I know the nun has just pulled out the big dusty TV with the tinfoil on the antennae, and that seeing me walk on the set is making all my friends go apeshit, right? So I do the trick, perfectly, and Ray Raynor looks at the cards, and he's being real nice, but he says: "But Timmy, that's not a diamond. That's an upside-down heart."'

'Ahhh shit,' I moaned.

'Yeah, I threw the goddamned cards on the ground and ran off the set crying. My mom took me home and I felt so fucking bad for my old man, you know, like I'd totally fucked up his gig and he wouldn't like me any more. And oh, God did I hear it from my class. You don't know how many asses I had to kick at school those next couple of days. And . . . I don't know, I waited for days for him to come home, but I never saw my dad again . . .'

He looked at me and grinned and then dropped his gaze to the candle.

' . . . *until*, until he walked back into the house one day when I was in the fourth grade – the last year I spent in Catholic school. Same story. Ray Raynor, Round Two. This time he teaches me a rope trick. And it's a good one. You take three different-length ropes, and twist them around in your hand and pull the jumble apart and it looks like they're all the same length. Same thing again – we get to the same dressing-room, my old man's smoking a Kool, but now he's wearing a black tux, and he tells me to do the trick for him. So I do, and I fuck it up completely there in the dressing-room. The ropes come loose from my hands at all different lengths like snakes and my dad, he goes kind of pale and says: "You're joking, right?" And I'm like, "Yeah, yeah, I'm joking."'

'Were you?'

'*Nah* I wasn't joking! I'd forgotten how to do the trick. But *fuck* if I was gonna fuck up again, man! Fuck *that*. So, again, same thing. I stand in the wings, wait for him to get done doing his intro, walk out there, and Ray Raynor's like: "Now, uh, I don't want to mess you up like last time, Timmy," and I just smile and start twisting the ropes without thinking, telling him – and myself – how I'm gonna make all these ropes the same length – him, and myself, and all the millions of people watching . . .'

'Including your class again?'

'Yeah, including my class again. Those bastards were taking

bets on how badly I'd fuck up. So I finish twisting them around, not knowing what the hell I just did and then I pull my hands apart and the ropes are stretched out taut, and I look, and Ray Raynor looks, and my old man looks . . . and they're all the same length.'

'Awright!' I hollered.

'Yeah. And then my mom took me home and I never saw my old man again.'

*

Somewhere around four in the morning I felt a tug on our tent rope, and the whole thing wobbled. My eyes snapped open from a muddy drunken sleep, and I sat up quickly, hitting my face on the damp canvas of the tent.

The candle'd burned out and it was dark and wet and cold in there. I heard Tim snoring next to me, before the whole tent shook again and he woke up as well.

'What the . . .'

I started untying the door-flap and he sat up too.

'Get the gas masks!' I shouted.

'Naw, shut up man, open that door.'

So I opened it, and saw the hairy back of a middleweight in army-issue boxer shorts walking down the line of tents, with arms held out in front of him like a zombie.

'That's fuckin' Mustafa, man!' Tim whispered, and it was indeed. He walked past all the little tents to the front, where the Drills slept in their heated twelve-man shelter, and then started walking around in little circles, sidekicking the canvas door with every revolution.

It all made sense in an instant – supposedly, sleepwalkers were kicked out of the Army. Me and Tim started laughing so hard and trying to hold it in that it hurt.

But it went on, and on and on. Those fucking Drills must have been sleeping like rocks not to hear Zack kicking their door. Finally, after about fifteen minutes there was a rustling around inside and Drill Sgt. Bean, a young black guy, jumped out with a long black flashlight raised like a club. He stopped, lowered the flashlight so it shone on Zack, and said:

'Gott–damn . . .'

At this point, for added realism, Zack started pissing on himself.

I was burying my head in Tim's shoulder to keep from exploding when I heard Bean shout:

'You nasty-assed muthaf . . . *get* yo' gott–damn pissed-on self out of here 'fore I . . .'

And another Drill shouted from inside the tent: 'Nice try, Mustafa! I don't buy it for a second. We'll deal with you later, dickweed.'

But Zack kept up the act until Bean jabbed him in the solar plexus with the flashlight again and again until he opened his eyes and tried to look astonished. Then Bean whirled back into his tent and back to sleep. Zack just stood there in the moonlight, his arms at his sides now, shivering.

I felt Tim suddenly pull me back into our tent and saw him quickly tie up the flaps.

'Don't let him know we're awake, man,' he said in a whispered laugh.

'Naw, man, we gotta let him know we *saw*,' I protested. 'Why not?'

'We'll let him know in the morning. That fucker'll wanna philosophize the whole experience with us, man, and we still got like . . .' he squinted to look at his watch in the darkened tent, ' . . . forty-five minutes to sleep.'

We heard him trudge back past our tent. He stopped and punched the canvas like he knew what we were up to, but we just lay there still, trying to keep from exploding, and, after a couple of minutes of silence I heard Tim start to snore.

I lay awake though. I was euphorically happy for the moment and I wanted to relish it. Zack was like human morphine, I swear to God. And Tim, the way he could endure anything and everything, was like a sturdy wooden crutch. I learned to use those guys for all they were worth, but it was only good to a point. As I lay there that early morning I thought back to Nuccio's ramblings about growing up with my father, and suddenly I was, I guess, just like Tim had been in kindergarten after the Ray Raynor fiasco – worried sick that I'd let my old man down. As much as I missed him it seemed to me right then that I would rather be dead than have him know what a loser I'd become. Even though my father had no idea where I was or what I was doing, I knew he never dreamed I'd be a fuck-up skinhead, hanging around on Belmont with Jason and those guys, talking incessantly about who was a Nazi and who wasn't. Getting arrested all the time. I didn't belong there and I didn't belong in the goddamned Army eating with my hands and shitting in the woods like a dog. I didn't even belong with Marie, for that matter, shacked up in a closet that still smelled like ferret. It was all wrong. Suddenly Mrs Kabushita's Buddhist congratulations made perfect sense. This was a 'beeguh benefit' after all. I belonged in school or something, where I'd be respected and where I could wave hello every morning to that nice girl I'd seen laughing in the paper.

Thinking of the girl, it suddenly seemed like I was suffocating in that tent. I sat up, untied the door-flaps, and crawled outside without stirring Tim. I stood up, barefoot in the cold sand wearing only my shorts, but as chilly and breezy as the pine-smelling air was, I still felt all closed in. The dark and heavy-bottomed early morning clouds rolled slow and low, just above the endless black treeline. All of a sudden there was so much that I wanted, and vague as it all was, I wanted it now.

My old man had his Lilac Farm, and I goddamned had to have my Deering Meadow.

BACK AT THE BARRACKS, Zack had various pamphlets and books hidden in his footlocker dealing with the philosophy of Objectivism according to Ayn Rand. Ayn Rand was very big on personal responsibility. Basically, she argued that if everybody spent enough time worrying about their own goddamn selves, no one would have to worry about anyone else. This made a lot of sense to me at the time, so I set out to test her theories immediately, and upped the ante with each passing day.

One of my boldest moves came when I walked into our Senior Drill Sergeant's little Company Office, snapped to attention, and informed him that I wanted him to make me the Fourth Platoon Guide. The position was temporarily vacant as the previous Guide, Private Leonard, had been stripped of his duties for not shaving his neck properly.

Senior Drill Sergeant Poole was a frighteningly intense man – black as pitch, with ropy veins of midnight blue bulging out of his thick neck and forearms. He responded to my request by looking up at me across his desk with a patented, saucer-eyed glower. This glare had turned countless recruits' knees to jelly with the sudden realization that the man, despite his crisply-creased BDUs and regimented love of procedure, might also be a psychopath. But there was something else in his eyes this day which betrayed him. He was amused at my request.

I myself did not find the idea of Alex Verdi, Platoon Guide, that funny. With graduation only a couple days away I had passed every inspection, aced the tests on Soviet tank identification, weapon assembly and first aid, earned Expert medals on the M-16 and grenade ranges, and, after a quite calculated approach, emerged from the final physical training test with the highest score – I held the title of Company IronMan, dammit. I had spent every free moment doing extra exercises, and when mealtimes came in the field, I sold my daily allotments of cake and Frosted Flakes and stuck the coins in my rucksack. Certainly Timmy Penn could do more push-ups and sit-ups than anyone, but once you reached the max score of seventy any more exertion was superfluous. And to be sure, there were a few gangly pituitary types in the Delta Company who could finish the two-mile run before me, but such narrow superiority was moot. *I* alone had maxed-out on the three basic tests of push-ups, sit-ups, and run.

I alone was IronMan.

'All right, Verdi,' Poole said, with a big-toothed, challenging grin that matched his crazy eyes, 'All right . . . you *got* it, dick.'

Senior Drill Instructor Poole was not calling me a penis, you understand; in keeping with recent military regulations that forbade the sergeants from calling recruits foul names, he was, with an acronym, bestowing upon me the highest of compliments. D.I.C.K. was short for Dedicated Infantry Communist Killer.

One of my first duties as Platoon Guide was to assemble a team to clean out a long-misused Battalion latrine in which the three toilets had been stopped up for some time (a fact that did not prevent harried, indiscriminate privates from continuing to use them until it became physically impossible to do so). Surprisingly, neither Tim nor Zack were at all flattered when I drafted them into an élite squad made up only of men I felt I could completely trust on such a mission. The operative tools for the task were canteen cups, plungers, and of course, our rubberized protective gloves and gas masks. When we arrived back at the barracks that night after lights out, Zack was not up for any Randian discourse, and Tim went without a word to the showers, and then to his bunk.

I had very little time for Zack and Tim now anyway. It seemed there was always some task along the lines of the latrine mission, or some form to fill out, and it took every last ounce of concentration and energy to keep from fucking something up. But I always made sure to shave my neck real good, and Poole told me in advance that, barring any half-stepping, I'd be awarded our Company's Outstanding Soldier Award for the cycle.

*

On the afternoon before graduation day, Drill Sgt. Poole burst out of his office and cast that horribly mesmerizing glare on our Platoon; first on the men, who were lined up in four neat rows in the Company area, then on me as I, Platoon Guide, stood before them with hands behind my back in a stiff at-ease position, then back on the men.

'Front-leaning rest!' he bellowed, and we all leaped into the push-up position.

'N-Now . . .' he began (he stuttered a bit when he was truly incensed). 'When I got here this morning I put a fresh copy of *The Columbus Times* on the front desk, *OK*? And now it's gone. And whoever *took* my copy of *The Columbus Times* wasn't even *kind* enough to replace it w-with his own copy of *Beaver Shot*, or a perfumed love letter from Susie Crotchrot back on the block, or any *other* contraband I *know* you Privates got stashed away up in those barracks. That's just not polite. I got nothing to read now. Nothing. But it's too late for the contraband now. My feelings are hurt. So I'm gonna give you all one chance to tell me where that paper is right now. One chance.'

I had my suspicions as to where it might be, but I didn't say as much. Nobody did.

'O-okay. Sometimes I exaggerate,' Poole said, after being met with a stony silence by the men. 'I'm gonna give you *two* chances. Two chances 'cause I know you *all* didn't take the paper, and because I know you *all* don't wanna be crawlin' with pain when you get back to your loved ones tomorrow night, and especially because I *know* how much you respect your fearless Platoon Guide here, Private Verdi.'

I could have done without the flattery right then.

'Two chances and this here is the second one right here. Going . . . going . . .'

'Private Mustafa's got the paper in his fuckin' pants, Drill Sergeant!' I was shocked to hear someone shout. I was even more shocked when I realized the voice was Timmy Penn's.

Poole called Zack up front and made him pull his pants down and give him the paper, but my eyes were on Private Penn as he stared unwaveringly straight ahead into space in the front-leaning rest position.

Telling Zack that he'd deal with him during lunch, Poole went back into the office with his crumpled *Columbus Times*, and I morosely got up and told the platoon to break down their rifles and give them one last immaculate cleaning.

After dropping the morning report off on the front desk, I walked through the crowd of seated soldiers as they wrestled with their weapons on the concrete floor and found Tim sitting in the back, his rifle already completely disassembled, each of its little parts laid out gleaming before him on a clean white towel.

'Why'd you do that?' I asked him, hurt. But I was interrupted by Poole who had burst out the front door again.

'Mustafa, where's the gott-damn sports section? Get up here!'

I saw Zack sigh in the corner of the company area and walk with head down to Poole, drop his pants again, and pull the missing section from his boot. Poole was nothing short of amazed.

'Private Mustafa, I *like* you. I like you so much I want you to accompany me down to the PX so I can get a new pen to fill out your Article 15 papers. Come on. Now, if I happen to drop any piece of this paper, I want you to catch it. If one piece of this paper touches the ground before we get there, I'm afraid we'll have to go beyond the Article 15 and just send you back to *day one* of the training cycle – that's four more months – for lack of discipline.'

And with that he began to walk out towards the road that led to the PX, shredding the paper into skinny strips and letting them fall away in the breeze. I watched him disappear over the hill as Zack followed, mostly on all fours, leaping wildly to catch each strip. Then I turned back to Tim.

'Now he's not gonna graduate!' I lamented.

'He's gonna graduate,' Tim said. 'They want him the fuck *gone.*'

'But he's our friend!'

'Look . . . *you're* Mr Army, man! All of a sudden this shit is real important to you for some reason, right? You're up for this award and shit. Poole was gonna *dump* you as Platoon Guide.' He began putting his rifle back together.

'I don't give a fuck,' I said. 'I thought you and me and Zack were gonna get an apartment together in Evanston. Make a skin outta him.'

'Are you fuckin' kiddin' me?' Tim asked, 'He's a fuckin' rich kid, man. Only rich kids act like that. I'm not getting a fucking apartment with that guy. Skins are strictly working-class, man, you know that.'

There was something uncharacteristically trite about his words, but there was also something hidden and genuine beneath them. I did not, by any stretch of the imagination, consider myself eternally working-class. That was one element of skinhead romanticism that I never bought into. It was several minutes before I spoke again.

'So what're *you* gonna do then?' I mumbled.

He sighed and looked up at me with a faint, angry grin. 'You're gonna move in with him?'

I shrugged and looked away.

'Listen to me, Alex, that guy's got a rich momma that'll pull his ass out of any crack he gets it caught in. You don't. You're working-class, man, like me. I've been talking to Texas Hector a lot and he's got some great connections in Mexico. He said we could go back with him for a while and work some things out.'

'And then what?' I asked, but it was a pointless question. I wasn't going to Texas or Mexico or anywhere but back with Zack to Evanston – to Deering Meadow. I was going to use my Randroid omnipotence and get into Northwestern University and finally start the task of finding out about that Harding County warrant and contacting my family. I had already tearily sent Marie a rambling goodbye-forever letter. I would have much rather just not addressed the situation at all and disappeared, but that didn't seem like the thing a man of integrity and values would do.

'And then . . . whattya mean "And then what?"'? Then we can unload as much shit in the city as we can fill a drive-away rent-a-car with and get a regular thing goin'. You know that. We'll be fuckin' flush, Degreaser.'

'We can't go back to the city though, Tim!'

'Ah come on, dude! What? Do you think they'll have "Wanted" posters up for us? Do you think anybody cares what we do besides Ugo? He probably doesn't even give a shit any more. We just gotta keep a real low profile until we make enough to go to India, man, and, ah shit, man . . .' He took a deep breath, and half-opened his mouth, as if to say something more, but all that came out was: 'Pfff.' That 'Pfff', I knew, was some condemnation of my character.

'What?' I watched him shake his head. As he looked up at me he wrinkled his reddening brow as if he were facing an adversary.

'You were never a fuckin' skin, man. You can wear the Docs and shave your head but that doesn't make you a skin.' And then, all at once, all traces of anger that were in his voice were gone. 'No man, I think you *should* go to Evanston. You should be in school, man. You should. Learn something for me, dumbass,' he laughed.

I thought for a moment, and – realizing that we probably wouldn't get another chance to talk before we graduated and went our separate ways – I started to stammer out an official goodbye. But he held up a hand and chuckled.

'Aw, c'mon, Degreasey. You're gonna be callin' me up in a couple weeks seeing if we still got a closet for ya at The Gorgon. We will.'

He began concentrating fully on his weapon, staring down the barrel and wiping at it with a rag, as if to say, as far as he was concerned, the conversation was over. But he wasn't quite pulling it off; he had that beat, deflated look – that dullness in his gray eyes – that I'd seen after we left his mother's place on Easter. I stood there for a few seconds, my face pulled tight, fighting angry tears. There was a lot I wanted to say to him, but it hadn't formulated itself into words. I almost said that *he* should be in school or something, too, but it would have sounded stupid, and it wasn't quite what I meant. I walked away from him to the other end of the company area, and sat down numbly next to Birch, who, with grease-stained cheeks, was still struggling with his weapon. In my current mood of sadness, Ayn Rand could kiss my motherfucking ass, so I reached over to help him.

'Happy to be going home, Verdi?' he said with a forced smile. Our collision during the gas attack had given him a permanent lump on the bridge of his beakish nose. Without really thinking I answered that yeah, I was fuckin' happy, wasn't he?

'Ah, I don't know, Verdi ... I'll tell ya, the days were hard here, but it seemed like everybody and everything had a purpose and, I don't know ... there's not much waiting for me back at home, you know?'

His words reeked of plagiarism. I'd heard those exact lines before in some war movie, or a television show. But I didn't doubt that his emotions were genuine. It occurred to me that people have a hard time expressing themselves, so they slap together bits and pieces of advertising slogans and soap-opera dialogue and Ann Landers advice columns and whatever, and, armed with that, they try and get as close as they can. Like Timmy with his skinhead schmaltz just then, and Marie back at The Gorgon, who reacted to my long-distance breakup letter by putting different dark and melancholy underground pop songs on her answering machine. Though I pumped countless quarters into the Company pay phone in the hopes of explaining myself after I sent that letter, she never picked up – never – but chose instead to lie there on her futon and let it ring, six times . . . then the click of the mechanism and the whirr of the tape and silently, to herself: *Do you see? This is how I'm feeling, this song says it pretty well, do you understand?*

Birch looked over at me with his skinny chicken neck and his pimply pale face – his camouflaged garrison cap pulled down on his long, narrow forehead, cocked at what the grade-B war-movie scripts would probably call 'a heroically devil-may-care angle', and asked me again if I knew what he meant about going home, and I didn't, not even a little bit, because, of course, I wasn't going home. I was going back to virgin fields of pure potential. I sat there and tried to reassure myself how very anxious I was to get there.

*

The last leg of the trip back was a Huey helicopter ride from Fort McCoy, Wisconsin to Waukegan. Zack slept heavily beside me. I sat awake, my rifle clasped butt-down between my legs, looking out the open side of the copter, down at the Wisconsin countryside, down to geometrically plowed farmers' fields, down to the green algae bottoms of murky ponds.

179

I watched, hypnotized, as tiny cars navigated themselves down twisted highways, and nearly fell asleep. Then I blinked and examined the terrain more closely.

'Fuckin' A,' I murmured, beneath the sound of the Huey's heavy metal blades chugging up the air. 'Fuckin' A, if that's not Route 41.'

As my gut tightened, I saw, far off in the distance, the tower of an amusement park. Much closer was a familiar-looking corn silo. Then the tiny cemetery, and behind it the meadow where I'd stood as a little boy, stood and looked up at the long rows of dark green helicopters that flew in low formation, across our property every other weekend.

I looked hard, and half expected to see myself down there, waving up and yelling and making machine-gun noises with my lips. I didn't see myself, of course, but there was something moving – a man or a boy or a dog or a deer. A dog I decided.

Then the clearing where the house and barn and stable had been came into sight. The fire had done its job. There was just a couple of vague rectangular foundation outlines, and rubble. The ruins of Lilac Farm. The abandoned retreat of my father, the haiku poet.

In the spark of one split second I felt a raging urge to whip the little canvas seatbelt off my waist and hurl myself down upon the land in one great act of revenge and instant atonement.

But we kept on flying and left the land behind.

PART THREE

'Not only does democracy make every man forget his ancestors, but it hides his descendants and separates his contemporaries from him; it throws him back forever upon himself alone and threatens in the end to confine him entirely within the solitude of his own heart.'

de Tocqueville, *Democracy in America*

I STEPPED OFF THE train in Evanston all juiced-up to 'seize the day', but the moments still each came and went like breath on a mirror.

I walked with Zack to the wooded edge of Northwestern's campus grounds. He had to register for spring classes. He pointed to a park bench by the cul-de-sac across the street and said to meet him there at dusk to discuss where we'd sleep that night. Zack had been banned from student housing after campus security found three hits of blotter acid in his closet, a paperback copy of *The Anarchist's Cookbook*, and something like 5,000 drying banana-skins.

My plan was to spend the day finding an apartment and a job, so I cut across a vast NU lawn and looked for a place to stash my Army duffel bag. I recognized a massive white-stone building and realized I was walking through Deering Meadow from the newspaper picture. I felt that surge of Ayn Rand omnipotence and smiled. I would work with a singular passion, and next fall, when I was a student *here*, who could say I hadn't made things right?

Behind a tiny old campus chapel, beneath two towering elms, I saw an entrance in a wall of high hedges. It led to a sort of labyrinth. Down one green corridor I found a worn stone bust of Shakespeare and turned to see a garden of flowers and lilac bushes, cherry trees in blossom . . . such a splash of sun and color all at once. I was in a place called Shakespeare Gardens in the springtime, and I was alone. I slung my heavy bag off my shoulder. Having traveled so far, with such a long, ambitious road ahead, what sin would it be if I sat on that stone bench over there by the violet patch and read for just a bit?

I cracked open *War and Peace* to where I'd left off on the train, and before long the stars replaced the sun. Breathing the scented night air, my eyes strained in the faint moonlight to read and re-read Pierre's dream:

'If it were not for suffering, a man would not know his limits, would not know himself. The hardest thing' (Pierre thought or heard in his dream) 'is to know how to unite in one's soul the significance of the whole. To unite the whole?' Pierre said to himself. 'No, not to unite. One cannot unite one's thoughts, but to harness together all those ideas, that's what's wanted. Yes, one *must harness* together, *harness* together,' Pierre repeated to himself with a thrill of ecstasy, feeling that those words, and only those words, expressed what he wanted to express, and solved the whole problem fretting him.

As Pierre woke up to his groom hollering something about harnessing the horses, I vaguely remembered I had to meet Zack. But as I stuck the book in my sack, and got up from the stone bench, I left Shakespeare Gardens drunk on flowers and the notion of harnessing ideas that could not be united.

Timmy Penn always said I lacked common sense. He worshiped common sense. Ayn Rand called Reason the only absolute. Mrs Kabushita said: 'Buddhism is Reason.' Reason is the golden fittings on my harness, the mathematical rhythm beneath everything that my father said I must confront . . .

I stepped blindly into Sheridan Road and the blue–gray blur of a honking car whizzed by, grazing the polished toe of my boot.

'Whah!' I cried, jerking upright, and my duffel-bag strap slid halfway down my shoulder.

'Holy fucking Christ!' I hissed, watching the car's red tail-lights shrink away. Then I continued crossing the road on shaky legs. *Almost snuffed out just like that! Idiot! What's wrong*

with you? Seriously. What's wrong with you? Wake up! So lost in
space a car nearly hit you . . .

That's when the next car hit me.

Actually, it slammed its brakes and skidded about fifteen
feet before the bumper basically tapped into my duffel bag,
but it was enough to knock me off my feet. The next thing I
knew I was sitting splay-legged on the pavement, staring
dumbly at the scraped heel of my palm. I looked up to see the
car – a red VW convertible – whine back in reverse. It
screeched still, jerked itself sideways – stopping traffic both
ways – then sped off down a sidestreet. Amidst all the honking
and blinking bright-lights I grabbed my bag and ran to the
other side.

I walked down the sidewalk poker-faced, ignoring all the
eyes of bewildered NU kids on their way home from classes,
but every step was a horrified test for broken bones. As I
realized that I wasn't really hurt at all, I nearly wept. I found
the designated park bench empty, and started to sit down,
when the sudden blare of a car horn made me leap up wildly.
Amidst all the cars parked around the cul-de-sac, a souped-up
old Chevy van with the words 'I Love Country Music!'
airbrushed on the side suddenly flashed on its dome-lights.
Out jumped Zack Mustafa, holding up his arms and nodding
triumphantly like some Turkish Mussolini.

'Friend!' he said. 'Check it out.'

With my mind still back in the middle of Sheridan Road,
we climbed in the back of the van. Two facing couches, a
mini-fridge, shag-carpet, and fake-paneled walls – some
anonymous redneck's mobile lovenest circa 1977. On the floor
was a bare twin mattress Zack had stolen from his old
dormroom.

'We can crash in here,' he said. I looked at him blankly.
'Until we find a place . . . I mean, you can have the bed. I'll
take a couch – you can have the bed.'

'How'd you buy this piece of shit?' I asked with suspicion, thinking he had blown his $1,500 enlistment bonus.

'Ah,' he shrugged, 'I blew my enlistment bonus.'

I threw my duffel bag down on the mattress angrily and gave it a vicious kick, bumping my head on the ceiling and biting the inside of my cheek.

'Mmmmmmmm!' I moaned, sucking my cheek and grabbing my head. I envisioned Timmy Penn, kicked back on his trapeze bed at The Gorgon, laughing at me.

'Fuck! *Zack* ... How the fuck are we gonna pay for a security deposit now? My bonus isn't gonna be enough by itself.'

He started to tell me his plan. We would buy some big tanks of nitrous oxide and turn the vehicle into a mobile whippets stand, which would generate all *kinds* of cash ... but I held up both hands and cut him off.

'Zack,' I said. 'Look ... I'm *not* livin' in a fuckin' VAN!'

He seemed completely confused by my outburst.

'Relax, friend,' he said. 'I'll ask my mom to wire me some money tomorrow. I hate to do it, but, whatever ... Come on, friend – relax. There's a keg-party tonight at Beta.'

I told him to go without me and curled up on one of the vinyl couches, using my field jacket as a blanket, silently cursing fuckin' Timmy Penn and his parting prophecy: 'You'll be back. Skinheads are working-class for life, Degreasey.' Like it was a *caste*. Like this was *Bombay* or some shit, and not America!

As soon as Zack left I knelt down on the mattress and chanted for an actual bedroom.

I also gave thanks for the second chance at life I got out there in the street. And the third chance too.

*

The ivy-covered Castle Apartments, with four stone turrets

186

looking down on a rose-garden courtyard, were just the type of quarters I'd dreamed of in my Sand Hill bunk. Zack furnished the place in ridiculous opulence with velvet love seats, cashmere Oriental rugs and brass-potted rubber trees that he stole night after night from the nearby Orrington Hotel's lobbies and hallways. A giant color TV appeared, courtesy of the Delts fraternity, with whom Zack apparently had some long-standing feud. I slept on the mattress Zack stole from his old dorm room, and, though I could not quite work this booty in with any of my newly-harnessed philosophies (except maybe skinheadism), I must admit I slept quite well.

I unfurled my long stored-away Gohonzon and hung it in an orange crate I'd nailed to the east wall of my bedroom, and chanted for a job. Zack saw a sign up on the door at a local NU hangout – ZB Treetz House of Sweets and Pancakes – so I marched right in and asked to see the manager.

Bob Stein, the owner, was short and thirty-something, with a boyish shock of black hair swept off to the side of his sullen, moon face. He took a long, hard look at my high-and-tight military buzzcut and spitshined jump-boots, then led me past tables of chattering NU students, through a back storeroom smelling of produce and milk, into a little office crammed tightly with a cluttered desk, one chair, and a dozen closed-circuit TV monitors.

His words were clipped with frustration.

'Look at this,' he said, stabbing a stubby finger at one black-and-white screen. A goateed character leaned half-asleep against the cash register. Another screen showed some back room where a kid in an NU sweatshirt pressed a teenaged girl up against a walk-in freezer door, kneading her buttocks as she squirmed and squealed without sound.

'Do they think I don't know what they're up to?' he asked me, then bitterly answered himself: 'They don't care. They steal, smoke pot back there, invite the bums in off the street for free food . . . In-credible.'

He shook his head and watched the screens in silence until (perhaps sensing how uncomfortable I felt standing there in that cramped little room) he forced his froggy mug into a smile and said:

'So, how do you like Heavenston?'

I forced a smile too and said I hadn't heard that term before.

Bob leaned back in his chair and explained how Evanston had long ago been a hotbed of Christian fundamentalism and was, in fact, the actual birthplace of the prohibition movement in the twenties.

'Hence the name: "Heavenston".' He smiled wryly. 'You couldn't even sell an ice-cream soda here on Sunday. It looked too much like a beer!'

We shared a little laugh.

'So,' he continued, getting rather excited now, 'to get around *that* particular law, a local merchant made a soda *without the soda water*, and served it in a dish. Hence the ice-cream "Sundae!"'

He roared with laughter. After a few uncertain seconds I too let forth with a belly laugh, because, as you know, I needed a job. Besides, seeing the guy's life calling, I could understand how such a tale might warm his heart.

Suddenly, he stopped laughing and looked dourly at the monitors again, shaking his head.

'*What* are they thinking?'

I surprised myself by saying:

'They aren't . . . they lack a philosophy based on Reason.'

He seemed too mesmerized by the snowy screens to hear me.

'I can't watch these things twenty-four hours a goddamn day! It's destroying my life . . . What I *really* need,' he said, as he swiveled his chair around to face me, and narrowed his eyes conspiratorially 'is a *night manager*.'

*

I operated as an undercover observer for the first week or so. Bob suspected his workers were doing a little pilfering. In fact they were robbing him blind. Each night, after the lights and cameras shut off, the staff would creep out the door, arms laden with entire hams, whole cheesecakes, cases of Diet Cokes, and anything else they could lug back to their dormrooms and sorority houses. Like demented little children, they stuck expensive product in the microwave 'to see what would happen'. Mounds of gummy bears became translucent rainbow puddles. *Galactic Jawbreakers* exploded like half-sticks of dynamite. I couldn't help but feel a pang as I watched. Bob had bragged to me that Treetz was the only shop this side of LA to carry *Galactic Jawbreakers*; they were his candied pride and joy.

Still, I couldn't bring myself to *tell* on anyone – to name names – but I finally did feel moved to hint to Bob why his whipped cream always lost its whip within a day or so of delivery. It was a flat-sundae mystery that was driving him to the point of nervous breakdown.

'They are sucking the nitrous oxide out of the cans with their *mouths?*' he gasped. 'With their filthy, herpes-sore *lips?*'

When I came into work the next night, a handwritten sign had been taped above the time clock.

ALEX VERDI is the new
NIGHT MANAGER
Please co-operate w/him fully.
Thank you,
B.S.

There was a new Sheriff in town. A half-dozen of the worst offenders quit immediately. When I interviewed potential replacements, I tried as slyly as I could to slip Ayn Rand into the conversation. This elicited little more than blank stares or outright looks of confusion. Except from Dewon Brown – a handsome, half-Jewish mulatto kid with biceps the size of big, brown hams. At the mention of Ms Rand something danced in his hard hazel eyes and soon the interview disintegrated into a lengthy, knee-slapping, high-fiving, Rand-roid bull-session. We both loved her fictional characters – the self-made mavericks who overcame all odds and smoked special cigarettes emblazoned with tiny gold $ signs. Dewon, who wanted to become a Hollywood film director, identified most with Hank Reardon, from *Atlas Shrugged*, who ignored the skeptics and invented a special kind of blue steel nothing could break. My favorite was the golden-haired Scandinavian – Ragnar Danneskjold – the capitalist-terrorist, who, with one pirate ship, went up against the guns, planes, and battleships of five collectivist continents, always eluding capture, slipping back through the tortuous blue fiords of his youth.

I scheduled Dewon to work full-time, never letting our nights-off overlap. Thus, seven nights a week, ZB Treetz was under the safe eye of capitalistic integrity.

I had a bedroom and now I had a job.

I gathered NU application papers and financial aid forms and bought some ACT study-guides, shooting for at least a score of twenty-nine. I spent hundreds of hours at the Northwestern library, using a forged copy of Zack's I.D. to check out materials. Sometimes, when the weather was nice, I'd take my books outside, through the labyrinth of hedges, to Shakespeare Gardens. I'd sit on the stone bench beneath the cherry tree and study. I'd read for pleasure too – mostly political stuff, but the idea of Shakespeare in Shakespeare Gardens was too cool to resist. Sometimes I'd just stare at the garden, at the trees and bushes in bloom. There were a few box-elders, looking weedy and out of place, and I remembered how my dad read in one of his *Stalking the Wild Asparagus*-type books that Elders were in the Maple family, and tapped table syrup from one with a finger-length of copper tube. I'd vow to begin the process of finding my family, as soon as I got situated here. Then I'd shake myself out of such reveries, and get back to the work – the *action* that would somehow make everything all right again.

Zack's I.D. also got me into the Patton gym, where I lifted free-weights every afternoon before work. Believe me, if you could have bottled the fog of pheromones swimming around in my new-found air of confidence, you'd have made a fortune. I saw the way the waitresses were looking at me differently. But I would no longer be so easily led from the path. In the past – whether it was pain-soaked longing for Marie, or animal lust for the Gorgon doxies I'd lured out to the fire-escape in pursuit of the Timmy Penn Skinhead Standard, or that simple bar-room flirtation the night we got arrested – my precious ambitions had always been wasted on skirts.

But things were different now that I had Ayn Rand.

Now every step was a sure, purposeful step, and each spare moment was filled. For instance, as I heard the ZB Treetz doorbells jingle that fateful afternoon, the cookies all were baked, the pastries pastried, the chrome counters and glass display cases sparkled, and I had just buried my nose in some scholarly discourse on Aristotle's Law of Identity when I looked up and saw Abby Rivers smiling.

It was that girl I'd seen laughing so happily in the Daily Northwestern picture at Fort Benning.

In the flesh, the clean and fresh-faced beauty born of wealth and good-breeding was blinding. But unlike most of the moneyed coeds, who purchased their sweets with a sour air of inaccessibility and reserve, Abby Rivers came right up to me like a city squirrel.

As she beamed and blushed and rolled her eyes down towards the countertop between us – fighting to keep the delighted corners of her small red mouth pulled down – I realized that the cool, pure pleasure coursing through me was naked. I was embarrassing her. As if to say in some pathetic way I was sorry, I went and made her frozen-yogurt sundae with *six* ounces of soft-serve, instead of the standard two-and-a-half, and topped it off with a ridiculously-generous extra-fistful of gummy bears.

Quoth the Bard:

> *My Reason, the physician to my love,*
> *Angry that his prescriptions are not kept,*
> *Hath left me. . . .*

At first I chanted that she and I would become great friends. Not boyfriend and girlfriend. Just buddies. Which was odd because she was such a knockout. Classic, All-American, long-legged, brown-bobbed. Not exactly my ideal look, but just about everyone else's.

'Well, this must mean I'm getting older and more mature,' I thought to myself, as I chanted one early morning and rubbed the prayer beads Mrs Kabushita had given me as a going away present back and forth between my palms. I'd thrown away the orange crate and built an actual presswood cabinet to hang my scroll in. Each morning I placed beneath it the standard offerings of fruit and evergreen and fresh water. Then I lit sandalwood incense and rang a tiny silver bell.

I wrote at the top of my list of weekly goals.

1) To continue chanting
2) To do my part for Kosen Rufu (World Peace)
3) To become best friends with Abby Rivers

Her yogurt trips to the shop became frequent, and soon she began stopping by just to see me.

She went to Lake Forest College, not Northwestern. Abby's sister, the other girl in that picture – the one with the big nose – went to NU. Her name was Sarah and she came into the shop with Abby a few times. She was a brooding, sarcastic, beady-eyed little thing and it was evident that she didn't like me at all, though it didn't much concern me. Nothing much concerned me when Abby was there.

Abby was doing an internship at an Evanston pre-school. When she stopped by the shop, we would sit at a small round table and talk. This is where the trouble started. She thought I went to Northwestern. And, well, I let her think it.

I didn't consider it a *lie* really, it was more of a . . . preview of the future truth. I would get into NU somehow. But the lies just multiplied, metastasized, and pretty soon I was not *really* a glorified soda jerk. No, that was just a ruse. I was, in fact, a secret psychological consultant for Bob Stein, and gathering material for my thesis (and eventual book). I was not a reformed skinhead either, but a graduate of Choate where I'd crewed. And father was not a Little Italy greasy-spoon restaurateur turned beatnik haiku poet, but a wealthy options trader who expected me to join the family business. But I kept on telling him, no, Dad, I want to be my own man.

Abby thought that was the greatest.

*

One night, near closing time, I heard the bells on the swinging glass door jingle and looked up to see an old man, on his way out, hold open the door for Abby as she rode into the restaurant on a shiny new mountain bike.

'Look at it!' she cried, riding across the black rubber mud mat towards the cash register, where I stood counting down the drawer.

'Hey,' I said, laughing nervously. Dewon, who was measuring out ice-cream for a milkshake, raised his eyebrows slightly. He nodded towards the hidden camera behind a hanging fern that Bob kept running at night. 'Hey,' I said, stepping around the counter, 'you can't have that thing in here.'

'Yes I can,' she said, laughing, making as if to ride right

down the center aisle and past all the staring faces of the customers. Most of the men looked like they wouldn't have minded.

I caught the bike by the back of its seat and laughed again, a little nervously, and said, 'C'mon.'

She dismounted and walked behind me as I wheeled the bike out onto the sidewalk, into the muggy night air. I gave her a quick once over: she was wearing sandals, a white leotard, a pair of huge and baggy blue nylon shorts, and nothing else. Her bobbed hair was pulled back into a short ponytail. As usual, her eyelids grew heavy and her lips seemed to swell as she basked for a moment in my trance-like gaze of approval.

Abby pointed to her new bike.

'I need to *name* it,' she said. 'Help me name it.'

I said that 'Sid' would be a good name and Abby agreed as she swung a leg up over the frame and straddled it. As she hunched over the handlebars, and placed one foot up on a pedal, the immense bagginess of those nylon shorts only barely hinted at the delicate, yet pronounced, curvature of her bottom. She was aiming at some effect with the obscuring hugeness of those shorts, but it wasn't modesty. I felt a strange sadness.

As she pedaled away without sitting, she looked back at me and yelled that she was having some friends over tonight and I should stop by after work – it would be fun.

After Dewon and I closed the shop I thought about running home to take a shower and change my clothes, but this was not a *date*. It was just buddies hanging out.

When I got to her fancy apartment building on Main, she buzzed me up and greeted me at the door with a hug. She had changed into a white, wide-necked t-shirt tucked into comfortable white jeans and let her hair down so that it brushed lightly against her shoulders. I noticed she had put some make-up on too. Just a little lipstick and some blue stuff in the corners of her eyes.

She pulled me in by the hand and introduced me as 'Alex from Northwestern' to the three interns from the pre-school she'd invited over. To my dismay, I already knew the black girl sitting on the couch rather well – from the Gorgon days. The fire escape one night. She left a pale blue ring of toothprints on the head of my penis. Marie had threatened me with a pair of scissors to tell her how they got there but I never said a word.

Though I'd been shaved bald back then, the black girl recognized me now. I could tell. But she was very nice and did not let on anything beyond the fact that she and I had already met, though she couldn't remember where.

'This is also something that happens when you get older and more mature,' I thought to myself happily.

The other two were guys – a big, softly muscular blond kid and a little dark-haired guy. Both were wearing khakis and pink oxford button-downs. I made a mental note to hit The Gap next pay check.

Everyone was drinking wine.

'I've got whiskey or beer,' she said, leading me into the kitchen and not mentioning the wine. As I stared into the refrigerator at an untouched six-pack and a still-sealed fifth of Jim Beam, I wondered if the two guys were their boyfriends. I also wondered if she'd bought the beer and whiskey especially for me.

A few minutes later, the two guys went home. That left me, the black girl who was named Lena, and Abby, who suggested we play a game.

She lit a fat white candle and set it on the floor in front of us, then turned out the lights. The game went like this: Abby asked some questions and Lena and I answered. One question was:

'Think of five words to describe your favorite animal, besides the way they look, and write them down on a piece of paper.'

My favorite animal had been Lovie. The mastiff who'd been

shot defending our home. All at once I saw it clearly – them dragging my mother and father from the house in handcuffs, carrying my sister off somewhere, all for a few green bricks of weed. Lovie was happier to die than watch it and her brains had spilt out red in the snow. During our last weekend-leave at bootcamp I paid an old biker in Columbus, Georgia, to tattoo the head of a snarling bitch mastiff across my left pectoral. I wondered what Abby would think if she knew. The simple truth was: my dad was a drug dealer and I had tattoos. But the simple truth was a lie.

'Five words,' I heard them both saying.

'Loyal, tough, mean, playful, loving,' I wrote, and slipped the paper to Abby, who read it, then clutched the paper to her chest and sighed:

'That means that's how *you* are.'

What else could I have done but hide? I asked myself, the guilt and hatred flaming up inside. *What can I do now?*

'Think of being locked in a shadowy room all alone,' I heard Abby saying. 'The room is empty except for a white chair facing an open window covered by a white drape that is fluttering in a cool, steady breeze . . . three words . . .'

Lena said:

'Fright, depressing, sad.'

I said:

'Ecstasy, calm, soothing.'

Abby leaned towards us a bit so that her bangs hung down and forward, and her pretty face was full in the glow of the candle and said:

'That's how you feel about *death.*'

I forgot about the fact that this was a mature gathering and drank the entire six-pack and a lot of the whiskey too, and passed out on the couch.

At some point, just before dawn, I jumped awake to see Abby walking in through the front door smiling.

'How are *you?*' she asked, flipping on the light.

'I'm fine, what . . . where were you?'

'I dropped Lena off, she needs to get up in the morning.'

'Oh,' I said, blinking at the light and sitting back down.

Neither of us said anything for a minute, then Abby asked what time I had to be in to work. I told her not until the late afternoon. She smiled, remembering something, and said:

'When I come visit you tomorrow I'm gonna ride my bike inside again.'

'No you're *not*.'

'Yep.'

'No y . . .'

'Yep.'

'No you're *not*!' I said, all the way awake now and laughing hard in spite of myself.

'Yeah I am,' she said, coming nearer, crouching down to my level, leading with her tiny, pointed chin. 'What're *you* gonna do? Hunh?'

'I . . .'

'Oh, I'm so scared Alex,' she said. 'What're you gonna do?'

Without really thinking I grabbed her around the waist and she fell face down across my lap. She laughed and squirmed around a bit and I tickled her waist. Her slim legs kicked up and down like a swimmer's.

I spanked her once across the seat of her white jeans. Suddenly her wet mouth was on my forearm. It felt like a toothless bite, but somehow it changed everything. She twisted around in my lap and leaned up to meet my lips with hers. Just before we kissed though, I never really knew for sure why, I covered her eyes with my hand so she wouldn't see me. This only made Abby want to kiss me more. She told me later that she thought it was sexy. Like maybe I blindfolded girls sometimes like in the movies. Sometimes I did. But this wasn't that.

THE SEX WAS ALWAYS mean and loveless and brightly-lit – all slaps and screams and mirrors and biting. But afterwards, in the dark, beneath cool, clean sheets, we'd talk long and softly, or, actually, most of the time Abby would talk and I'd listen.

A row of streetlamps lit up the private parking lot beneath her fourth-floor window, so the room was almost, but never quite, pitch black. She'd shower after sex and lie there on the soft bed with wet hair, smelling of baby powder, and speak secrets into the darkness – some big, some small, but each one plucking luxuriously on some delicate string deep inside her.

'When I was little,' she'd whisper in my ear, in the tiny, raspy, little-girl voice she only used alone in the dark with me, 'I used to sneak into the laundry room and smell my dad's undershirts. Oh fuck yeah,' she'd purr, 'I loved it.'

It usually started with some small and goofy confession like that: how she sometimes had sex dreams involving some mysterious, unfriendly older lady, though the whole idea left her cold in the waking hours; how, as a child, she would get the neighborhood kids to play house with her and act out scenes which always revolved around the same basic theme: she was the kid in the family, she'd misbehaved in some way, and somebody had to give her a spanking.

She'd caress my tattoos and remember the one night she came to the shop after close, stripped naked in the back room, and asked me to sodomize her on the smooth, bleached planks of the pastry table. Had I done that to other girls? Had I tied any up? Fucked any *really* hard?

The subject matter usually got heavier as the night went on – her real dad's secret coke addiction that ruined his life, her sister Sarah's emotional problems as a kid, how her new step-dad's unbelievably rich family had never really accepted the Rivers sisters – but even when she started sobbing uncontrollably, the mood there in the dark was as breezy and electric as a summer storm.

Sometimes though, she'd remember (as if she'd never quite realized the fact before) that everyone she talked about was going to die someday, and suddenly the night would be the way its badrappers are always painting it: cold and hollow and frightening. That's when I'd start talking, digging deep to try and breathe the life back into it with a steady stream of metaphor given in as calm and warm a voice as I could muster.

'Remember what I told you about babies, baby?' I'd say, reaching out in the dark for her, pulling her close.

'No,' she'd whimper. That meant: 'Yes, but tell me again.'

'Well,' I'd say, 'you know, you remember . . . how I said that I saw on TV how it's very scary for a baby to watch its mom leave the room they're in because the baby's brain can't, you know, comprehend the . . . I mean, the room is like the baby's entire *universe*, right? So when the mom leaves the room, to the baby it's like she stops existing.'

I'd pause for a second, and Abby wouldn't say anything, but she'd squeeze my hand beneath the covers in quick pumps, like some reflexive code.

'And that's why I think death scares us so much,' I'd go on. 'Our brains are too small to understand that it's no big deal to die – that dying is just like growing up. Nothing ever ends.'

'But how do you *know*?' she'd say, in that raspy voice.

'I just do,' I'd say, because, of course, how *could* I know such a thing? But I will say this, the fact that I was lying alone in the dark holding Abby Rivers made such optimism come very easy.

Then she'd pull my hand to her face, and I'd feel her still damp hair fall across my fingers, and she'd fall right asleep. I'd

listen to her breathe for a while and then, eventually, I'd drift
off too.

*

My ACT scores arrived in early summer. Zack tossed me the
envelope and I savagely ripped it open, then stared in shock
until he took it back from me and whistled.

'A *thirty-four?* Friend, you're *in!*'

I picked up the phone and made an appointment with an
admissions counselor for that afternoon before work.

Ms Peterson was tanned with long, brown, cover-girl hair
and a natural-linen pants-suit that said: *Stylish? Yes. Feminine?
Definitely . . . but nobody's fool.* She leaned against her office
doorway talking into a cordless phone and looked right
through me as I approached her door, like I was one big
argument she didn't want to hear.

She clicked off the cordless phone but never moved from
her doorway.

First of all, she explained, staring at my file folder, turning
it back and forth with her wrist as if uncertain where to even
start, I had actually earned too *little* money the previous year
to qualify as an independent for financial aid. She dismissed
the ACT scores, and pointed to my non-existent academic
records.

'What I'd suggest you do,' she concluded, 'is attend a junior
college for a few years – prove yourself academically – and
then re-apply. But even then, there's no guarantee you'll get
in. It's highly competitive.'

I started blankly into her eyes as they widened to punctuate
her frank tone – the white grooves of crow's feet expanding
and flashing in her tanned face like little hand-fans. Though I
wouldn't realize it until much later, the teeth of some rusty
inner-gear clicked a notch in the wrong direction just then. I
turned and left without a word.

200

It took a long time to walk to work. I found it hard to even muster up the motivation to move my feet. I slid my card up and down in the timeclock slit until the teeth finally chomped down on it. I found Dewon in the back room, sitting on the pastry table, curling a pair of thirty-pound plastic pails of cookie dough till the veins popped up in his ham-sized biceps. Other employees spent their fifteen-minute breaks smoking or on the phone; Dewon worked out.

I slid up on the pastry table next to him and watched morosely until it seemed those muscles would tear out from their taffy-colored casings. Then he dropped the pails, buried his head in his arms, and groaned. I'd groaned that groan. It was the angst-drenched cry of a frozen-yogurt boy with stellar expectations.

He jumped off the table and grabbed me by both shoulders.

'Ohhhhh . . . I gotta DO IT, boyeeee!' he wailed, shaking me like a rag doll. Do it, as in win big like an Ayn Rand hero.

'Come on!' I snapped, stiffening in his grip. 'I mean it! I'm not in the mood.'

'Well get the fuck in the *mood*, man!' he said, shaking me harder, 'We gotta DOOO IIIT!'

'Alright!' I cried. 'Alright, fucker, that's it.'

I lunged and grabbed his left leg, meaning to take him down, but he clamped one of his massive arms around my neck and squeezed mightily. We danced around the backroom like that for a while, careening off of giant oat barrels, putting new dents in the battered walk-in freezer door.

This sort of thing occurred so often as to qualify as ritual.

Our dance abruptly ended when Dewon stepped into an empty dough-pail and slipped onto his back with me on top of him.

'Get off me!' he grunted. I rolled off and lay next to him, panting heavily and staring at the high white ceiling.

'I hate Steven Spielberg!' he cried.

'What're you *talkin'* about? Yesterday he was your fuckin' idol . . .'

'Naw, fuck that punk-ass,' he panted. 'Do you know, do you know that when Steven Spielberg was *thirteen years old*, his parents bought him a Crystal-sync 35 millimeter camera – and when he made his first film they rented out a big-ass theater and invited all his little-kid friends to come see it with *popcorn* and *jujubes* and the *whole shit?*'

If Dewon felt intimidated by such advantages, well, he was conceived in 1967, shortly after his mom (a gorgeous Northshore Jewish girl) saw his late father (a much-heralded black be-bop jazz drummer) jamming one night in an underground Hyde Park nightclub. Hyde Park. It must have been some kind of place. The way Mickey Silver talked about it to my dad, when recalling their tales of beatnik glory, it sounded like some great society within society, where poetry and racial harmony were the standard. Anyway, when Dewon was born, neither side of the family had much to do with his parents anymore. It was a pretty lean childhood.

I looked at Dewon as he lay there staring at the ceiling. We shared the same thirst for class. But the thing in him was better than it was in me. One night he made a deal with one of the customers – this rosy-cheeked kid, a music major at NU. The kid practiced clarinet late at night across the street from Treetz – in the towering old brick building everyone said was haunted. On the night I'm speaking of, Dewon made the rosy-cheeked kid an extra-thick milkshake, and, after we locked up the shop that night, he told me to follow him across the street. We sat on the grass beneath the music building, and way up high I heard a creaky window slide open. Then the clarinet strains of *Tosca* came falling down upon us for nearly an hour.

Dewon moved his eyes from the ceiling to me and groaned.

'I am twenty-one years old, man,' he sighed, 'time is running out!'

This was my cue in the ritual to remind him of our theory

that people who had the world handed to them on a silver platter were actually at a *disadvantage*. His life experience and unshakable resolve would enable him to someday make even *better* movies than Steven Spielberg. I told him all that, but I was just as much speaking to myself.

Why was I giving up so easily? That NU lady obviously shot me down because I didn't have the money – just the sort of trifling obstacle an Ayn Rand character would *laugh* at. But what kind of an Ayn Rand hero begged for what he wanted, on his knees, muttering some hocus pocus at a box?

If I could get the money, all of it, and talk to a different counselor . . . Quick cash. That's all I needed. I thought about calling Timmy Penn. I thought about it every day, actually. But *not* calling him – completely disengaging myself from that scary nocturnal Gorgon world of skins and punks and other creeping street flotsam was the very cornerstone of my plans.

So I called up Zack instead.

When I locked up the shop that night, Abby was waiting for me in her Audi. We went back to her apartment, and there was Sarah, slouched on the couch in front of the TV, with her short-chopped, dyed-black hair and her sloppy thrift-store duds. She lived in an NU dorm, but the Rivers sisters were leaving for the Hamptons the next afternoon to visit their mom for a few weeks, so she was sleeping over.

Again: Sarah had a big nose, and rather beady, close-set eyes. I reminded myself of these facts as a sort of weak comfort whenever she got my goat, which was often, as getting my goat was a sort of passion with her. To Sarah, I was simply some cretin her sister was fucking, and, during our inevitable verbal jousts, I rarely did anything but fortify that image.

I had told Abby *not* to tell Sarah that I went to NU – lest word get out and the employees at ZB Treetz I was studying for my thesis (and eventual book) stop 'acting natural'. I figured the fewer people Abby told, the less likely it was somebody – namely Sarah – would tell her I was a lying sack of shit.

I sure told some doozies, but I was *thorough* about it.

When we walked into the living-room that night, Sarah didn't even look up, just said, in a real bored voice, 'Hi Abby,' and then, after a few seconds, like it was a chore, ' . . . hi Alex.'

I ignored her and sat on the opposite end of the couch while Abby darted into the bathroom to take a quick shower. Kate, Abby's little black kitten, came running to me across the hardwood floor from the bedroom. Abby had asked me to name that cat, just like Sid the mountain bike. I wasn't much for felines – or housepets in general, for that matter, since the Gorgon days when Corny's ferret Fido used me as a giant salt-lick – but this kitten actually played fetch with me. Seriously. That night it was a little rubber squeak-monster of some sort. I threw it in the kitchen and that goddamned kitten brought it back to me in her mouth. I considered Kate a big improvement over Abby's previous pet, which had been a big, fat, domesticated chinchilla that sat in its cage and crapped and rarely did anything else besides wrinkle its nose occasionally. Then, one day, Abby brought it to show the kids at the preschool, and one of them fed it a crayon, and it died. I found both the Rivers sisters on the couch that day crying their eyes out, and when I frantically found out what the tragedy was, I was so relieved that I made some sort of a joke, and Sarah called me 'an asshole'.

After a few minutes of playing with the kitten, Abby came out of the bathroom in her robe with a white towel on her head. She sat down between Sarah and me on the sofa and asked her sister: 'Whatchya watchin', honey?'

Sarah gave a little laugh and said, still without taking her eyes off the screen, 'You want to know the truth? I'm watching beer commercials. It's really interesting. Apparently, all boys have to do is drink a certain brand of beer and hordes of bikini-clad women will come and give them *head* or *fuck* them or something.'

'Yeah, you're right,' I said, 'getting a chick drunk has never helped a guy get laid before.'

Sarah just looked at me like she was amused and amazed. 'You're scary . . .' she said, and I nodded. 'Why do you feel compelled to defend . . .'

But I cut her off.

'Why do *you* feel compelled to bitch about only those kind of commercials? Are you saying they're the only ones that are full of shit?'

Sarah said they were definitely in a full-of-shit category all their own.

'Well, what about tampon commercials?' I said. 'I mean, you're obviously on the rag, and I don't see you riding a horse through a field of daisies.' .

'Alex!' Abby screamed, but she was giggling.

Sarah grinned too, for a second, in spite of herself, calling it 'hilarious' that I would assume such a thing just because she was disagreeing with me.

'Boys are so predictable,' she said.

'Predictable?' I said. 'Whaddya call getting cranky on exactly the same day every month?' I chuckled. I thought that was a pretty good one.

'Yes, the same day every month,' she said, 'the same day every month, unless, unless . . .' (she sang this part and poked Abby in the side with one index finder) ' . . . unless something happens. Isn't that right Abby? Did you tell him yet?'

I felt my entire body go numb. I turned and looked at Abby and said, very weakly, 'What?'

Then both of them burst out laughing. It was just a joke.

'Boys are so predictable,' Sarah said again.

Sarah's joke weakened me considerably and took the wind out of my angry sails. Feeling defeated, I looked for an easy way out of the razor fight.

'You don't like me very much, do you, Sarah?'

'Of course she does,' Abby said, looking over at Sarah like she'd better second that.

'Oh, I like you, Alex,' she said. 'I just feel sorry for you, that's all.'

I didn't say anything. Just fixed my eyes blankly on the TV screen. But Sarah wasn't through.

'I mean, do you know the way you *look* at people? You look at every woman like you could *fuck* her if you wanted to, and every guy like you could kick his *ass*.'

I clenched my teeth and smiled a little, but still kept quiet.

'What you *really* need,' said Sarah, 'is for some woman to kick your ass, and some guy to fuck you like you've never had it before.'

Maybe Abby could sense me really get my back up over that one, because when I opened my mouth to answer Sarah, she got pissed for the first time that night and cut me off.

'Alex! Would you just stop?' she said. 'Jesus!'

My face stung as if she'd slapped me.

'Actually,' I said, getting up, 'I'm gonna get out of here.'

'Well, hey . . . *there's* an idea,' Sarah said.

'Sarah!' Abby said, 'Alex, no, c'mon . . .'

My eyes rested on Sarah's cut-off, camouflaged pants. They were a pair of my Army BDUs I'd let Abby borrow.

'Nah,' I whispered, and walked out the door.

I got about half a block down the street when I heard her tennis-shoes pattering down the sidewalk. I stopped and saw her running after me, hair wet and stringy, wearing a tennis-style skirt, fumbling to pull on the thin white windbreaker she'd bought for sailing. The fact that she knew how to sail made her seem all the more angelic.

I fucked her in the alley behind her apartment, up against the bricks behind a dumpster. She wrapped her legs around my waist and I pulled her panties to the side. She came hard in about three minutes, grinding the top of her head into my collarbone like a mortar pestle, then went completely limp. But I remember thinking I could have done better – had I *ripped* those panties right off of her, shit . . . she might have lost *consciousness* or something. I zipped up and made a mental note for next time. Genius is in the details.

We ended up spending the night on my stolen bed, which seemed like a bad idea, but, to my relief, Zack was gone and didn't come home at all that night.

We held each other in the dark and she cried that she didn't want to leave the next afternoon, so I told her about Shakespeare Gardens and promised her a champagne picnic breakfast there in the morning.

I awoke face-down in my pillow, mourning the outcome of a dream. Abby called from the Hamptons to say she was never coming back. For a few full seconds after waking I was paralyzed as some gland secreted searing liquid grief into my veins. Then I blindly reached beside me in the bed and found a small, warm buttock.

She arched herself against the press of my palm and gave a lazy morning purr when the phone rang from somewhere on the floor beneath our crumpled clothes.

She shot up to a sitting position and gave me a hurt, accusing look, recognizing the very real possibility that it was Bob Stein calling to see if I could come into work. She was tired of me breaking dates for that stupid job. But Bob had given me a chance and I was grateful, so I had a hard time telling him no. He knew that, and capitalized all the time.

The phone continued to ring.

'You *said*,' she said with a forced cry. A thick strand of hair was hanging out the corner of her mouth like a pipestem, and her face was covered with pinkish pillow wrinkles. But, what can I say? She still looked beautiful. 'You *said*.'

'Just tell him I'm not here,' I whispered, as she found the phone and snatched it.

'Hello . . .' she said, like a tough guy, fist-twisting the sleep from her eye.

'No, he's not!' she shouted, then the anger melted into confusion. 'No . . . uh huh. Yeah, *okay* I'll tell him.' She hung up, still puzzled.

'That was your friend Zack. He said if the phone rang today to answer it like this: "Hello, The White Truffle." He said he's trying to buy some . . . nitro zoxide tanks or something?'

I kept a poker face as I reached over to pull that hair-pipe out of her mouth. I had rekindled Zack's interest in the scheme to turn his van into a mobile 'whippets' stand. He could spend the summer traveling to Grateful Dead shows, partying and meeting neo-hippie girls, and I, as the chief investor, would raise some badly-needed capital.

'Hmmmmmmm,' I said to Abby, without showing much interest. 'That's odd. Heh, heh. He must be joking. That Zack.' The phone rang again and I snatched it.

'Hello, The White Truffle,' I said, somewhat bitterly, then winked at Abby.

'Hello? Alex?' It was Bob Stein.

After promising we'd have that champagne picnic the very moment she got back from the Hamptons, I had her drop me off in the alley behind ZB Treetz. As I walked away she rolled her window down and called to me.

When I got back to the car she was staring at her steering wheel.

'Were you scared when Sarah said I was pregnant?'

Was I scared? Yes. But not in the way they thought. I just imagined the entire skyscraper of bullshit I'd constructed suddenly collapsing on top of me.

'Scared?' I said. 'No.'

'You turned *white*,' she giggled. 'You blanched. That's what blanching means.' Then she bit her lower lip and said:

'What *if*, though? Would you have wanted me to have an abortion?'

'Of course not.'

'What would you do?'

'Marry you!'

'No, I mean, yeah . . . but, what? Would you quit school? Would you go into your dad's business?'

I looked at her, blinked, and couldn't help but grin.

'Something like that,' I said, and leaned down to kiss her goodbye.

ONE AFTERNOON, A FEW days before Abby was due to return from the Hamptons, I was pumping cookie dough in the back room at work when Dewon came in on his night off and gave me two weeks' notice. Taken aback, I asked him why. A broad smile broke across his somber caramel face and he gripped his powerful hands around my wrists excitedly.

'You ain't gonna believe this shit – I'm going to USC in the Fall.'

'UIC Circle campus?' I said, blankly.

'SC, man, S. University of Southern California!'

He was going to live with an auntie, and was eligible for all kinds of scholarships. He'd been keeping the plan under his hat for a long time. Didn't want to jinx himself.

'Wow,' I said numbly. My immediate reaction was one of hurt, and I was disgusted with myself for being anything less than overjoyed.

'Gotta go, bro!' he smiled, giving my wrists a final pump, then turned for the swinging steel door that led to the front.

'Dewon,' I called, when I got my voice back. 'I'm going to a house party over on Foster after work. It's right on the corner. Meet me there. We'll have some beers – celebrate.'

Dewon wrinkled his nose.

'Aw I don't know about that, V, I ain't into hanging out with all these NU gumps drinking warm keg beer. Don't worry, we'll hook up before I take off.'

I shrugged as he left.

'Whatever,' I said, quietly.

I wasn't too hot on going to the party myself but the plan to turn Zack's van into a mobile whippets-stand fell through, so we were going to try selling pot. A pound with our name on it was due to arrive at the Beta fraternity later that night. While Zack bought the weed, I'd already be at the party drumming up business. Then he'd show up later with quarter-ounce baggies.

I sighed heavily and pinned my nameplate to my T-shirt. As I was tying an apron on I heard the sorority-squeal voice of one of the nightshift girls – Zabrina. I looked up front and saw her standing behind the register talking with a customer. Zabrina was wearing white boxer shorts (against the rules) with purple NU Wildcat paw prints across the butt, a pair of flip-flop sandals on bare feet (against the rules), and her frizzy brown hair hung down loose to the middle of her back (against the rules). But it was the conversation she was having with the wealthy old lady across the counter that really set me off.

'I mean, really,' the lady was saying, 'the last time I came in here a small frozen yogurt was ninety-five cents.'

'You're totally right,' Zabrina sympathized, leaning her elbows on the counter and putting her chin in her hands (against the rules). 'I'm appalled. Bob Stein is just *greedy*. Everybody hates him. We're all totally disgusted here.'

I waited till the old plastic surgery victim cluck-clucked her way out the door before calling to Zabrina from the back room.

'Zabrina. C'mere.'

'Hold on.'

'C'mere!'

'Hold. ON!'

So I walked up behind her while she pretended to fill a napkin dispenser and said:

'Zabrina, you don't talk to the customers like that.'

She turned around and faced me, all floppy T-shirt, tits and indignation.

'I have the right to say whatever I *want!*'

I was getting hot.

'You got the *right*? Nah – if you got a problem with the way Bob runs his business, you got the *right* to walk *right* out that fuckin' door.'

'Who are you, Alex? Hunh? Who are *you*?'

'I'm your . . . night manager, that's who!'

We were loud enough now that the daytime/general manager, Raphael – a short and chubby mustachioed Mexican guy – came over to see what was up. He always hung around a little late to flirt with the coeds who worked the night shift.

'What is going on up here?' he laughed.

'I think it's wrong, Ralph,' Zabrina whined. 'Bob raised the prices again and I just think it's *wrong*.'

'So buy your own fuckin' restaurant,' I said, throwing my hands up. 'And *give* the goddamn food away. You know what you sound like, Zabrina? You sound like a . . . oh, wait a minute, I forgot: you *are* a silly college girl.'

'Alex . . .' Ralph said, stroking his mustache nervously.

'Don't you talk to me like that!' Zabrina cried.

'I'll talk to you any motherfucking way I want.'

'Alex! You stop . . . it is unprofessional!'

'Okay,' I said, 'then do me a *fucking* favor wouldjya, Ralph? Call Bob up right now and tell him how unprofessional I'm being, alright?'

This was a blatant threat. Would Bob consider it more professional to take girls out for drinks while they were on the clock, like Ralph did before Bob hired me? To steal whole hams and entire cheesecakes and cases of Diet Coke for sorority parties like Zabrina did before Bob hired me? To invite the insane and filthy bums that prowled Evanston's streets inside for free food so they could sit around and pick at their scabs and shout absurdities at the customers like the entire waitstaff did for kicks before Bob hired me?

I never told on anyone, because that's not the way I was, and, besides, to tell you the truth, I didn't much like Bob

Stein. I thought he was a paranoid asshole. But I was starting to see how he *got* that way.

'Zabrina,' I said, settling down a little. 'What if Bob was *your* dad? Wouldn't you want him to have a successful business?'

'Psh . . . Bob has enough money. He's rich!'

'How the . . . how much money is *enough* Zabrina? Hunh?'

Ralph was scared I'd tell on Zabrina – scared he'd lose a nubile body to leer at and brush up against every afternoon – so he said:

'I'll take care of it, okay Alex? Zabrina, he's right. It's Bob's store, he make the prices.'

'I mean it's not the fucking *proletariat* we're serving here for Christsakes,' I started up again. 'It's mostly your BMW-driving sorority sisters. Maybe Bob wants to buy *his* daughter a BMW someday.'

'Alex!'

I angrily grabbed a white-handled brush from beneath the register, went in back, and started scrubbing beneath the steam counter. As I got down on my hands and knees I thought of the late Ms Rand, and smiled grimly.

'Ayn, baby,' I thought to myself, scrubbing away, 'I know you were an atheist and all, but I hope you're somewhere smiling down on me. 'Cause no one else is.'

I didn't speak a word to anyone for the rest of the night. Just cleaned and counted the cash register periodically and went about my business. But a couple of minutes after close I saw Zabrina with her green 'Theta' windbreaker on, making a beeline for the door, so I asked her:

'Is everything done?'

'Yes,' she snapped, offended, and stomped out the door, leaving me there by myself.

I walked around the empty restaurant and, of course, nothing was done. I filled the napkin holders, turned off the yogurt machine, put the lemon squares in the fridge, and slowly walked toward the deli meat-cutter with a sense of dread. My fears were justified. The whole thing was splattered with dried beef blood, and when I flipped down the safety cover I saw a sick mixture of congealed meats and cheeses. Easily a twenty-minute job.

I was in a hurry to get to that party, so, to save time, I turned the blade on and held the abrasive pad against the side of it while it whirled.

Perhaps you can see what's coming. I cut my thumb almost down to the bone and my own blood spattered the machine.

'SON OF A . . . !' I screamed, but stopped myself, and listened to my voice echo off all the stainless steel in the empty shop. There was a time when I would have torn that place apart in rage and stalked out never to return. But I was different from that now. I had responsibilities.

*

I sat at the party on a couch that reeked of bong water. The couch was flanked by two high-tech stereo speakers that blasted a teeth-rattling barrage of angry black rap nationalism.

'FIGHT THE POWER! FIGHT THE POWER!'

A guy who stood in the arched doorway of the crowded room pretty much epitomized the curious blend of East Coast old money and quasi-hippiness that ruled the scene there. He was tall and healthy-looking, with a neat brown ponytail pulled back from his well-bred, high-cheekboned face. He had all the accessories – a short string of tiny, colored beads around his neck, a Grateful Dead T-shirt underneath a thrift store suit vest, and a pair of ripped and faded (but very clean) Levi's cuffed at the bottom so everyone could see his brown suede Birkenstock sandals.

When I'd arrived at the party my crudely-bandaged hand was throbbing horribly, and looked like something you'd bring home from the butcher. I should have gone to the hospital, but the bleeding had stopped so I went to the basement and drank down four quick jumbo–cups of warm keg beer, then headed upstairs with two more full ones. There I sat with the hippie snoots for nearly an hour, waiting for Zack.

'FIGHT THE POWER! FIGHT THE POWER!'

My stomach was empty, so the beer started hitting me fast.

A very pretty girl, wearing a gauzy floral smock dress, smiled from across the room and started walking towards me.

'I know you,' she said, brushing back a mass of shiny blonde bangs with one hand, and pointing a lit Camel filter at me with the other. I hid my bandaged hand between my legs and kept it there, though holding it low like that made it throb all the more.

'Where do I know you from?' she said, still smiling as she sat down beside me. 'I've been wond . . . Oh *I* know. I know. You work at Treetz.'

I sensed a trace of well-hidden disappointment in her voice.

'I'm the . . .' I shrugged, smiling weakly, 'night manager.'

'Oh,' she said, 'do you go here?'

'Here' meant Northwestern University.

'Yeah,' I said.

'Are you in a house?'

I shook my head. There were still some lies even *I* couldn't bring myself to tell a girl.

'Oh,' she said, 'well good for you.'

There was a kind of uncomfortable silence after that, as the girl looked across the room, and, I figured, tried to think of a polite way out of the conversation.

'I'm going to go get a beer,' the girl said, turning to me. 'Do you know where it's at?'

'It's down in the basement by the band,' I answered, almost without looking at her. But she was hard not to look at.

'Would you like one?' she asked, just to be polite. They're all very polite, I thought to myself, these fucking jerks.

'Yeah,' I said, suddenly smiling. 'Bring me two.'

*

The room cleared out a little bit when she was gone. A couple of black guys knelt in front of the stereo and looked at all the different CDs, mocking most of what they saw, and bitched loudly when someone came over and changed the station from WRAP, or whatever they were listening to, to the college station. Tall lanky guys, one black as coal and the other a few shades lighter than Dewon. They were wearing tri-colored African pendants around their necks, and NU black student union T-shirts that said things like: 'Black By Popular Demand,' and 'It's a Black Thing, You Wouldn't Understand.' The kinds of slogans that used to make Timmy Penn's blood boil: *"'Stop black-on-black crime,'" he'd sneer, reading the El poster aloud, adding his own embellished subtext: 'Attention Brothers! Save our culture – stick to muggin' honkeys and raping white bitches.'*

I looked at the two Afrocentric types as they flipped through the CDs and wished Dewon were there. He liked to fuck with guys like that. He didn't go for separatism. 'I'm global,' he once told me, 'that's why I get *all* the bitches.'

A very stoned-looking couple sat on the couch across the coffee table from me, sort of lounging all over each other. The guy was feeding her some line and the girl nodded, looking rich and bored. I decided to wait a bit, and then tell them about the skunkweed Zack was bringing. They were pretty far gone already though. A thin guy in a striped oxford and blue cardigan, who sat next to them, looked at the two, then looked at me, smirking knowingly. He seemed all right. He was neat, with very short brown hair. Sort of like Mr Rogers, I thought. But he looked intelligent and nice at least, so I smirked back.

The girl in the gauze dress came back, to my surprise, with three plastic cups of keg beer. She put one on the coffee table, sat down next to me, and handed me the other.

'Here ya go, Alex,' she said.

I smiled with surprise in spite of all my sourness and asked her how she knew my name.

Her eyes wandered down to my chest, where the nameplate still stuck pinned in my shirt, and she shrugged.

'I'm Heather,' she laughed. It was an easy, friendly laugh, but I found it insulting nonetheless.

A pop song featuring the peppy nasal voice of some British guy came on, and Heather's smile grew even broader.

'Mmm,' she said, through a mouthful of beer. 'Oh, I *love* him. Do you know who this is?'

I shook my head as I drained the first of the two jumbo cups. It was going down real easy tonight. The more I drank, the less I felt the steady pulse of pain in my thumb.

'It's Billy Bragg. He's a Socialist.'

'Yeah?' I said, 'Well *fuck* him then.'

'Oh no,' she said, 'he's good. He's rewriting the *Internationale*, you know? The Communist workers' song?'

'Well,' I said, setting the cup down and reaching for the full one, 'hopefully he'll OD soon or something.'

She was intrigued at the oddity of my views. She shifted around sideways on the sofa and leaned back a bit, grinning at me curiously.

'Why do you say *that*? Because he's Communist?'

'Isn't that reason enough?' I said, 'Communism is evil shit.'

She smiled as if I were claiming masturbation led to hairy palms.

'Do you *know* it's evil? I mean based on your own experience?'

'No, not based on my own experience.'

She held up her palms and shrugged happily, as if she'd proven her point.

'Then who are *you* to say?'

'Who am *I* to say? You know who I am to say,' I set the cup between my legs and tapped my name tag. 'Alex Verdi, remember?'

'But, I mean, never having lived in a Communist country, to apply our cultural ... It's just, you can't view it through a subjective lens like that. It's like Ronald Reagan calling Russia an "evil empire".'

'It *is* a fuckin' evil empire,' I said. 'What are you *talkin'* about? They got fences around these countries and if somebody tries to leave, they *shoot* 'em. They shoot their own people for trying to *leave* for crissakes. I'd say that's pretty fuckin' evil.'

'But you have no idea what it's like to *be* them,' she said, still with that friendly smile, as if going easy on me in light of my charmingly rustic views. 'You can't judge cultures you know nothing about.'

I frowned and rubbed my chin.

'Well you know what, Heather ... that's interesting, because in *my* culture ... I mean, in my homeland, which is many moons from here, we take pretty girls like you and ... slice their clits off.'

I brought my hand up and made a plucking gesture just under her nose, as her facial expression did a one-frame switch from sickly-sweet to icy-cold.

'Get. Your hand. Away from me. Now.'

'Okay,' I said, and let my hand drop to within inches of her lap, then quickly pulled it back and showed her the end of my thumb as it protruded from between my second and third fingers.

'Hey look! Gotchyer clit, Heather. Gotchyer clit!'

She tossed the remainder of her beer in my eyes and stood up.

'Hey, whattya gettin' all pissed about?' I shouted after her, wiping my eyes with the back of my bandaged hand, and waving my own beer at her with the other. 'Huh? Don't you start gettin' all subjective on me, Missy!'

I swigged deeply and grinned at her over the cup. Perhaps there is no need, but I'll say it anyway: I was getting *plowed*.

Heather stopped in the arched doorway and conferred angrily with a big Nordic-looking dude with blond locks that hung nearly to his shoulders. He looked up at me with raised eyebrows.

'Whattya lookin' at, ya big Viking!'

Everyone in the room looked over at me – the blacks by the stereo, the stoned couple on the other couch, Mr Rogers.

The Viking took a step towards the coffee table.

'What's the problem, dude?'

'There's no problem,' I said. 'Unless you're a fuckin' Communist. *Then* you got problems. You a fuckin' Communist?'

The Viking flared his nostrils and suppressed a grin, then cast a quick look around the room, as if to communicate his realization that I was a harmless nut.

'No, dude, I ain't no Commie,' he said, flashing a campy peace sign at me. 'Democracy all the way, my man.'

'Ah, fuck Democracy too,' I said, and drained my last beer. As the Viking rolled his eyes and grinned a tremor of laughter rippled through the room.

'Dude,' he said, 'why don't we go get you another beer for the road?' A few more quasi-hippies appeared in the doorway to see what was up.

'What's so funny?' I asked. 'What the fuck is Democracy? It's mob rule. What's so fuckin' great about that? Democracy makes *you* a criminal every time you suck the bong, Viking, ya big fuckin' hippie. Democracy is sodomy laws – it puts laws on how you can fuck. I mean, shit, Democracy gave us fuckin' *slavery*.'

'You tell 'em dawg,' one of the blacks laughed approvingly. I turned and narrowed my eyes at him. It was the light-skinned one that said it.

'Was I fuckin' talking to you?' I asked him. 'No, so shut the fuck up.'

His eyes opened wide with exaggerated shock, and he

219

looked over at his friend as if to verify that he wasn't just hearing things.

'Whaddayou bitchin' about?' I asked him, 'The only reason you're *goin'* to this school is 'cause you're *black*.'

His bottom lip dropped and he shook his head incredulously.

'Aw hell no,' he said to his friend, pressing his palms flat to the floor, preparing to get up. '*Hail* no . . . I know this fool ain't trippin'.'

'You heard what I said. You already gettin' special treatment, but you want more. You wear all that shit like you think you're *owed* somethin'.'

He and his friend stood up and approached me. I stood up quickly and stumbled slightly as I felt the full effect of the beers.

'Hey,' the Viking called out, but the lighter-skinned black kept approaching till our chests nearly touched. He stood about a head taller than me, and his friend, who stood behind him, was just as tall.

'I *am* owed something, stupidass,' he said, rocking his face back in forth in mine, just like a hotdog Drill Sergeant I'd had at Fort Benning.

'What?' I inquired.

'Forty acres and a mule.'

He smiled tightly and nodded, as if proving some point. I spread my arms out baffled.

'Pshhh . . . You don't even know what the fuck I'm talkin' about do you?' he said with disgust. 'You pathetic.'

'Forty acres and a *mule*? I don't know . . . let me guess: *this* . . . is one of those *black* things I wouldn't understand?'

'Naw . . .' he said, leaning forward. Our noses were almost touching now. 'It's a *white* thing, mothafucka – you *betta* unnastan'. 'Cause you a white-ass honkey cracker mothafucka.'

'And you, sir, are a credit to your race.'

The Viking stepped between us and the black guy pointed at me over his shoulder.

'You throw around cliché talk like: "You think you're owed something," and you don't even know that your *own government* promised each freed slave forty acres and mule. But it was all just talk, just like you're all just talk. Shit. Do I *think* I'm *owed* something? I *am* owed something: forty acres and a mothafuckin' mule.'

'Nah,' I said, 'you're pretty light-skinned . . .'

'*What?*'

'I'd say you're only owed twenty acres and a donkey.'

You'd be hard pressed to find another man who's left eye has absorbed as many surprise blows as mine has. I think it was the other black guy – the one who hadn't said anything – who leaped over everybody and nailed me, but I never saw it coming. It was something else. His arm must have been six feet long. My head snapped sharply to the right and my body followed. The next thing I knew I was staring up at a circle of angry faces with my good eye. Viking was pointing down at me and yelling:

'You. Out. NOW!'

Off in the distance I heard one of the blacks howl and crow: 'And that was a left, dawg, a *left*!'

Somebody stepped on my injured hand and I shrieked. As I tried to get up several hands grabbed my clothing roughly and started dragging me towards the door. I closed my eyes and stiffened my legs, then dug my heels into the carpet. As they shouted at me one calm voice separated from the rest.

'I've got him. It's all right. C'mon. Leggo.'

The hands started to release me and soon only one palm rested on my shoulder. The person guiding me towards the front door was Mr Rogers.

'It's all right,' he said, with a look of concern. 'C'mon.'

He pushed the screen door open and I stumbled drunkenly down the concrete steps to the lawn. The night air felt like a cold slap against my cut and swollen eye. I turned towards the house and imagined calling Timmy up at The Gorgon. He and a couple carloads of skins would come down here and destroy the place. But I hadn't talked to Timmy in a long time.

'Fuckyooooou!' I shouted impotently at the house.

'Shhh . . .' Mr Rogers said, stepping in front of me. 'C'mon. It's all right. I understand.'

And the strange thing was, he sounded as if he really did understand exactly what I was feeling. He put a hand on my shoulder and I opened my mouth to speak, then closed it and shook my head.

'I know, I know . . .' he said.

To have emerged from all that with even just this one ally meant everything to me right then. I closed the eye that wasn't already swollen shut and nearly wept with gratitude as my thoughts sloshed together in a dark drunken swamp. I imagined I was lying on the grass somewhere with Abby in my arms. Then I felt her lips press gently against my own. That is to say, I felt lips and imagined they were Abby's.

They were not Abby's lips.

My eye snapped open and I saw Mr Rogers with his eyes closed, kissing me.

'What the fuck?' I yelled, hopping back and throwing my hands up defensively. His eyes flew open in terror, as if he had just made a very, very big mistake.

'I . . . I . . .' he stuttered.

'What the *fuck*?' I said again, wiping my lips with the back of my good hand.

'Am I deluding myself?' he asked. 'I mean, I thought what you . . . the things you were saying in there . . . Oh God. Oh God.'

The look of anguish on his pale face in the moonlight was sobering, and strange. I dropped my hands down to my sides and stood transfixed. It was like looking in an emotional mirror.

'I . . . I thought I saw something in your eyes earlier inside,' he whispered miserably. 'I . . . oh God . . . you're probably disgusted by me.'

Suddenly, I felt completely deflated. 'Nah,' I said. 'Nah, man, I ain't disgusted by you . . . I mean . . .'

'Oh God,' he moaned. 'When you were talking about the *sodomy laws?* I'm an idiot.'

'No, look. I think what you were seein' in my eyes was that I *liked* you . . . you know. I mean like a friend.'

Boy. I didn't know what else I could say. But I felt like I had to say something. Just then, in deus ex machina! fashion, Zack's 'I Love Country Music' van came rumbling up in front of the house, shone its headlights on us, and honked.

I looked at Mr Rogers, who avoided my gaze and walked back into the house. I never saw him again.

The side door to Zack's van slid open and out jumped Dewon, wearing acid-washed jeans and a matching jean jacket with no shirt.

'You said Foster, V!' he shouted happily. 'This is Hinman. Just lucky I saw the love-mobile drivin' . . . whoa man, what's up with the eye?'

I shook my head and said nothing.

Zack got out of the van and he and Dewon came up close enough to see that it had swollen shut. Dewon stood up straight in realization, and his massive chest bulged impressively in the moonlight.

He grabbed my elbow and began leading me towards the house.

'C'mon,' he sighed matter-of-factly, 'let's go fuck somebody up.'

I stopped and pulled my arm free.

'Naw man . . . no. Let's just fuckin' get out of here.' I looked at Zack. 'Go sell some shit and I'll just walk home.'

Zack crossed his arms and shrugged.

'There's nothin' to sell. The guy never showed.'

Dewon grabbed my wrist and pulled it up. A fresh stream of blood trickled down my forearm.

'Man your eye is fucked up and your hand is all bleedin' and shit . . . what is *up* with you, bro? Hunh? Talk to me.'

'It's a white thing . . .' I said. 'You wouldn't understand more than half of it.'

He shoved me gently towards the van.

THE FIRST TIME abby told me that she loved me, we were sitting on a big, flat, shoreline rock on Northwestern's Lake Michigan landfill. The sun was going down and the lake was flat and purplish. From a distance we must have appeared quite the picture of tranquility on that breezy, late-summer day – her young, willowy frame stretched out luxuriously between my splayed legs. She rested the back of her brown-bobbed head against my chest while I leaned back on my palms supporting both our weights. We'd been sitting there like that for quite some time, though, and my aching wrists were secretly turning to Jell-O.

Time had passed since the night of the fight. My thumb was all but healed and only a faint yellowish tinge remained beneath my eye. Abby, of course, was shocked to see it when she returned from the Hamptons. As usual I just made something up. I forget now what.

'Oh, Alex,' she suddenly sighed, looking out across the calm waters towards the northernmost curve of the Chicago skyline, 'your campus is so beautiful. I'm jealous.'

I told her that, ah, it wasn't *that* beautiful – Lake Forest College had a pretty nice campus too, didn't it?

Rather than answer that question directly, she suddenly dove into a rehearsed-sounding monologue, the gist of which revolved around the fact that she suspected she'd been *mildly* dyslexic as a child, and the fact that she was even *going* to college at all was something of a miracle actually. There was something in her whole presentation and posture that reminded me of Billy, the black-and-white sheepdog my family had raised in the country. Once, when he was a puppy,

225

he hurt his paw and we nursed him with special attention and soft-toned words. After that, whenever we caught him doing something bad, he'd immediately start to limp.

I began to wonder where all of this was going with Abby, and where it was going was: she had applied to NU as her first choice of schools, and she didn't get in. She hung her head and clenched the muscles in her delicate shoulders and neck, as if anticipating a blow.

'Do you think I'm totally *stupid* now?' she asked, mournfully.

'Do I think you're stu . . . No! What kind of a . . .'

'Ohhh,' she sighed again, 'you're really a good person, Alex. You are. You're going to be a great man and . . . I'm just totally *jealous* of you.'

This would have probably been an opportune time to make a certain confession of my own, but instead I snapped at her.

'Would you just shut up with the jealous shit? Jesus!'

She twisted her neck around and looked at me with hurt brown eyes.

'Look,' I said, in a gentler tone, 'I don't want you to be *jealous* of me, ya know?'

'But it's a *good* jealous, Alex. It is. It *totally* is. It only makes me love you more.'

I pretty much had to kiss her after that, seeing how, as I mentioned, this was the first time she'd actually said she loved me. I wasn't much in the kissing mood, though.

This lie was going to continue, evidently, indefinitely. Her confession just seemed to highlight the ludicrous nature of our relationship.

'Why would you want to go to this school anyway?' I asked her after a while. 'Isn't your sister always going on and on about how much she hates it here?'

'I don't wanna talk about her,' she said quickly, and after a pause, added, 'What about *your* sister Alex? You've never even told me about her.'

I silently cursed myself for ever mentioning the fact that I had a sister. But somehow I felt that if I laid down the bones of my life pretty true to form, it was okay to be a little creative in the way I fleshed them out.

'Tell me about your sister,' she said again.

What's to tell? She's in some foster home. Can we leave it at that? I did.

I looked out at the lights that were just starting to twinkle in the Chicago skyline and opened my mouth to speak, but at first no words came out. Then I began, like I began before with all the other stuff.

'My sister,' I said, 'is studying ballet in San Francisco . . .'

I was staring across the kitchen table at my father and something seemed vaguely alien and disturbing about him. Though nothing in his mannerisms had changed, he seemed oddly troubled. Rather than dwell on all this unpleasantness I concentrated on eating breakfast. Raw goat's milk and wild strawberries. But I couldn't help myself from glancing up at him every now and then with frightened curiosity. The breakthrough came when Stacy crawled up in his lap, her blue baby's eyes narrowed into a startlingly adult look of alert concern. She began stroking his face – his jawline and smooth upper lip.

'You shaved your beard!' I blurted out, without thinking. It was the first time I'd ever seen his entire face.

We stayed there sitting by the lake until nightfall, then walked back to Abby's. I immediately went to the fridge and got a beer. All there was was some Rolling Rock that must have been Sarah's, but I grabbed a bottle anyway. When I got back to the couch I didn't say much to Abby – just petted Kate the Kitten in my lap, drank the beer, and looked at the TV screen. I wasn't paying much attention to what was on, though – my stomach was too full of icy-hot anxiety for me to do anything much but scheme. I thought of Timmy Penn, and big puffy-faced Texas Hector, our friend from basic training, and how he always laughed at the prices people paid for weed in Chicago, saying how he set people up with all they could drive away with for practically nothing. Coke and E too. Anything. Anytime. Tim was probably making a killing right now driving back and forth from Mexico. I thought of the born-big frat guys who were always over at my apartment buying dime-bags from Zack, saying how they could move pounds and pounds of the stuff if it weren't for 'the drought'. That was all those small-time weed-merchants talked about – 'the drought'. Shit, I'd think to myself, they just don't know the right people.

'You know,' I'd just recently said to Zack, 'if I were to call up Tim, we could all take a plane to Houston, load up a drive-away rental car with shit, drive it back here, and sell it in one day.' That way, I figured, I could pay for tuition to NU night school. *If* I got in.

'Yeah,' Zack had said, 'but if we got caught our lives'd be ruined.'

At that point we both silently asked ourselves: 'What the fuck am *I* talking about?' and switched back to our normal personalities.

'You're absolutely right,' I said, 'it's not worth the risk.'

'But man, seriously,' Zack said, getting excited, 'what are the odds of getting caught? Pretty slim, friend.'

That was one of my little subconscious tricks – I'd plant seeds in that crazy bastard's head and then slowly let him 'talk me into' doing things.

As I thought of all this at Abby's place that night, I tipped back the beer and kept on staring at but not watching the TV screen. I wished the beer was colder or I was thirstier.

' . . . you know?' I heard Abby saying from a zillion miles away.

I nodded, 'Yeah.'

'What?' Abby said.

'You're right,' I said.

'What was I just talking about?'

' . . . you know,' I said.

'You weren't even *listening*,' she whined.

'Abby, wouldjya c'mon, I'm trying to watch this.'

'You're trying to watch this? This?' she said, getting up and walking until her finger actually touched the screen. I focused in and saw a True Value Hardware commercial for The Garden Weasel.

'Stop watching stupid TV and look at me!' she whined louder, walking back to me and climbing in my lap. I clenched my teeth and strained my neck to the right so that I could still see the TV. I started to tip the bottle of Rolling Rock back again but she slapped it out of my hand so that it banged against my teeth and spilled all over my chest and leg.

I grabbed her by the shoulders and shook her and shook her in white-hot silence as hard as I possibly could and almost enjoyed it until I saw this look on her face – this look I'd seen as a kid in cowboy picture books on the bug-eyed faces of shot-dead outlaws, the look I'd seen once in a K-Mart checkout aisle when a white-trash polyester mom shook her little boy just the same way I was shaking Abby right then.

An open-mouthed look of complete and goddamned near-divine helplessness.

I pushed her off my lap onto the couch and raged through the living room – slicing up the air with wild Tae Kwon Do kicks and mighty roundhouse swings. I wanted very badly to smash something but everything in that place – the furniture, the entertainment center, even the paint on the walls – was so nice that I ended up grabbing the door frame to the kitchen with both hands and smashing my forehead against it again and again until the next thing I knew I was lying on my back, staring up at Abby, and thinking to myself for some crazy reason that I hoped the kitten hadn't seen me act that way.

Abby knelt down beside me holding her hands to her mouth. I told her I was fine.

'Just stay there,' she said, and went into the kitchen to get some ice for my head. But when she tried to twist the plastic tray her hands were shaking too badly and she dug her chin into her chest and bunched up her face to keep from crying. She lost the battle with one giant sob, and I got up and went to her, my brain rolling loosely in my skull. I hugged her for a while and then stooped down a bit, lifted her up in my arms, and walked with her out of the kitchen, through the living room, to the bedroom.

'You're crazy,' she kept saying, biting her lower lip and nearly hyperventilating as I sat down on the edge of the bed and undressed her.

'Yeah, I know,' I said, quietly, as I pulled her shirt up over her head and unbuttoned her jeans. 'Straighten your legs out so I can get these off you. I know, I know I'm crazy.'

Sometime around midnight I opened my eyes to the blackness of her apartment and slowly made out the outline of Abby standing naked, about fifteen feet from the foot of the bed, in the arched doorway of the room. Behind her the faintest blue glow of a nightlight seeped out from underneath the bathroom door.

At first — you know how it is — I tried to place who she was and where I was and all that, but once I remembered I realized that something strange was going on. I lay completely still. She stood there looking at me for a pretty long time, then slowly backed towards the bathroom door and opened it. As she turned and slipped inside, the soft blue nightlight shone against the curves of her slender legs and ass and I could see her holding the cordless phone. As she pulled the door shut I leaned over and felt for the bedside phone, picked it up off the receiver, and pressed my thumb down hard on the red-lit MUTE button.

I was still tired enough to be pretty calm, but as the sound of eleven digit-tones came over my end I wondered who the hell she was calling. After a couple of rings I heard a fairly deep woman's voice answer sleepily.

'Mom?' I heard Abby say.

'Abby?' the voice came back, a little worried, and then turned sort of cold. 'Did you call me and wake me up to slam the phone down in my ear again?'

'Yeah, Mom,' Abby said, in a hoarse half-whisper, 'yep, *that's* why I called.'

'Don't you ever . . .'

'Mom.'

'Why are you whispering?'

'Mom.'

'Oh for Christ's sakes, Abby. Oh for Christ's . . .' She laughed short and sharp. 'Oh, this is lovely. Mike is spending nearly a month in Japan and Taiwan, in part so he can afford to pay my daughter's tuition and rent so that *she* can shack up with an unstable Italian with bad teeth and tattoos.'

I had never heard myself described quite like that before and I couldn't help but grin in the dark as my thumb grew sweaty on the button. Then my eyes stung and I blinked and remembered how Tim had fronted me the money for those root canals and I'd never paid him back.

'I love the way you say "my daughter", Mom. If he doesn't consider me his . . .'

'Oh, Abby, how can you even say that? After all he's done? Huh? How can you even . . .'

'Mom, you've never even *met* Alex.'

'Your sister has been filling me in on what I already know from the way you've been acting lately.'

'That little bitch.'

'She's worried about you Abby.'

'Oh Mom. She's jealous. She's always . . . you're both always . . .' She was starting to cry a little and her mom's voice toned down a notch.

'Abby, I don't think it makes her *jealous* at all to see her only sister with a person who makes her cry and starts *shouting* at the slightest provocation. Oh honey, I don't doubt that he's

231

a nice boy. I'm not saying that . . . I'm just saying you could do a lot better.'

'Oh, Mom,' Abby said, a little calmer now, 'you just don't know.' *Go on*, I thought, getting pissed that she wasn't saying enough in my defense.

'I *do* know. I do know, Abby. Are you forgetting that I was married to your father for *ten years*? Have you completely forgotten what he . . .'

'I don't wanna talk about it,' Abby snapped, and started sniffling again.

'Of all the boys . . . the *men* there at your school and your sister's school, too, who would give their eye-teeth to . . .'

'To what?' Abby scoffed.

'To treat you right, Abby.'

'Who? Like Steve? Like Richard? Great, Mom. You just *loved* Richard didn't you? He sucked.'

'You *liked* Steve a lot, you know that.'

'He sucked too.'

'Listen to me honey,' her mom said, and I was struck by how genuinely sincere she sounded – how very worried she really was. 'Before you left for school four years ago, you were *convinced* that you wanted to marry Roger. Remember? And I told you what I thought, and you screamed at me and said you hated me. Now think about it. Can you imagine if you had married him? Can you *imagine*?'

'Roger loved me . . . he loved me.' It was all she could do to say it without sobbing.

'Oh honey, of course he did. Of course he did. And I'm sure Alex loves you much more than even you could ever imagine. I know he loves you very, very, very much. You're probably the most special person he's ever met. But honey, that's not reason enough to be with someone. Don't you realize what you're doing? It's terribly fatalistic. You're not making any decisions here. None of this is your choice. *He's* choosing you.'

'Yeah, well Mom . . .' she said, and her voice was filled with bitterly sarcastic accusation and she was crying hard now. I could hear her through the phone, and I could hear her through the door that still glowed faintly at the bottom with blue nightlight. ' . . . Mom . . . maybe *I* don't make such good choices, you know?'

After she came back to bed and fell asleep, and after Kate the Kitten tired of jumping on the lumps my feet made underneath the covers – thinking they were mice – I lay there in the silence, my mind racing wildly. Slowly the confusion transformed into a wired sort of temporary bravado as I saw that there was only one thing I could do.

I slipped off the mattress without waking Abby. I quickly got dressed, and walked down the block to the payphone beneath the Main Street El stop to call Timmy Penn. He would know what I should do about this mammoth trap I'd created for myself. Or else he'd say: 'I-told-you-so, Degreasey, come on back to The Gorgon – let's make that money quick and get the fuck to India.' And so what if he did?

'Yeah . . . *fuck* this place,' I said out loud, with a nervous laugh, brushing relieved tears from my eyes as I called the Gorgon hallway payphone outside Tim's bedroom and let it ring perhaps twenty times. It was nearly one o'clock in the morning and I figured things must be reaching fever pitch at the club. Someone finally picked up, and, despite the pounding bass-beat in the background, I realized immediately it was Marie.

'Is Tim there?' I asked in a gruff voice, but she knew it was me and immediately began crying.

'What's the matter,' I asked her flatly, not wanting to get into ancient history right then.

'I'm pregnant!' she hissed.

I wondered how that could be possible. She and I hadn't seen each other for close to a year. But I was not to blame for this one. It was Timmy Penn. And Timmy Penn, she told me, was in Vandalia prison, serving three-to-five for narcotics.

233

WHEN I HUNG UP THE phone with Marie I numbly climbed the stairs at the Main street El stop and rode the train down to Belmont. It hadn't been a year so I was still officially in exile but Ugo and Nuccio could fuck themselves.

The streets and sidewalks of the old neighborhood were crawling with small packs of young skinheads. I didn't recognize a single one. They were all fresh-shaves; little suspender-wearing, suburban Q-tips with stiff new Doc Martens, and strange acronyms sewn across the backs of their bombers – SHARP, SHAC, GASH, GOSH, etc. As I turned down Sheffield, a barrel-chested young black skin jarred me with his shoulder as he passed with his crew. I just kept walking. So much as a sideways glance and they would have jumped me and booted me, all of them. I knew.

'I know that motherfucker,' I heard one of them say, and I picked up my pace. 'He's fuckin' white-power, dude!'

'You're high, dude,' another said. 'That pussy-ass Gap-pants-wearin' motherfucker?'

Their argument drowned away into the other street sounds as I slid through the crowd and approached The Gorgon. Some new Asian guy with a short black ponytail stood in the entranceway with folded arms, along with a kid with longish red hair. They were telling some drunk he couldn't come in.

As I got closer I saw that it was Aladdin and Kirk.

'Hey!' I said, surprised, and they gave me a quick, wide-eyed glance before the drunk regained their attention.

'You wanna go right now?' he taunted. 'I'll take botha you faggots!' He was a disheveled redneck in his late twenties with shaggy brown hair and some sort of a giant, inflamed-looking pustule just to the left of his nose.

Standing there in front of The Gorgon sent me back in time and almost instinctively I stepped between Kirk and Aladdin and right up to him.

'What's the problem?' I asked.

As a newcomer from the street, the man saw me, I guess, as a potential ally, and began to indignantly explain himself in an alcoholic slur.

'This fuckin . . .' he said, pointing to Aladdin, '*chink*, this fuckin' chink is a racist, man! He won't let me in because I'm white. Because I'm fuckin' white! This chink is a fuckin' racist!'

I stared directly at that oozing, grape-sized pustule and asked which chink he was talking about.

'That one!' he shouted, pointing, of course, at Aladdin.

I looked at Aladdin who, still with folded arms, was staring across the street, ignoring us.

'Oh, *that* chink? No, he's not a racist. You know what he is?' I whispered, winking slyly.

'What?' The man said, swaying a bit.

'He's a *pimple*-ist,' I sneered.

He stared at me for a second or two, digesting my words, then raised his hand and roared something about it being a boil. He swatted the infected area violently and swung his other arm at my head. I ducked and spun behind him and took him down easily and I felt truly good for the first time in a while. Then I felt arms around me, pulling me off, and the man stumbled away down the street, throwing threats back as he disappeared into the night.

'Hey chill out, Alex, my man,' Kirk was saying gently in my ear, 'Re-the-fuck-lax, man.'

'What's goin' on? Hunh? What's goin' on?' I heard someone asking excitedly, and turned to see Jason. He was sporting neat, middle-parted hair with a dandy's thin sideburns, a black

235

motorcycle jacket, flared jeans, and a pair of expensive-looking suede cowboy boots.

As Aladdin and Kirk informed Jason what had just happened, he held up a hand and interrupted them, looking my Gap chinos and polo up and down sarcastically.

'Whoa . . . What's with the image, brother?'

'What are *you* talkin' about, Tex?' I snapped, looking *his* duds up and down. I wasn't in the mood for his shit. I nodded up at The Gorgon: 'This place gotta mechanical *bull* now or what?'

'Guy,' he scolded, nodding towards the drunk as he stumbled off, 'that aggro stuff is *totally* old-school.'

'Really, Degreasey,' Kirk added, 'I'm getting sick of *defending* you when people start talking about what an asshole you've become.'

'What are you *talking* about?' I said, defensively.

'See? There you go again.'

And so they began breaking my balls as they always had.

'No, seriously dude, what have you been up to, my man?' Kirk asked, extremely interested.

'Well . . .' I sighed, but he immediately cut me off.

'Oh, cool. So *anyways* . . .' and he turned his back on me and began talking to Aladdin, then spun around, laughed, and embraced me. They all did.

We talked for a short bit until they asked if I'd heard about Timmy. My mood darkened and I nodded.

'You know about Punch, too, right?' Aladdin asked.

'No, what?'

'He's *dyin'*, guy,' Jason whispered. 'He's down to like ninety-five pounds. 'sgot the virus, Holmes.'

I looked at my feet and no one spoke. Finally I looked up and asked where Marie was.

Aladdin gestured with his eyebrows.

'Up in her room, Degreaser.'

I found her sitting in the dark on her futon, staring at the window as a northbound train rattled past. We hugged in silence and I felt her warm tears running down my neck.

'Are you still chanting?' she finally asked, and I lied by nodding slightly.

'I am so stupid,' she wept. 'We started doing photography together and he said we'd get an apartment and have our own darkroom. Pfff. He said we'd go to India together.'

She rolled her eyes in bitter self-mockery.

'He said there's some *bird* there that's never been photographed . . . Do you know what that cocksucker said when he called from Cook County and I told him I was pregnant? He said I was a slut and he didn't give a fuck *what* I did about it.'

My eyes focused on her. Even in the dim light she was clearly showing. I felt my jaw tighten, and, as the whole situation finally sunk in fully – that Timmy had slept with Marie, that he was in prison, that my inner debates regarding the pros and cons of going to Texas with him for the drug-buy had been moot all along, that we had our tickets to Alaska in our pockets that night and I had ruined it all – I realized that the summer was over and time had passed and certain things were gone forever. I pinched the bridge of my nose with a thumb and forefinger and squeezed my eyes shut to keep from crying. With Marie sitting right there, I didn't feel I had the right.

'What are you gonna do?' I finally asked her quietly, without opening my eyes.

'Ha! I'm *having* it,' she said defiantly. I looked and her blue eyes shone in the dark. 'You think I'm gonna kill this thing just because its father is an ASSHOLE? A scumbag, cocksucking . . .' And she began to sob again on my shoulder, rambling on about how this was just how it had been with *her* mother and father.

'Another white asshole,' she said. 'He owned a bar or some shit and he was *so nice* to my mother. She would tell me the story over and over so I'd learn what lying faggots men are – how he took her out to the Indiana dunes with a six-pack and a blanket and told her he loved me . . . *her* I mean, and fucked her *one* time. Stuck his dick in her and got her pregnant and when she told him . . . he did just what Timmy's doing right now only I *know* where that asshole is! He can't disappear like my dad. I'm gonna stick this so far up his ass . . . I hope he dies though. I do. I hope he gets fucked up the ass so many times in prison he dies!' she shrieked, choking for air.

The violence and futility and amplitude of her words made my ears ring and I suddenly – for a split second – felt like slapping her across the face with all my might. Instead I took a deep breath and said that Timmy hadn't meant what he said. Could she imagine the pressures he felt, knowing he was bound for prison?

My words didn't sway her, but my tone seemed to calm her a bit.

'Thank God my mother is dead,' she said, taking a normal breath, and swiping her knuckles across her eyes. 'That's all I've got to say. If there was one thing she ever wanted me to learn . . . Did I ever show you a picture of her?'

I was glad that she had calmed down and that the subject had veered somewhat from Timmy, so I told her that she hadn't, but I'd like very much to see one. She dug around in her little chest of drawers and pulled out a stationery box. She thumbed through Polaroids of me and her, me and Timmy, *her* and Timmy, Corny and Jermaine, pausing now and then to make a crack or chuckle. She reached a white envelope and pulled out a handful of old black-and-whites. The first one – shining with excellent preservation, trimmed with white lace – showed a young black woman with a straightened bob hairdo and doll-like, rounded features. She was lovely and snub-nosed and I could not take my eyes off the photo for a long while.

'She's beautiful, Marie,' I finally said.

'*Was* beautiful,' she corrected me, 'yep,' and flipped through the rest of the pictures which mostly featured her mother and older black people I didn't know.

'Here's the asshole,' she said, placing her thumb directly in the center of a Kodachrome snapshot of a young white man in a button-down oxford and thin black tie. His hair was short and neat and brilliantined to the side and as she removed her thumb from his face I saw her moist thumbprint define itself, then dry into an all but invisible trace.

All I could think as I stared, riveted, at the man's soft and heavy-lashed blue eyes was that it was not so strange. I forgot to breathe or blink and thought of nothing other than the fact that it was not so strange. I told myself perhaps a thousand times in that minute: it was not so strange. I had come back alone to the city – the city where I and my father were born – to search for a sister, had I not? It was not so strange that in the very vortex of lost midwestern kids I had found one.

I first noticed how badly my hands were shaking when I tried to put my token in the slot at the Belmont station for the return ride to Evanston. Marie's cold-lipped goodbye kiss had frozen my cheek, and the rest of my face and neck was going hot and tingly.

When she showed me that picture of my father – younger than I'd ever known him, clean-shaven, but him – I'm sure the shock was naked on my face, but Marie was too consumed with her own troubles to notice anything. A state of mental overload – an unfocused but visceral paranoia – blotted out all thoughts but escape. I grabbed Marie's hand as she continued chattering and flipping through the photos and told her in a strange voice that I had to go. She nodded, without looking up at me, then stood and walked me to her door. It was in this zombified fashion that I made my way back north.

It was nearly four in the morning when I reached Howard Street and crossed the platform to the Evanston shuttle. I was the only passenger so I mumbled 'Man Street' to the conductor and she took me there, express.

As I stepped out at Main, I realized that there wasn't anywhere I wanted to be. Not Abby's, not my own stolen bed. The two-car shuttle rolled off north and I sat down on a bird-stained bench, put my face in my hands, and stared ahead blankly, through the spaces between my splayed fingers.

My eyes locked onto a ghostlike figure across the tracks, beneath the other platform. I lifted my head from my hands a little bit and saw a pale white possum staring back at me, frozen. It clutched a hunk of French bread between its claws, and gnawed at it every so often, but never took its flat black eyes off of mine. In the distance, a car waited for the red light at Chicago and Main, stereo blasting. A heavy bass line throbbed through the otherwise quiet night like the beating of some massive heart. Then the car drove off. I tried to hold the possum's stare, to communicate with my eyes the fact that I wasn't after him or his bread, but he turned his bristly white back on me anyway, and slunk and lumbered down into a crater he'd dug in the black earth beneath the platform. I closed my eyes and put my head back in my hands.

About fifteen minutes later the shuttle came back again from the north. It stopped momentarily and I heard its doors open up in invitation. I felt the muscles in my legs flex, as if some part of me forgot for an instant that I couldn't go back to The Gorgon. Then the doors slid closed and the cars rattled back towards Howard Street without me, and soon it was very quiet again.

I made no attempt whatsoever to direct my thoughts in any linear fashion, so they seeped into one another, and superimposed, and blossomed within blossoms like a dream.

When I was a boy, our gander Charlie was as tall as me and, with wings held out like an airplane, he chased me and bit me and it wasn't funny at all and the point of this and the rest of this story is not to make you laugh but the few times I've told it I think people thought I was trying to be funny. Like a nightmare Dewon's face was when I told him. And Abby's. Peculiar looks, disturbed smiles. That's what life is like when you're ill. A joke that fails. To the unwell every smile is just the baring of flashing teeth. Their irony and camp are cold wet bricks in a clean fake fireplace. But the story itself as I said is not meant to be funny or sarcastic and it has no point, but its pointlessness is not the point either. The gander loved my father. He would stop at my father's boots and hunch down and ruffle his feathers in submission. One day we went down to the pond for a swim and as I bobbed close to the silty shore, hidden in cat-tails, I saw my father in a deadman's float reach out and grab the gander by the tailfeathers and Charlie began to beat his wings in a furious flash of white against the sun until together they became a sort of slow but steady propulsion craft. Like that, white wings humming, Charlie pulled my father around the entire circumference of our little pond, until they reached the widening traces of their own wake, and that is the story I like to tell but rarely do as it seems to bother people.

The first snowfall.
Its cold scent makes me almost
Remember something.

won second place in an international haiku contest. Have you heard it? My father wrote it. He said English syllables are a lot longer than Japanese syllables, so a lot of experts feel that English haiku should have fewer than 17 syllables. It's an art to find the right length and balance in English haiku because the syllables vary so much more in length and stress.

The wood
He cut for a fire
Is turning gray.

won first place in the same contest the following year. My dad wrote that one too. It was a very esteemed international haiku contest. Not some run-of-the-mill haiku contest.

Cat prodding mouse
For another spurt of life
To play with.

Won second place in the same contest the same year. 'This is quite a coup,' the editor of Haiku magazine wrote my father.

I heard a pounding which I realized were footsteps coming up the corrugated steel steps at Main Street and I raised my head from my hands just in time to see a rather wild-eyed skinny black man in an army jacket trotting towards me. When he saw me open my eyes he extended a hand which I shook dazedly.

'Ronnie Jaspers,' he said. 'Pleased to meet ya.'

'. . . Alex Verdi,' I said, and finally had to pull my hand away from the man's grip.

'Just got out,' he said.

'Got out?'

'The Marines,' he said, nodding down at his camouflage jacket. 'I was a Green Beret.'

The Green Berets, of course, are an Army unit. Not Marine. Not that that was my only clue something was not quite right with the man.

He began to slowly pull his other hand out of the jacket, and I instantly sat up straight with fear. He then abruptly yanked his fist all the way out, and I flinched considerably.

'Look,' he said, opening his hand, and displayed a palmful of strange coins. 'I been all over the world – Mexico, France, China . . .'

He had rehearsed this. But to what end?

'I been all over the world, and then I get back . . . I was up on Howard Street,' he said, looking south down the empty tracks. 'and some *mutha*fucka took my fifty dollar bill. I was up on Howard and that nigga *took* my fifty dollar bill.'

He reached into the breast pocket of his jacket and produced a retracting razor boxcutter, then pushed the slanted silver blade out with his thumb.

'I'll kill a mothafucka . . .' he said, slicing an imaginary neck about a foot away from my face. I slid down the bench a bit, and stood up about four feet away from him. He stood between me and the staircase.

'I mean . . .' he said, reaching into the pocket where he'd put the coins and pulling out another boxcutter, '. . . I ain't playing. Went and took my fifty dollar bill. I'll kill somebody.'

Like a brief cold chill the thought passed through me: if I

was wearing my skinhead boots and bomber and my head was shaved, the man wouldn't be doing this. Whatever this was.

I stared down at his feet, which were clad in ragged vinyl loafers and no socks. I looked into his eyes as if to ask what exactly his intentions were, but they weren't clear just then, and I must admit they never got any clearer. There was pleading in his bloodshot eyes, and friendliness, and, I felt at the time, menace.

What do you want, my eyes incessantly asked, but he seemed unsure himself as he took a step closer to me, still slicing the air up slowly with the blades. I considered whether I should try and bolt past him, or cut across the tracks to the east platform. I had always been terrified of the deadly third rail.

'I been all around the world,' he said, and his voice broke a bit as he added: 'and I ain't playin'. I need some mothafuckin' money now.'

He was afraid of what he was doing. Suddenly afraid of me.

A white-hot flash of what seemed to be a lifetime's worth of wrath pumped heavily into my veins whatever secretions make a man want to fight very badly.

Are you threatening me, motherfucker? I asked with my eyes, feeling my nasal passages expand and clear. *Me? With a couple of fucking boxcutters?*

I stared him directly in the eyes and made it very clear as I stuck my hand into my baggy pants pocket that I was reaching for a weapon. All I had was a pack of smokes, however, but how was he to know?

His eyes were glued to my pocket as I stepped towards him to make my way to the stairs. Instinctively it seemed, he dropped one boxcutter and grasped my pocketed wrist in his shaking hand. I tried to knock it off with my free hand. I saw the other razor coming for my face and reached up to stop it with my palm. The blade punched deep and my knees almost buckled from the pain.

I roared something unintelligible and, head down, dove

forward at his legs. He toppled backwards to the platform, then immediately spun around to his stomach and tried to crawl out from under me. I tied his legs up with my own, however, and punched him as hard as I could in the back of his skull. The explosion of pain in my fist competed with the screaming puncture wound in the pad of my other hand.

He struggled with enough energy to drag himself, with me on top of him, across the platform, towards the staircase. As we scraped forward I continued to punch him in the back of the head though my fist felt crushed after the first few blows. They must have been registering, because he stopped crawling and managed to twist around and slash up at me with the razor. I tucked my chin in and felt the blade dig across my scalp before I grabbed his wrist with both of my hands.

He tried to peel my fingers away with his free hand, and as we struggled for the blade he slowly got his legs free. We rose to standing positions on the platform, which provided him with an opportunity to kick me in the balls.

Though I didn't release his wrist, I sank to my knees and the kicks kept coming, driving me steadily backwards, until the wooden planks beneath me disappeared. I fell backwards off the platform to the first rail, pulling the man down on top of me.

I lost my grip on his wrist as we hit the bed of sharp white stones between the rails in a tangle of limbs. As he tried to crawl out of the jumble with two free hands, I looked for the blade. I found it lying loosely on my belly, near the edge of a long, jagged rip in my polo, tinged along the edges with pink, and steadily expanding into a rose-colored stain.

Holding the boxcutter now, I leaped on him again as he sluggishly crawled away, and slashed at the back of his jacket wildly, exposing three stripes of insulation. He spun to his back and flailed up at me spastically. Though in court I lied and said I didn't remember what happened next, I do. Quite vividly. As he sat up, reaching for me with both hands, I slashed him once across the cheek with the razor. He brought his hands to the wound and I stood up, hurling the blade down the tracks into the darkness.

I wiped at the mask of blood pouring down my forehead and doubled over with nausea from his groinkick. The man rose to all fours and reached as if to crawl across the tracks towards the other platform. I aimed a kick at his ribs. Before my toe reached its mark, though, I saw white sparks and a white flash seemed to light up the inside of my skull.

The voltage running through him had been enough to throw me backwards. I woke to a burning stench and heard the shuttle train behind me, almost too late. I'd be trapped if I rolled under the platform, so I tried to climb back up on it.

The conductor hit the brakes, but the train kept screeching towards me. I pulled my torso up to the planks, and crawled towards the stairs, trying to get the rest of my body out of the way, but the front car clipped my heel and sent me spinning up and around and headfirst into the side of the car.

When I regained consciousness this time I was lying beneath the bench, and the train was pulling into the Main Street stop again, as if the whole thing had been a dream. But the mask of blood had grown sticky, my polo shirt was sopping, and I heard sirens blaring from the street, so I tried to get to my feet and run. I was slipping in and out of some sort of twilight though, and my left leg wouldn't move, so I dragged myself blindly towards the stairs. The train doors opened and I heard a shout and the barking of a dog as the K-9 security guards released its leash. I reached up for the stair-bannister, the dog was upon me, and we tumbled together down the steps. I felt the claws on my back and the cold steel muzzle-cage on my throat and I smelled the dog breath, hot on my face. Then I closed my eyes and I slept for a very long time.

PART FOUR

'You common cry of curs . . . I banish you!'
. . . there is a world elsewhere.'
William Shakespeare, *Coriolanus*

IN MY PREVIOUS STAYS in hospital rooms I had always found the weary smiles and deadpan bedpan humor of doctors and staffers and candy-stripers kind of depressing. But I must admit I missed it now. When dealing with a patient who is handcuffed to his bed and awaiting trial for killing a man, the faces of those who re-plug your IV tubes and change the dressings of your wounds and stick state-of-the-art thermometers in your ear are grim and dutiful.

I yearned for a little phoniness.

'How are you feeling today?' now clearly meant: 'How soon can we OK your transfer to Cook County Correctional?' So, of course, my answer was always: 'Worse.'

But, under professional care, no amount of willing can prevent flesh wounds from healing. My fever progressively went down, the slashes sealed, and stitches were plucked out daily from my hands and scalp and stomach. The train had snapped my leg-bones in three places, but they were clean breaks, and the plaster was due to be sawed off the day I received my only two visitors.

A slight woman with short, graying hair and a gangly adolescent girl with a self-conscious, smart-ass grin walked into my room that morning. A full minute or so went by before I comprehended that the kindly-looking lady was my mother and the gum-snapping teenager with the big blue eyes was my sister Stacy.

My mother walked up to the side of my bed, while Stacy hovered in the background cautiously, averting her gaze – first pretending to be very interested in some spot on the wall, then, realizing she was failing, yawning in a tortured attempt to keep a desperately unwanted smile off her round and pretty face.

In light of my predicament they both seemed to be trying hard to hide the fact that they were very happy to see me again. They didn't cry though. Just patiently answered my questions.

My parents were divorced. The property was in my mother's name and the split had been part of my father's successful plan to save the farm. But things can be both true and false, and my mom and sister made it clear the marriage was over for real. My father's plan required that my mother testify against him. He'd been sentenced to two years in a minimum security prison, and was due out in a few months. My mother sold the land immediately to Mickey Silver, who sold it back to my father. My mom agreed to wait until my dad's release before suing him for alimony.

Ah, that Verdi imagination.

They had an apartment in Uptown on Argyle, right in the heart of New Chinatown. My mom was waitressing.

'What about the foster home?' I asked, and Stacy rolled her eyes. They'd had a rough time of it, but she'd never been in foster care.

'So . . . how's school?' I asked her, and she rolled her eyes some more, and chewed her gum.

My mother smiled uncertainly and looked at her, and then back at me again.

'What?' I said.

'Nothing,' my sister sighed.

'She got suspended for a week,' my mother ventured with wide eyes.

'For what?' I asked incredulously, my sibling blood boiling with instinctive indignation.

'She threw a rock at somebody at recess.'

'Who?'

'Pedro.'

'Who the fuck is Pedro?'

'He was throwing rocks at *me*,' my sister said, with a thirteen year old's impetuous shrug. 'Just cuz I've got better aim . . . Whatever.'

'Somebody throws a *rock* at you, tell the fuckin' principal!'

'He's not gonna do nothin'!'

I narrowed my eyes hatefully.

'What – was it because you're *white* he threw rocks at you?'

'No,' my mother said. 'He's . . . Pedro's your friend isn't he?'

Stacy shrugged again.

'Are you like the only white chick there?' I wanted to know, working on my theory.

'That's not it,' my sister said, impatiently. 'He's just a jerk.'

'Well . . .' I said, nodding my head, 'you tell fuckin' *Pedro* that your brother is a *vicious killer* and I'm gonna get him if he doesn't watch out.'

I meant it somewhat as an ironic joke, but it didn't go over too well. Both of them looked at their feet uncomfortably.

'Was it in the papers?' I finally asked them quietly. 'Is that how you knew I was here?'

'There was one little thing in the Metro section,' my mother said, still looking down. 'We were packing some stuff and Stacy saw the name. At first I didn't even think it was the same Alex Verdi.' With a dubious stare, my sister looked at the pink scalp scars on my shaven head, and asked if I was really a *Nazi*?

I sighed, and mumbled that I was *not* a Nazi, and what had happened was an accident, sort of, and the police had agreed to abandon the direct application of the hate crimes law, and even the murder charge – if I'd cop a manslaughter plea. The man I'd killed was a convicted felon, and a mental patient, but they wouldn't accept the self-defense plea – not with the injuries to the back of his head, and the slash on his cheek, and my own skinhead history. Everything was coming back in a swirl. The man was dead, I suddenly acknowledged fully. The skinny crazy-eyed man whose face came back to me now like an old friend was dead. And I had killed him. Outside the hospital, everything but that man's life was continuing in an unbroken flow.

As Stacy dubiously and impatiently listened to my explanations – surveying the entire room with those blue eyes that were at once dubious and bored and highly alert – I abstractly noted how much her nervous mannerisms reminded me of Marie's. As the full weight of that thought took hold, I lost my train of thought and stopped talking.

'Does *he* know?' I suddenly asked.

He didn't. Yet. They came straight to the hospital when they found out.

'I don't want him to find out about this right now,' I said.

'*I'm* not gonna call him,' my sister said.

I hadn't heard from Abby, and was sure I never would again, though I would in fact see her one last time. Zack, I would learn much later, had done his best for me. Disguising himself as his late father, he tried to draw cash from one of his mother's CDs to get my bail, after which he planned on driving me to the Mexican border in his van. But he'd been found out and arrested and his mother threatened to press charges if he didn't enroll in a six-month rehab program in Vermont. As I lay in that hospital room though, both Zack and Abby seemed like characters from a brief sad dream.

Marie, though, was more than that to me.

I thought of Tim's baby she was carrying, and I thought of the picture she had shown me of her mother. I looked at my own mother, and she looked back at me sadly and apologetically, as if she had failed in some way, as if she'd been anything other than a woman who left her home in the city to rise at dawn and milk the goat for her childrens' breakfast.

'Ma,' I suddenly said, 'I don't want you or Stacy comin' to

the trial or anything, and I don't want *him* to find out about this.'

It suddenly occurred to me that if Marie had heard about this – and she undoubtedly must have, she kept scrupulous tabs on skinhead violence reports in the media – she would probably show up at the trial. She might meet my ma and Stacy, and they could bond in some way, and inadvertently put two and two together. I envisioned it all and told my mom again that I didn't want them at the trial. I had to either think up the perfect way to tell Marie, or else keep the secret forever.

'Ma,' I said. 'I love you and I'm sorry . . . I'm sorry. Please do this one thing for me. Please. Don't come to the trial. And let *me* tell him. Give me his address there and I'll write him a letter.'

My mother started crying and said she was scared for me and maybe he could help somehow.

'What did I just say, Ma? Huh? Do *not* call him. Don't!' I shouted, and enraged by my rage and my inability to handle the complications of my senses, I brought my free hand to my face and covered my eyes.

After a few seconds I felt my mother's trembling fingers on my wrist, and without moving my hand from my face I called my sister over to the bed as well. I leaned over and tried to hug them both with one arm, and they hugged me back stiffly and uncertainly.

'I don't wantchya to worry. I've got a deal worked out. It's a good deal so don't worry.' I wasn't lying about having a deal in the works, but it was not a particularly good one. The public defenders I'd talked to on the phone said the prosecution would offer a five-year sentence for the manslaughter plea.

'I love you, I love you, I love you,' I murmured over and over again. 'Please don't throw any more rocks,' I finally said to Stacy, and laughed, far too hard. They laughed as well, too hard.

Before leaving my mother carefully wrote my father's address on a scrap of paper and placed it in my hand. When they left I stuck it in my mouth and ate it.

*

When I got to County a guard had our whole group strip naked, one layer of clothing at a time. I was given a baggy orange jump suit, then led to a large holding cell on the first floor. I found an empty spot on the wall and sat.

After about half an hour a black man, about my size, walked up to me.

'You sittin' in my spot,' he said.

I got up and found another spot across the cell from him. A few minutes later he stood before me again.

'You *still* sittin' in my spot.'

I stood up and stared him in the eyes dully, not quite straight on. My left leg felt shorter than my right. It still does.

'Well, just go back to your other spot,' I said, 'and I'll keep this one warm for ya.' Had he been much bigger, maybe I'd have kept moving to every new spot in the jail. But, like I said, he was just my size.

He stared at me crazily with big round eyes and I laughed. Leaning my face closer to his I told him:

'That's funny,' I said, 'you look *just* like the brother I just killed.'

'Awright,' he said, expanding his chest and squaring his feet.

'No, wait,' I said, trying to sound cool, but my lips were quivering. It was nervous energy, and fear, but also some kind of immature pleading of injustice. There was no pleasurable rush though. That wouldn't come anymore. I just felt like crying from fatigue. 'I mean, am I supposed to be scared of you just because you're *black*? Is that it? I'm *not*. I mean, it's no disrespect. You just don't *look* like much is all.'

That would have done it. The thick, hanging, crucial second had come and gone, but just then a short, muscular black man came trotting towards us shouting: 'Yo, yo, yo, yo, yo! Hold up. Hold up a second there.' And as soon as he arrived, my adversary turned on his heel and strolled away.

'Hold on my man,' the new guy smiled, clapping me on the back. 'Was he messing with you?'

I nodded blankly.

'Well, he ain't gonna mess with you no more, awright? You don't need to be kickin' nobody's ass in here. You got enuff problems, brotha, without whuppin' that nigga's ass. Am I right? I know, I know how it is . . .'

He proceeded to tell me how the gangs had marked their territory in the building. This first level of the jail was 'Folks Floor'. The third level was 'People Floor'. It suddenly occurred to me that the confrontation and this guy's timely intervention had all just been some good-inmate/bad-inmate orchestration. My heated inner-rages of injustice and racial tension and my own uncertain manliness had all been conjured up by the mechanized ritual of a jailhouse political party.

The Folks, he told me again, ran this floor, and I would be all right here if I was down with them. If I had friends with The People up on Three, that was where I'd have to go. There was also the second level, where the 'Neutrons' stayed, but Neutrons had no pull, so that was the shittiest place to be – fewer lights, no phones, no reefer for sale; the Neutrons were the last to eat, etc.

The Neutron floor was not the place to be, of course, but, nevertheless, that was where I decided to stay until I was convicted of manslaughter and shipped to Stateville for five to seven.

I talked to my terrified mom on the phone a few times. She asked if I had written my dad. I said I had, and everything was all worked out, and I'd see her soon. She sounded doubtful, and I suspected from her tone that she was going to contact him. She and my sister did keep away from the courtroom, though. So did Marie, which had me perplexed. I even called The Gorgon once, and left a message on her machine. But she never showed up.

Despite the fact that I was plea-bargaining, I spent a full month being carted back and forth across the street to the courtroom at 26th and California. I made every trip in handcuffs and leg-chains. Just standard procedure, the guards had nothing against me. In fact, I even befriended a couple of young bailiffs – one black and one Puerto Rican. They overheard a Neutron buddy of mine – a Mexican kid named Manny – schooling me on what Stateville would be like as we waited one day in the holding cell behind the judge's bench. They came over and broke Manny's balls for a while. And then they started in on me. Telling me how I wasn't getting any pussy for a long time. Telling me about all the young prostitutes they banged in the witness waiting-room right next to our cell. Gradually, over the weeks, they learned my whole story. Rodney, the black bailiff, had spent a semester at Northwestern, and we would tell Louis, the Puerto Rican, about all the fine-ass lookin' women that went there. Louis, a thin boy with a thin mustache, once told me he was a spiritualist – he believed the air in the courtroom and the jail was choked with the spirits of the dead, swirling around us even as we spoke. He was also very horny, and never tired of Rodney's tales of female conquests. I mentioned Abby Rivers, and they both called me a liar and pressed for details. Talking about her all the time woke certain things up, and I realized how horribly I missed her.

I don't think Rodney or Louis ever quite believed me fully, until the morning of my sentencing date, when I scanned the audience, as usual, looking in vain for Marie, and instead saw Abby Rivers sitting in the back row.

As soon as I was sure it was her, my head instinctively

jerked back around towards the judge's bench. I kept my eyes riveted there, heart beating, the whole morning while the judge talked to my public defenders and read their briefings. Before the actual sentencing, the judge announced that in five minutes the court would take a twenty-minute break.

Rodney came up to where I sat and spoke without looking at me, which is the way we usually conversed when court was actually in session.

'So, you goin' away tomorrow, huh Verdi? No drama, though, you know what's up.'

'She's *here*,' I whispered desperately.

He almost looked at me.

'*Who?*'

'Abby . . . she's all the way in the back. Skirt-suit. Charcoal gray pinstripes and . . .'

'Awwwshit . . . yeah, I see her. Hell no. Damn.' And he immediately crossed the courtroom to tell Louis. Louis, who stood slumped up against the wall, straightened right up when Rodney whispered in his ear. Louis mouthed: 'Where? Where?' until he saw her.

They came over to me right before the break began, talking a mile a minute.

'Aw man, I don't believe this shit – she's *fine*, dude,' Louis said. 'You wanna take her to the witness room? You can do it, man. I'll take care of you. It'll be your going-away present.'

'Shit, man' Rodney said, 'she ain't here to go to no *witness* room. Look at her man, she's pissed. He didn't call her *once*. Made her look all stupid. She gonna come up here at the break and curse him out. Then maybe spit in his face.'

'Aw no, man. She *into* it. It's romantic, man. She's gonna have a *lover in prison*, dude . . . She's gonna write to him every day, and cry to songs they listened to when they was togetha.'

'Naw, man these bitches ain't like that, I'm tellin' you. She's *pissed*.'

'I will *bet* you man . . .'

257

'Shit – I'll give you *odds* mothafucka. Two–to–one. I'll put twenty to your ten she tears him a new asshole then stomps the hell outta here.'

'Naw man, she's gonna say: "Oh, I'll wait for you for–ev–ah, baby . . ." '

'Shiiit . . . you might as well give me that ten right now, fool . . . Aw shit, there go the judge. Here she comes.'

They sauntered away as I heard the click of high–heels get closer and closer behind me, then stop. I didn't turn around until I heard her sniffling.

'Whatsamatter?' I asked her, testily, as I swiveled around in my chair. She was all done up like the rich–bitch knockout I'd described her as. Her hair shiny and perfect and flipped up at the ends. Make–up, nails, the pinstripe skirt–suit crisp and tailored so that Rodney and Louis and everybody else could see just how dynamite her body really was. I felt a stir in my crotch and I was angry because when I looked in her eyes I knew that Rodney was right. Sort of. She really was mad, but she was playing it up to hide her own guilt too.

'You want somethin'?' I asked her.

She gulped for air.

'C'mon, speak . . .' I said.

'You *lied* to me!' she said, and dropped her chin to her chest.

'Yeah, well . . . you said you'd always love me, no matter what – you remember saying that? Don't you remember?' It was at this point that I realized I was taunting her. 'Still love me? Hunh? Well, I guess we both lied then, eh?'

'I *do* still love you, Alex!' she sobbed, and looked as if she might collapse right there in the aisle.

I would have lifted her over the waist–high wooden barrier and rocked her in my lap, but for the handcuffs. I leaned against the polished wood that separated us, and whispered: 'Listen, we can go to the witness waiting–room back there. We'll be alone . . .'

258

I had really only meant so that we could talk in private, but she raised her chin and looked at me with mascara pouring down her smooth, rosy cheeks, then shook her head.

'Not like that, Alex . . . I don't love you like that anymore.'

I chuckled bitterly.

'So, when we were in bed together that night,' I began, 'and you *begged* me: "Promise me you'll always love me." What? Were you, like . . .'

'Stop it!' she shrieked.

I 'shhhhh-ed' her and looked back at Rodney and Louis, who stood against the judge's bench listening, then jerked their heads to the side as if oblivious to our presence.

'It's no big deal, Abby. I understand. I was just some guy you were fucking. It's no sin just to fuck a guy. I'm just a little pissed that you don't have the decency to come back to the witness-room for a few minutes and fuck a guy when he's really in need, you know?'

Abby had had enough.

'You *lied* to me about *everything* . . .' she said, and turned to leave.

'Nah, not about *everything*,' I said through my teeth. 'I told the truth about always loving you. I told the truth about that. That's why I lied about everything else, you fuckin' bitch!'

She stopped. I watched her back heave for a full minute

When we got to the witness waiting-room she hastily stepped out of her stockings and took her panties down, still crying. She pulled a chair out from the meeting-table for me to sit on. I held my cuffed hands up above my head as she unzipped my jump suit all the way and knelt to put my cock in her mouth.

She sucked – tears dripping onto my belly, until I was ready for her. Then she got up, turned her back to me, pulled her pin-striped skirt up above her bare and perfect Northshore ass, then lowered herself down onto me. Of all the new positions I taught her, this had been her favorite. She said it made her feel the naughtiest. But I think this time she was just doing it so she wouldn't have to look at me.

She leaned forward and balanced herself on the table-edge, sniffling and let loose with an occasional sob as I slowly thrust.

When it was over, she sat on my knee with her head on the table and basically *wailed*. I felt like bawling, too, to tell you the truth, but something was stopped up inside me, and all I could do was put my cuffed hands around her neck and tell her again and again that I loved her. After a while she turned and wrapped her arms around me.

It's hard to describe a goodbye-forever hug, but you know it when you feel it.

When Louis brought us back out to the courtroom, she walked straight for the little door in the barrier without looking back.

'Didn't even kiss my man goodbye,' Rodney said to Louis, holding out his palm for the ten. 'C'mon mothafucka, tell me honestly you think he's ever gonna see her again.'

Louis crossed his arms and stared at Abby's back.

'Yeah, but, dude . . . she *did* him in the witness-room, man. C'mon.'

Rodney eyed the long tear in her black stockings as she turned on her heel and walked out the door to the lobby. Then he shrugged a little as the judge came back in and said:

'Yeah . . . I guess we gotta call that a push.'

. . . BUT IT'S GONNA BE even worse for a white boy like you. Cállate Carajo! Listen to what I'm *telling* you, man. A lot of them black dudes, when they get hold of a pretty white boy inside, they be like: '*Payyyyyyback!*' I'm not saying it's right. You said every baby's born with bad karma, and we just gotta each accept it and deal with it. Well just remember that when some big black mothafucka's all in you ear like: 'You *my* bitch now, white boy!' Ain't it just a funny-ass joke on the outside, though? But that shit's not funny once you seen a bunch of black dicks all dripping with some white boy's shit and blood. I know you'd never let that happen to *you* though – you'd *die* first, right, bro? Only it ain't your choice. You can't just decide to *die* when they hit you over the head with a dumbbell bar and you wake up with your head smooshed between two pillows and a dick in your ass and your ass all bleedin'. A big black mothafucka tearin' up your asshole waxing yo' ass like you a bitch, probably pumping you full of AIDS. And after all the brothas've fucked you and knocked your tonsils black and blue they start doin' things like . . . pissing in your mouth and – Don't alright-alright me, blood! You ever swallow piss? Had you ass so tore out they had to sew it back *into* you? That how you wanna spend the next five years? Then I don't know . . . kill yourself right now, shit . . . I don't know what to tell you bro, I'm thinking out loud. I ain't never been to Statesville neither, that shit's *uncivilized*. I got a few homies though, and I'm gonna see what I can do for you when we get there, but I'll be straight witchyou: first and foremost I'll be takin' care of mines. I gotta heart, bro, but my heart belongs to my asshole . . .

Before Stateville, we spent a week at the Joliet Correctional Center for Reception and Indoctrination, where they told us not to join a gang.

I found a small silver screw my last night there. I found it beneath my bunk half-covered in paint-dust. I wondered if a screw would be of any special worth at Stateville, so I spat on it, and wiped it on the orange leg of my jump suit, and resolved to ask Manny in the morning. Then I lay on my back in my bunk and twirled the screw between my thumb and forefinger, gazing as the pointy stem seemed to climb and climb to escape its threads. Then my eyes grew heavy and I fell asleep.

They took Manny's group before breakfast, so I tossed the screw in the grass as they led us out to the bus. It probably wasn't worth anything. A little screw. But I just figured I'd ask. Manny had gone on and on about the magnified worth of things in prison. Seventy-five dollars for a chapstick cap full of marijuana shake. More than that for a three-pack of Trojans. But Manny was gone and there wasn't anyone else I could ask.

The grounds of Stateville are beautiful and manicured. Beds of show-flowers amidst blue-green lawns. Inside though, just like in the movies, everything is gray, and the sound of every action is followed by a hollow echo.

The admissions process was not unlike the first day of the army. Only the guards didn't yell like the Drill Sergeants had. They didn't need to raise their voices to let you know they could hurt you; they didn't need to shout to create a mood of fear and sobriety.

As I shuffled through the outfitting room a blank-faced man let his eyes flit over my frame for less than a second, before deciding my approximate size. I was the same size I'd always been. I'd tried hard to bulk up at Cook County. I'd tried lifting weights and doing push-ups and eating other inmates' leftover slop. But I just got harder and tighter. If anything I was thinner now. The blank-faced man reached beneath his counter and handed me two pairs of stiff denim pants and a couple of shirts, some socks and some underwear, and told me to drop my sweat-soaked jumpsuit in the hamper.

A nervous nausea had been building all morning. My face quivered ridiculously, and I fought to control it. As I stepped into one of the outfits I saw a guard with several rings of keys on his belt come in from a side door. The noise of the cellblock came in with him. Shouts and unidentifiable clanks and laughter. He shut the door behind him and began whispering to another guard.

Like a recurring dream, where I remembered each segment an instant before it happened, I stiffened as the first guard checked his clipboard, looked up, and jutted his chin to point me out. The other smiled grimly and beckoned me over. Before getting to him I sank before a trash can and vomited up some of the nervous knot in my stomach. Several of the other prisoners jeered and booed.

The guard, a husky young white man, led me outside to C Block, a five-tiered circular building. It made sense, Manny said, how violent criminals were kept in a special block. We entered, and an intense human racket came from all directions, yet there were very few inmates in sight. A fat black man sloppily mopped the main floor. A thin Hispanic kid in a white dago-tee, rested his elbows on the second-tier rail, staring abstractly down at me and my guard. As we climbed the stairs towards the fifth and top tier of C Block, the sound of sparrows chirping separated from the cacophony around me. Birdshit stained the handrails and cold air from the high, broken windows rushed in all around me. For all the fresh air though, this place stank a horrible unwashed human stink beyond anything I'd experienced at County. This was an aged reek, and I was struck with the fact that if I lasted long enough, I'd get used to it, as one eventually gets used to anything.

The guard knew exactly who I was.

He spoke with exaggerated good ol' boy amusement, like some guard he'd seen in a bad prison flick. 'Aw, they gonna *like* you, Verdi. Aw, yeah. Just tell em what a tough guy y'ar. Some big black buck starts gettin googly-eyed in the shower, you just tell em what yer in for. Tell im: "I done killed a niggah—niggah . . . I'm a big tough skinhaid."'

His laughter bounced off the slimy walls of the staircase, and we reached the fifth tier. I blinked hard and tried to concentrate. There was something false in his tone – like a Drill Sergeant's. Something insincere and staged about his meanness.

'Aw, yeah . . . ha ha ha. You gone have a good time. You got five years to meet everybody. Aw, yer gonna make some lifelong friends here, Verdi, in five years.'

Sixty months. One thousand, eighteen hundred and twenty-five days. I'd be twenty-five years old when I got out. I divided it all up at County. My only visitor there had been Mrs Kabushita, who, I figured, had read about it in the paper. I looked at her through the glass between us and asked if she was gonna *congratulate* me on this big benefit. I'd only meant it as a joke, but when she shook her head and smiled, her flashing black eyes were moist. No, she said, but I *should* welcome this experience. If one could chant a thousand Nam-myo-ho-renge-kyo's in fifteen minutes, a million in 275 hours, how many could I chant in five years? And how, as a Bodhisattva of the Earth, might I help my fellow prisoners erase their own bad karma?

I figured not letting any of them rape or kill me would be a good start.

Above the sparrows' chirping and the disembodied inmate sounds, my guard's bootsteps clip-clomped like a horse trot. Like a metronome backbeat to his rehearsed-sounding terrorism.

'But your best friend of all, though – the guy you ain't never gone ferget – that's gone be your cellmate. I already told him all aboutchya, an' he's *real* excited. He's waitin for you right now. Skipped breakfast and everything just for the occasion. He promised to be a gentleman and take things nice and slow. If I told him once I told him a hundred thousand times: when a new boy says no, he *means* no. Plain'n simple.'

I leaned over the railing and dry-heaved, but nothing came up. The guard chuckled with disgust.

'Shit,' he said, and waited for me to finish.

We walked down the north end of the fifth tier, passing empty cell after empty cell, when he suddenly grabbed me by the collar and halted. He walked a step or two ahead and stuck his head through the doorway of a cell. It was the next-to-the-last cell on that side. He called:

"Scuse me, anybody home? Special de-livery.'

The guard pulled me by the collar and shoved me roughly into the cell. A set of bunk beds in the corner. The lower bunk neatly made and empty. On the top bunk a bare mattress and a man in a black hooded sweatshirt lying on his side, his broad back facing the doorway.

The guard called again and the man stirred. He tensed up and brought his hands to the hood, as if he hadn't wanted to fall asleep. Then he rolled over so abruptly to face us that without thinking I stepped backwards and clenched a fistful of the guard's shirtwaist in fear.

'Inmate! *Git* your fuckin' . . .'

As the guard reached for his stick the man on the bunk spoke in a hoarse, serious tone.

'It's all right, Ford! I'm sorry . . .' He sat up and pulled the hood of his sweatshirt down. 'Chill out, Degreaser.'

Before I could fully digest that this stocky, raspy-voiced man was Tim Penn, he sprung off the edge of the bed with both palms, and landed flat-footed before me.

'Put this on,' he said hastily, yanking off the sweatshirt. I heard Ford's bootsteps disappear behind me and stared open-mouthed at Tim as he stood there in a sleeveless white undershirt, pulling the tangled sweatshirt right-side in again. He had several new tattoos running up and down his meaty arms. White Power stuff. Aryan Brotherhood inscriptions in unreadable Old English script. The crucified skinhead on his right shoulder was altogether blotted out by a thick blue-black swastika.

'Don't ask me *one* fuckin' question, Alex,' he said. 'Just shut the fuck up and listen.'

I looked dumbly into his eyes, which seemed grayer now. Though I don't remember saying anything, Tim gave a humorless laugh and said: 'Don't thank God, Degreaser. Thank The Brotherhood.'

Then he put the sweatshirt over my head. In that blackness, before I could even poke my head through, he began giving me instructions.

*

I walked, head down, face hidden by the hood, to the ground floor of C Block, and found the exit to the yard Tim spoke of. Outside in the bright sunlight, amidst the blue-green lawns and splashes of wildflower beds, milled groups of prisoners – blacks with blacks, Hispanics with Hispanics, and in each group the occasional white who, to me, looked punked-out and used. Chanting under my breath, I headed to where about a hundred white men monopolized the northwest corner of the wall and contemplated all that Tim had said.

Indeed, there was nothing divine or even lucky about this intervention. Marie had written Tim about my situation repeatedly. She had known all along, scolding Tim in her letters that *he'd* turned me into a murderer and as karmically bankrupt as he was he'd better see to it that nothing happened to me. At Vandalia Timmy had fought a black guard, and now he was here, with the violent criminals – with me. That he was here didn't matter, Timmy said. That he had arranged all this with white guards sympathetic to the cause meant nothing. The Aryan Brotherhood was his family now, and the family took care of its own. Without family here you were a slave, you were livestock.

And I wasn't family. The only thing that mattered was up to me alone.

The Aryan Brothers stood in their corner, sat on benches, conferred, exercised. Up above them, on the walkway of the wall, stood a guard with a rifle. He looked out across the yard like a hunter. Oddly like a protector.

As I neared the group a tall, pock-faced man recognized the sweatshirt and drawled:

'Morning, Brother Penn . . .' and brought his fist up lightly to his chest.

I looked down and nodded, but forgot to return the salute. I walked a few more steps and felt an arm on my tricep.

I whirled around and slapped away the pock-faced man's hand.

'What's your deal boy? Who the fuck're you?' He drew back, but didn't look the least bit scared.

'I'm a white man, Brother,' I replied.

'Then why you hidin' your face like you ashamed of it?' he said, reaching for my hood. I swept my wrist up and out and batted his hand away. A short, bald-headed man in his fifties, and an olive-skinned man of undetermined age, flanked Pockface and stared at me curiously.

'I ain't never seen you before, Brother,' the dark man said, chewing slowly on some gum. 'Who invited you to be here in the Brotherhood corner?'

'I'm here to see Frank Pritzger,' I heard myself saying.

The dark man stopped chewing for a second as if reflecting, then started up again and said: ''s he expectin' you?'

I shook my head.

'He'll wanna see me,' I said. Tim said I should come alone, to show I had balls. But I suddenly wondered if he had stayed away because he feared I'd come across as soft. Or because he thought Frank wouldn't forgive me.

The shaved-headed man slipped away into the crowd, while the dark man fixed a cold look on me.

'You look like a piece of shit,' he informed me, at length.

'I am,' I said. I don't know exactly what that meant, but I said it confidently and with a taunting smirk.

'Where the fuck're you from boy? Where's your cell? I ain't never seen you here before.'

'With the birds,' I said.

'The birds?'

'Up with the sparrows.'

'You're talkin' out your ass, boy,' the dark man said, chewing faster now. 'You think you're funny? Get the fuck outta here.'

He glanced up towards the man on the wall, then reached for me. I stepped back lightly, bumping into a large man with shaggy salt-and-pepper hair. I spun around wildly and stood sideways between the two men.

'Yo, I just wanna see Frank!' I said slapping my chest with both hands. To my ears, I sounded ridiculous. 'Why you actin' like I'm here to visit your *bitch* or some shit? You wanna go? Come on then. What's the matter? Your kick-start broken? Come on. If you're a frog, then jump!'

The dark man stepped towards me and I grabbed a fistful of his denim shirt. Pockface shrank back and Salt-and-Pepper threw a big arm around my neck, cutting off my air-supply. Then I heard Frank's voice, and the man let up a bit on my throat. I twisted my head free, but several hands clutched at my clothes. I saw Frank's clean-shaven, square head come cutting through the crowd. He looked healthy and well-fed, and milk-white from lack of sunlight.

'Who?' I heard him ask. 'Which one?'

He turned to face me. The tattoo of a blue-winged Nazi

Luftwaffe icon spanned the length of his forehead, with a circled swastika centered right between his eyes, like a brand.

'What's your business?' he asked, peering into the face-hole of my hood. 'Who are you? You got a fuckin' name, Brother? C'mon, talk to me. What's your name?'

'You don't know my name, Frank?' I said, shaking my head. 'I gotta tell you my name?'

'Yeah, you do . . . what's your fuckin' name, dude?'

'You don't wanna know my name.'

'Just tell me your name,' Frank said, as if he'd suddenly decided he was reasoning with a madman. 'You look like shit, Brother. You've got good blue eyes, but with those dark circles you look sick. You on drugs? Tell me your name and then you can go get some sleep.'

'You ready?' I asked him, and pulled the hood down. 'Remember me?'

'No, Brother, I don't. What's your name?'

'My name's Alex Verdi,' I began. 'My girlfriend was Marie . . . the mulatto chick. Remember? I thought fighting you guys'd make me a hero.'

Frank's small brown eyes slowly lost focus as he no doubt thought back to the Belmont days; me hand-in-hand with a mixed girl; the fight in his apartment. As I continued, I spat each word with bitter self mockery.

'But I wasn't anybody's hero. Everywhere I've ever been, people looked at me like I was scum. Dirty. All I ever asked for was an even break, but people never cut me any slack, they just took care of their own. Who's *my* "own", Frank? Who'll take me anymore in this country?'

I chuckled and looked him right in the eye like Tim said I should.

'So here I am, Frank,' I shrugged, and spat on the ground. The fact that *everything* depended on this moment actually made it easier. I couldn't fuck up, so I wouldn't. 'Killed a nigger. Cut his throat and tossed him on the El tracks like garbage. Think you could use a guy like me?' I laughed. 'Make the call, Frank. You want a white working-man's revolution? I'm your man. You don't want my help? Cut my fuckin' throat right here and now. I'd understand you wantin' me dead . . . but just say the word and I'll be down with you to the death.'

Frank focused on me again. His pupils hardened. He reached out with both arms and gripped my shoulders and cried out my name with characteristic intensity and melodrama.

'Alex. Alex . . . Every word you . . . we're the same, Brother . . .' He hugged me and all other hands released my clothing as he continued with a breathy voice in my ear:

'I swore I'd fucking kill you, Brother. And Brother Penn too. Especially him. But *he* learned the truth at Vandalia. He wouldn't lay down for it, so they sent him here. He came to me just like you. We're from the same mold, Brother – you and I and Brother Penn. And together . . . it's destiny. It is. We were destined to be great men – you and I and Brother Penn . . . Brother Penn most of all. He's a leader. But *this* is where his country wants him. Right here. And you, Brother – you're . . . an angel . . . a thinker . . . you *are* heroic of soul and yet . . . here you are. But together we're strong. You believed in all the lies once, so you know them better than I ever could. This is the start of it all right here, Brother . . .'

Frank pulled away from my ear with a grim expression and called to the dozens of hard white faces nearby: 'Make Brother Verdi feel welcome. He's going to be staying with us for a while.'

When I got back to the cell later in the day, Tim was leaning his desk chair back on its rear legs, reading. I sat on the lower bunk and recounted in low, relieved whispers how I'd pulled it off. He listened with a set jaw, not taking his eyes off the *Kung Fu Dragon* magazine in his lap and nodded every so often in approval. He had changed. He was quite beefy now, as opposed to strapping. He was hard-looking. When I finished filling Tim in on the details, I caught sight of my own face in the worn, metal side-panel of his locker. The softness and roundishness I had always wished away were gone now too.

Tim pointed the rolled-up magazine at me and said with a harsh whisper:

'*You gotta quit actin' like you're actin' and believe that you believe.* You can't have it both ways. There's no gettin' over on anybody . . . not in here.'

I snorted involuntarily.

'Believe I'm a *Nazi*?'

The magazine came flying at me, its pages aflutter, and Tim stood up red faced and hissing.

'If you wanna talk like a fuckin' *faggot* we don't need you in the Brotherhood! You can go live with the niggers a couple tiers down. *They'll* take good care of you!'

There was genuine hatred in his voice, and, at the same time, a contrivance of tone; like the guard who brought me here. Was he even really sitting there? The last two hours had been a drunken walk through a house of mirrors.

'Quit bullshittin' yourself, Alex. Frank wouldn't've fuckin' believed you if *you* didn't believe every word you told him. You gonna sit there and tell me you didn't really *feel* it?'

'Yeah,' I whispered, 'yeah, I *felt* it. I lied to myself till I felt it. It's called acting.'

'No – you fuckin' asshole – right *now* you're lying to yourself.'

He locked his blue-gray eyes on mine for several minutes, then dropped the glare to my chest, shook his head, and took a breath.

'You're lucky, man,' he said, with less venom. 'This is only my second day back in general population. I was in the hole for four weeks. You weren't originally due for another couple of days.'

I finally had a chance to get some answers.

'What happened at Vandalia?'

'The niggers run Vandalia,' he said. 'I took out a gangbanger nigger hack, they sent me here.'

'A guard?'

'Pff . . . 'guard'. Guy was a fuckin' nigger Vice Lord. Me and one of his homeboys were going at it, and he starts hittin' on me with his stick, macing me . . . I snapped his arm and they called it attempted murder. Eight more years it got me. Then *here*, two niggers tried cutting me last month and now one of them's walking around with an eye missin'. Now I'm up on charges for that! I'm never getting outta here.' He laughed. 'I'm gonna grow old in this place. I'm gonna be like the Birdman of Alcatraz and shit. Trainin' the sparrows to crap on niggers . . . Fuck it. I'm better off here in this hellhole with the Brotherhood than in Vandalia alone. I would have hung myself there. I mean it – knowin' they'd fuckin' kill me sooner or later, or fuck me in the ass.'

'I mean . . . how did ya know what was goin' on with *me* and everything?'

His eyes shone with suspicion, as if I might be fucking with him.

'I told you, Marie,' he finally said. 'I told you – she writes me letters. I don't usually even open 'em. Like I said, you're lucky.'

'I never heard from her *once* when I was at County,' I said, astonished. I paused and thought, then opened my mouth to speak again, but Tim pointed a warning finger at me and shook his head.

'Degreasey, I'm gonna tell you this *one time*: don't fuckin' discuss that cunt. Ever. Awright?'

He spoke low, and his voice was all but swallowed up by the clanks and screams and laughter of C Block. He looked up. There were two men standing in the doorway.

It was the pock-faced man from the yard and a younger guy with light orange hair and matching lashes, who inquired:

'Brother Verdi?'

'That's your boy, Peachy,' Pockface grinned, pointing at me. He swayed a bit. Like he was drunk. The orange-haired boy held a leather pouch the size of a purse, and Pockface held a large, sopping-wet section of faded blue terry-cloth.

'Gotta put some ink on you, boy,' Pockface said jovially, then walked across the cell and sat down next to me on the bunk.

'"Boy?"' Tim inquired angrily, his face hard and red as brick again.

'Oh, I know he's *your* boy,' Pockface said, throwing an arm around my shoulders.

Tim glared at me to react.

'Get your fuckin' . . .' I said, shrugging off his arm and facing him. 'What'd you fuckin' say?'

'Naw now, ah hahaha! C'mon, Brother. Sheeit, Peachy – poke some holes in Brother Verdi here 'fore he *explodes* on us. C'mon now . . . Brother.'

Peachy knelt down before me and opened his leather pouch. It was filled with various sharp-pointed tools and a black plastic film container. Dark blue ink oozed out from beneath its lid.

'Brother Southard,' Tim said, standing before us, 'you fuckin' refer to Brother Verdi as Brother fucking Verdi, or you'll be up for chastisement.' When the Brotherhood ordered an errant member to be chastised, three or four Brothers would show up at his cell and kick his ass. He would stand still and take it.

'Aw hell . . .' Southard said. 'C'mon, Brother Verdi, take yer shirt off.'

I looked at Tim, who nodded.

'Did you hear me, Brother Southard?' Tim asked, as I unbuttoned the denim shirt. 'Are you clear on what I'm sayin'? 'Cause I'm not gonna say it again.'

'Yeah, it's clear, Brother Penn. Shit, just re-lax fer a second. Goddamn, Brother Verdi, have a drink.'

He held up the towel to my mouth. I looked at Tim who frowned and nodded. I opened my mouth and Southard wrung out a shot of some horrible-tasting alcohol directly onto my tongue. I swallowed and grimaced as it burnt a trail to my stomach.

''s made outta potata skins,' Southard grinned, squeezing a shot into his own mouth. Then he rubbed the towel across the faded anarchy sign on my right shoulder.

'Aw, what's this shit? This's gotta *go*, Brother Verdi.' Southard said, and draped the wet cloth around my neck.

'Wait a minute,' I said, suddenly comprehending what was about to happen. 'Nah, what the fuck? I don't want any tattoos, man. Not with that dirty-ass shit you got there.'

'Just relax,' Tim said.

'I don't wanna get fuckin' AIDS, man!' I said, stalling. Peachy displayed a small Bic lighter and began to singe the blackened tips of several tools.

Southard chuckled.

'This what gonna *keep* you from getting AIDS b ... Brother Verdi.'

There was no getting out of it. Peachy pulled a black magic marker from the case and drew a fat swastika over my old tattoo. Then he dipped his tool into the ink, and poked a hole in my skin. Dipped and poked. Dipped and poked. Hundreds of times. It burned badly and the blood poured.

In the midst of the job, Timmy suddenly slapped Pockface on the back, as if deciding to forgive him.

'Come on, Brother, sing us some Hank.'

Pockface leaned forward drunkenly and began to rub one of Peachy's tools back and forth across an iron air-vent cover in the wall. Back and forth in a steady high-low, up-and-down rhythm. Then he started to sing.

> I can set-tle down
> and be do-in' just fine

till I heeeaar an old freight
rollin' dowwwwn the line

He had a good, deep, trembly voice, and he was very serious about it. So absurdly good and serious it distracted my efforts to think of a way out of this. His song rose above the prison racket and sent chills through me. Peachy kept on poking and dipping.

Then I hur-ry straight
home and pack
And if I diiiidn't go
I b'lieve I'd blooow my stack.

I glanced at Tim, and he gave me a certain old look of his. The sarcastic grin, the jut of the chin, and the dart of the eyes that seemed to say: 'Check out *this* character.' But this particular sneer of his was always wrapped around admiration. It was a look of backhanded respect he reserved for losers who managed to walk through life with a certain ridiculous dignity; not because they were undaunted by what the world thought of them, but because they had no idea. It was the look he gave the other skinheads that first night they came across Alex Verdi, the de-greaser.

I love you bay-beee
but you gotta un-der-stand
when the Loooord made me
he made a raaaamblin' man.

I squeezed some more potato liquor into my mouth and caught a sight of my shoulder in the metal locker. Still working on the first arm of the swastika, Peachy had all but covered up my old anarchy sign. I watched the dark flow of blood and ink roll down the reflection of my arm for a while. Then I closed my eyes and relaxed.

A WEEK AFTER HE GAVE me the swastika tattoo, Peachy had his head caved in by a couple of blacks with lead pipes. They got the white guard Ford too, as he was leading Peachy and some others through the tunnel to the evening meal. Ford had been very good for the Brotherhood, and what was good for us was bad for the blacks. There was no middle ground in Stateville.

A month after that my father came to see me.

I saw him sitting in the mist-like cigarette smoke of the crowded visit room. A short letter had arrived from my sister a few days before. My mother had gone to see him before his release and told him. He mimed an animated hello and quickly stood up, then looked down to see if he'd dropped anything. He seemed to have grown rather thin in the couple years since I'd seen him. The fleshy warmth of his hand in mine brought me out of an underwater dreamstate. We sat down close to one another on folding chairs, amidst the raucous laughter and bickering, the wailing of children.

'How are you, Alex?'

'Ah . . . you know how it is.'

'No, I *don't*. Where I went was nothing like this. Nothing. I'm serious. How are you?'

'I'm fine. I really am.'

'We've got a lot to discuss, so . . . but why didn't you contact me earlier? I could have done something. Why did I have to find all of this out so long after?'

It took me a while to find the right words. He waited.

'I . . .' I began huskily, then, after a very long pause, sighed through my nose and grinned. 'I kind of had it in my head I'd be a great man the next time I saw you.'

277

I'd always felt a certain juice flow through my veins after the survival of some catastrophe, a certain relief, an inability to wipe the smirk off my face. This right here was similar, but different. This right here was the giddiness of resignation, and the release of defeat. All my lies were public now, all my secrets revealed. Except one, that is.

My dad didn't see the humor.

'Alex, you're *going* to be a great man, it's never too late for that,' he assured me softly. 'I'm very proud of you.'

I chuckled again. It wasn't a mean laugh. I couldn't help it. It just seemed like a funny thing for him to say right then.

'No, Alex come on . . .' my dad said, almost pleadingly. 'It's never too late. It is *never* too late. You're very young. This isn't permanent. Jesus Christ, you should have contacted me, Alex . . . but it's not too late. I'm gonna get you out of here. Or transferred at least to some . . . no, we're gonna get you out of this, Alex, don't you worry kid, I don't care if I've gotta sell the goddamn farm to do it . . .'

I blinked blankly.

'I'm sorry about the buildings.'

'What?'

'Burning down the house, the barn, the stable . . . I thought they were gonna take 'em.'

'Oh . . . they weren't worth anything. It's the land . . . I tried to find out where you went but, God . . . I was in jail. Your mother was in and out too. We tried to locate you. We tried. But I had no idea. It doesn't matter. That's not important right now. We've gotta get you out of here. Now, Gene Nuccio told me that the previous trouble you got in wasn't . . .'

'You talked to Nuccio?' I smiled. It was pleasant to think of him for some reason.

'Yeah,' my father said emphatically. 'After your mother finally told me I looked him up right away. I didn't . . . I mean,

I didn't know if he would be any help, but we have to explore all our options. So far he's our best bet. He seems to like you.'

'He likes *you*,' I laughed. 'He told me all about your *beatnik* days.'

I didn't mean to say it with such obvious subtext, but my father gave me a wary look. After a split-second of consideration, I took the leap.

'Did you ever have any kids besides me and Stacy?'

His wary glance melted into a curious, wounded look.

'What in the world did Nuccio tell you?'

I shrugged. Then, as briefly as I could, I told him about Marie. He did not react like a man who had finally been found out, or anything like that. He just froze with surprise.

Then he shook his head.

'Wait a minute,' he said. There was a thickness in his voice and I could tell he felt betrayed. Here he was trying very hard to help me, and suddenly I interrupt to reveal I've joined the conspiracy against him.

As he slowly recounted his side of the story, I closed my eyes, swept over with a great feeling of grief. Not just for him, but, at the time, it seemed, for the entire world. Since I came to Stateville, Mrs Kabushita had sent me Buddhist literature every week. I read the stuff from cover to cover, and chanted. I chanted for forgiveness for joining the Brotherhood. I chanted to avoid situations of confrontation with the blacks. I vowed to become a Bodhisattva of the Earth – man's highest calling short of actual Buddhahood. A Bodhisattva devoted his minutes and hours and days to relieving the suffering of his fellow man. But how did one do that? How could one act and be sure that one's best intentions weren't only *adding* to the suffering?

My dad spoke softly, but his face grew red with indignation. 'I dated her a few times, then one morning, a couple years later, out of the blue she showed up at the restaurant asking to borrow some money. I had plenty by then, so I gave her some.

She didn't seem to want to leave ... We drove out to the Indiana dunes and ... about a year later I got a call. It was her saying she had had my baby. Obviously she was ...'

He paused, thinking back to her.

'You thought she was trying to gank you?' I said, opening my eyes.

He looked up at me blankly.

'She was after money,' he said. 'I mean, she had other boyfriends. I had only been with her that one day. I was young and I had worked really hard. I was just married to your mother, and she was pregnant with you, and I didn't want to lose all that I had. I didn't want to get taken for a ride. Once you've got something, Alex, everyone changes, everyone has a scheme. That's one of the reasons I moved us out to the farm. I wanted to make myself very distant from all of that, and create a situation where we could have something good ... And, for a while there, you have to admit, we did.'

'*Detach yourself from barbarians and beasts*' I said. '*Follow the creative energy and return to nature.*'

My dad smiled, surprised, and seemed to relax – to forgive my betrayal – just a bit.

'Yeah – Basho ... You remember that from out there?'

'Nah, I ... there's a lot of time to read in here ... It's no scam though, Dad. About Marie I mean. I mean, you'd just *know* if you saw her.'

He shook his head and looked at his hands. 'She sent me a picture once. The girl was *black*. I know, I know – she still *could* have been mine. Could have been. It just seemed so unlikely. She had plenty of lovers and I only slept with her that *one time*.'

'It's true, though.' I said.

He looked at me and for the first time seemed to consider the possibility, then abruptly changed the subject.

'Alex, you surviving this depends on one thing. No matter what happens, even if you feel like you've got nobody backing you up, you've got yourself. You've always got yourself. And you've got me. Remember that and we'll beat this thing. We'll beat it just like we've beaten everything else.'

He laid out his basic plan for getting me out. Before he rose to leave he asked me for a number where he could reach Marie.

*

Before he was transferred to Stateville, Timmy had it good at Vandalia. All he did was pick cherries all day. That's the kind of place it was – safe and easy. But there was trafficking going on there like anywhere, and Timmy had his own thing going. The gangsters didn't like it and they had the black guards backing them up. When Timmy broke the guard's arm, it immediately put him in good standing with the Stateville Brotherhood. By the time I arrived he was a high-ranking officer of sorts. Kantz, a fortyish triple-murderer, bald-headed and massive from decades of weight training – his body literally covered with White-Power ink – was in charge, but I rarely saw the man. Frank Pritzger called the shots in our sphere. But Timmy answered to no one. He had earned acclaim for never backing down to the blacks, and had spent months in the solitary hole for it. The Brotherhood had grown significantly in strength and confidence since Timmy Penn arrived, and everyone looked to him now as the real leader. You could tell this bothered Frank, but I had to hand it to him – the good of the Brotherhood really did seem to be more important to him than personal power. Slightly.

Whereas before Tim had been ambivalent about race, he now spoke of blacks only with the bitterest venom. He said it was simple self-defense. Blacks had openly declared war on the white man and war was fine with him. I asked him about Marie and the baby occasionally, and each time he warned me more and more vehemently never to mention it again. The last time he nearly attacked me. But he checked himself, and backed off. Marie was the past, he said quietly, and we were done with the past forever.

But no one is done with the past forever. Not until they die. Not even then. Life is eternal. I studied all that Buddhism, remember, so just trust me on this one. Otherwise you're going to feel very silly some day. And if I *am* wrong, well, you'll never find out.

I was to blame. I realize that. I came up with the whole idea after finally getting a letter from Marie. She addressed it 'Dear Brother' and it took me a while to catch the significance. Everyone called me 'Brother' now and I thought she was mocking me. She wasn't. We never actually dealt with that in the letters though, but instead talked about Buddhism, and the baby. She'd had a boy and moved to Evanston. She had started nursing school. I had a sense my dad was helping her out after the windfall subdivision of Lilac Farm.

We conspired by mail. She came as my visitor on the same day Tim's mom came to see him. I told Tim it was my father that was coming, and he said he looked forward to meeting him. That would have been strange to see, Tim and my father shaking hands.

*

We entered the room and there sat Tim's mom with Marie. They both were glowering. In Marie's arms was a baby boy with skin the color of caramel, lighter than Dewon's. I heard Tim exhale in defeat. Then he drew in a deep breath, as if to steel himself.

He sat down across from his mom, crossed his arms, and stared at her stonily. As his mother shook her head at him and scowled, he violently held his palms up, shrugging.

'*What*?'

This startled Mrs Penn, and she turned meek.

'Timmy, don'tchya even got a kiss for yer ma?'

Tim started a sigh, then checked it, and leaned forward to peck his mom on the lips. The kiss quickly melted to a tight embrace, and Timmy cradled his mother's graying head against his breast in silence for several minutes as she sniffled softly into his shirt.

Then he leaned back again and folded his arms, not once looking at Marie, who rocked their child and flushed with indignation. Her blue eyes shone as with fever.

'Timmy, don'tchya want to hold your son?' Mrs Penn asked pleadingly. Tim's expression stayed stony, and she looked to me for help. 'Shouldn't he hold his son, Alex? You're a good boy. Don'tchya think he should?'

My eyes flitted momentarily to Marie, then to the floor. I shrugged and mumbled:

'I don't know ... If he *wants* to.'

'Well of *course* he wants to!' Mrs Penn exclaimed. 'Timmy, take that boy in your arms right now!'

Tim scratched behind his ear, and shifted as if preparing to leave.

'Timmy! Say somethin' at least.'

He looked at his mother with a blank countenance.

She leaned her head towards Marie and went on.

'I got this girl cryin' on the phone to me every night, that my son won't have nothin' to do with his own baby! My *son*!' she said, and began to cry angrily. 'I let you get away with a lot when you was growin' up, Timmy, but not *this*.'

'Yer wastin' yer time here, Ma,' he said, and once again hunched forward to stand. Tim's mother jumped up first, though, and dropped to her knees before him.

'Do I gotta beg you, Timmy? You gonna make your old lady beg?'

'Oh what the fuck is *this*?' Tim exclaimed, looking around the room exasperated.

'This is yer ma, Tiger,' she wept, then gestured towards Marie. 'Do I gotta tell you who *she* is too?'

Tim shifted his eyes to Marie, who stared him down coldly. He gave a short laugh and rubbed his forehead.

'Nah ma, that's Marie the ice-queen. Ma, I gotta go.'

Mrs Penn turned to Marie and pulled her wrist.

'C'mon, Marie, get down on your knees with me. He wants us ta beg him. There didn't used to be a boy who loved his momma more, but now he don't care about you *or* me. You ought to be *ashamed*, Timmy Penn. C'mon, Marie.'

Clutching the boy to her chest, Marie sunk to her knees beside Mrs Penn. Her blue eyes softened with pity.

Tim stood up.

'Timmy! You're gonna listen to me! You're gonna hold that boy right now or I swear to God I'm gonna kill myself. I'm gonna go home and jump out the window eleven floors! You think I'm kidding? I got nothin' to live for. My own son don't even respect me.'

With a pained smile Tim reached down and held his mother's small hand in silence, then turned his head to break her gaze. His eyes fell down on the child, who was looking up at him attentively, with wide-set blue eyes.

Tim began breathing hard through his nose at a quickening rate, then bit his tongue and stopped breathing altogether. A red stain washed up his neck and across his lean face, his nostrils flared, and his jawbone protruded from his cheek. Suddenly he brought the crook of his bicep up to his brow and flexed his arm to shut his eyes from our view entirely. Alarmed, I leaned close and saw his trembling lips thin out, then purse in agony. As the tears began to drip and disappear into the folds of his sweatshirt, Marie handed the child to Mrs Penn. She stood up and wrapped her arms around Timmy's waist. She spoke low into his ear for nearly a minute.

'Ah, fer chrissakes, Ma!' Tim shouted, pulling back from Marie with an attempt at a laugh. He wiped his face roughly with his sleeve again and again, chafing his face, then looked at his mom.

'Gimme him.'

I turned and saw a group of inmates, including Frank, being buzzed into the room.

'Frank's coming with some guys,' I whispered.

'Let 'em come.'

Marie stood up and extended the child. Frowning, he took the boy in his arms, then reached down with a long index finger and tickled the boy's palm till he grasped it with his own tiny fingers.

'Got a good grip,' he said, looking down at me. I was the only one still sitting. Before I could grin or say anything back, Tim exhaled long and hard. His flushed red face had turned ashen, and his lips looked bloodless and white. He pulled the boy up and planted a dry kiss on his forehead.

'God help ya, kid,' he said, and handed the boy back to Marie.

*

That night he and I sat in our cell on Timmy's bunk and he spoke loudly – with animated urgency – about the troubles that were building with the blacks, and not once of his baby or his mom or Marie. He spoke of how we needed to stop being so picky about who we recruited – we were losing ground to the blacks every day and things would get worse soon if we didn't make some big moves fast. We needed more guards, we needed more money. It all came down to money. We needed to contact every White Power group in America for funds. There were hundreds of them. And they weren't just a big joke any more – they were organizing together and planning big things. Not just in America but all across Europe. I was good at writing – I could draft the letters.

It was then that I first revealed to Tim that my dad was

285

working with Nuccio on a deal to pay someone off and get me transferred, then released in about a year. He stopped talking for a moment and looked at me. I looked away guiltily, afraid he might ask if there was any way he could get in on the deal. In the one phone conversation I had had with Nuccio, I started to mention something like that, but he cut me off sharply and barked that it was time I quit acting like a kid.

But Tim just nodded soberly and said:

'Well that's real good, Degreasey. Jump on that. Maybe you can help us more from outside anyway.' He laughed. 'Hey, see if you can find *my* dad. Maybe he's still a magician and he can like, *levitate* me outta here or some shit.' Then he went on planning aloud:

We needed to take the offensive. Catch the niggers by surprise and take as many of them out as we could, as quickly as possible. He talked loudly, and he continued to talk even after he saw Frank standing in the doorway to our cell. Behind him were Byrnes, Pennington, and the pock-faced country singer, Southard, all of whom buried their hands deep in their pockets, and seemed a little nervous to be there. Southard even shrugged a bit when Timmy looked at him, and nodded dubiously at the back of Frank's head.

'You don't gotta knock, Brother Pritzger, c'mon in.'

'Get up, Brother Penn.'

'Can't ya see I'm in the middle of something here, Bro?'

'I can *hear* you telling lies to Brother Verdi, if that's what you mean. Don't listen to this fucking traitor, Brother Verdi.'

'What'd you fuckin' say?' I asked, getting up from the bunk, but Timmy put his hand on my shoulder.

'This doesn't concern you, Brother,' Frank said to me. 'You weren't the one standing in front of a hundred people today crying in the arms of a nigger. You weren't the one holding a nigger baby in your arms. We're not here for you. We're here to administer chastisement to Brother Penn for disgracing the Brotherhood.'

'Ha!' Timmy said.

'Get up, boy,' Frank sneered. 'And try not to bust out crying again like this afternoon, would you?'

'Pfff . . . *Boy?*' Tim scoffed, and stood up. I tried to stand too, but he pushed down on my shoulder with all his weight. " '*Boy?*" *You're* gonna chastise *me*, Pritzger? Howzat? You only got, what? three guys with you? And they're not even *with* you. Don't you see it? They ain't gonna do nothin'. Those are *my* men. They don't respect you, Frank. They're just here to see what you'll do.' Tim looked down at me. 'Last time he and I went, he had half a dozen guys with him, remember Alex? And I scattered 'em all like pigeons!'

He turned to Frank and screamed, veins and sinew bulging in his neck, blood racing to his cheeks:

'*Alone* I did it!'

Frank looked back at Byrnes, Pennington, and Southard, amazed. 'You hear the way he talks to us like we're niggers? Are you hearin' this?'

With one swift sliding motion, Tim glided in and clamped an under-the-armpit headlock on Frank, then twisted back fiercely towards me, tossing Frank over his hip – flat on his back on the concrete with a loud slap.

As Tim straightened up from the throw and towered over Frank, there was a hollow punching sound and the clean tip of a sharpened piece of steel emerged from his solar plexus. Maybe the inner light goes out the instant the dying begins, I can't say, but when Tim's questioning eyes locked on mine and the dark spot spread out across his torso I couldn't hide what I knew. He cupped his hands over the tip of the blade, lips parted, and the death roar came out a muted sleeptalk sigh. His eyes closed as he fell forward onto Frank. Southard released the handle of the weapon and stepped in, straddling their bodies, and placed one boot on the back of Timmy's neck. I stood, legs heavy as if waist-deep in water, and shouted:

'Hold on! Hold on! Hold on!'

'Hold on!' Frank shouted, too, sliding out from underneath Tim's body with horror. 'Hold up! Oh . . . Jesus.'

I fell to my knees beside him in a fog, blinking hard in an attempt to comprehend, and for several seconds we all stared in silence.

'He isn't dead yet,' Southard said, peering down at the spot in Tim's twitching back where the makeshift knife handle – a mop-stick wrapped thick with masking tape – stood upright.

'I wonder how long it'll take,' Pennington said matter-of-factly, then knelt down with us.

''s hard to say,' growled Byrnes. 'Could take long, could *not*. Let's get it done.'

'Leave him!' Frank whispered.

I grabbed the handle with both hands and pulled, but my arms felt weak, and the handle came loose from the blade. Tim's body was still. I stared hypnotized as the handle and my hand shook into a blur.

'Give me that, you idiot!' Frank said, gingerly snatching the handle. He stood up and tossed it to Byrnes. Frank was crying a bit and looking particularly crazy.

'He's dead,' he said.

His words began to bring me out of my stupor and before concrete hatred or sorrow could take hold I prepared to spring up at Frank and tear out his throat with my teeth.

Byrnes suddenly knelt down very close to me and said in a calm, steady whisper: 'You got a deal comin' down from Chicago. Everybody here knows it. You tell the hacks what you just saw, it's off. Believe me. They'll pin it on you. We'll tell 'em how *we* saw it go down – you and Penn had a lover's spat. Happens in here all the time. You'll get the chair, if you're lucky. Otherwise you'll spend the rest of your life in here a nigger bitch.'

Frank waved him off. 'Do like I said,' he told them, and yanked my arm. He pulled me out of the cell, and the others stooped to grab fistfuls of Tim's prison suit. As Frank and I walked down the tier I turned and saw the three of them heave Tim's body through the rails, then walk away quickly. His body hit heavily, and shouts echoed from below.

While we waited in the gym, word spread. Others in the Brotherhood formed small groups and stared at Frank with hard eyes. Even Kantz, it was said, was angry. But Frank could talk, and he did, of Timmy's tears in the arms of Marie and the living bundle of treason he had held up for all to see – the caramel-colored baby. He talked and talked until only I, it seemed, remained unswayed, but impotent, nearly catatonic – torn between my well-being and my physical ache to kill him. It was a bonedeep, never-ceasing ache to avenge . . . to make up for all that I had caused, once and for all.

Frank gave me every opportunity, following me every-where, speaking in sympathetic, repentant tones – even as I listened to Marie on the payphone a few days later, and heard of the grand and motley funeral procession that had followed Timmy's casket down Sheridan Road to his North Side grave. Right up until my transfer to Vandalia came down a month later, Frank spoke incessantly, obsessively, and with great sadness of 'The Brotherhood's pride . . . our dead Aryan brother . . . the great white warrior . . . King of the Skinheads . . .'

Timmy Penn.

EPILOGUE

'I would not be surprised, if you would find – if you live long and become an artist – you'll be an artist in spirit whether you are in fact or not – you'll find a decided drift towards decadence.

Hatred, cruelty – taking the place of tenderness and the attempt at understanding. It's easier.

A good many things may make it so. Industrialism, city life. The growth of advertising and publicity.

Fake figures always being built up by publicity – in the arts – in government – everywhere.

Everyone really knowing.

The answer being cynicism.

That's the easy way out.'

Sherwood Anderson, letter to his son

It's my first Christmas out and I sit at Marie's dinner table after dessert. My dad, on a nearby couch, cuts a rather austere figure – thin, with a neatly-trimmed silver beard and mustache and eyeglasses. He's working on a novel, and devotes the rest of his time to the stock market. His ex-wife, now working at a bank, sits across the table listening patiently to a drunken Mrs Penn, a soft-spoken, sentimental lush. His blue-eyed daughters Stacy and Marie gulp coffee, laughing nervously in the intensity of their sisterhood. His grandson Timmy Penn sits still and radiant, like some little bronzed boy, pondering the meatless dish his mother prepared for him an hour ago.

I stand up, a little drunk on wine, take my suitcoat off, and hang it on the chairback. Marie's eyes lock on my empty shoulder-holster.

I'm working my way through junior college as a launderer's bagman for Gene Nuccio – the hairy, Sicilian bear. The money is good and I will reapply to Northwestern in the spring.

'Where did you put the gun?' Marie hisses, glancing across the table at Timmy.

'I stuck it under Timmy's pillow . . . Whattya think? It's locked in the desk!'

She shakes her head and begins clearing the table, muttering that I'm not a Buddhist. Marie isn't hip to the concept of 'harnessing'.

'Who says I can't chant *and* wear a gun?'

'Me!' she says.

'And the Shakyamuni Buddha!' says Stacy, who idolizes her half-sister. 'This is Marie's house – that's her son.'

I refill my wine glass and shrug.

'I don't hear any complaints when I write the checks for Timmy's Montessori school . . . I didn't hear any this morning when Timmy opened up that top-of-the line laptop.'

Stacy informs my dad that his son is a materialistic braggart. I shrug again, unashamed. My dad nods with mock disappointment:

'Alex has what I call a "Cronus Complex" . . .'

Cronus: the Titan who castrated his father Uranus to become king. It is both a joke and his genuine theory about me.

My mother's small voice rises in my defense.

'If he's *got* any complexes, where do you think he got them?'

My dad nods gravely, as if thinking back.

'You're misinterpreting your own creation,' I laugh, tongue thickening with wine. 'Everything I do is to please *you* . . . you're in my head . . . not as a rival – as an *audience*.'

'Ohhh my God, I'm gonna puke,' Stacy says.

'Me too,' my dad says.

'I'm not saying I'm happy about it!' I say. 'It's a curse. I'm cursed with this Audience Of Dad.'

Mrs Penn suddenly lets out a drunken sob and clutches a fistful of her gunmetal hair.

'What's wrong, Gramma?' Marie says, off-handedly, stacking the dirty dinner plates.

'What's the matter, Joyce?' my father asks, concerned. He isn't used to her outbursts.

'Oh,' she sniffs, bringing a napkin to her nose. 'I'm just listenin' to youse, thinkin' . . .' The rest of us exchange wry looks, and then she gets the words out: 'Little Timmy ain't never gonna *have* that audience.'

Marie blinks, then continues stacking the dishes. I feel that old, dangerous heat in my face. Tim Penn is dead and buried, but unavenged.

*

Two more Christmases went by and another was almost upon us when my dad passed in his sleep from a heart attack. He was sixty. I cared for his affairs, and numbly went back to my own.

One of the things I do for Nuccio is watch over his investments. He invests in nightclubs. One of them is The Gorgon.

Punch is long dead. I'm glad I was locked up while he died. That way I can remember him plump and resplendent, the amorphous mother/father figure of that fever-dream Gorgon family.

The new crowd is young professionals with moussed hair and leather jackets, Doc Martens they bought at Fields. Vintage Harleys lined up out front. Poseurs. I'm not putting them down, though; I try to look a certain way, too. My teeth are capped and I don't go outside anymore without a suit on and if I meet a girl I even use a face-tanner sometimes. I'm just saying, The Gorgon is the kind of place a skinhead wouldn't be caught dead in.

So I was surprised when I stopped a certain blue-eyed kid from entering the club one night. I was on my way out with Nuccio's cash and I saw a boy with a shiny scalp and SKINHEAD tattooed across his throat in Old English letters. A few steps behind him, cap pulled low, was Frank Pritzger. He looked scragglier. Like he'd been sick.

I put my palm against the kid's chest.

'Private party,' I said.

'Ah, c'mon, man,' the kid smiled. 'What's the *real* reason?' I saw in his eyes that weird sense of validation skins get from being so universally unwelcome.

Frank's eyes met mine and the Glock strapped beneath my armpit grew heavy.

'The real reason?' I said. 'Okay, the *real* reason is . . . you're not Aryan enough. Sorry.'

The kid's eyes went blank and Pritzger started chuckling. He raised his hat brim above the Nazi eagle tattooed across his forehead, then looked at the boy and nodded towards me: 'Underneath that suit there's some beautiful White-Pride ink.'

He stared as if he could see right through my imported Milano silk. But I had paid through the nose to burn them all off with lasers. Only the snarling bust of Lovie the bitch Mastiff remained. I felt sweat run underneath the holster and roll down my side.

'C'mon,' the kid said. 'We just want to go inside, hand out a few flyers.' He held up a stack of Nazi propaganda, taunting me to impress his mentor. He looked about seventeen. Runaway. Thin with a rosebud complexion. Soon enough he'd be in Stateville; them staining him with Brotherhood tattoos, or pissing in his mouth.

'Get the fuck outta here!' I screamed. Exchanging sly smiles, they shuffled off with the ominous promise that they'd be back. Skinheads are forever shuffling off, promising they'll be back.

They turned the corner towards the alley and suddenly I was trotting after them, reaching into my coat.

But, dizzy, I had to stop and lean one hand against the cold bricks of the building. *Every day, after classes at Northwestern, I walk Timmy home from school. He sits on the radiator in the mudroom and waits for me. Today he wasn't there. I sprinted to Marie's and found her in the kitchen and him writhing in sheets on the couch, his golden skin mottled with chicken pox and smeared pinkish with calamine.*

I stared at the corner that Frank and the boy had long since rounded, then I caught a Loop-bound El. I rode and watched through my dark transparency reflection as paint-peeling back porches rolled by. Then I put my forehead against the cold plexiglass, closed my eyes, and wept.

The stops on my daily train ride will forever wait for me like trip-wired infusions of old shames and heartbreaks and ecstasies; nothing ever allowed to heal or fade completely.

But the city's physique invariably brings calm. Iron and stone and glass and light at night. Gold lights and red lights. Bolts and bricks and bridges. Steel sidings.

Everything clean in its utility.

AMERICAN SKIN

DISCUSSION POINTS

1. How does the author set up the story of the narrator Alex in the first few paragraphs of *American Skin*? Using the details De Grazia provides, what kind of person does Alex seem to be?

2. What comes to mind when Alex, in one breath, says, "Aside from my dad, who was in prison at the time, I looked up to Tim more than anyone"?

3. Because Alex encounters so much violence in the city, do we suspect that he might be heading for a life where violence is a necessity? When Alex first meets Tim and the other skins on the train, what are his impressions of them? What if he had met some Hare Krishnas, young Christians, or another gang—would he have been attracted to them?

4. What do you think of Alex's musings early on when he is sitting with the skins in the break room at the factory and imagines "the life of an anti-Nazi skinhead to be several times more romantic than that of a First World War ambulance driver or a freedom fighter in the Spanish Civil War"? Taking his age and situation into account, is he somehow predisposed to joining the skins?

5. Were you aware that there are anti-Nazi, or Swazi, as well as multi-racial skinheads? What would have happened if Alex first met the white power ("Swazi") skinheads?

6. Tim says that skins are strictly working-class. From what we know about him, does Alex seem like a working-class guy? Are you surprised with Tim's affinity for Alex? Although in a flashback Alex initially refers to Tim as "Timmy," he later calls him Tim throughout most of the story, until they get to basic training. Why is this, and what effect does it have on our perception of Tim and the evolution of Alex's relationship to him?

7. What is the dramatic effect—and poignancy—of Alex being stuck on the sidewalk in between the Nazi-skins and those who reside at the club Gorgon? Why does Alex burst into tears after Tim acknowledges him inside the Gorgon, and why is this so unexpected? Does this scene help the reader relate more to Alex and the alien environment of the skins?

8. What are the differences between the Swazi leader Pritzger and Tim, and their offers to take care of Alex? How are Alex's biological and adopted skin "families" alike? How are they different? For Alex, what, if any, familial roles do Punch, Marie, and Tim play? What is Alex's role? Do you agree with Alex when he says he had already run away from home in body and Skinheadism was just his mind catching up?

9. Discuss Tim's often touching relationship with his alcoholic mother. Are you shocked when Alex discovers the identity of Marie's father? Or that Alex ends up being related to Tim's son? What do you think of De Grazia's use of this classically tragic, and epic, plot twist?

10. Does the quick intelligence and depth of knowledge of the skins surprise you? How does De Grazia use Alex's philosophical and literary references to reflect his upbringing? Considering the reader's lack of exposure to Alex's father throughout most of *American Skin,* do Alex's interior monologues and relationships with others help to shed light on his father's influence on him? After everything he's been through, why does Alex still feel a sense of guilt over his family's plight?

11. Discuss Alex's sudden change from a high-school student to skinhead and his realization that someone is afraid of him simply because he donned a costume of boots and bomber jacket and had shaved his head. Can you relate to this experience of judging someone by how they look? Why does Alex claim that the unearned nature of his tough guy rep would come to secretly bother him in an almost pathological way? Do you agree that his reputation as a tough guy is unearned? Does he look tough but not feel tough?

12. What is the significance of Alex's connection to the mob guy, Nuccio? What about the retelling of the story of Icarus and the references to Ayn Rand? What about the fact that Alex was always subconsciously getting himself into conversations about his dad?

13. Is Alex's attraction, and adherence, to the routine of the Army the same thing that drew him to the skinheads? What contributed to Alex's failure at becoming a Northwestern student? Why did Alex lie to Abby, and why does he return to Tim and the skins?

14. Does Alex have to sink to the bottom and land in prison for murder to become the man he was destined to be? Are you surprised that Tim is in prison and helps Alex, and that Tim becomes a Swazi? What do you make of Alex's survival in prison and his allegiance to Pritzger? Does Alex's letter to Marie cause Tim's death, or did Tim's actions cause his own demise? Knowing the Swazi culture, why did Alex write to Marie? Does this reveal a fatal flaw or his inherent need to do the right thing?

15. In the end, does Alex really save himself or did he need many oth-

ers to do it? Are you satisfied with the book's finale and Alex's coming full circle and chasing off some young skins?

16. Discuss the quotes from Kerouac, Chekhov, de Tocqueville, Shakespeare, and Sherwood Anderson that start off each part of *American Skin*. How do they frame, and color, the story that follows, or the story in general? What is the significance of De Grazia choosing each of these literary giants who are also penetrating social commentators?

NOTE FROM THE AUTHOR

I intended for *American Skin* to be an epic coming-of-age tale—contemporary, but in the tradition of the classic stories that made me want to be a writer. To me, the "adventures of" picaresque is an exciting form because it lets a writer realistically explore many disparate corners of society, and, at the same time, allows for a touch of the Romantic, the mythical—particularly when the protagonist is an impressionable adolescent. I experimented with a number of points of view before deciding on the first-person fictional memoir. The Alex Verdi who tells this story is an older and (somewhat) wiser person looking back from a distance. Often, however, the narrator is swept up in reliving the moment, and the distance is not that great.

Discover more reading group guides on-line!
Browse our complete list of guides and download them for free at
www.SimonSays.com/reading_guides.html